Deliverance Valley

By

Gladys Smith

1999 Winner of the Women Writing the West's
WILLA CATHER AWARD
FOR BEST MASS MARKET PAPERBACK
"RIVER OF OUR RETURN"

ILLUSTRATIONS BY JOHN FAWCETT
Prize-Winning Western Artist

A Log Cabin Book
Hamilton, Montana

Deliverance Valley

By

Gladys Smith

ISBN 1-931291-27-6

Library of Congress Control Number: 2003100219

Publishing Consultant: Stoneydale Press Publishing Company,
523 Main St., Stevensville, MT 59870 Phone: 406-777-2729
Email: stoneydale@montana.com

LOG CABIN BOOKS
1026 Tammany Lane
Hamilton, Montana 59840
Phone: 406-363-3024
Email: logcabinbooks@cybernet1.com

Dedicated to the memory of my father-in-law,
Archie A. Smith,
whose unforgettable journey from West Yellowstone
to the Bitterroot Valley in 1898
inspired me to write this novel.

And dedicated to Tawn, my husband's remarkable mountain-horse,
who shared our wilderness adventures.

Chapter 1

Southwestern Montana, 1898

Eight years on a homestead had taught me to reject the loss of my animals as unthinkable until faced with fact. I'd thawed frozen calves and orphan lambs at my kitchen stove, believing that if I willed it and worked hard enough, I could keep them from slipping into oblivion. Yet once again, death had crept onto the flat with its brazen hunger and threatened to snatch one of my flock.

The babe lay still, wrapped in a crimson film, the last of three lambs to slip from the birth canal. The mother sprawled nearby on a bed of straw that reeked of birthing and damp hair. She panted from the ordeal and from the late August sun that struck the thin walls of the shed.

I could have strangled the ram who'd escaped the neighbor's farm and planted his seed off-season. I would have waited another year to breed the ewe. She was too young for easy delivery, too exhausted and bewildered from the birth of triplets to care for the clumsy babes. So far she'd survived, the lambs healthy, searching for nourishment. Except the one.

I scooped the babe from the straw, brushed the shiny film from its face with a towel, and blew a puff of air into its nostrils. It quivered. I sent another puff of life into its lungs and rubbed its chest. A pulse trickled beneath my fingertips. With a shudder the lamb seized life.

"That's the way, sweetie. Hang on. Life isn't half bad."

I wiped the rest of the film from the silky hair. A little girl lamb, the tiniest I'd ever seen. She had an adorable wrinkled face, eyes like buttons, knobby knees. She flicked her ears, and I kissed them. As always, bestowing the gift of breath and a warming touch brought a remarkable bliss.

"What a dear thing you are, my little lamb. Jessie has a little lamb, little lamb, little lamb, Jessie . . ." The melody strung thin from my lips, as it would from a child, rather than from a tired woman of forty-three.

The babe wriggled in my arms. "Coming to life, are you? Shall we see if you can suck?"

Nudging aside the other lambs, I pressed the tiny mouth on one of the ewe's teats. The lamb jerked her head aside and pushed backward.

"Try, sweetie, you need the nourishment."

I tickled her velvety lips and pressed them against the hot, tense udder. They quivered, nuzzling for milk. The precious colostrum dribbled into her mouth. Not to be denied, the other lambs crowded in, bleating. Rivalry for the ewe's milk would put the runt at a disadvantage, but bottle-feeding would help her survive.

The suckling lambs plucked at the ewe's nerves. She thrashed her legs and tried to rise, fell back, tried to rise again. Next time she made it to her knees. A lurch and she gained her feet. Pressing against the shed's rough planks, she swerved to keep the babes from her udder. I pulled her against my legs and held her to let the lambs suckle.

Some ewes balked at motherhood and had to have it forced upon them. I found their lack of interest unbelievable. Mothering was in my nature, not a conscious effort, but a need. Perhaps it had always been there. More than likely it had grown through the years, especially after the birth of my only child when I lay in a half-sleep, death hovering near. I'd wakened to find the child gone. My husband, Ben, told me she'd died at birth and that I'd never be able to conceive again. The fact had haunted my days and nights, the long weeks and years. I hated the truth of it. It had coiled around my heart and crippled my feelings. I still yearned for the child I'd never hold in my arms.

I might have to teach the bleary-eyed ewe about motherhood, but, by heaven, I'd not let fate steal the product of her womb as it had mine. I released her with a hug. "Don't despair, Belinda. I'll bring fresh water and mash."

The lambs had tired and lay snoozing on the straw. While they slept, I'd milk the cows. First I'd change into my house dress. I'd found the ewe in painful labor when I rode my buckskin in from school; now blood stained my blouse and brown denim skirt.

I carried the little lamb to a side pen where she wouldn't be trampled and gave her another kiss. "I'll be back, sweetie, with a bottle of fresh cow's milk."

As I stepped from the lambing shed into the sun's raw heat, the clop of hoofs and the honk of Clay Turner's bulb-horn came from the base of the drive that led up to my home on the bench. Clay contracted with the Post Office in Darby, a few miles to the north, to deliver mail three times a week to distant homesteaders. Evidently, he had a package too large for the box.

My big yellow dog, Duff, deserted his post outside the lambing shed and raced down the drive to meet the mail wagon. With a thought toward my appearance, I pulled strands of damp strawberry blond hair from my face and tucked them into a French braid. I could do nothing about my clothes.

It seemed late in the day for the mail wagon. The sun had already dipped into the West and hung over the ragged peaks of the Bitterroot Range. Three hundred yards to the east, its slanted rays glittered on the river, where the stream meandered free of cottonwoods and pines. Beyond the river, the brushy, rock-pegged foothills of the Sapphire Mountains shouldered abruptly toward the smoldering sky. Lightning had struck Idaho last week, and smoke from a forest-fire had blown in from the south, tainting the breeze.

The sound of the stream's riffling waters drifted to my ears along with the whine of saws, the thud of lumber, and the smell of fresh-cut pine from a sawmill a half-mile downriver. I cherished this southern end of the Bitterroot Valley. My husband, Ben, now in his grave, had bought the ranch site more for its setting at the base of Trapper Peak and its nearness to his livery in Darby than to raise livestock. Timber covered most of the parcel. There was little grazing land, yet enough pasture for milk cows, sheep, and hogs. In good years I sold butter and cheese, wool, and weaner pigs.

Clay had reached the top of the drive and was reining in his dappled grays near the barn. The horses swelled their dusty sides and blew great breaths. Duff circled the wagon, thrashed his tail, and whined. My twenty-year-old buckskin, Zeb, galloped in from the back pasture, whinnying, and craned his neck over the fence. Cows and sheep in the field behind the barn were not as curious. They looked up briefly and went back to their grazing.

"You're late, Clay," I said with a grin. "What happened? Did the grays go on strike?"

He gave an ironic laugh and snugged the reins around the brake handle. "My Percheron got the colic. I had to give him the treatment."

"I hope he's all right."

"Stubborn as ever." Clay was a big, bluff, hearty man with crinkly brown hair beneath his slouch hat. He pointed to my clothes. "Looks like you been butchering."

"Lambing."

"A late start for lambs. They'll have to race winter."

"It wasn't my idea. The neighbor's ram got loose."

The wagon was a converted hay wagon with arching ribs that supported a canvas in bad weather. Clay rummaged behind the seat, grunted out a package wrapped with brown paper, then set it on his knees so his far-sighted eyes could read the label.

"Are you Jessie Tate of Darby, Montana?" Clay liked to prolong his deliveries with a tease.

"You know very well, Clay Turner," I said with a laugh.

"It's from that aunt of yours in Maryland."

"More books I hope."

He handed me the package. Heavy.

"Got a letter here for you." He took a tan-colored envelope from a wooden apple box beside him on the seat and held it at arms length to check the address. "Here you go."

I studied the front of the envelope. "It's from my brother, postmarked Monida. He must be at his cow camp." I felt an uneasiness, a foreboding. Gabe had been ill for some time.

"You been there?"

I looked up from the envelope, my thoughts distracted by the possibility of bad news. "Been there?"

"At the cow camp."

"No, but they say it's beautiful. It's in the Centennial Valley, on the border between Montana and Idaho. Near Yellowstone Park."

"I know all about it. Worked on a ranch there for a couple of years. Gets cold enough in winter to freeze a cow's tail off." Clay spat a string of tobacco juice over the side of the wagon box and loosened the reins. "There's a package here for the school. Too big for you to carry on horseback. Is the door open up there?"

"Always."

"Then I'll set it inside."

I pictured the log schoolhouse two miles upriver, where I acted as shepherd for twenty squirming, sniffling children, ages six to fifteen. I'd accepted the summer position to cover the losses caused by a harsh winter. Some of the children were sweet as sugar cake, others ornery as teased snakes, the pride of a handful of settlers in the upper valley. I was fond of them all.

The wagon wheels clinked gravel onto the rims as Clay urged the team down the drive. I called Duff back to his duties and bent to stroke the heads of two mother cats heavy with kittens. They'd run from the barn and rubbed on my legs, mewing. Hogs squealed in their pens near the lambing shed. Rhode Island Reds scooted toward me and clucked for grain.

"You'll need to wait, girls. I have a letter to read." I set the package on a bench at the front of the barn and sat to tear open the envelope.

The words on the enclosed foolscap were sparse, written in the scrawl of a failing man. *Jessie, please come to the Centennial. The brain tumor is about to do me in. I need you to look after my affairs. Kitty needs you, too.*

I let the letter drop to my lap and held it with trembling fingers. Gabe had always hated to ask favors. I could only imagine the despair that had prompted him to write. In my mind's eye I saw him as he was when I visited his Dillon ranch last Christmas, thinner and paler than before, lacking his usual vigor. He'd suffered headaches and nausea but hadn't yet taken to his bed. Kitty, a child dear to his heart, was forever at his side, doing his bidding. In June he'd written to say the headaches had become fierce, his vision and memory blurred. Still, I'd hoped a miracle would save him. Now this letter . . .

It seemed only yesterday I'd mourned the death of my husband, though four years had passed. The thought of losing my brother, my childhood companion and friend, brought the familiar ache of loss to my heart. I wanted to go to him, but how could I leave the homestead?

I looked about at the chores needing attention—young lambs to mother, cows to milk morning and night, arrangements to make for the last cutting of hay, beans to pick and can. Later, there'd be apples to make into sauce, potatoes to dig, fences to mend before the ground froze iron-hard, and on and on. I was blessed with good neighbors, but I couldn't ask them to help for long. They faced their own deadlines.

Beyond all that, five days of school remained before I could send everyone home with a kiss and a hug and file reports with the Clerk of the Board. And there was the threat of Carver Dean's return along with the dismal prospect I might have to sell. That possibility had shrilled down from the Yukon in the form of Carver's letter to my dead husband. A former mining partner, Carver had been in the Yukon for several years and didn't know Ben had died.

I'll arrive in the Bitterroot next month to collect the five hundred dollars you owe me, he'd written. *If you don't pay, I'll go to the sheriff with that secret of yours. You wouldn't want me to do that to Jessie, would you*?

Despicable man. He'd bled Ben for years. He could no longer hurt Ben, but he could ruin me if he proved the money was for something other than blackmail. I'd have to sell the place to settle the debt. So far I'd rejected that idea. I'd dug my roots into this valley, and it would take a team of horses to tear me loose.

Leaving for just a few weeks would put the homestead in jeopardy, yet as I listed mentally what I must do today and tomorrow, I heard my obligation to the homestead recede to the back of my mind. I thought of Gabe and Kitty and recalled how they clung to each other like roses to a trellis. I thought of the pain Gabe had endured, weighing that against the consequences of my leaving home. My feelings allowed no alternative. As soon as school was out I'd leave for the Centennial.

Chapter 2

I tried to leave my worries about the homestead behind. No easy task. But it helped to know my neighbors watched over the place. I was grateful. As the Monida-Yellowstone stage lurched to a stop beside a pole gate, my mind locked with dread on another worry. Did Gabe live, or had the tumor taken its course?

The driver leaped from his perch and opened the coach door, the wind fluttering his yellow hat and duster. "This is your stop, Mrs. Tate."

"Excuse me," I said to the gentleman sitting beside me. He and the other passengers on the crowded stage were headed for Yellowstone Park and the amazing sights some attributed to the devil. I thought their dress out-of-place, more suitable for a night at the opera than for an outing in the great outdoors.

The driver helped me down from the stage, saying, "Wish they were all as light as you," then went to the rear boot and tossed my dusty baggage onto the road. Next minute, he'd urged the clattering team toward a stage stop a half-mile distant. I felt abandoned on the sun-baked road, alone in strange country.

Not for long. Horses trotted through the fields of bunch-grass and sage, whinnying a greeting. Most were chestnuts and bays, their hides like oiled silk. Some had the sleek lines of thoroughbreds; others were stockier Percherons and crossbreeds. The last were part of a herd Gabe had produced by crossing thoroughbreds with mustangs to create a sturdy mountain horse. They gathered at the corners of a jack-leg fence.

"Hello there, beauties. I can see the Centennial agrees with you."

A loud trumpeting turned my eyes to the north, where a family of trumpeter swans had cut the gleaming surface of Upper Red Rock Lake and were folding their wings. Nearer shore, mallard ducks and their noisy offspring dabbled for insects. The lake filled much of the valley, but in the surrounding sage and grasslands deer and antelope fed amid herds of long-horned cattle. To the north, across the lake and the aisles of sage and tall browning grass, the slopes of the Snowcrest and Gravelly Ranges lay in a blue haze.

This valley received from six to eight feet of snow in the winter and only a few settlers stayed year-round. Most of the cattle belonged to Beaverhead Valley ranchers who used the Centennial as summer range for their herds. My brother, Gabe, was one of them. Each summer he trailed stock from his Dillon ranch up Blacktail Creek to feed beneath the sheltering mountains. Here he'd built his cow camp.

I saw it south of the gate—a cabin and several log soddies peering through a haze of smoke at the head of a meadow. Beyond the camp a barrier of soaring cliffs frowned down upon the valley, one towering wedge veiled in mist.

Gabe's stock dogs, one black and white, the other a blue Australian shepherd, raced down a wagon road to warn me off. Frightened by their barking, a cow moose and calf trotted from the meadow into the safety of an aspen thicket.

"Easy," I said as the dogs ducked through the gate. "You'll scare everything off." They wagged their tails in sudden recognition and sniffed my skirts. I stroked their heads.

I'd boarded the stage in the cool of morning. Now it was noon, the September sun warm on my cheeks. I smoothed wind-blown hair from my face and tightened the pin that held my green toque in place. The skirts of my traveling suit had collected a layer of powdery clay during the forty-mile trip from the railway station at Monida and they appeared gray rather than green. I shook them out.

"Come, friends," I said to the dogs, "take me to Gabe and Kitty."

I opened the groaning gate, reset the horseshoe latch, and, leaning against the weight of my carpetbag and satchel, began the quarter-mile trek to the cabin. The horses followed, trotting along behind the fences on each side of the drive. The dogs jogged at my heels, grinning as dogs do. The wagon road was nothing but two ruts gouged into an aisle of grass where horses had been allowed to graze. I skirted piles of dung.

The barking had alerted Kitty to the fact I'd arrived. I recognized her lean figure and boyish stride as she headed down the drive, the sun glinting on her red braid. Her hair was three shades brighter than mine, the color of a carrot. Her name was Kathryn, but everyone called her Kitty. She'd just turned fourteen.

I set my bags on the ground and waved. "Hello, Kitty."

She tossed a wave. "Hi, Aunt Jess."

She continued down the drive, her stride loose, almost a swagger. She'd worked with Gabe from the day she could toddle and she felt at home in the outdoors. She could rope, tame broncs, and handle a herd better than wranglers twice her size. She worshiped Gabe. He worshiped her. She'd been the leaven in his loaf, the special ingredient that seasoned his life. I envied him.

The dogs raced up the drive to meet Kitty and bounced up and down in greeting. She threw a stick for them to fetch, taking her time to reach me.

"It's good to see you," I said with a hug. Her response was a brief circling of her arms around my waist, a reluctance carried over from the past.

She gave me a sketchy smile. "Glad you made it, Aunt Jess." The smile didn't carry into her voice. There was little welcome there. Each time I made a pilgrimage to Gabe's Dillon ranch I sensed she'd grown more distant. I could blame it on a growing independence, a wish to ignore ties she had no desire to perpetuate. More than likely it was a hardening of her sense of injustice. Whatever the cause, it saddened me.

She stuffed her hands into the pockets of her jeans and stared at me from under the turned-up brim of her ranch hat. In Kitty, I saw myself as a girl, though not such a tomboy—the same straight, lean figure, the same round freckled face and flat blue eyes. The resemblance was so striking that when she was an infant I'd thought she should be mine. Usually her eyes shone like new buttons. Today they were full of gloom.

"How was the trip?" she asked.

"Long. Wore me to a frazzle. But I saw some beautiful country." Some 340 miles of it I recalled with a sigh, a three-day trip by stage and rail. I felt as squeezed of fiber as a worn dishrag. I was sure I looked the same.

"How are you, Kitty?"

She gave an indifferent shrug. "Tolerable, I guess. You know . . ." Her face expressed the sorrow she chose not to put into words. She picked up my satchel. "C'mon, I'll show you the cabin."

As we walked I tried to make conversation. Kitty replied in monosyllables and shot guarded glances my way. She'd grown a couple of inches in the last eight months I judged she was an inch shorter than my five-foot-three. Her legs were long for her torso, her arms ropy, the muscles beneath her jeans taut, similar to those of boys who spent their time chasing cattle, forking hay, and chopping wood. If it weren't for the tiny mounds beneath her plaid shirt, one would have thought her a boy.

A cross-fence prevented the thoroughbreds and crossbreeds from following us further, but cow ponies of various colors trotted through the yellowing meadow grass and stood at the fence that bordered the drive. Snorts came from their wet nostrils. Their tails switched at flies. Though curious about me, the ponies were more interested in Kitty. She whistled a greeting.

"Which of these do you ride?" I asked. I'd seen her ride at the Dillon ranch. She could mount a horse bareback like a jumping spider and tear off across the fields as if part of the horse.

"I ride all of them," she said in her careless way. "Mainly that little paint." She pointed to a fidgety, short-coupled mare, her sleek hide splotched with white, brown, and orange. "Her name's Trixie."

The name sparked a memory. Gabe and I were towheaded youngsters of perhaps six and seven, racing our ponies over the wooded greens of our childhood home in Maryland, laughter rippling in our wake. As we grew older, Father had bought us the finest hunters and jumpers, the hottest racers for Gabe. But on that day, he'd brought home two of the finest ponies on the east coast.

"Gabe used to have a pony named Trixie," I said.

"Yeah, I know." A smile flickered across Kitty's lips, then faded.

"So . . . how is your father?" I'd dreaded asking.

Kitty seemed just as reluctant to answer. "Oh . . . all right, I guess."

"I'm anxious to see him." True in one sense, not in another. I could imagine Gabe as a withered version of his former self.

"He's snoozing now. He had to whiff some of Yeng Sang's opium." Her voice wavered. "He hurts real bad."

"I won't bother him, just look in."

We were nearing the mouth of a canyon that crawled down the

mountainside and spilled a meadow into the circling woods of quaking aspen and pine. A family of sandhill cranes feeding at the head of the meadow gabbled with annoyance and strutted into the woods. On a flat above the meadow, Gabe had built an assortment of sheds and corrals and a log cabin with sod roof. Nearby paddocks held a few thoroughbreds, a milk cow and calf.

Gabe's wife, Amy, had always stayed at the Dillon ranch to tend the vegetable garden and cook for the hay crews. The minute I walked into the cabin I could tell she'd had no part in making it a home. The small sitting room with its splintery floor, shallow loft, and single uncurtained window, had the feel of a bear's den.

From the kitchen came the clatter of pans and the spicy smell of stew. I stepped into a room twice the size of the sitting room, its roof at a slant. A dusky lean-to. Near me stood a worktable, two crude cupboards, and a wood range, the source of the smoke that veiled the meadow. A long table covered with white oilcloth filled the far end of the room.

Yeng Sang, Gabe's housekeeper, stood at the worktable, his queue like a black stripe down the back of his shan. He was cutting biscuits from dough he'd rolled onto the surface of the worktable and flour coated his hands. I liked Yeng Sang, admired him for his ability at the stove and for the infinite patience he'd shown Gabe and Kitty.

"Hello, how are you?" Pleasure at seeing him filled my voice.

He bobbed his head in respect. "Just fine, Missee Tate, just fine. Good you come. Now Mister Gabe find peace."

"I truly hope so." I plucked a piece of dough from the flattened circle and tucked it into my mouth. It had a buttery flavor.

"You hungry, Missee Tate?"

"Starved."

"Dinner ready soon." He pressed the end of an empty baking powder can into the dough to make a circle. "First you see Mister Gabe."

Kitty had put my bags on a cowhide settee and was leaning against the far wall of the sitting room. "Pa's in here," she murmured. Her young eyes reflected the misery that lay beyond a door.

The bedroom held no comfort—two slab benches and a lodgepole bunk. One bench supported a kerosene lamp and a flaming incense candle, the other a blue water pitcher, basin, and towel. No window. The chest of drawers appeared to have been left in the rain at some time. The wood had warped and separated at the grain. Hooks on the wall held denim trousers and shirts. The room seemed as spotless as a crude cabin would allow, yet the smell of urine mixed with the fragrance of burning incense and the scent of vinegar.

Gabe lay asleep on the bunk, a shadow of the man I'd seen last Christmas. His once round face was thin, his skin blue-gray, his eyes sunken deep within bony sockets. He lay still as death, but his breathing betrayed him. A gray wool blanket rose slightly with each faint, wheezing breath he took. I caught myself trying to breathe for him.

Gently, so as not to disturb him, I pulled the blanket from his chest and saw the flannel covering of a flaxseed-vinegar poultice. I replaced the blanket and felt his forehead. Hot to the touch.

I turned to Kitty, her lean figure outlined in the doorway. "He has pneumonia. He should be in Dillon, under the doctor's care." The whispered words hissed from my lips.

Kitty gave her head a determined shake and hissed in return, "Pa wants to bide his time here. Yeng Sang's medicine is as good as the doc's." Obviously upset by my remark, she slipped from the room.

Yeng Sang knew a great deal about Chinese herbs and potions as well as medicinal plants that grew wild in southwestern Montana. Still, I thought Gabe should be under a doctor's care. Tomorrow I'd ride into Lakeview, a tiny settlement the stage had passed a few miles back, and ask if I could send word to the doctor in Dillon. I had no idea whether he'd come this far or what he'd charge. In the meantime, I'd see if the store in Lakeview had quinine, paregoric, and camphor in stock.

Swallowing back a mix of sorrow and irritation, I looked down on the ruins of a man who'd once had the strength and tenacity of a bulldog. At one time our hair had been the same reddish-blond. Mine had grown darker over the years. Illness had streaked his with silver. He'd shaved his beard, but bristles covered his chin. He had the face of an eighty-year-old rather than a man of forty-four.

The symptoms had first appeared two years ago, but the tumor must have existed before then. Besides searing headaches and loss of memory, he sometimes lost the sight in his left eye for three or four hours at a time. He'd seen doctors statewide and in southern Idaho, had tried legitimate treatments as well as those of quack doctors. He'd even written a famous doctor in Pennsylvania who'd done some brain surgery. When he'd learned the slight chance he'd have of surviving an operation, he'd chosen to die a natural death, rather than one from a surgeon's knife.

I touched his hand, wishing my love could make him well. In reality there seemed nothing I could do but let him rest.

I'd reached the door when a hacking cough made me turn. Gabe's red-veined eyes had opened a crack and stared at me as a calf stares in bewilderment at the first human it encounters. He pulled a stick-thin arm from beneath the blanket and flipped bony fingers in my direction. "Who are you? What are you doing in my bedroom?" The wheezy voice carried feeble outrage.

I returned to the bunk and took his hand. Unlike his forehead, it felt like ice. Veins stood out like rivers on a parched plain. "I'm your sister, Jessie. Come to make you behave." I tried to put humor on my face and in my voice.

"Sister?" He jerked his hand away and tucked it beneath the blanket. "Don't have a sister, not even . . ." He seemed to have lost himself in thought or forgotten what he was going to say. His eyelids closed over glazed blue eyes. His head turned to the side.

Last Christmas he'd asked the reason for decorations and gifts. Now he couldn't remember his own flesh and blood.

Chapter 3

I was still at a loss when Kitty appeared in the doorway. "Pa's feeling the opium," she said. "Might as well let him snooze."

I walked into the bear's den, taking careful note of the furniture for the first time—three chairs and a settee made of lodgepole, a pot-bellied stove against the back wall. A patchwork quilt and a painting I recognized as one of Kitty's watercolors provided the only bright spots in the room.

"Do you want to put your things away before dinner?"

I gathered from Kitty's tone that she was in no hurry, but I said I wanted to unpack and that I'd like to wash and change my dusty clothes.

"We haven't fixed a bed yet. Would you rather sleep up there"—she pointed to the loft, the sod roof so low I'd have to stoop to move around—"or in the bunkhouse?"

I glanced at the flimsy ladder leading to the loft and decided against it. "Are cowpokes using the bunkhouse?"

"They're out on the range. Won't be back for a few days. There's a wall down the middle, so you'll have one side to yourself." She picked up the satchel. I followed with the carpetbag.

At the upper end of the flat stood a privy, a squat log barn with grass and purple asters growing in the sod roof, and a tiny cabin Kitty laughingly called Yeng Sang's dog house. The bunkhouse perched on a rise across from the barn. The bark on its logs hung in gray shreds. Benches lined the walls.

Rufus, Gabe's Australian shepherd, had remained at the cabin in a sad-eyed vigil, but Penny, the black and white shepherd, had settled in front of the bunkhouse to await the men's return. Her bushy tail raised dust when she greeted us, grinning. Black markings that arched over her eyes gave her a quizzical look.

I bent to pet her. "I'm glad you came to the Centennial. We'll have a good talk one of these days." We'd been friends since the Christmas she strayed onto Gabe's ranch and I'd tamed her with scraps from dinner.

I set my carpetbag on a bench, Kitty the satchel. She gave one of the rough-hewn doors a hard shove. "This side's been closed since last summer."

I stepped across the threshold into the reek of mouse urine and stale tobacco juice. A spiderweb caught in my hair. Other webs hung from the beams, snaring flies. A pot-bellied stove in the center of the room had the look of a pregnant sow. On its lid, a teakettle and coffeepot collected dust. Four lodgepole bunks lined the walls, above them shelves for cowpokes' belongings. Mattresses and bedding hung from the ceiling in pole frames, a protection against mice and pack rats.

We pulled a mattress and bedding from one of the pole frames and went outside to shake the blankets. Kitty took one corner of a gray wool blanket, I another. "I s'pose Pa's going to make you sell the ranch," she muttered without preamble.

"I have no idea."

"I heard him talking to some braggy mine owner before he got real sick. The fella wants to summer his racehorses here." She grunted with each tug on the blanket.

"Sounds like a good buyer for the place."

She stopped shaking the blanket and scowled. "Pa don't have to sell. I can run the outfit."

Kitty knew a lot about ranching. But to take command? I told her it would be too much for someone her age. Especially a girl.

"I know a kid took over when his pa died."

"Is his mother living?"

"Yes."

"It makes a difference when you have a grown up's help."

There were other problems besides Kitty's age. I hesitated to speak of them for fear I'd say something Gabe wanted kept from the girl. On the other hand, she needed to know if she was to understand the situation.

"Has Gabe told you about his debts?"

She shrugged. "Guess he owes some money." Her face said she knew more than she wanted to admit. We'd shaken the blanket and brought the corners together. Kitty left me to fold it while she took another blanket from the bench and held a corner for me to take. "I could sell all the cattle and raise horses."

"It's hard to make a living raising horses, especially thoroughbreds the bank owns. Your father spent too much on racehorses. Not enough on cattle."

"What's wrong with buying horses? Pa likes them. So do I." Her tone was sullen, defensive.

We gave the blanket one last shake. I tucked it under my arm, took the other blanket from the bench, and stepped into the bunkhouse.

Kitty shuffled in behind me. "Pa's sold all the racers," she said sourly. "Don't know why. I could take care of them." She scooped a handful of kindling from a box next to the stove and stuffed it into the stove's black gullet. "He's going to keep the crossbreeds, though. He wants me to have them."

I assumed she meant the thoroughbred-mustang crosses Gabe had bred for use on mountain trails. I'd expected them to be sold with the rest of the stock.

Kitty took a log from a stack beside the door and gave it an angry shove into the stove, jarring a pipe that poked through the low ceiling. "Don't know why I'm telling you. You don't care about horses."

Resentment started a slow burn on my cheeks. "A lot you know, young lady. I rode every day when I was a girl. My father taught me and Gabe everything he knew about horses." I threw a blanket over one of the bunks and pulled it into place with sharp tugs. "I used to be as crazy about horses as Gabe was."

"I bet you couldn't go into the wilds and pick out a good mustang —rope it —tame it—teach it to do what you want."

I had no good answer for that. It was clear Kitty had been worrying about losing the horses for weeks, nursing a grudge. She was using me for a whipping boy. I threw another blanket onto the bunk.

Kitty took an empty bucket from beneath a wash-stand and stood there sulking. Her sullen gaze traveled from the doorway to my bunk and back again, as if she were searching for another reason for argument. The one she found took a different tack.

"I bet you won't stick around to help me. Like Ma and Pa. Won't be around when I need you." Her mind seemed to travel in circles. She had a habit of returning obsessively to things that upset her.

I sat on the bunk and gave it a pat. "Come sit down. Let's talk."

She just stood there, a pout on her face.

"Try to understand. I grieve for Gabe, too. I love him dearly. I've come a long way and left pressing matters behind to help him out." I paused, searching for the right words. "You can be difficult or you can make things easier for everyone. For Gabe's sake, I hope it's the latter. I have no intention of crossing you just to be perverse. I never would. But I plan to do what I think is best for Gabe and for you."

Silence.

I studied the downcast eyes, the slumped shoulders, the slight frame trying to become that of a woman. A wretched time for the youngster. "Despite what you think, dear girl, I love you as if you were my own. I'll make you a good home in the Bitterroot. And I'll always be around when you need me."

She stared at the floor a long, troubled moment, sucking in her cheeks to keep her chin from trembling. "It doesn't matter. Pa isn't going to die. I won't let him." She turned aside, lifting the bucket. "I'll fill this so you can heat water."

"You needn't bother. I can . . ." I left the rest unsaid. She'd walked out the door.

I watched her descend the rise and cross the turn-around to a pump that stood in a patch of grass near the cabin. Her cow ponies, grazing in a field of mountain timothy, looked up and whinnied. They loved her. She loved them. Losing even one horse would trouble her. So much loss to eat away her spirit. So much uncertainty. She was like Gabe—he'd always lashed out at others when he was hurting.

Phantoms from the past came to sit on my shoulder as they always did when I was with Kitty—the dark events that had robbed me of my child, another tragedy that had robbed Kitty of those she loved. The latter had taken place six years ago, when I was visiting Gabe's Dillon ranch at Christmas-time, Gabe in the South gambling on horses. Amy and the children became desperately ill with diphtheria. I tended them with loving care, disinfected everything several times each day, tried to keep the film of death from their throats, but I was able to save only Kitty, the eldest of three girls. The others I laid to rest one by one, leaving part of me beneath each mound of earth.

I'd stayed with Gabe and Kitty until chores at the homestead demanded I return to the Bitterroot. I'd considered taking Kitty with me, but the separation from Gabe would have shattered her. She needed him desperately. He needed her and wanted her to follow in his footsteps. Now he was about to fade from her life.

* * *

Gabe slept the afternoon away. When he woke from his drug-sleep, Yeng Sang insisted he, not I, tend Gabe's bodily needs. "Man not like for woman to see him naked."

While Yeng Sang played nurse, I stoked the fire to reheat the stew for supper, set the table, and readied Gabe's tray. Yeng Sang had grown a surprisingly large crop of potatoes, carrots, turnips, and onions, the season too short for other vegetables. Except for the garden harvest, I'd discovered the larder had grown lean. When I questioned Yeng Sang about it, he said stoically, "An empty house needs no grain."

Because Gabe had little appetite, Yeng Sang had prepared an onion soup with Chinese herbs. I carried the tray into the dusky bedroom, where Gabe lay propped against a folded pillow. He seemed to recognize me. At least he didn't question who I was or why I was there. I set the tray on his lap and leaned forward to kiss him on the forehead.

He flicked me the semblance of a smile. "It's good to have you here."

I patted his arm and returned the smile.

He took a few sips of the clear soup and munched absently on a soda cracker. "I'm not hungry these days. Stomach's always upset." It showed in his loss of weight and in the skin that lay in wrinkled folds.

"A little broth won't hurt. You need to keep up your strength." I moved the pitcher and basin to the floor and sat on the bench. "I wish you'd stayed in Dillon. You need a doctor. Heaven knows if I can get one to come a hundred miles."

His lips tightened. The red-rimmed eyes narrowed. "I don't want a doctor. What's the use? Yeng Sang can see to the pain and fever. I'll not . ." Wheezing, he lay back against the pillow.

I held his hand and kissed it.

"I need to talk of other things while I can," he said faintly. "I'd like you to visit Glen Peterson . . . he has a ranch down the road . . . agent for Marcus Daly, the copper baron. The elevation here will develop his racehorses' lung capacity." He paused to suck in breath. "Daly's buying the cow camp and the Dillon ranch. You see to the paper work."

"I'll see Peterson first thing in the morning. Don't worry yourself." I reached out to stroke his forehead.

He caught my hand, his clasp feeble as willow sticks. His hollow eyes searched my face. "Jess, please take Kitty to the Bitterroot. Take care of her."

"Of course. I've wanted her for years. If I'd known you were . . ." I was about to say "in such a bad way," caught myself, began again. "I should have taken her with me at Christmas-time."

"No, I needed her. . . a good girl." He hesitated. "I want Kitty to have the crossbreeds . . . give her a start on life. I want you to drive the herd to the Bitterroot."

I sat speechless, unbelieving.

Drive the herd to the Bitterroot? Impossible!

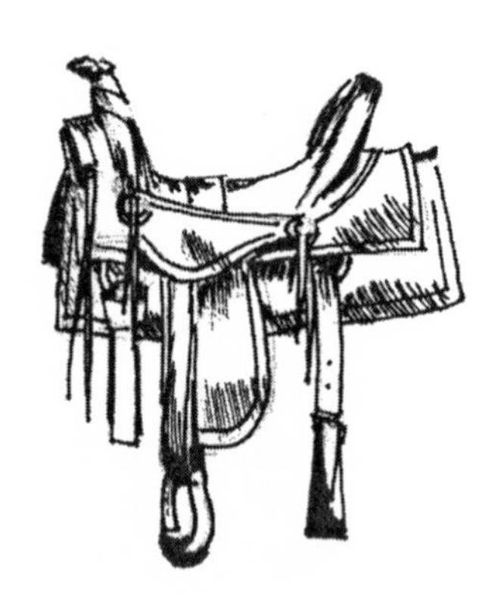

Chapter 4

I raised my arms in protest. "How can you expect me to trail a herd that far? It's two hundred miles, likely closer to two hundred fifty, most of it in the wilds. Mountains steep enough to slide a grasshopper."

"I've sent horses to the Bitterroot before. A hard trip, but you can do it."

"Who'll help?"

"Kitty's as good as three men."

I rolled my eyes toward the ceiling. "I can't. I love you Gabe. It tears me apart to see you like this, but you ask too much." I got to my feet and paced back and forth. I felt guilt for having refused, blamed Gabe for having asked.

"It's not for me, Jess, it's—"

"I haven't enough pasture." Again I threw up my hands. "I'd have to buy hay. I haven't the money." An understatement.

"You can sell the crossbreed geldings to the army, the war with Spain's increased the demand. Please, Jess, I don't want the herd to go to a stranger . . . somebody who won't treat them . . ." He closed his eyes and took a long, gasping breath.

I touched his arm. "I'm sorry I've upset you. We'll talk later."

His eyelids flew open. "I need to talk now." He pulled me onto the bunk beside him and fixed me with his bleak stare. "You know how to breed horses and how to keep them healthy. I want you to take them. I won't rest unless you do."

"You're being unreasonable. Even if I were willing, it's getting late in the season. Hardly the time to start a trail drive. How long would it take? Maybe three weeks? It'd be October before I could leave here, almost November before I'd reach . . ." I broke off as it occurred to me I was setting a time for Gabe's death. I looked aside, hoping to hide the thought.

He turned my chin with his bony fingers so I had to look into his eyes. A tear leaked over his eyelid. "Please, Jess, the herd is all I have to give Kitty. Don't deny me that."

The plea went straight to my heart and struck the scars of my youth. "You call it a gift? I say it's a millstone around Kitty's neck. It'll drive her to the poorhouse, like it did Father. Like it did you. You should have thought of Kitty's welfare when you were frittering away your money. If you want to give her something, sell the herd. Give her the money for an education."

"A girl doesn't need one."

"She has as much right as any boy. She's bright. She could become a teacher, a nurse, even a doctor. Don't pass a father's and grandfather's obsessions on to your child."

"Everybody has an obsession, Jess. Kitty has a right to choose hers. She loves horses and has a magic way with them . . . you did, too, when you were young."

Young? It seemed so long ago. I saw myself in one of our Maryland paddocks, calming a stallion who'd gone berserk. I heard his screams, saw the savage glint in his eyes. I heard my girlish voice speaking softly, offering reassurance, afraid, yet pretending courage.

"What's happened to you, Jess, and your passion for horses?"

It took a while to sort the cause from other dregs of the past. When I replied, I spoke slowly, almost against my will. "I suppose it was all the heartache, the hard times and disappointments, the need for the pennies to go elsewhere."

"I've faced hardship, too. I didn't lose my passion."

"Ben taught me to keep a wary eye and tight hold on the purse strings. It meant the difference between going to bed hungry and having a few beans on our plates."

"Ah, yes. Practical Ben." Emotion had turned Gabe's eyes into filmy puddles set in dunes of gray. He sighed and waved a hand. "I'm tired. We'll talk later." Then, as I fixed the pillow and helped him stretch his withered self between the blankets, "Don't close your mind, Jess. Think on it."

* * *

I knew better than to stress a sick man, but I couldn't abide the fact that Gabe had nothing to leave Kitty but a herd of horses she couldn't feed. For years, his extravagance with racehorses and his disregard for family had turned my respect into disappointment. Yet I still loved him, always would.

I should have held my tongue.

Feeling a terrible remorse, I headed for the porch at the front of the cabin to be alone. As I passed through the bear's den, I stopped to look into the kitchen. Yeng Sang and Kitty sat at the table, eating warmed-over stew. A fresh pie sat between them. I caught the aroma of brown sugar and apples. Before Gabe had lost his appetite, he'd loved pie. He'd lured Yeng Sang from a large cattle outfit because of his ability to make a flaky crust. Pie had no appeal for me at the moment.

A horse-gnawed hitching post, well, and water trough stood a few feet from the cabin in a patch of trodden grass. A dipper hung from the pump's shaft. I squealed the handle up and down to fill the dipper, drank the icy water, then sat on the edge of the porch. A cricket chirped in the dark world beneath the floor. Penny lay at my feet, snoozing, a black and white rug. Rufus sprawled beside me, his blue-gray muzzle warm on my thigh. Clearly, he missed Gabe and needed someone near.

The sky was tinged a soft yellow, the orange ball of the sun about to drop behind a flat-topped ridge to the west. Pines growing along the meadow's western border sent long, pointed shadows onto the amber grass.

I sat there a long while, drinking in the smell of sage and yellow tansy, letting my mind drift with thoughts of Gabe. I wanted desperately to remember him as he had been, not as the shell of a man he'd become. When young, he'd been frisky as a colt, charming, my father's pride and joy. I looked to the north, across the sweep of grass, sage, and clear mountain waters and imagined that the sundollars sparkling on the surface of Red Rock Lake were shimmering on the Susquehanna River. Rather than herds of free-roaming cattle, I saw hundreds of blooded horses wandering the greens of Father's Maryland horse farm. I wasn't heir to the estate, but Father showed almost as much interest in me as he did in Gabe where horses were concerned. Against Mother's objections, he taught me to ride and let me haunt the stables. Mother considered me a tomboy. When she insisted I go to finishing school, "so they can make you into a lady," I went, kicking and screaming.

Yeng Sang dragged me from my reverie, a long-stemmed tobacco pipe in one hand, a crockery bowl filled with stew in the other. He offered me the steaming bowl with a hand that smelled of onion. "Nice evening, Missee Tate." I invited him to sit beside me on the step.

We spent a moment talking about the evening. I thanked him for the stew and dug in so he wouldn't think me ungrateful. The smell of turnips filled my nose. From the kitchen came the clatter of pans and the sound of plates settling into a dishpan.

"Is Kitty washing the dishes?" I asked with surprise. She'd only help me under protest.

"Girl need to know how to cook and wash dishee," Yeng Sang replied around the pipe stem. "One day may cook for big man." Yeng Sang often bragged about cooking for a "big man." When he'd worked for the largest cattle outfit in southwestern Montana, he'd acted as camp cook for Teddy Roosevelt on a hunting trip into the Big Hole Valley.

I smiled at the thought of Teddy—a man we Montanans considered a neighbor because of his ranch in the Dakotas—and at the idea Kitty would hire on to cook for him, or anyone else for that matter. "She's all wrapped up in horses," I told Yeng Sang. "It's enough she knows how to cook for herself." I paused, thinking of the difficult days ahead. "It's going to be hard on her—Gabe's death. I hardly know what to say to her."

Yeng Sang took the pipe from his mouth and blew a cloud of acrid smoke. "You not be sad," he murmured. "Life, death, allee same . . . all from One." He studied me from the corners of his slanted eyes. "No need worry 'bout Kitty. She strong inside. Worry not good. Must sleep with no dreams. Wake with no worry."

* * *

Yeng Sang's advice was easier said than done. I spent half the night fretting about Gabe's plea for the herd, about things to be done around the cow camp, and about my homestead. I hated to ask my neighbors to milk and tend the lambs and garden for long. I worried that some calamity would befall my beloved animals. I worried, too, about Kitty, wondering how I could bring balance into her life. How would I keep her from making decisions that would turn into a bed of thorns?

First thing in the morning, I studied the ledgers and legal papers Gabe had brought with him from Dillon. As I checked for accuracy, I discovered a pattern of reckless ventures that had amassed an appalling amount of debt. Like my father, he'd allowed his passion for thoroughbreds and gambling to drown good judgment.

Gabe and I didn't discuss the herd of crossbreeds that day, though he asked if I'd thought about trailing the herd to the Bitterroot. I merely said I needed more time to think. A stalling tactic, designed to avoid stress.

Later that day, I rode into Lakeview on a buckskin named Bannack, posted a letter to a doctor in Dillon, and was told by the storekeeper that no one had ever dragged the doctor this far from town. "Chances are, you'll recover or die before he'll come to the valley."

I called on Glen Peterson, agent for Marcus Daly, the copper baron who planned to buy Gabe's land and string of racehorses. Peterson had all the papers ready for the transfer. There was no payment made. The agreement called for Daly to pay all debts held against the cow camp and the Dillon ranch. Despite his will against it, I hoped to persuade Gabe to sell the crossbreeds as insurance for Kitty's future.

Meanwhile, I'd ready the ranch for the new owner. The cabin was Yeng Sang's domain. He'd hung quilts, blankets, pillows, and towels on lines strung between the cabin and privy and they made a rainbow of color as they flapped in the breeze. I'd clean the barn, sheds, and bunkhouse. The barn had the most clutter. I dressed in one of Gabe's plaid shirts and a pair of his jeans, pulled the belt tight to keep them from slipping from my hips, and started work on the barn.

Gabe was in a drug-sleep, Kitty in a corral gentling a mustang captured before the men left on roundup. That morning she'd brought Chinook, a retired racehorse, the thoroughbred sire of the mountain horses, from the range on the hogback west of the meadow. She'd treated a cut on the chestnut's leg and left him stabled in the barn so the cut would heal. Worried about the mares left on the ridge, he raced back and forth in his stall, kicked at the walls, and bugled to his harem. They responded with squeals that shrilled across the meadow.

I'd never seen Chinook. Gabe had always turned the herd onto winter range by the time I visited at Christmas. As I peered over the stall door at the pacing stallion, I thought I was seeing a ghost. This horse had to be Fury, one of my father's stallions, my favorite. Chinook's coat was the same shade of brownish red, glossy as freshly-polished boots. He had the same star on his forehead and white stockings on all four feet, the same sleek body and long legs that helped thoroughbreds fly over the ground. Fury had been an enigma. He could be gentle as a lamb and affectionate, but turn into a demon when a mare was near. I wondered if Chinook had the same temperament.

It'd been ages since I'd calmed a nervous stallion, but my father's voice whispered instructions from the past. "Listen to what the horse is telling you. Make him comfortable. His strongest instinct is to survive. Let him know he can survive with you."

I spoke to Chinook softly from behind the stall door. "Easy, boy. I'm not going to hurt you."

He paced the stall, churning bits of straw into the air, his neck arched, tail plumed.

"You're going to be here for a while, so you might as well relax."

He shook his wavy red-brown mane and whinnied toward the hogback.

"Your lady friends aren't going anywhere. They'll be waiting." Likely with mixed feelings about his return. Stallions could be tyrants.

I'd brought some raisins to snack on. I dumped several into the palm of my hand and held them over the stall's half-door to lure Chinook.

He drew his head back and crouched, legs braced.

I didn't move. "Come, I'm your friend."

He stretched his neck to catch the scent of the raisins, the long hairs on his nostrils quivering like a May fly's antennae. I held my hand still. Gingerly, he closed the space between us. When his moist nostrils touched my hand the strange smell seemed to startle him. He jumped backward, thought things over, then stepped forward to whiffle up the raisins.

"I'm coming in to talk, so don't be afraid." I opened the stall door and crept inside.

Chinook circled for a few minutes blowing and sniffing before he relaxed and let me stroke his neck. He lowered his eyelids, mouthed my hat and sleeve. He seemed as changeable as the weather, one minute threatening a storm, the next as calm as a windless lake. I'd been told he was born during one of nature's phenomena called a chinook, hence his name. It seemed appropriate. A chinook was a wind that could streak in from nowhere, blow its warm breath over the frozen Montana landscape, thaw two feet of snow in an hour, then fade to a soft zephyr.

Chinook's injury oozed blood through the bandage. While I replaced the dressing, he stood with a patience and gentleness remarkable for an ungelded horse. He even ran his flaccid lips over my hair and collar in a show of friendship. When a brindle kitten scrambled under the door to rub against his leg, he picked it up gently in his mouth and held it out all slobbery for me to take. The simple gesture captured the mother and lover in me and melted my heart. I began to see Kitty's and Gabe's side of the argument. This was a horse worth keeping.

When ready to clean the stall, I turned Chinook into a corral that ran across the back of the barn. Excited to see his mares on the far ridge, he trotted back and forth along the fence, filling the air with snorts and whinnies. His hoofs clapped on the hard-packed earth and kicked up the smell of wet dung.

I was scraping the tines of the fork along the dirt floor to collect urine-soaked straw and manure when a man's voice came from the doorway at the front of the barn, the pitch raised to carry above the horses' clamor. "Hello there."

My heart gave a leap. I could imagine one of Gabe's creditors come to collect a debt.

Turning, I met the inquiring gray eyes of a man who'd stooped to peer through the open doorway—Levi's jeans and jacket, embossed riding boots, grizzled black hair and handlebar mustache. He was slender with a slight middle-age paunch, and tall enough to fork a horse without stirrups. His frame seemed fluid somehow.

"Sorry, I didn't mean to scare you."

"That—That's quite all right. I just wasn't expecting—rather, I was expecting—" I found myself at a loss for words, suddenly conscious of my appearance. I thought I must look like any other cowhand who worked in mud, dust, and manure. I brushed bits of hay from my shirt.

The man raised bushy brows in an expression that said he was surprised to find a woman cleaning the stall. "Would you be Mrs. Breen?"

"I'm Jessie Tate. Gabe is my brother."

"I see. Then I'd best introduce myself." He removed a gray Stetson. Tanned skin below his white hat line betrayed work in the outdoors. He was no debt collector. "My name is Dillard. Sam Dillard?" He said the last as if he hoped it would spark a memory. "Did Mr. Breen receive my letter?"

"I have no idea. I just arrived yesterday."

"Then you probably don't know why I'm here."

I looked at Dillard in question. "Why are you here?"

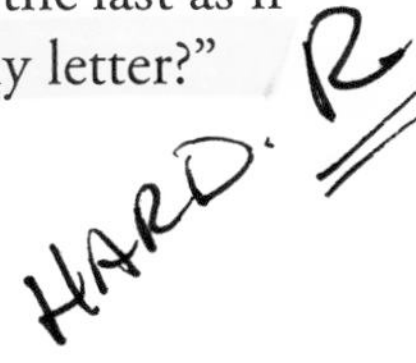

Chapter 5

Dillard flipped his hand in the direction of the crossbreeds' range on the hogback. "I've come for my horses. The Chinaman told me to talk to the lady in the barn."

His horses? "You mean the racehorses. I thought they belonged to Marcus Daly. Are you one of his men?"

Dillard gave a little snort. "Hardly. And I'm not into racing."

"Then which ones are yours?" Gabe had told me each wrangler would keep the cow pony he was riding, Kitty the three ponies in the pasture. Other than the crossbreeds Gabe wanted for Kitty, that left only some mules and Percherons.

"I've bought the herd of crossbreeds. The ones bred for work in the mountains."

"There must be a mistake. Gabe told me—" I clamped my mouth shut before I said something that might cause a misunderstanding. I had no idea what explanation Gabe would offer.

Dillard looked at me as though I were missing a lobe of my brain. "Maybe I should talk to Mr. Breen. Where can I find him?"

"He's in the house, but . . ." I moved toward Dillard, wondering how much I should say about Gabe's condition. "Who are you?"

"A cattle buyer from Colorado. In my letter, I said I'd come today." An apologetic smile spread across the kind, sober face. "I hope I'm not putting you out."

"Did you know about Gabe's illness?"

"He was having headaches when I was here a year ago. Are they still causing him fits?"

I stepped outside and stood next to Dillard. "He's dying," I said glumly. "A brain tumor."

The long planes of Dillard's cheeks went slack. He gave a long, low whistle. "That's a gut-twister. I'm sorry." He stared at the cabin on the far side of the turn-around, running his fingers across his mustache in thought. "It's a bad time for you. I don't want to butt in."

"There isn't going to be a better time."

"Then I'll collect my horses and be on my way." He turned to leave.

"You're not driving them all the way back to Colorado, I hope."

He stopped in mid-step and shook his head. "I've bought a piece of land in the Big Hole. I need to put up corrals and a cabin before the first deep snow."

"You'll be pushing it. The Hole can get a hard snow any time now."

Dillard frowned toward the ridge that held most of the crossbreeds. "Then I'd best get at it." He pulled his far-seeing gaze from the horses and turned it on me. "Could I talk to Mr. Breen? I'd like to give him a check for the balance I owe. I'll need a bill of sale, papers on the stallion. Maybe you could see to that."

"He's sleeping right now." I wanted to stall Dillard until I spoke to Gabe. "I'll finish here. He may be awake by then." For me, the sale would be a godsend, but I knew someone had made a mistake. I took a water bucket from inside the door and held it out. "How are your muscles?"

Dillard grinned. "Good enough to haul water."

While he scooped bits of hay from the water barrel in the stall and filled it with fresh water, I filled the manger with hay and tossed in a few potatoes to kill intestinal worms.

When I led Chinook into the stall, the sun pierced a narrow window and sparked into vibrance the reddish hues in his coat. Dillard stood outside the half-door, his arms crossed on the top-brace. His eyes gleamed. "I wondered if that wasn't my stallion carrying on. What a beaut. I got me a couple of good saddle sores looking for a stud like him."

"Quite an investment."

"My boy's footing most of the bill."

"Still a big investment." I couldn't imagine Gabe selling Chinook for less than six thousand dollars. The ledgers showed he'd paid eight thousand for the retired race horse. "Is your son a breeder?"

"A surveyor. He's contracted with the government to survey southwestern Montana. I'm going to retire so I can help." Dillard's voice was medium in pitch. In addition to weariness, the Texas drawl carried a trace of sadness or disappointment.

From the troughs at the corners of his mouth and the furrows that creased his forehead, I judged him to be about fifty. A little young to retire. "Why do you need so many horses?"

"We'll have a big crew."

I removed Chinook's halter and draped it across the half-door, scooted a pan of linseed meal into the corner. "Won't a stallion cause problems?"

"I'll keep him at my place in the Hole while the other horses are out in the field. The survey'll drag on for several years. Some of the horses will go lame or wear out. Chinook'll grow the herd."

I opened the half-door and walked through, closed it. Dillard leaned across it again while Chinook edged over to sniff his outstretched hand.

"He's a fine thoroughbred. Nice head—straight, lean. Eyes big and alert. He has a lot of depth through his girth. His coat's silky." Dillard stroked the long, sloping shoulders, studying them with eyes that reminded me of light shining through smoky quartz.

"The grass here makes his coat shiny. It packs more energy than grass at lower elevations." Speaking as if I were an expert, I went on to name the different varieties and what they did for a horse. Dillard nodded as if he knew it all.

He straightened, groaning a little as he pushed on the small of his back. "I've already put in a long day. Shall we see if your brother's awake?"

I spent the short distance between the barn and cabin wondering how I could prepare Gabe for Dillard's surprise visit. At least, it had come as a surprise to me. I had no idea whether Gabe would remember the man's letter or that he'd bought Kitty's crossbreeds. Neither Kitty nor Yeng Sang had mentioned anything. Evidently, Gabe had told them nothing. If he had, Kitty would be even more furious with the world.

Dillard had tied a saddle horse and a sturdy brown packhorse to the hitchrail in front of the cabin. No sign of another rider. I wondered how he'd manage the herd by himself. "Did you come alone?"

"Got a Mexican wrangler, Benito. He's watching some little gal gentle a mustang. Reminds me of my daughter. She'd put a red rag to the bull at the flick of an eyelash." I detected a grim edge to his voice.

When Dillard and I stepped into the dimly lit bear's den, he took off his hat and squinted to adjust his sight from the bright outdoors, registering shock when he saw Gabe hunched on a lodgepole chair. He was coughing, a wadded bandana handkerchief at his mouth, the patchwork quilt thrown over his lap. He appeared more the Grim Reaper than a man. No chance for me to speak to him in private.

Yeng Sang scuffed about in the bedroom, changing the covers on the bunk. He'd set a pail and mop just inside the sitting room door. A slop-jar stood beside them, smelling of urine and Lysol. I wavered between the need for apology and the desire to ignore it. I ignored it, and went on to introduced Dillard and explain why he was there.

Gabe wrinkled his brow. The bony hands in his lap shook. "What are you trying to pull, mister? I didn't sell the crossbreeds. Never would. They belong to Kitty."

It was Dillard's turn to frown. He towered over Gabe, the heavy brows drawn into a hedge across his forehead. "Last summer you wanted to sell. Said you were desperate for money."

"I never saw you before."

"What kind of bullshit is that? I spent two days here looking over the herd."

Gabe leaned forward in the chair, trying to raise himself to challenge the lofty Dillard. "You're a liar. I've never laid eyes on you."

"I'd say you're the liar, sir." The words were measured, resolute. Dillard's face had turned as red as a newborn's. The lines at the bridge of his nose were etched deep. "I know you're sick and might have forgotten, but I have proof." He pulled a wallet from inside his denim jacket, took out a folded paper and handed it to Gabe.

Gabe studied the paper with scrunched-up eyes, tilting his head forward and backward while he held the paper at varying distances. He handed it to me with disgust. "Can't see anymore."

"It's a receipt," I said after I'd scanned the page. "Mr. Dillard made a partial payment of six thousand dollars for a herd of thirty-five thoroughbred-mustang cross, including all foals born this summer. Three thousand of that applies to the six-thousand-dollar selling price of Chinook. He's to pay the remaining six thousand dollars owing on the herd and stallion before he takes possession. It's dated July twentieth of last year, signed by you."

"It's a forgery," Gabe said with disgust.

"On the back is a list of the horses in the herd."

"I tell you, it's a forgery!"

Dillard stepped toward Gabe in anger, caught himself, edged backward, and stood with nostrils flaring. "You think I'm some greenhorn you can flim-flam. You honor the sale, sir, or I'll go to the law."

"Go right ahead!" The words retched from Gabe's lips like vomit. He choked, then broke into a lung-wracking cough.

I took Dillard's arm. "Let's step outside."

He didn't budge.

"Please." I pulled on his arm. He went grudgingly, scowling back over his shoulder at Gabe.

Outside near the hitchrail, I told him about Gabe's lapse of memory, the reason he wanted Kitty to have the crossbreeds, and my reason for wanting them sold. "Don't take the horses until Gabe remembers the sale. It would be less upsetting for him." And for Kitty, I thought. She'd be furious, however it came to pass.

Dillard untied the rope that held the packhorse and passed it through a ring on the sorrel mare's saddle. He'd calmed somewhat. "I can appreciate the fix you're in, but I don't have time. Most I can wait is two days." He untied the mare and hoisted himself into the saddle.

"Where will you be if I want to reach you?" I hoped there'd be no need for that.

"I have a friend at Henry's Lake. That's near the park. I'll bide the time there."

"Maybe you should look for other horses," I said with reluctance.

"I've already rode over the whole state, half of Wyoming and Idaho. I'm not going to let this turn into a wild-goose chase. Your brother's crossbreeds are just what my boy needs for rough country." He gathered the reins and clucked at the mare.

I grabbed the bridle to hold her in place. "There's something else you should know." I hesitated, steeling myself for his anger. "There's no money for a refund."

He sucked in a breath. His eyes sparked outrage. In one movement, he took my hand from the bridle and dug his heels into the mare. "I'll give you two days. Then I take the horses."

Chapter 6

The hours sped by as if they were hares and I a tortoise trying to keep pace. Gabe still had no memory of the sale of the crossbreeds, nor could I find it listed in the ledgers. No record of a bank deposit. I'd begun to think he might be right about Dillard, except the man seemed an honest sort.

My heart ached at the sight of Gabe near death, yet I couldn't promise to take the herd to the Bitterroot knowing I'd have to break the promise. Not only did I lack the money for feed, but Carver Dean's threat of blackmail loomed dark on the horizon. I tried to prepare Gabe for the possibility the horses belonged to Dillard but could make no dent in his resolve. I didn't dare try too hard, as it upset him. I had little chance, anyway. Pain seared through his head so relentlessly he spent most of the time in a drugged stupor. I wondered how long he could endure.

Dillard's wrangler, Benito, had told Kitty about the sale, and she was incensed. Every time we spoke, she made some argument against it. She was still brooding the second morning of Dillard's allotted time as we headed down the drive with oats for a few of the crossbreeds kept separate from the rest of the herd.

She darted a sullen glance my way. "You let Dillard have the horses and I won't have anything to do."

"I have no choice. He bought them."

"That's what *he* says. Pa says he's a liar."

"He has a receipt."

"Could be a fake."

"True. He may be a crook."

"You know he is."

"I know nothing of the kind, but I'm going to learn the truth." I saw no point in further wrangling. We'd been over this many times. "You'll have plenty to do in the Bitterroot," I said, reaching for the positive. "You can tend the cows and sheep. Hunt and fish." I knew Kitty lived to work in the fresh air and beneath the blue sky. I purposely omitted indoor activities, except to say, "There's school. We're thinking of having two terms, one in the fall and one in the spring."

She crinkled her nose as if she'd smelled a skunk. "I don't much care for school. Anyway, I'm not going to the Bitterroot."

"Gabe wants you to go. I do too." *More than you know.*

She made no reply, simply stared sourly at the path her feet were taking. Why would animals accept my affection while this niece of mine would have none of it? If only she'd open her shell a crack and let me in.

We'd reached a pasture that held several geldings and fillies as well as a mustang mare heavy with foal. Farther west, Chinook's harem of eight mares and their foals grazed the open hogback. Several exiled yearlings and two-year-olds grazed higher on the grassy ridge. Sight of them brought a vision of the acres and acres of pasture they required, the tons of winter hay, of which I had little. Thank heaven for Sam Dillard.

Chinook's demanding whinny blared across the fields. The mares stopped grazing and raised their heads to answer their lord and master.

"He doesn't like to be separated," I said.

"They're his. He doesn't want any harm coming to them."

I pointed toward the pregnant mare, a light bay. She was feeding at the back of the field that held the small group of crossbreeds. "Looks like she's due soon."

"It's Chinook's catch colt. Lilly usually throws a chestnut like Chinook, but sometimes a dun. Pa'd rather the foals were dark. The army buys them when they're four-year-olds. It likes dark horses, harder to spot from a distance."

"Why the crossbreeds?"

"They're good for riding in rough country. They can climb like mountain goats."

"They get that from Chinook?"

"He passes on his smarts and big lungs, his easy stride. The way they hang onto a steep trail comes from the mustang mothers. Steady as a rock. Nothing rattles them."

Kitty dumped a pail of oats in a feed trough attached to the fence, then banged on the bottom of the pail. Lilly, the pregnant mare, whinnied and headed in our direction at a full-bellied trot. Several sleek chestnut and bay fillies and geldings trailed close behind, all of them nickering, leaving brown trails in the morning frost.

Kitty's face clouded as she watched them run in. "I can't believe they're sold to Dillard. I could earn me a living growing the herd."

"It takes money to make money."

Her reply was a sullen snort.

"The money Mr. Dillard owes would pay for a college education. You could train to be most anything you want. There are even women lawyers now."

She turned to glare at me. "Who wants to be a lawyer? What I want is to raise horses. And by God nobody's going to stop me."

I stood still, watching Kitty march up the drive toward the cabin. With each of her determined steps it became clearer the grim days ahead wouldn't be easy. Events had ripped her heart's cloth, and there was nothing I could do to mend it. It seemed that by waiting for Gabe to remember the sale of the horses, I'd helped with the tearing. What on earth could I do to ease her heartache and narrow the chasm that separated us?

Barren at forty-three, I could no longer carry the seed of life, but I could act as medium, the one who nurtured and sustained. I could thaw a freezing calf by my stove on a bitter February night and suckle it from a bottle. I could tuck lettuce seed in the earth, give it a drink, and watch it shoot fingers of frilly green toward the sun. I could slip my arm around shy first-graders and open their minds to possibility. I'd find a way to nurture Kitty, too. Despite her acid tongue, she was mine to care for. We were the last of the Breens, she and I. We'd carry on.

As if my thoughts had traveled on the breeze, Kitty stopped abruptly. She spent a moment looking my way, then rushed toward me, her arms spread wide. Without a word, she threw her arms around me, lay her head on my shoulder, and drenched me with tears. I had no idea what had caused her change of heart, nor how long it would last, but it seemed her troubles had become more than she could bear alone. I wanted to take her home, where I could protect her from life's agonies and show her its promise.

I pushed strands of orange hair from her forehead and kissed it, as I had when she was a little child. "Don't you worry, Kitty. We'll make it through all this. We're strong, you and I. We'll find a way."

Chapter 7

Concerned about what the next morning would bring, I kept busy as an anthill. A subdued, silent Kitty helped me clean the rest of the barn, sorting out tack I could use in the Bitterroot and that which would stay with the new owner. She seemed preoccupied while she worked, hardly raised her eyes from her plate at the supper table, and climbed early to her bed in the loft.

I went to bed early as well, but worry disturbed my rest. My thoughts twisted and turned, traveling in circles. Kitty's words—*I want to raise horses. And by God, nobody's going to stop me*—rang in my memory's ear.

Gabe had spent fifteen years developing a horse for mountain trails, one with superb lung power, stamina, sure-footedness. When he bought Chinook, he'd found the sire of his dreams. He'd captured the best wild mares to breed to the stallion. Well-muscled, their smaller size was a good balance for Chinook's sixteen hands. For Kitty—more than her passion for horses, or the means to earn a living—the crossbreeds symbolized her father. If she owned the herd, she could keep Gabe with her, at least in spirit.

"These crossbreeds are the best I've found for traveling canyon and ridge top," Dillard had said.

He wanted them. Needed them. Kitty wanted them. She needed them for a variety of reasons. I needed the money from the sale of the herd for Kitty's future.

So what should I do?

I tossed, tangling my sheets, arriving at a different decision every half-hour. Just before dawn I settled on a compromise I could live with. My responsibility was no longer to Gabe. His life was in the shadows. I would act on Kitty's behalf. That meant supporting her dreams as well as helping her find balance in her life. It meant I must convince Dillard to take half the herd—he'd paid for that—and to find more horses elsewhere. No easy task. It meant helping Kitty face the reality of owning half the herd. The task no easier there.

Despite my will against it, morning arrived, bringing a headache. The clock I'd set on the floor beside my bed in the bunkhouse read four A.M. I'd set the alarm for five, but I hadn't slept all night.

Leaving Gabe to finish his drug-sleep, I drank three cups of Arbuckle's while I baked a coffee cake, set bread to rise, and boiled potatoes for a big salad. Gabe's wranglers would arrive in a few hours to collect their belongings and paychecks. After driving the cattle to Monida for shipment, they'd expect a big meal.

"They'll be hungry enough to eat plates and all," I said to Yeng Sang.

He'd visited a Chinese friend in Lakeview during the night and was hung over from drinking too much rice whiskey. He sat at the kitchen table, his head resting on his arms. I'd pushed cups of tea in front of him and glasses of buttermilk. In between naps, he'd downed them obediently and graciously.

Yeng Sang had two vices—no, three: rice whiskey, opium, and gambling. I'd been told he indulged them rarely, then with abandon. Most of the time he was perfect help. Priceless. No matter how many extra to cook for and clean up after, he never complained. The kitchen was never in disorder. Last night was one of those rare occasions when he'd heard the owl hoot. It was likely Gabe's condition had led to that.

Gabe's faint rasp drifted through the doorway. Yeng Sang roused. "Yes, Mister Gabe. I come." And to me as he shuffled around the room gathering a towel and pouring water from a bucket into a pitcher, "Last night I sorry for Mister Gabe. I drink too much whiskey. This morning I think 'bout death. I think Mister Gabe once was nothing—no body, no spirit. The One give him shape, mind to think with, spirit. Now he change again—go to other world, find peace. It is the way. I sad, but it helps to know this."

The simple, eloquent speech caved my chest and started it heaving with grief. I hid my tears behind a handkerchief. "I've failed," I said after I'd swallowed back my sorrow. "I came here to make things easier. Instead, I've made things worse."

"Even wise men sometime play the fool. You have done what you could."

I shook my head dismally. "One way or another I'm going to make things right."

Yeng Sang turned and focused his deep-seeing eyes on mine. I had the feeling he was looking down the road I would have to travel. "Do not worry. Your heart will show the path to follow." Then over his shoulder as he stepped toward the door, "Please to fix tea for Mister Gabe. Maybe cracker. Maybe he not want either."

The wall clock chimed seven times. Despite the clatter of pans and bits of conversation with Yeng Sang, no sound came from the loft. I wouldn't wake Kitty. Yesterday had been difficult. Today could be worse.

A loud bawling erupted at the barn. Ordinarily, milking Daisy was Yeng Sang's job. I'd milk today. I checked the cooler in the small spring-house off the kitchen, found a pitcher of milk left from yesterday, a little buttermilk, and a jar of butter. Good. We'd not have time to skim or churn today. I shrugged on Gabe's sheepskin jacket and pulled on a woolen cap. The corner of the kitchen held a collection of milking tools. I took a two-gallon pail and headed for the barn.

Daisy had raised her bawling to a higher level of distress. "I'm coming," I yelled. "Be patient."

The kittens knew it was milking time and scurried into the barn ahead of me. The sidebarn that held the stalls was quiet—no stomp of hooves, no nickers. I stepped to the doorway and looked inside the icy cave. No reddish brown head peered over the stall door. Was Chinook sick? I rushed over and stared inside. Empty. Perhaps Kitty had slipped from the cabin without my knowing and returned him to the hogback.

The rack that held her saddle was empty. A few halters were missing from the wall pegs, some hobbles—I had no idea how many—and at least one bridle, perhaps more. Why had she needed all that tack to return Chinook to the range? A frightening possibility shot to the surface of my mind.

Hoping to find Kitty or to question Yeng Sang, I hurried back to the cabin. I found neither one there. When I climbed the shaky ladder to the cabin's loft I wasn't surprised to see an empty bed.

Kitty, what on earth have you done?

I rushed down the drive, scanning the pastures at the far end. Fog blanketed the lake and reached long tendrils up the gentle slope to the main wagon road. A few gray wisps drifted across the lower pasture. Not enough to obscure the view. No fillies or geldings, no pregnant mare. Only the mules and Percherons in the field across the way. I grasped at a straw to keep hope from drowning. The crossbreeds could be lying down; there was enough mist to hide them. I ran farther down the drive, toward the dark shapes of cattle hulking on the edge of the fog.

From the east came the clatter of hoofs, the rattle and creak of harness, and the crack of a whip. A bright red shape loomed through the mist. No crossbreeds raced along inside the fence and whinnied as they did four times a day when a stage rumbled past.

When I reached their pasture I saw hoofprints leading from the gate into the drive and onto the wagon road. Perhaps Kitty had driven the fillies and geldings to the hogback to join the rest of the herd. But why would she take a pregnant mare from the safety of the pasture? I ran down the stage road toward the hogback following prints overlain with those of cattle, spooking longhorns from the murky fog. My frantic breath raked at my lungs.

Wraith-like mists rose from the grayness and transformed pine and aspen at lake's edge into phantoms on the prowl. The chatter of waterfowl traveled beneath the fog and reached my ears loud and clear—much like the gabbling of a crowd at the county fair. I felt the damp. Smelled it. Not a good day to find horses.

A half-mile down the road, I reached the gate that opened onto the hogback. It was closed, but hoofprints told a story. Horses had come through the gate and headed west with those from the pasture. When? Impossible to tell. Piles of dung lay damp in the road, but fog would have kept them moist, with no night wind to dry them.

I recalled hearing whinnies sometime during the night, the sort one heard when coyotes were on the prowl. I'd heard no hoofbeats. Anyone could have taken the horses from the pasture a quarter-mile distant. Only Kitty, with her skill in handling horses, could have slipped Chinook past the bunkhouse without my knowing. The fact loomed stark. Kitty had taken the entire herd.

She'd left after nine o'clock that night, when I'd gone to bed, and before four-fifteen in the morning, when I'd returned to the cabin. She could be several hours away and still on the move. I had no idea where she was headed. I hoped she wouldn't go far. But there was the possibility I might not find her until late in the day or even tomorrow morning. I'd prepare for a long ride. That meant packing a bedroll and other camping gear.

My stomach sank at the thought, my head reeled. Which held first claim on my attention, Gabe or Kitty? Life or death. If only the hours would stand still for a while and give me time to care for both, time to think and plan. But time had a habit of rolling along, oblivious to my needs and my wishes. I'd do the best I could with the time I had.

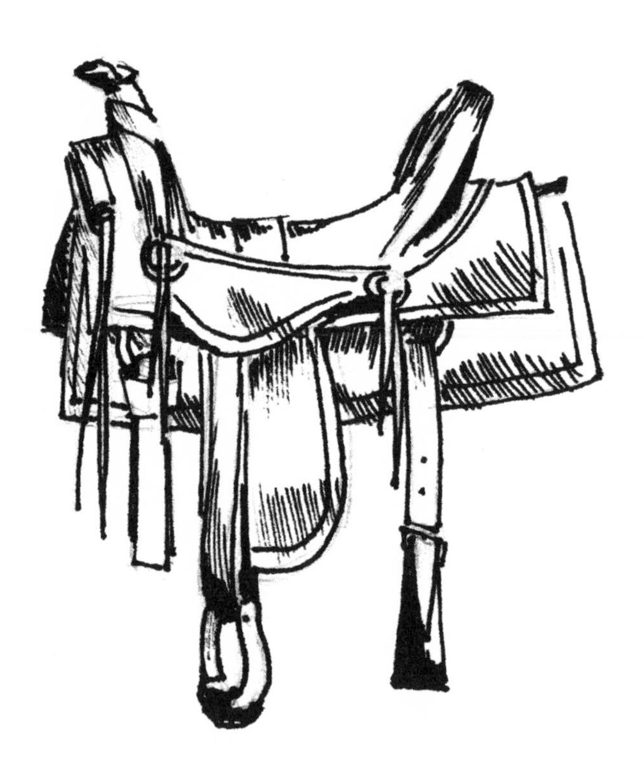

Chapter 8

Yeng Sang had revived enough to put a fresh flaxseed-vinegar poultice on Gabe's chest, and the smell swept up my nostrils as I entered the bedroom. He'd propped Gabe's back with pillows so he could drink a cup of tea, but Gabe had slid down the pillows and lay with his eyes closed, his neck at a painful angle. Light from the oil lamp flickered on the logs like candles at an altar and breathed yellow life into his sunken face. Seeing him lie there, awaiting death, brought a sudden weight bearing down upon me, as if all the world's pain had crept into the room and sat on my shoulders.

I rearranged the pillows while Gabe stared at me through glazed slits. He moistened his lips with a reluctant tongue.

"Would you like some tea?"

He stared at me slow and unblinking, the ghost of a man trying to get his mind to work. No recognition in his eyes. No understanding.

"Is there anything I can do?" I picked up the cup of lukewarm tea. "Can I heat the tea?"

He raised bony fingers from the bed and wagged them. "Who . . ." His unsteady gaze crept over me until a glimmer of recognition came to his eyes. "Jessie?"

"It's me." Tears spilled down my cheeks. I wiped them away with shaky fingers.

Gabe looked slowly around the room as if his eyes had missed something. "Kitty?"

"She's outside." An evasion, but true. I wouldn't tell him Kitty had ridden off with Chinook and his harem.

"I need to see her."

"She has a chore to finish." Another white lie.

He tapped the edge of the bunk. "Then you. Come sit."

I settled on the bunk and smoothed a wisp of downy, gray-blond hair away from his eyes. His skin was cooler today, but pneumonia had taken its toll. I had the feeling it would be a last goodbye. My chin trembled.

"Don't be sad," he said. "I want to die . . . the pain . . ." The words came so softly I could hardly hear them. I leaned closer. "Take good care of Kitty." His lips quivered. Tears made wet trails through the bristles on his cheeks. He drew a wheezing breath and sighed. "I was stupid . . . selfish . . gambled everything away . . . left her nothing."

"Gabe, please. You don't have to—"

"I want to confess," he said with a burst of energy. But it had been too much. He tilted his head back and lay a moment struggling for breath. I took his hand. Nothing but bones covered with a thin layer of skin.

"That man, Dillard," he said with eyes closed. "The crossbreeds are his. I lied so Kitty could have them. He's paid for half. Don't take his check for the rest . . . give them to Kitty."

"I'd already decided to give her half. It's as good as done." More truth in that than he knew.

Again he struggled for breath. He seemed unable to say more. I didn't press him. Rather, I bided my time, searching the dresser for papers on Chinook. I found them in an envelope hidden among some long johns. It also held a copy of Dillard's receipt. I tucked it into my shirt pocket, wondering what Gabe had done with the elusive six thousand dollars. He'd probably gambled it away or bought another racehorse. Part of me was furious. The other part felt only a deep, deep sadness.

The lamp sputtered. Gabe motioned for me to dampen it a bit. I did, turning the corners of the room to shadow, stealing the life from Gabe's face and transforming it to ashes. As before, a great pain washed over me, the icy dread of death and of the unknown.

Gabe focused his eyes on me with great effort, as if the strain helped bring thoughts to the surface of his mind. "Promise you'll take Kitty and half the herd to the Bitterroot . . . take Yeng Sang too."

I dropped onto the edge of the bunk and took his hands. "I'll not leave you here alone."

His eyes opened to red-rimmed slits. "Do you want me to die in peace?" I nodded. "Then do as I ask."

I raised my hands in a hopeless gesture. "I have no idea what Dillard will do."

"Try begging."

I flicked a wan smile, then sat in silence while another worry twisted through my splintered thoughts. "What route should I take to the Bitterroot?"

"Go up Sheep Creek to Simpson Creek, then down the Medicine Lodge to Bannack. You know the way from there . . . my friend, Hal Sherwood, has a ranch two miles west of Bannack . . . you can rest up there . . . maps are with my papers." He squeezed my hand—to receive courage, I thought, as much as to give it. His eyes receded even more darkly into their sockets. "I'll be with you," he whispered, "sailing on a cloud . . . riding the ridge tops."

Tears clawed their way up my throat. I looked around the room, searching for something on which to fasten my gaze. It settled on the lamp, which blurred before my eyes.

Gabe's cheeks slackened into their hollows. "It's all right Jess . . . we all die sometime."

For a long desolate moment we sat, thinking our own thoughts. I took out a handkerchief to dry my eyes and bent to kiss him goodbye.

He put a feeble hand on my arm. "Don't go yet. There's something I must tell you. I should have told you long ago, but I loved her too much. . I couldn't let her go." Chin trembling, he pressed his head against the pillow and leaked tears that pooled in the hollows beneath his eyelids.

His confessional tone made me search his face in question. I stroked his forehead. "Maybe you should leave it unsaid."

"No!" he blurted with an unexpected show of strength. "I'm not going to die with it on my conscience. Even if it makes you hate me."

"How could I hate you? For God's sake, Gabe, what is it?"

The tortured seconds dragged by while I waited for an answer. Gabe couldn't seem to look me in the eye. He wiped his eyes and nose, finally gathered his courage on a long, wheezing breath. "I . . . I stole your child, Jess," he said with self-spite. "Me and Ben."

I sat breathless, too dumbfounded for speech. When words came, they stammered from my lips. "Wh-What do you mean, stole my child?"

Gabe looked up then and seized my hand with an imploring grip. "Don't blame us, Jess. You were so sick from giving birth we thought you'd die . . Amy was at my house, her baby dead. She was delirious like you, but with more chance to live . . . it didn't seem wrong." He choked back tears and swallowed.

A wave of disbelief washed over me, carrying me to the brink of a terrible rage. "Are you saying Amy's baby died, that Kitty is mine?"

"Yes, God forgive me."

I thought a sledge hammer had struck me. The confession had sent all the heartache from the past, the grief, the terrible longing plunging down around my shoulders. I saw Kitty at Amy's breast and thought of what I'd missed. How many times I'd imagined that child at my breast, imagined her cradled in my arms.

I tried to picture the days after the birth of my child—not as I recalled them, for I had no memory of the events, but as Ben had described them. He'd said that half the time I was out of my head, the other half lying like a corpse awaiting burial. When I was strong enough to walk, he'd taken me to the graveyard in what must have been a sham of sorrow—his, not mine. My grief was real. I recalled kneeling at the tiny granite slab to lay a bouquet of wildflowers and to kiss the stone.

Ben had said it was better to have lost the baby than me—*If that had happened,* he'd said, *I would have curled up and died.*

I wondered now, as I faced the grim truth, if death wouldn't have been a better fate for both of us, rather than live the lie, rather than live all those years with that other secret eating at our souls.

Gabe's trickle of a voice wandered into my musings, drawing me back to the present. "Say something, Jess. Say you forgive me."

A heavy weight had settled on my heart, an unbearable burden of disbelief, anger, and disappointment in those I'd loved. Slowly, still not quite believing, I turned my eyes on Gabe. Behind the bleak face I saw a stranger, a man I'd never really known, a thief, a destroyer of lives.

When I opened my mouth to speak, my hollow voice seemed to rise from someone else's throat. "How could you have done such a thing? To me. Your sister. We were—I was—oh, Gabe, how could you?"

I pushed off from the bunk, and leaning against the wall, beat on a log to give vent to my anger. My head reeled with images of the past, with the facts of Gabe's confession. The only bright spot was the fact that Kitty belonged to me. My daughter. My very own child. I'd often had the uncanny feeling Kitty was mine, that a certain twist of her head and look in her eyes reflected a spirit born of me rather than of Gabe and Amy.

"It was Ben's idea," Gabe said through my distress. "No excuse for me, but the truth. You know how he hated to have you pregnant with—with that cad's baby."

I spun as bitterness took an iron grip on my feelings. "Why take it out on me? It wasn"t my fault I was—"

"Ben couldn't live with a child of rape. He was a proud man . . . he saw a chance to be rid of the baby and help Amy at the same time."

"Help Amy?" I said with outrage. "What about me? Grieving all those years for the child I thought I'd lost." I bent over Gabe, hands propped on the bunk. "Do you know what it's like to be barren? Yearning. Longing. No child to fill my woman's needs." I straightened to wipe the sweat of anger from my upper lip. "You men are all alike. Selfish. Uncaring."

"Please don't hate me, Jess. You'll be fine. Kitty'll be happy to know her mother is alive . . . happy to be with you."

"That's easy enough for you to say. You haven't felt the sting of her resentment." The torment of the past few minutes had taken its toll. The starch had left my knees. I dropped onto the bunk and glared at the wall, unseeing. I thought of Kitty alone in the wilds, driving a herd of spirited horses, facing unknown dangers. *My child* out in the wilderness.

"I'm sorry for all the pain I've caused you," Gabe said. He put the handkerchief to his cracked lips and coughed. Tears seeped from under his crepe-thin eyelids.

I studied his ashen face for a long second, and searched my feelings. Wretchedness poured from my heart. "I doubt I'll ever be able to forgive you, Gabe, but I understand why you took the baby. I know it was Ben's doing. I can even understand how he felt." I recalled the other desperate act Ben had committed because of me, the secret that haunted our days.

My thoughts swerved abruptly to the third person involved in the switch of babies. "Did Amy know?"

Gabe shook his head, a slight, grim wag of denial.

"Kitty?"

"I could never bring myself to tell her."

"So it's up to the victim to right the wrong. That figures." I let sarcasm ride the remark. "Now isn't the time to tell her. She's too filled with grief

"Forget what's over and done, Jess. She needs you. This is your chance to be the mother."

To be the mother? Oh Lord how I'd wanted that.

As much as my heart fought showing Gabe any charity, I knew it might be our last moment together. I didn't want to have regrets. It would take more constraint and compassion on my part than I could imagine, but deep down I wanted it. Hesitantly, I leaned forward to wipe the tears from his face, my hand resting on the blanket that covered his chest. I felt something hard beneath the wool, the shape familiar.

With a feeling of dread, I pulled back the blanket and saw what I already knew was there. "Why do you have the gun?"

Gabe shrank from the directness of my gaze. "F-For protection." The way he stammered and the way he looked aside confirmed my instincts. He had something other than protection in mind.

The bones seemed to leave my flesh, my heart to burst from conflicted feelings. My first impulse was to take the revolver. My hand rested on the cold metal while my mind drifted into the past, then into the future. The present was almost beyond enduring.

It's wrong, my conscience screamed. *Let his Maker take him in due time.*

Then as I thought of the pain Gabe had endured, the hours, the days, the years of it, I realized he had the right to die as he chose. I'd not interfere.

His eyes closed wearily as I pulled the blanket over the gun. "Jessie?"

"Yes?"

"I want you to sing a hymn . . . maybe Rock of Ages."

How could I sing at a time like this? Sorrow and outrage had swollen the linings of my throat.

"Please, Jessie. Your angel voice will make me think I've flown to Heaven."

Lord! How could I sing? How could I forget the terrible events that tore at my feelings?

I breathed deeply, trying to keep emotion from clogging my throat, swallowed once, twice, three times before the frail melody strung from my lips. "Rock of ages, cleft for me, let me hide myself in Thee. Let the water and the blood from Thy side, a healing—" My voice wavered, choked. I swallowed, then went on with effort. "Be of sin the double cure, save from wrath and make me pure. Should my tears . . ."

The words, so appropriate for what had just transpired, were more than

I could bear. I gave my brother one last kiss, one last despairing glance, and stole from the room.

Chapter 9

I was still in the grip of shock and grief when I headed for the barn to saddle a horse and pack the camping gear Yeng Sang had gathered—so preoccupied I nearly missed seeing Sam Dillard. He stood at the hitchrail at the front of the cabin, wiping his mare's face with a cloth that drifted the scent of camphor and cedar oil. The air had begun to warm and black flies clung to her eyelids. Dillard's wrangler waited at the edge of the fog bank that had crept to within a hundred yards of the cabin. He slouched against a fence rail, watching his pack animal and dun saddle horse graze on the short-cropped grass.

When I walked up to Dillard he took obvious note of my distress. "I've blundered again. Is it a bad time?"

"Gabe's failing. He . . ." My throat clogged on the rest.

"I'm sorry. Very sorry." He sounded genuinely sympathetic. "Not a time to be messing with horses." He folded the cloth and tucked it into an oilskin pouch. "By the way, where are the crossbreeds that were in the lower pasture? I didn't see them on my way in."

If Dillard had ridden in from Henry's Lake he would have seen only the tracks leaving the pasture at the foot of the drive. That was enough. I felt lame. Any other time I might have eased into the truth. This time, I blurted it out. "They're gone. Kitty's taken them somewhere."

Dillard's eyes became large gray question marks. "Why? Where?"

"I have no idea."

"You mean she just took off with them, didn't say anything?"

"That's right."

"Maybe she turned them in with those on the hogback."

"They're gone too."

"She stole them?" His face was turning red.

"She thinks they belong to her."

There was silence. A long, startled moment of it. Dillard stared at me tight-mouthed, jaw tense. The tendons in his neck stood out. "Now what am I supposed to do? I've been more than patient. Lost valuable time." His lips quivered beneath his handlebar mustache as though he was trying to keep from saying something he shouldn't. When words came, they were measured, the rasp of breath behind them. "You have no idea where she's taken them?"

"None. I was going to follow the tracks."

Dillard sucked air in sharply through flared nostrils. "Does Mister Breen recall selling the herd?"

"Yes—yes he does."

"Well, at least that river's crossed." He gave a sarcastic laugh. "Now all I have to do is find the herd." He stared out across the valley, his face dark with angry thoughts. "When did she leave?"

"Sometime between nine last night and four this morning. I learned of it about an hour ago."

His head spun toward me. "Good God! Maybe eleven hour's head start." He jammed the pouch into his saddlebag and gave the buckle a determined tug. "I'll need the papers on Chinook and a bill of sale for the herd. I'll give you the check for what I owe." He reached inside his jacket.

"I don't want the check." I paused, steeling myself for an even harsher exchange. "Gabe and I have agreed to let you have half the herd. You've already paid for that. The other half belongs to Kitty."

Dillard shot me a look that mixed disbelief with outrage. "That wasn't the agreement. You saw the receipt. It was for the entire herd." He pulled a written check from his wallet and thrust it into my hands. "This pays for the herd in full. Now I'd like the papers."

I shoved the check toward him. "I can't accept it."

He pushed my hand aside. "Nor will I accept its return."

"Then you leave me no choice." Slowly, deliberately I tore the check into bits.

Anger rippled Dillard's jaw. He wiped spittle from his lips with a long, calloused finger. "You're a determined woman, Mrs. Tate, but I'll not let you get away with this. I intend to have those horses. They're rightfully mine."

"*Half* are rightfully yours."

He thought about that, gritting his teeth. "Then I demand the certificate for the stallion and bill of sale for half the herd—mares, foals, fillies, colts equally divided." I could almost see the steam of anger rise from beneath his jacket. To his credit, he didn't shout, but it was obvious he fought the urge.

I, too, kept my voice down. "I'll not surrender any papers until I find Kitty and know she's safe. It'll be easier to divide the horses then, judging each on its merits." Still riding the crest of my courage, I added, "I'm sure Kitty will want the stallion."

"Oh no! The stallion's mine. I've paid three thousand on him. I'll pay the rest when I see what shape he's in."

He leveled one last scalding look on me, untied his horses, and mounting the sorrel clucked her into a fast trot. A few seconds later he'd disappeared into the fog.

* * *

I think moments arise in each life when doing what one must seems impossible. Such a moment struck me full bore with the muffled report of a revolver. Gabe and I had been brother and sister too long. Despite his confession, I wanted desperately to return to the cabin, scoop him into my arms and weep. It was all I could do to keep from it.

The fog had cleared, and as I rode out the drive, Gabe's embered eyes bore into me from the tawny meadowlands, breaking my heart, nearly snapping my mind. I vowed I'd not let that happen. I'd survived trouble in the past and hadn't cracked beneath the strain. Nor would I now. As Yeng Sang had put it in his quiet way, I'd reach out and do what was needed.

I'd salvage the best of Gabe for Kitty to cherish, help her to understand that all humans had failings, that they had weak threads in their fabric. I had mine as well. I could only hope my weak threads would hold strong for the uncertain trip ahead. My comfort lay in the knowledge Kitty was mine, the daughter for whom I'd yearned.

Yeng Sang would attend to Gabe's burial. After that, he'd pack his belongings along with items I wanted and follow the herd's trail. I'd left a piebald cow pony and pack mule for his use. I'd write a friend in Dillon and ask her to send a few things from the main ranch to the Bitterroot—Kitty's belongings and some of Gabe's, as well as a few treasured items that had belonged to my parents. I'd left paychecks for the wranglers and final cleaning instructions for Yeng Sang. I hoped I hadn't forgotten anything, but in my fractured state of mind that was likely.

I'd chosen to ride Bannack, Gabe's buckskin cow pony. Yeng Sang had told me the gelding was raised on the Sherwood's ranch and named for the nearby town, that he was a good pegger. "Mister Gabe say, 'that horse can turn on a dime and toss back nine cents change.'" Yeng Sang had gone on to say the horse could climb without working up a sweat and could keep his footing as well as a mountain sheep. I hoped that was true.

I'd failed to coax Rufus from camp, but Penny had followed gladly. She trotted alongside Bannack, a dog grin on her face. My pack animal was a brown mule called Shorty. Though smaller than most mules, he was well-muscled and alert. He carried my carpetbag and satchel, food, a small Army field tent, as well as halters, ropes, hobbles, and stakes for picketing horses. I'd keep his lead rope in hand until I learned his ways. If he proved steady, I'd loop the rope around my saddle horn or tie it to the ring in the saddle, a Denver style with side skirt and fenders.

To anyone passing, I'd look like a cowpoke, from Gabe's denim jacket and jeans to his brown felt plainsman's hat. Around my waist I wore a holstered Colt .45 double-action revolver. Yeng Sang had insisted I take it along to scare grizzlies on the higher slopes and to kill rattlesnakes at the lower elevations.

I'd tied Gabe's sheepskin jacket and slicker behind the saddle and strapped a pair of binoculars around the saddle horn. I'd considered bringing a rifle, but thought the scabbard might catch on brush. As it was, Bannack carried a load. My saddlebag was filled to bulging with human and horse medicines, dried apples and raisins, sandwiches, newspaper cut in sections for toilet use, a leather pouch that held Gabe's important papers.

It was late morning when I arrived at Lakeview. Several men and women strolled past the store and the half-dozen cabins that fronted the wagon road. Tourists. I could tell by their well-tailored traveling suits and the women's ruffled parasols. As I drew abreast a smithy, I understood why they were dawdling about town. A crimson coach sat crippled in front of the blacksmith's shop, the wheels on one side removed and leaning against the wall, the frame resting on blocks. A forge glowed red in the gloomy interior, sending a curl of smoke from a stovepipe at the back of the smithy.

A large, barrel-chested man with a thicket of red hair and beard worked near the open doorway. He'd set the strap from a thoroughbrace on the anvil and was hammering on it with a sledge. A blacksmith would likely notice everything that went on in town. Interrupting his work, I asked if he'd seen Kitty ride by last evening.

He straightened from his work and rested the sledge on the anvil. "'Twas quite a ways after dark, though the moon was full . . . mebbe ten or so." His voice had the lilt of the Irish. "I was working by lamp light to get that onto the blocks." He motioned toward the crippled stage.

"Was she running the horses?"

"Sure was. The lass—I'd thought her a lad at first—comes pounding down the road on that stallion o' Gabe's, a raft o' horses behind her. I thought me eyes were playing tricks. Kind of eerie, that time o' night."

"Was she managing all right?"

"Just fine. She was ponying a big bell mare. The rest following meek as lambs." He resumed pounding, grunting information with each swing. "I tried to get the lass to stop. She just waved and went on her way. Kitty's a fine girl, she is. I been fretting about her ever since, but had no time to ride out to Gabe's."

"It's just as well. He's . . . he's passed on."

I thanked the blacksmith for the information and told him not to worry about Kitty, I'd find her. It concerned me that she had more than twelve hours head start and that she might run the horses too hard in her need to escape. Still, I relaxed somewhat, knowing she had them under control.

A rising breeze had sent the lake fog scurrying. As I rounded the bend north of town, it riffled the waters that spread before me. High overhead it drove clouds shaped like ghosts across the sky. Their flat, gray bottoms trailed thin sheets of rain that never reached earth. I wondered if others would see them as ghosts, of if they appeared that way to me because of Gabe. Perhaps I'd see ghosts lurking everywhere. I hoped not.

* * *

Two days had passed and I hadn't caught up to Dillard or Kitty. Had Dillard found her and taken his herd onto the Big Hole? If so, where was Kitty and her part of the herd? Perhaps he hadn't caught up to her yet. Though anxious to find them before Dillard caused trouble, I didn't want to tire my animals. I kept Bannack at a fast walk, trotted him now and then, and stopped often to let him rest.

I'd come to love Bannack in our two days together. I found myself speaking to him often, singing melancholy songs for his twisting ears to fathom. If something spooked him, I needed only to say, "Easy boy, it's all right," and he'd calm down. His measured hoofbeats, his breathing, the ebb and flow of his muscles, the slight sway of his rump, had a soothing affect. It helped me to relax and eased my grief. It even helped me to forget my anger. What was done was done. Bolstered by the reality that Kitty was mine, the ride filled me with an unexpected sense of release and freedom.

The herd of crossbreeds had left the stage road near Monida and turned north, cross-country, following the Red Rock River through a wilderness of low hills and prairies that connected the Centennial and Red Rock Valleys. Pronghorn bucks tore through wheat-colored grass and sunflowers to collect their harems. Blackbirds flocking by the thousands skimmed the tips of the tall grass.

Thirty-five horses had left prints and sign easy to track, except for a half-mile stretch where a herd of cattle had stomped through the dust, and several miles where an isolated thunderstorm had beaten the grass level with the ground. In both instances I trusted my instinct that Kitty had continued to follow the river

We'd traveled for miles and miles with no sign of a house or human, everywhere leaping jackrabbits. The Centennial Range had grown small at my back. The eastern slopes of the Tendoy Mountains loomed at my left shoulder. I had a sense of boundless sky.

When the river turned into the shallow trough of the Red Rock Valley I stopped at an abandoned way station to get my bearings. Just west of the station railroad tracks gleamed in the bottoms, the Utah Northern Railway I'd ridden from Butte to Monida. The tracks, the river, and a wagon road seemed wed, meandering together like giant snakes. A steam engine labored up the long slope to the divide between Montana and Idaho, the sound heard and lost, then heard again on the fitful wind.

The crossbreeds had crossed the rail and wagon roads to head west on the Sheep Creek trail. My map showed that the trail cut through the Tendoys into the high river basins to the west, one of them the Medicine Lodge which Gabe had mentioned.

Driven by a terrible need to find Kitty, I'd skipped breakfast that morning and started off down the river when dawn was nothing but a gray pencil-stroke of light across the eastern horizon. I worried, too, about

Chinook's injured leg and about the pregnant mare. I hoped she wouldn't foal before she reached a place of safety. Every expectant mother, human or otherwise, deserved a place of quiet and safety to give birth.

By the time I'd traveled a mile up Sheep Creek, my stomach growled from hunger. An old fire ring on a bench above the creek offered a place to boil coffee, fry bacon, and heat beans in the can. Breakfast over, I sat on a rock, brushing my hair, running my fingers through the reddish-blond waves that resulted from a braid. I'd walked down to the creek to wash the pots and pans and had set them to dry beside a canvas pack that lay open on the ground. The fire had dwindled, but pitch on one large branch smoldered, spitting ribbons of pungent smoke into a gusting wind. Shorty and Bannack stomped impatiently at the end of their leads near the fire ring.

"Quiet down, boys," I said. "We'll find grass up the creek."

Bannack noticed someone riding north on the Monida road before I did. He let out a loud whinny that brought my head around. I went for the binoculars strapped to the saddle horn.

By the time I'd focused the glasses, the traveler had turned onto the Sheep Creek trail and was a half-mile away. The glasses revealed a man of average size astride a ribby black that carried bulging saddlebags, a bedroll tied behind the saddle, and a rifle in a scabbard. He trailed a large burro with pack boxes slung on each side, its color a flea-bitten gray.

I'd learned to protect myself since Ben died, but not in the wilds. I hoped the man would ride on without noticing me, but my animals' whinnies and brays made that impossible.

As the man turned his mount up the slope onto the bench, Bannack continued to whinny and Shorty to bray, the black horse and burro to answer. Penny slinked around, snarling, tail curled between her legs, unusual behavior for her. I rose, putting the final plaits in a French braid and tying it with a boot lace.

The man brought the black to a blowing stop a few yards away and adjusted his seat, creaking the saddle. One stirrup was broken down to iron and weathered skirts were in need of an oiling. The man was just as time-worn—scrawny, with brazen eyes that squinted from a long wind-cracked face. Sparse teeth grinned at me through a tangle of gray beard. His canvas pants and red wool Mackinaw carried the ground-in filth of weeks or years.

He rested a hand above a holstered revolver. My hand crept toward the butt of the Colt .45. His grin spread. "I ain't going to hurt you." He tipped a battered slouch hat. "Name's Buck Riley. Yours?"

I could see no reason to answer. But I did, loud and clear, a forced boldness.

"I thought I smelled coffee on the air. Could you could spare a cup?" His voice had the sound of gravel rolling along the bottom of a stream.

"Sorry, but you're too late. All that's left is over there." I pointed to the coffee grounds I'd heaped near the roots of a sage.

"In that case, I'll build up the fire and boil my own." He dragged a leg over the saddle and eased himself to the ground.

I felt a nudge at the back of my mind, the third or fourth reminder I was alone. I doubted I could stop Riley from making himself at home, but I could leave. "Help yourself. I'm on my way out."

I picked up the can of Arbuckle's and a box of matches I'd left by the fire and put them in the open canvas pack with the pots and pans. When I returned for the muslin-wrapped bacon and bread, Riley had tied the black to a sage bush and was stacking twigs in the fire ring.

"I didn't mean to run you off." His brazen stare crawled over me. "I was kinda looking forward to company, 'specially a nice-looking gal like you. Pretty hair, good shape." He puckered his lips and spat a brown splotch on the ground.

Something told me I should work faster. I fastened the buckle on the pack and hooked the heavy canvas bag on Shorty's packsaddle. Riley brought a crockery jug from his packbox and walked toward me. The stench of whiskey, grit, and sweat lay heavy on his clothes.

"How's about a slug o' whiskey?" He held out the jug.

"No thanks. I don't drink." I looped a strap around Shorty's pack to keep it from flopping up and down.

Riley shoved the jug closer. "You'd like this. Warms the blood, if you get my drift. Got me a still at my diggings."

I backed toward my horse. "You're a miner?"

"Yep. Got me several claims up Sheep Creek. This time o' year I work the roundups. I got a job as cook's helper a couple days north o' here. I'll head there soon's I drop this stuff off at my diggings." He slung the jug onto his shoulder, twisted his head around and took a long draught. It ended with a smack and sigh that flowed into a question. "Where you headed?"

"I'm following a herd of horses."

"I saw the tracks. Quite a bunch."

"I'd better be on my way, or they'll get so far ahead I'll never catch them." I untied Shorty and Bannack, yanked the stakes from the ground, and wedged them between ropes that held the pack in place.

Riley took another drink of whisky and wiped his mouth with the sleeve of his jacket. "No need to hurry. Them tracks ain't going nowhere. Why not sit a spell? A man gets lonesome out in the Basin. We can travel a ways together."

"It's nice of you to offer, but I really can't wait." I climbed into the saddle and prodded Bannack down the slope.

"If you should change your mind, I won't be far behind," Riley called out.

Not if I can help it, you old flirt. You're too free with the jug.

Chapter 10

I kept Bannack and Shorty at a run for about a mile, then slowed to let them blow. I hoped I wouldn't meet other men on the trail like Riley. Likely, he was harmless, but I didn't want to find out.

We'd left the land of sage and grass and entered Sheep Creek Canyon. For several miles, the creek flowed deep, green and meandering through its narrow gorge, the sidehills a jumble of rocky cliffs, talus slopes, brush, and pines. Now and then the banks opened onto meadows fed by hillside springs. There, shiny range cattle lay on the grass, chewing their cuds. Some of them hauled themselves from the ground and glared at us for having disturbed their rest. A badger sulked into its den beneath the sage.

We met a solitary human, a dark-bearded freighter in mud-spattered boots, chaps, and a crumpled pie-tin hat. He led a string of mules with empty pack-saddles, canvases folded and tied on top. We stopped to talk about the weather and our reasons for being in the canyon. His was a once-yearly trip with supplies for three homesteads up Sheep Creek; he was on his way back out.

He motioned up the creek to where the canyon opened onto a broad, lush meadow. "There's a ranch at the head of that meadow. You being female and alone, you might want to leave the trail and ride up over that hogback." Again he swung his arm, this time toward a broad ridge coming in from the northeast. "Folks at the ranch are friendly enough, but they're a rough bunch. Rumor has it they're cattle rustlers. Probably wouldn't do you no harm, but no sense taking a chance."

I scanned the hogback, judged it three-quarters-of-a-mile to the crest. I said I was afraid I'd lose track of the herd I was following.

"Where's it headed?"

I explained that I had no idea.

"Except for the ranch, there's no grazing to speak of until you reach the junction with Simpson Creek. Likely the horses won't stop until then—that is, if the rustlers don't get a hankering for them. The old pioneer road to Bannack goes along Simpson Creek. If you go to the crest of the hogback and head due west you can't miss it."

I did as the packer suggested, using clumps of bitterbrush and mountain mahogany as a screen to prevent anyone in the bottoms from seeing me. The rise in elevation allowed me to look down on Sheep Creek and the large green-gold meadow. The only activity near the ranch house was that of horses roaming the meadow, mainly paints, not the color of the crossbreeds.

The directions the packer had given to find the old road were accurate. From the crest of the ridge, I looked down on a sagebrush flat, perhaps ten miles across, walled on the west and south by the barren, pyramid-shaped peaks of the Continental Divide, on the north by the western swing of the Tendoys. It took my breath to look west. It filled my heart to look north or south.

At the base of the hogback, the Sheep Creek trail intersected a north-south wagon track that left Sheep Creek to follow a small stream. The track looked old, overgrown with bunch grass and sage. Three trails entered the road from the west. From the crest of the ridge, the five routes of travel resembled the threads of a giant brush spider.

Two men had stopped at a little spring-fed creek that flowed down the hogback into Simpson Creek. They'd picketed their horses near the road and were unrolling their bedrolls onto the grass. I slipped my binoculars from the saddle horn and saw the men were Dillard and Benito, about a half-mile away.

Dillard apparently sensed my eyes upon him. He looked up the slope in my direction, took a spyglass from a saddlebag lying nearby, and appeared to focus on me. I thought it amusing—Dillard staring through a glass at me, I at him. He waved. I waved back.

I reflected on the meeting with Riley, on the packer's warning about the rustlers, and was tempted to join Dillard. Resisting the idea, I spread my bedroll in bunch-grass near the source of the spring, a quarter-mile above Dillard, a stand of bull pines at my back. The previous night I'd slept in a downpour, the tent walls flapping in a gale. This evening, there was no threat of rain, no reason to raise the infantry tent.

I was weighing whether or not to build a fire when Dillard walked from behind willows that lined the creek. Penny growled and barked, then recognized him and wagged her tail. I'd halfway expected him to climb the hill to speak to me but had no idea what face he'd put on things.

"Evening," he said, working for breath. He tipped his hat.

"Care to sit down?" I motioned toward a sturdy log resting on the ground near an old fire ring. Evidently a sheepherder or hunter had camped there in the past, perhaps a prospector.

"Benito's waiting supper. I came to ask if you'd like to share our camp."

I considered it briefly before I motioned toward my bedroll and the animals picketed up the hill. "I'm already set up for the night. Don't really feel like moving. It's nice of you to ask."

He rubbed the thin lips below his handlebar mustache in what I read as disapproval. "A woman shouldn't be in the wilds by herself."

"I know, but circumstances—"

"You'd think your brother would've sent someone else."

"He knows I can handle myself."

"Couldn't you have brought some ranch hand along?"

I explained that the men were away from the cow camp and I couldn't await their return.

"What about your husband? I'd never let my wife go into the wilds."

"He's dead."

He gave an apologetic grunt. "Sorry. I didn't mean to . . ." He let the rest trail off.

"I have to admit Ben wouldn't have approved. Since he died, I've done things I had no notion of trying when he was alive." Most times I liked making decisions on my own. I hadn't realized how the dark side of the marriage had stifled my spirit. I likened my rebirth to a moth emerging from a cocoon.

Dillard had been studying me, running long fingers across the black stubble he'd grown in the last three days. "I still think you should've stayed at home."

"I was anxious to find Kitty."

"Little rebel." He shook his head and clucked his tongue. "How can one little gal handle that many horses by herself? Must have somebody with her."

"You don't know Kitty. There isn't anything she won't try."

He gave a silent laugh, reflecting on some private thought.

"She's brash, but she can be sweet as a lamb. Right now, she's filled with grief and afraid she'll lose the horses. I worry about her."

"You need somebody to worry about you." His eyes glimmered with friendship, a change from that last day at the Centennial. "Gotta be careful. A woman can get too brave." He stretched his back and rotated his neck. "If you should change your mind, you're welcome to join me and Benito." He turned down the slope toward his camp. "We'll be leaving at first light. You can ride along if you'd like."

"Thanks, I might do that." Then, in afterthought, "I didn't expect to catch you until I found Kitty."

He stopped, turned slightly, feet braced against the rocky slope. "My horse threw a shoe and I had to reset it. Wrenched my back."

"You should've let your wrangler do it."

He gave his head a quick wag and started angling down the hill. "I don't trust other men with my horse."

The comment reminded me of Ben. He'd always had a firm notion of how things should be done. Dillard's manner hinted of a more pliable nature. Where Ben had always moved in a determined, purposeful way, Dillard had an easy stride and supple frame, a gentle quality, though this evening he walked a bit gingerly, as if he favored his back. Circumstances permitting, I could like the man.

* * *

After a quick supper of cold beans, bread, and canned tomatoes, I lay in long johns and a shirt, watching the sun sink beyond the divide, my head on the fleece-lined jacket I'd rolled as a pillow. The sky faded from lavender to steely gray then slowly flushed the color of a ripe peach. Blue shadows of dusk gathered on the Bitterroots and crept across the valley onto the mountainside.

Coyotes yipped and howled on the ridge above me, perhaps a wolf or two. At my side, Penny growled a weary answer. I reached over to stroke her floppy ears. "You tell them, girl. We don't want any wolves around here."

Below us, Dillard's campfire flickered and someone strummed on a guitar. After three days in the wilds with my spirits in a dungeon I longed for human companionship. I wished I had the gumption to move camp.

Buck Riley had said he was going to boil coffee, but he should have reached Simpson Creek by now. It occurred to me he might have seen where Bannack and Shorty left the trail to climb over the hogback. On the other hand, with all the other tracks, he might not have noticed. I told myself I was worrying for naught and ought to get some rest. Tomorrow could be another long day. It seemed Kitty had some distant goal in mind. But she appeared to be in charge of the herd. The tracks didn't stray far from the trail. I didn't know which was the greater of the emotions that swelled my heart—admiration, love, anger, or concern.

Soft measured breathing rose from Penny's sprawled body, but sleep eluded me. As the night wore on, heartache settled with the weight of a cast-iron kettle, and I wept quiet tears. When someone you love has been ill a long while, you expect death, even consider it a godsend they no longer suffer. Still, it comes as a shock, especially in the shadows of confession.

From thoughts of Gabe my mind bent toward the Bitterroot, speculating on Carver Dean's arrival. How could I raise five hundred dollars other than by selling the place? I could think of no way. I wondered if yesterday's thunderstorms had hit the homestead and ruined the second cutting of hay. I wondered if the ewe had accepted the lambs, and if they were doing well. I was certain the runt would still need a bottle. Sweet thing. I wished I was there to help. I couldn't believe I was this far from home, sleeping in the wilds, taking risks Ben would not have allowed me to take.

I'd never seen air as clear as that in Montana's high country, the millions of stars and the depth of sky. As I lay on my back watching the stars pale in the light of a rising moon, night sounds reached my ears as if they were inches away. I could account for the sound of the spring bubbling from the hillside and for the whine of wind in the trees that rose in dark shadows at my back. I knew the screech of a great-horned owl. The snap of a twig and limbs brushing against each other could be caused by the horses moving restlessly at the end of their tethers, or by some wild creature on the prowl—even a man. The uncertainty prickled my skin. The fear of things unknown. Unseen. Lurking in the shadows.

I lay tense, dreading the long nights that lay ahead, nights filled with anxiety and exhaustion. The wind had quieted to a whisper. No sound from Bannack and Shorty. I wished for morning to come so I could be on my way. The cold of the earth had seeped into my bedroll, my long johns, and into my flesh.

Then I heard it—movement almost beyond hearing. A step—silence—another step.

I strained to hear, tight with alarm.

A long skulking silence, the sigh of the breeze, then steps.

Something was out there in the dark. I pulled the revolver from under the jacket and propped myself on an elbow to listen. An owl hooted from a treetop. I sensed the glide of broad wings overhead.

Penny sat up, hackles raised in the moonlight. She growled.

My heart raced. Breath rasped in my throat.

Something brushed against the ground. So near I thought I could reach out and touch it. I sat bolt upright, revolver tight in my fist.

Chapter 11

"Who's there?" I could hardly speak.

No answer.

Twigs snapped. Penny growled and barked.

"Who's there?" My voice was louder, sharper.

A man stepped from the shadow of the pines and stood wavering in the checkered moonlight. The smell of whiskey and the reek of his unwashed body rode the air.

Penny charged and nipped his pantsleg. The man gave her a clumsy kick that knocked her to the side and brought a yipe. She kept her distance but continued to growl.

"Damn it! Call off your dog. It's me, Buck Riley." He carried what appeared to be a jug. Moonlight reflected from the glazed sides.

I doubted a grizzly would have caused more alarm than this man who'd crept up on me in the night. My finger tightened on the trigger. I could hardly swallow.

"What do you want?" I was afraid I knew the answer.

"I heard the wolves. Reckoned you might need somebody to look after you." He spoke with the slurred effort of someone who'd drunk too much whiskey.

"I don't need help."

"I brought my jug. We could cozy up a bit." He took a couple of wobbly steps toward me, offering the jug. The smell of whiskey grew stronger.

I jerked the gun forward. "Stay back!" The glint of moonlight on the barrel seemed to spur Riley to do as I ordered. I wanted to light the small lantern at the head of my bedroll, but I didn't dare lay down the gun. "How did you know I was here?"

"Followed the tracks up. Saw you make camp." He hiccuped, swallowed, ran fingers through his long beard. "I'm camped just around the bend." He jerked a thumb toward Sheep Creek Canyon. "See some fool's stopped down below." He flapped a hand toward Dillard's camp. "It's getting too crowded 'round here."

He made a move to sit on the saddle lying nearby.

"Stand over there." I jerked the revolver toward a spot in full moonlight. Riley attempted to follow the direction and stumbled over a rock.

The sudden move startled Penny. She lunged.

Riley's boot thwacked her lamely in the side. "God-damned cur! That's no way to treat a body."

Penny inched back a foot or two, snarling, the hair ridged on her back.

"Ma'am, call off your dog. Don't know why you're so plumb afraid." He gave a suggestive chuckle. "'Cause you're in the moonlight with a man?" He raised the jug to his lips, drank, wiped his mouth with the back of his hand. His breathing was heavy. "Something about a full moon...warms the blood . . . makes a man hanker after a woman."

I pulled my shirt down as far as it would go over my long johns and got to my knees. "I want you to leave. Now!"

"You gonna make me walk all the way down the hill for nothing? I'm all wore out." He made another wobbly move to sit on the saddle.

"I told you to leave!" I aimed the revolver at the ground near his feet and pulled the trigger.

The noise stunned me. The recoil jolted my arm. The flash dazzled my mind. Penny yipped and went *ky-yi*-ing into the woods.

Riley staggered to one side. "Whyn't you put that down. Next time you might not miss."

"I didn't miss. I just wanted to scare you."

Down the slope a twig snapped. I thought I heard a footstep.

Riley didn't seem aware of either. He raised an arm in mock surrender and laughed. "Awwright. But you don't know what you're missing. I know how to please—"

A tall shadow exploded from the darkness, took Riley by the collar, and slammed a fist into his jaw. There was the sound of bone crushing bone. Riley fell. The jug landed several feet away with a thud and rolled down the slope into some sage.

The shadow bent down, took Riley by the front of his jacket, and hauled him, swearing, to his feet. The shadow raised a fist.

"That's enough," I hollered. "He's drunk."

There was more scuffling. Riley fell to the ground, flailing his arms and legs. Debris crackled underfoot. Dust filled the air.

"Do you have any rope?" The rasping Texas drawl was Dillard's.

"In the pack." My voice shook. I pulled on my jeans and boots and groped blindly in the pack. "There's two kinds here."

"Bring all you have."

I took two lengths of lead rope and a length of hemp rope to where Dillard hovered over Riley in the moonlight. He was blowing gusts of air to slow his breathing. Riley sat on the ground, muttering.

"Hold your gun on him," Dillard said. "I'll tie him up."

Dillard fastened Riley's wrists together at his back with the hemp rope and began to pin his arms to his sides with a lead rope. "What's your name?"

An unintelligible grumble from Riley.

"Answer me." Dillard jerked a knot tight at Riley's back.

"None o' your damned business!"

"He's Buck Riley," I said.

"You know him?"

"I met him on the trail this morning."

"That figures." Dillard groaned to full height. "I'd take him to my camp for the night, but he's too drunk. I'd have to carry him." He nodded toward the bull pines above camp. "I'll tie him to one of those trees up there."

Riley squirmed in his bindings and grumbled, "How long you going to keep me tied?"

"Till you sober up."

He licked his lips. "How's about my jug?"

"No jug. But I'll find a soft place for your rump."

Dillard hauled Riley to the edge of the woods and pushed him to the ground, his back against a pine. He went around the trunk with a length of rope, securing the prospector to the tree. Penny slinked out of the dark woods and growled, backing off when Riley spat at her.

"We'll leave him there until morning," Dillard said as we descended into the patchy moonlight at camp. "I'll tell Benito where I am, then come back to stand guard."

"Riley can't cause trouble now." Part of me wanted privacy; the other part wanted protection.

Dillard must have heard the uncertainty in my voice. "It wouldn't be right to leave you alone. A grizzly might come along." I thought I saw a grin flick across his lips.

"I can take care of myself."

"Helps to have two." Dillard paused to let his gaze rove the shadows around camp. "You stick tight," he cautioned. "I won't be long."

"Mr. Dillard," I said as he turned to leave. "Thanks ever so much."

He looked back over his shoulder. Again, I sensed that faint grin in the moonlight. "No problem."

* * *

By the time Dillard returned, I'd built a fire within a ring of shale. I couldn't offer comfort, but I could provide warmth. I sat with legs crossed, shoulders hunched, on the log at fireside. He stood across from me, warming his hands. He'd pulled on a long, dark wool poncho. I'd thought he'd bring a blanket or two for a bed, but evidently he intended to sit through the early morning hours, or use the heavy poncho as a blanket. He'd checked on Riley and found him in a drunken sleep. I could hear the man snoring.

I stared absently into the flames, listening to the crackle of burning limbs, my face warmed by the heat, my back chilled by the surrounding dark. The glittering bowl of the heavens reminded me of the vastness of time, of Gabe, Ben, and other souls long departed. I felt ageless, a tiny speck in the sands of eternity. I sensed the presence of men who, for eons, had sat beside campfires and wondered about the heavens and about the purpose of life. Perhaps the flames had lulled them into an inner peace, while on the edge of their awareness night creatures circled the fire with a soft tread.

Dillard and I had said little since he'd returned. He sighed as he lowered himself onto the far end of the log, his long legs jackknifed in Indian fashion before him, his rifle propped on the log. He yawned, stretched.

"I'm sorry I spoiled your rest, but I'm glad you came along when you did." My mind sorted through the sequence of events. "How did you get here so fast? I'd hardly shot when you came."

"I heard my mare tromping around in her hobbles and went to put her on a picket. She'd leap-frogged half-way up the hill."

"All the better for me."

He yawned into an unrelated question. "Has your husband been dead long?"

"Four years." I looked beyond the fire, where the flames cast dancing shadows onto the sagebrush. Ben's face danced with them, resolute, lined with care. Having heard a confession that involved him in a heartless act, I felt less affection. "In some ways, it seems like yesterday. In other ways, a lifetime."

Dillard leaned forward and folded his arms across his knees. His mouth firmed perceptibly in the glow of the fire. "How long did it take you to get over it?"

"I'm not over it. Just learned to get along."

"Did he die of illness—accident?"

"A heart attack. He suffered from rheumatism. I guess that weakened his heart."

"Too bad." Dillard rubbed his chin. The orange firelight waxed and waned over his thin face. "Then this thing happened with your brother. But I guess you expected it—his dying, I mean."

"His death wasn't a bolt out of the blue like some. Still, I doubt a person is ever ready for death. I didn't give up hope until it became a fact." I saw no need to mention suicide. I felt like a hypocrite for speaking of grief when resentment toward Gabe played tug-of-war with love.

As I searched those feelings, I looked out across the broad sagebrush flat to the distant peaks, the exposed granite silvery in the moonlight. Dillard, too, was silent. I felt a surprising companionship with this man and hoped we'd not clash over division of the herd. I thought of the day at the barn and my instant impression of a man saddened or disappointed.

"Have you lost someone recently?" I asked.

"My wife, last fall . . . my girl, the year before that."

"Oh, Lord, I'm so sorry. Life can be unfair." I paused. "Your wife died from . . . ?"

"Heart disease."

"And your daughter?"

"Drowned in the river." He turned his eyes toward the arch of jeweled black velvet. In the firelight I saw his Adam's apple move above the poncho.

"I shouldn't have asked."

"No problem." He sighed. "Guess I have a ways to go before I can handle it."

I stared once more into the fire, reflecting on real losses I'd endured and on the loss that had been a deception. "It's bad enough to lose a spouse or parent. Losing a child is almost beyond enduring." I looked up, searching his face. "That's why you're here." More statement than question.

"I thought it might help if I left Colorado. My son and I can get to know each other again."

"Winters in the Big Hole aren't fit for man nor beast."

"It's central to where my boy will be surveying. There's lots of good grass."

"The Bitterroot is milder in winter."

"So I've heard." He stretched his long legs out in front of him, reached inside his wraps, and brought out a pipe, a tin of Prince Albert, and a match. He poured tobacco into the bowl. "You live in the Bitterroot?"

"I have a homestead in the upper valley."

"Will you stay on there?"

"As long as I can manage. I make ends meet—barely."

"Maybe you should move on, like me."

"Sometimes I get discouraged and think I should. But I love my homestead. I grit my teeth and hang on, keep learning from my mistakes."

He lit the pipe and sucked on the stem in thought. "Sometimes quitting is the hardest thing to do. I tend to wrestle with a problem even when it's got me thrown, with its horns at my head."

I gave an apologetic laugh. "Like now, with Kitty and the herd?"

He looked my way and said with a twitch of smile, "Yeah, like now."

Chapter 12

To make certain Riley would cause no more trouble, Dillard roused him when dawn was a faint banner of gray along the eastern hills. He returned him to his camp on Sheep Creek, waited for him to pack his burro, and started him south on the old wagon road toward his diggings. Now, our concern was finding Kitty.

Dillard led the way on his sorrel, trailing the brown. Benito brought up the rear on his dun, leading the other pack animal. I rode in between, ponying Shorty. The road was a couple of weedy ruts. In the 1860s, when the gold town of Bannack was capital of the territory, freighters had used the road to enter Montana. The thoroughfare was abandoned when gold was discovered in Virginia City and other routes were established. Named for a tribe of Indians, the mining town of Bannack was located fifty-five miles north of the Sheep Creek trail's intersection with the road. Gabe had said the Sherwood ranch was near that town. It would take at least two days to reach it.

The rain that had prompted us to wear our slickers hadn't lasted long enough to wash away the herd's tracks. They were headed north toward the Medicine Lodge. Dillard didn't hurry, but he barely paused to rest in mid-afternoon. Bannack's hide had grown hot beneath my legs, and sweat darkened his neck. I was sore and constantly shifted my weight in the saddle. My stomach said we should stop to fix supper. Yet Dillard rode on until we climbed a saddle through broken hills and dropped into the Medicine Lodge Basin. There, we wedged our way through a band of sheep, irritating the herder and his dogs.

Medicine Lodge Creek was as small as the one we'd left behind, perhaps six feet wide, willows and wild roses growing along the banks. Indian tribes had left signs of old encampments—rock chips from tool making and circles of rocks that had secured the skirts of tipis. I'd heard there'd been buffalo in the area at one time. A sign on a graying board confirmed the notion. It pointed toward a U-shaped cliff at the head of a draw. The faint handwriting said BUFFALO JUMP. Some freighter or prospector had likely put the sign there during the height of the gold rush.

A few miles north of the saddle, we came upon two brown-skinned men standing on the grassy creek bank, willow fishing poles in hand. They'd dropped their hooks into waters that riffled from a branch creek into the Medicine Lodge. Their faces were more well-defined than those of the Flathead Indians who traveled the Bitterroot, their features angular, carved rather than molded. They wore calico shirts and black denim trousers, a little ragged at the edges. A high-crowned black felt hat topped the raven braids of one man. Both figures had the accumulated girth of middle age.

Dillard stopped to ask the men what they hoped to catch.

"*Tsa pank,*" said one of the men, his face without expression.

"Trout," said the other man in the same guttural tone. Both gave their attention back to the creek.

I rode closer and asked hopefully, "Have you seen a girl trailing a herd of horses?"

The man with the hat pointed down the Medicine Lodge with his chin. "Girl with Tendoy. Not far."

My heart raced at the thought we'd found Kitty, but I couldn't imagine what she was doing with Tendoy, chief of the Lemhis. The government had trouble keeping him on the reservation in Idaho. When I lived in Dillon, I'd met him when his little band camped at Gabe's ranch during their fall hunting and gathering trip through the Beaverhead Valley. I doubted he'd remember me. Ten years had passed since I'd left Dillon.

Tendoy was intelligent and strong-willed, much revered by his people. A kind man, but I had no idea how he'd treat a girl in possession of a band of spirited horses. He and his tribe survived by trading horses for white man's goods. They owned hundreds. I doubted he'd steal Kitty's horses, but he might claim a few as condition for her release.

Bannack needed little prodding to move faster. He flared his nostrils to catch an elusive scent and pointed his ears forward to gather sounds ahead on the road. Feeling the same excitement, Shorty trotted alongside, braying like a banshee. I waved my arm and yelled, "Get back!" Bannack swerved his rump and struck out with a hind foot to let the mule know he should keep his distance. Dillard's horses showed a similar unrest.

A mile farther on, the creek flowed into a nest of low-lying hills and gentle draws, the bottoms lush with grass. Grazing in one shallow draw, in a state of constant movement, was the reason for Bannack's excitement. Most were Indian ponies—small, raw-boned, angular, the kind that could race like the wind, that liked to strike, kick, and bite at will. At least a hundred. Some of them were misshapen things with wild eyes and potbellies. Many were splotched with color.

Four bronze-chested boys in their early teens sat astride horses on the outskirts of the herd. They kept watch in a casual way, slouching on their horses' bare backs, dangling their legs down the ponies' spotted flanks. A rope with a nose loop was the only control over their mounts.

The Indian ponies snorted and whinnied when they caught our scent. They pranced around. The herders shot to life, waving hide whips in the air, yelling to keep the horses bunched.

Horses staked at the back of the draw pulled on their ropes and squealed. They were larger than the ponies, handsome, well-bred bays and chestnuts. A lone chestnut stomped around in a sagebrush corral and screamed his anger at the world.

Dillard pulled his sorrel up short. "I'd swear that's my stallion in there."

"I see Lilly and some of the younger crossbreeds out among the Indian ponies." I saw no foal and was glad. Lilly might yet make it to safety.

"Son of a gun! I believe my entire herd's out there rubbing noses with those rag-tags." Dillard gave the pack-horse's rope a jerk and prodded the sorrel into the draw. Chinook bugled when he saw us and slashed at the encircling sagebrush fence.

Bannack followed Dillard's sorrel, churning up dust. Some of the crossbreeds seemed to recognize his scent and trotted out from the milling herd to meet us. They circled, nickering, pawing up bits of sod. The smell of their dander and sweat was strong.

One of the boys raced up on a short-coupled pinto and lashed at the crossbreeds. Dillard rode alongside the boy and yanked the whip from his hand. "Stop it! Those are my horses."

"You go! You go!" the boy yelled. "Make trouble with ponies."

"Not until I've collected my herd."

"Half are Kitty's," I yelled above the bedlam.

Dillard hadn't heard me, or pretended he hadn't. "Why are my horses in with yours?" he demanded of the boy.

The young man eyed Dillard with a fierce brown gaze. He was about Kitty's age, dressed in government-issue black denim, a plaid shirt tied around his waist. His face was a shiny dark bronze, sullen. "Girl bring horses down road to Tendoy's camp. Stallion fight with Tendoy's horses. Chief keep girl and horses till he find out if they are hers."

"They're mine and I'm going to cut them from your herd." Waving Benito forward, he urged his sorrel toward the milling crossbreeds.

The boy nudged his horse alongside. "You see chief first," he hissed. "And give back whip."

Dillard reined in the sorrel. "No whip until I see this chief of yours. Where is he?"

"Down creek. Not far."

Dillard grunted. "That's what your elders said a mile back." He turned the sorrel. "Wait here, Mrs. Tate. I'll see what sort of mischief we're dealing with."

"Oh, no." I spun Bannack around. "I've come too far to let you and Tendoy decide things without me."

Dillard's eyes flashed. He gave a soundless snort. "Suit yourself."

A mound of glacial debris kept me from seeing the Indian camp, but I smelled it, a smoky, burnt-leather odor. I knew it wasn't far when we came upon several small children and their dogs playing in the creek. The children's glistening brown bodies were naked as newly-hatched sparrows, welted with insect bites. Despite the onset of evening, they splashed each other, squealed, and shivered as we passed.

Penny was having trouble with ribby mongrels who bounced around her yapping and baring their teeth. She'd charge them; they'd run off a ways and tear back.

I waved an arm at them and yelled, "Leave her alone." They ignored me.

The gray and yellow dogs were still pestering when we rounded the glacial mound and saw the Lemhi encampment spread before us on a grassy bench overlooking the creek. A variety of smells filled the air—wood smoke, meat dripping fat onto coals, the stench of human waste from clumps of tall sage and willows.

There was a murmur of voices, laughter, a baby's cry of hunger, the yipping of dogs. A few horses staked near the lodges whinnied. Bannack answered and jerked his head up and down.

Dillard showed Benito a grassy spot on the creek bank where he could make camp and stake the pack animals, then he and I rode onto the bench. On the way we passed a couple of parked buckboards and farm wagons. Two more battered wagons stood at the rear of the bench.

The dozen cone-shaped lodges appeared to have been raised years ago. Piles of wind-blown dirt and tumbleweeds had collected around the skirts. The hide coverings and tiny forests of poles that poked from openings in the top were bleached from the elements. A few tipi rings—circles of rocks used in the past to hold down the hide skirts—formed tufted humps amid the trampled grass. A few old frames had been allowed to rot and collapse with age.

Smoke lazed upward from three of the twelve skin lodges and from sagebrush fires burning in the space in between. A large hide pot on a willow frame straddled one fire. From it steamed the odor of meat and sage. Metal pots hung from other tripod frames. Chunks of meat skewered on ramrods hung above pits lined with red-hot coals. Iron teakettles, coffee-pots, and enamelware basins lay on the ground near the fires.

Two lodges appeared to have been raised this season, the poles covered with canvas, the doors rolled up and tied. We stopped at the larger of the two and dismounted. The front quarters of a deer hung from a pine near the lodge. A wrinkled crone looked up from hanging strips of venison over a drying frame and jabbered something to a toddler. The boy had been carrying a black and white spotted pup on his back like a papoose. He set the puppy on the ground with the rest of the litter and ran into the tipi.

While we waited for some sort of recognition, curious Lemhis gathered around us, some of the older members of the clan scarred with pox. Girls carried hide buckets of water. Women trudged in with dead sagebrush. Men of various ages stood watching us, arms folded across their chests, most dressed in calico, black denim, striped shirts. Their eyes showed nothing, no past or present, but seemed to be waiting for something big to happen.

I heard a rustling sound inside the lodge. The toddler babbled in his native tongue. A man's quiet voice answered. Then someone shuffled toward the door.

Chapter 13

Chief Tendoy stooped through the lodge's doorway and straightened to an impressive height, his back as erect as the pines on the ridge top. His manner was one of quiet pride. If I hadn't known his history, I'd never have guessed he was in his sixties. The only wrinkles in his firm bronze face were two trenches that curved around his mouth. They accentuated high cheekbones and a wide, resolute upper lip. A handsome man, well-muscled beneath his black denim trousers and vest. His only ornamentation was a bear-claw necklace that hung over a red-striped shirt.

"Me Chief Tendoy." He jerked his chin toward Dillard who stood loose-limbed at his horse's side. "You?"

"Sam Dillard." He held out his hand. Tendoy made no move to shake it.

For a long, steely moment, the men took each other's measure, Dillard with his translucent, keen-sad eyes. Tendoy's widely-spaced black eyes seemed to regard Dillard with indifference, yet with the soft wisdom of the ages. I'd never seen authority conveyed with such clarity, yet with such lack of animosity, without a word being spoken. It showed in each man, in the cast of his shoulders, neck, and jaw, the expression in his eyes.

Dillard ended the appraisal by propping his hands on his hips in a deliberate way. "I've come for the horses you're holding. They're mine."

"They're not yours!" A familiar red head and ropy frame burst from the tipi and took a stand beside Tendoy.

Kitty was scrawnier than ever, and dark circles lay beneath her pixie eyes.

Other than that, she appeared normal, except she wore a buckskin vest decorated with porcupine quills over her plaid shirt. Part of me wanted to throw my arms around her and declare I was her mother. The other, wiser part of me, said to bide my time. Kitty was in no mood to accept the startling news, nor would it help to impose such a scene of revelation on Dillard and Tendoy.

The chief frowned at Kitty. "I tell you stay in tipi."

"And let him steal my horses?"

"They're not her horses. I bought them." Dillard took the receipt from his wallet and offered it to Tendoy. "Here's proof."

Tendoy held the paper at arm's length, squinted at it for a few seconds, then nodded to a slender young woman in the flock of Shoshonis. She read the receipt, translating it into Tendoy's native tongue. As he listened, Tendoy ran his fingers absently through the tips of grizzled hair that hung loose over his shoulders.

"It's a fake," Kitty said before the girl had finished. "Pa told me so."

"It's not a fake. I have a copy of it." Leaving Bannack ground-hitched, I walked up to Kitty and slipped my arm around her shoulders. "Don't worry, we'll work this out." She shrugged off my arm with the old hostility.

The faintest of smiles flicked across Tendoy's lips. "Girl thinks she big chief. Not listen to Tendoy or to woman." The smile spread to include his eyes. "Tendoy like this girl. Not afraid to bring horses from beyond the mountains. No help. She brings honor to her father."

"Then why don't you—"

"Shh," I hissed to silence Kitty. For the moment she held her tongue, staring daggers at everyone.

Tendoy fixed his gaze on Dillard. "My granddaughter says you buy many horses. I think you pay too much." He made a sound that was half-grunt, half-laugh. "White man foolish with money. The more he has, the more he wastes. Like the squirrel who stores more nuts than he can use in four winters, then loses most to the bear."

Dillard seemed unabashed, slightly amused. "I'd say the squirrel shows good judgment. By storing more than he needs, he satisfies the bear and has enough left for himself to keep from starving."

Tendoy appeared to chew on that thought a second before he turned his eyes on the receipt. "Maybe you *temaah*. Maybe you write this. Maybe Gabe Breen not the man who signs his name."

Dillard snatched the receipt from Tendoy. "I don't lie, sir."

"He does lie!" Kitty said in outrage. "They're my horses, not his."

"I can settle the matter." I didn't know if Shoshoni tradition allowed women a voice in disputes, but I'd speak anyway. "Half the horses are Mr. Dillard's."

"Only because you refused my check." Dillard turned his sharp glance from me to Tendoy. "Chief, you heard what's on the receipt."

"Aunt Jessie!" Kitty said, wild-eyed. "You're not going to let him take them?"

"Only those he's paid for."

Tendoy studied me with curiosity, as if he'd taken real notice of me for the first time. "I see you before. Many moons past."

"I'm Jessie Tate, Gabriel Breen's sister. I owned a boarding house in Dillon. I baked sweets for you and your people."

Tendoy's eyes reflected a moment's puzzlement, then lit with recognition. "Ah. You good cook." His deep-chested voice was cordial.

"Do you remember Kitty from the ranch? She raced ponies with your grandsons."

"*Haa*, Gabe Breen good friend. Girl say he sick from black spirits. Tendoy sad. She say Chinee cook make medicine for Gabe. Tendoy like Yeng Sang. He play poker like fox."

Dillard gave the brim of his hat a quick push upward with a thumb. "Chief, could we get on with this business? Like I said, the horses are mine." The Lemhis at our backs had begun a loud muttering. Tendoy surveyed their rapt faces and crowding bodies and motioned us inside. "Come, we talk where there are not so many eyes to see, not so many ears to hear."

The smell of leather and smoldering sage met us as we entered the tipi's dusky interior. Baskets along the fringes of the room gave off the grain-sweet fragrance of seeds and berries. A fire ring claimed the center of the lodge. A couple of chipped crockery bowls, spoons, and ladles and a few tin plates and cups sat in an enamelware pan near the sputtering fire. To the right and left of the ring lay pallets of brightly striped woolen blankets. Along the back wall, stood a row of leather pouches and a rawhide parfleche.

Two women in red calico rose from their work near the fire ring and without expression backed to the rear of the lodge. One had been sewing on a soft leather moccasin. She held a large curved needle threaded with a strip of rawhide. I guessed she was Tendoy's age, but she looked older, her hair gray, her skin wrinkled. Indian women showed their age sooner than the men, especially those who'd lived a nomadic life before being sent to reservations. The other woman appeared to be much younger, the mother of the toddler who hugged her side. Her fingertips had turned orange from the rosehips she'd been grinding on a stone mortar.

Tendoy lowered himself onto a bearskin rug on the far side of the fire ring and sat cross-legged, his broad shoulders against a reed backrest. He motioned Dillard to a place at his left. The women sat on their heels at his right and resumed their work. He nodded Kitty and me to a rush mat on the near side of the fire. I sat on my heels as it seemed the accepted position for women. The toddler curled up on one of the pallets and closed his eyes.

Dillard sat with his long legs crossed like Tendoy's, his Stetson in his lap. "Now, can we settle this, Chief?"

"First we smoke pipe, so words speak truth."

"I have things to do. I want to check my horses."

"Can wait till next sun. Soon no light. You smoke. Let tobacco give comfort." Tendoy took a pipe from a hollowed stone near the fire, the bowl of smoothed volcanic rock, the stem of arrowcane. A white-tipped eagle feather and a hank of black horse-hair dangled from the stem. Obviously an everyday pipe, not one of the ornamental peace or prayer pipes I'd seen among the tribes. Tendoy pointed the stem toward the points of the compass, toward the earth and sky, then filled the bowl with tobacco. He handed Dillard the pipe and a punk stick to light it.

Dillard drew on the pipe several times, sending acrid smoke ribboning toward the open canvas flap at the peak of the lodge, then returned the pipe to Tendoy. The taste of tobacco had whetted his habit. He reached into his vest pocket for the necessary supplies, and soon his pipe was sending the aroma of honeyed tobacco into the air to mix with that of Tendoy's dried kinnikinnick and bark.

Tendoy's granddaughter left her station near the doorway to speak to someone outside and returned to sit on her heels. Near her stood a tripod made from lengths of skinny pine. The frame held a bow, a quiver of arrows, and a battered rifle. Gathered neatly beside the tripod lay two saddles with blankets, bridles, halters, ropes, hobbles, and stakes for picketing horses. I recognized Gabe's rifle in a riding scabbard. Likely a mix of Kitty's and Tendoy's paraphernalia.

Kitty squirmed beside me, tapping her fingers on a bony denim-covered knee. "I wish they'd hurry up," she grumbled under her breath.

"Relax," I whispered. "As Yeng Sang often says, 'With time and patience the mulberry leaf becomes silk.'"

"I'm no mulberry leaf."

Dillard seemed just as restless. "Can we get started?" he said with a loud smack on his pipe.

Tendoy remained calm, his dark, liquid eyes reflecting deep thought and enjoyment of his pipe. "You show paper that say horses belong to you. White man's papers not always speak truth. Tendoy learn this many times." He pointed his chin in my direction. "Tendoy let woman speak."

The older woman raised her eyes from her sewing in a look of surprise and spoke to her husband in clipped, guttural words strange to my ears. Tendoy replied firmly, in kind.

"When do I get to talk?" Kitty prodded.

"Girl must learn to wait, like bird that stands all day on one leg, waiting for fish to come. I have heard what you have to say. Now I listen to woman you call your aunt."

Again, I wanted to shout to the world that I was her mother. Instead, I said as evenly as possible, "Mr. Dillard tells the truth. My brother sold him the horses last summer." I went on to explain the terms of the sale, that Gabe had spent the money from the first payment, that I'd destroyed the second check. "A tumor in his head made Gabe sick and forgetful. When Mr. Dillard came to Gabe's cow camp to claim the horses, Gabe couldn't remember the sale."

For Kitty's sake I perpetuated the lie. It would make no difference in the outcome. "Gabe was dying when I left him." I felt Kitty quiver at my side and sensed her gaze rivet on my profile. "He'd lost all his money and had only the horses to leave Kitty. He wanted me to return Mr. Dillard's check, so she'd own half—"

"He wanted me to have all of them! Not half. He said—" Kitty shut her mouth on the rest, strangling on tears.

I slipped my arm around her shoulders. This time, she didn't resist. I bent my head close and whispered, "I found a copy of Mr. Dillard's receipt and showed it to Gabe. He admitted that Dillard has legal claim to half."

Dillard overheard. "I have legal claim to all." His face had darkened.

"And what is Kitty supposed to do? Fade into the dust? How can you deny her a small inheritance?"

"I have a son to consider. As far as I'm concerned, the matter is closed." He clamped his mouth shut and got to his feet.

"Sit, Mr. Dillard." Tendoy's tone was resolute, his eyes commanding.

Dillard made no move to sit.

"You stand in Tendoy's tipi. Your horses walk my camp. My word is law here. If you wish to keep your horses, do as I say."

Dillard stared in outrage. "You threaten robbery?"

"Tendoy speaks of things as they are. When in shelter of my village, you do what I say."

"This is America. Ruled by law not one man's whim." Dillard steamed toward the doorway. "In the morning, I'm going to collect my horses."

"Sit, Mr. Dillard." Tendoy's voice was unyielding.

Dillard stood at the doorway, obviously weighing the alternatives. He didn't leave; neither did he sit. He simply stuffed his hat on his head at a rebellious angle and stood facing Tendoy like a bristled porcupine, arms folded across his chest.

"Let Tendoy tell about white man's law." The chief spoke in a firm, measured way. "It says my people must stay on reservation. There is little game, little to eat. If we travel to find game, we break law. We need money for food. Instead of money, white man trades bad whiskey for the few things we have to sell. Whiskey is white man's broth of hell. My men get the drinking sickness." His wife raised her eyes from her work. A tremor crossed her face. It seemed she'd experienced this sickness in her husband.

Tendoy went on to speak gravely of the Indians' way of life before white men forced them from their lands, his low-pitched voice resonating in his nose. He took his time, pausing between sentences to smoke his pipe and think, or to give his words added weight. Now and then his eyes spoke of feelings he could not express in words.

Dillard seemed to listen against his will, annoyance on his face. Kitty and I sat quiet as robins with a hawk on the wing. At least I did. Kitty squirmed and fidgeted in silence.

After one pause, Tendoy's gaze settled on Dillard's tall, lean frame as if he represented the past, alive in the present. His eyes kindled with resentment, then flamed into anger. "White man greedy! Want to kill everything. He stupid! Damned stupid!"

Dillard snapped a reply. "Most men I know shoot only what they intend to use."

"Your people bring men from beyond the mountains. They pay big money to shoot, shoot, shoot." Tendoy made a sweeping gesture toward some imaginary landscape, a movement born of such fury it startled me. "If white man hunted like Indian, buffalo would still send dust clouds into sky." He nodded in the direction of the creek bottom. "Beaver would still make lodges in stream. Many moons ago, Dillon was nothing. Just grass on the prairie. No white men. Indian trails meet there, then go past land of steaming waters to Crow country. Flathead, Shoshoni, Nez Perce, ride together in peace. The trail this deep." He used his hand to indicate a depth of three feet. "In Crow country, buffalo run from sky to sky. Now, no more buffalo. No more meat for Indian. *Pisoaima! Pisoaima!*"

I squirmed, collective guilt weighing on my conscience. Dillard's jaw rippled.

Tendoy waited a long while before he said more. Then, with a dismissive jerk of his arm, "Enough talk. Tendoy listen to girl. Listen to woman. Listen to you, Mr. Dillard. I will think on this. When the sun shows his face above the mountain tops I will decide what must be done." He took a nail from his pocket and dug at the ashes in his pipe, making it clear the visit had come to an end.

Still numb from his oratory, we were slow to move. "*Kaihkwa*. You go." Tendoy lifted his chin toward the girl. "My granddaughter will give you food and drink. I smoke prayer pipe. Ask the One in the Sky to show the way."

Chapter 14

To prevent curious Lemhis from gazing down on me in the night, I pitched the tent on the creekbank, the smell of willow strong on one side, sage on the other. Dillard and Benito spread their bedrolls about a hundred yards down the creek. We'd spoken little while we ate at the granddaughter's lodge. I was sorry for the trouble between us. Except for his stand on the horses, Dillard seemed a man of honor, someone I could trust.

Kitty refused to bed down in the tent, saying it was "sissy," the need to prove herself as tough as a man ingrained over the years. Penny lay in vigil beside her, growling softly at two young Lemhi men who'd stationed themselves near the tent, likely at Tendoy's orders. They lay jabbering, wrapped in their furry robes. Now and then their laughter riffled through the canvas walls, a vulgar amusement punctuated by obscene noises that imitated body functions.

I lay in my bedroll fully clothed except for boots; the incident with Riley had taught me that. My stomach was filled with the stew I'd eaten—rabbit and grouse flavored with sage and thistle root—my mind filled with worry about the morrow, my ears with the restless thud of Bannack's and Shorty's hoofs. Earlier that evening I'd fought an irrepressible urge to take Kitty in my arms and tell her I was her mother. She was full of resentment and would likely reject my claim. I wasn't sure I could handle that. I'd wait for a more peaceful time, when we'd patched our differences and I could speak more easily of the dark events surrounding her birth.

It had been bad enough when she'd accused me of neglecting Gabe, by saying, "Why aren't you back at cow camp, taking care of Pa?"

The charge had taken me by surprise. With all the argument about horses, we hadn't discussed Gabe's death. "I—I was worried about you. So was Gabe. He was dying . . . I doubt he lasted more than a few hours." I saw no need to tell of the suicide.

"Why didn't you stay until then?"

"He said he'd have no peace unless I found you and took you to the Bitterroot. By the way, where were you taking the herd?"

"To Sherwood's ranch near Bannack. Then I was going to ride back to Pa." A moment of silence. "I don't believe he's dead," she'd said, sniffling. "You're just saying that to get me to come with you."

I'd tried to convince her otherwise. When she'd defeated me on that score, she'd turned to a different argument. "I bet you're hoping the chief'll give all the horses to Dillard. Then you won't have to bother with them. That isn't what Pa wanted." There seemed no limit to her vengeful tongue. I'd like to think it derived from the darker side of her parentage, not the Breen's side. If I hadn't loved her so, I'd have packed my bags and gone on my way.

Disturbed by these thoughts, I slept little and rose when I could no longer tolerate the feel of the hard, cold ground, especially the places where I'd failed to clear away pebbles. I pulled the collar of the fleece jacket up around my ears and nose, jumped a narrow spot in the creek, and walked to a draw opposite the Indian camp where junipers offered privacy for my toilet. Then I sat on a rocky outcrop to watch the night pale to an obscure gray.

A few bars of pink lay below the morning star, hinting of sunrise and a clear day to follow. To the north, perhaps a half-mile away, mountain sheep walked single file up the rim of a bluff, dark silhouettes against the northern gloom. In the shallow draw to the south, the band of horses appeared as a mass of shadowy forms, constantly on the move. Their soft nickers drifted on the breeze.

The gray wash of light outlined the conical tipis on the bench. On the flat below them, my tent assumed a black shape. Penny had followed me up the hillside and had returned to guard Kitty. I saw her pacing around the tent, a furtive sentinel. A shot of flame said Dillard or Benito had built a fire. The smell of burning sage wafted my way on the western breeze. The fire grew until I could see Dillard's lanky figure etched against the flames.

I longed to speak to him. I wanted to reach an agreement before we spoke to Tendoy, but I'd wait until he was ready to face the day.

The air hadn't the bite of extreme cold, yet I looked forward to warming myself at my campfire. First, I'd take Bannack and Shorty to water and for a few mouthfuls of grass. Then I'd check on Lilly, the pregnant mare. The cross-country trip might have sped things along. If she hadn't foaled during the night, she could at any time. In Maryland, we would have babied her and kept careful watch. We would have fed her mash made from grain, wheat bran, and slivers of carrot. Here in the wilds of Montana, she had to fend for herself.

Kitty was still sleeping when I returned to the tent after checking Lilly. Obviously, she'd rested little on the way here and not much the night she'd spent in Tendoy's tipi. A few Lemhi men had roused from their sleep. They stood, yawning, stretching, facing the east, seeming to wait for the sun to crawl above the eastern hills. When the first long rays pierced the sky like spokes of a golden wheel, even before the crown of orange appeared, they raised their arms to the east, palms upward, and began to sing a long, repetitive chant. The guttural chant had slight melody, yet was pleasing to the ear. The song pulsed across the basin along with the sound of a flute that was clear as the call of a lark, plaintive, reedy, then floated skyward to meet the dawn.

I'd read about countries where people worshiped the rising sun. In China they rang little bells. In Japan they said prayers. In India they offered flowers. I'd read that some American Indian tribes held a newborn up to the great orange ball and said the child's name, so the sun would know the baby.

As I watched the colors take over the sky, it was easy for me to feel the morning's magic. On one hand, it created a feeling of hope. On the other hand, it aroused such a sadness that a melody rose from my heart: an earth song, a sky song, a song of love and mourning, of remorse. While I sang, the pink dawn flowed across the basin, the soft colors waxing and waning. There was a primeval sense of waiting, of suspended time, of nature put on hold.

Their chanting ended, the Lemhis lowered their arms, patted their chests, and hurried down to the creek. They took off their shirts, splashed their faces and chests with creek water, and dried themselves with their shirts. A few women had wakened and moved about on the bench tending fires. It prompted me to build my own.

I traveled far from camp to find dead sage—fuel near the Lemhi village was long gone. When I returned with an armload, Kitty had crawled from her bedroll and pulled on her jacket. Her long braids were frizzy from tossing in bed, her eyes partly glued from sleep. The smudges beneath them weren't quite as dark as yesterday.

"Good morning. I'll have a fire going in no time." I tossed the armload of sage to the ground. "Are you hungry?"

She yawned and shook her head. "I'm going to check on Chinook and Lilly."

"I was just up there. She seems tired, starting to bag. We'll need to check on her often."

Kitty shot me a look that said, *What do you think I've been doing all along?* "I'll talk to Chinook, let him know I'm still around." She whistled Penny to her side.

"I wouldn't go up there alone. Wait until we've had some breakfast, and I'll go with you."

"What's to hurt? I came all the way here by myself." She stuffed her hands deep into her pockets and pulled her head forward to loosen the braid caught under her collar.

"The herders might resent you. They didn't like my being there."

"Won't bother me." The bitterness in her voice revealed the depth of her wound, the fact that she'd lost the person who'd been her universe. The trip across the mountains and her encounter with the Lemhis had done nothing to lessen that. It seemed the horses had become a way to keep Gabe alive in her heart. Nothing I said would change that. Not yet.

I watched her walk off up the creek with Penny, putting on a bold front despite the fact her world had come crashing down around her shoulders. Somehow I'd find a way to ease her heartache. After all, I was her mother. Mothers were supposed to be able to do such things. A rebellious youngster was no different from a fractious filly or heifer. The latter two I could handle, but I could hardly put a rope around a girl and lead her to shelter.

Chapter 15

"What have you decided?" Dillard aimed the question at Chief Tendoy as we stood before him, our cheeks as taut as the canvas of his tipi.

"I tell you later. I want to take better look at animals that have caused such war between you."

I'd had no chance to speak to Dillard about the horses. The chief had sent for us before I'd finished my breakfast coffee, the sage casting leafy shadows onto the sunlit flat. I'd set my cup aside and, leading my horse as Tendoy had asked, followed the messenger through the frosted grass onto the open bench above the creek.

Tendoy faced us, standing tall in a striped shirt, black trousers, and a deerskin jacket decorated with small blue and white trade beads and porcupine quills. Evidently, he thought the occasion special enough to wear the jacket.

"Come on, Chief, you've had all night." Dillard's drawl was emphatic. "This business makes me feel like I have one leg tied."

Me too, Mr. Dillard. Me too.

Tendoy stared at Dillard from under his heavy brows, seeming to weigh what he should say, or if he should speak at all. "I sit in doorway long time smoking pipe. I watch star that does not move. I watch moon. Watch horse spirit gallop across the heavens. Horses will show Tendoy the way."

He started off through the camp's clutter, his stride slow, somewhat stiff. He stopped now and then to introduce this son, that nephew, an uncle, several grandchildren, giving them instructions in Shoshoni. I'd have wagered they already knew his decision.

Three of Tendoy's sons and two nephews went to the rear of the bench to gather saddle horses. The older grandsons grabbed rope halters from the dark interiors of tipis, then followed Tendoy in a loose group, shirtless, wearing jeans and worn cowboy boots. I wondered how they could go without shirts in the chill morning. A few dogs, mongrel herding types, followed at their heels.

Dillard restrained his sorrel and his own long stride to keep abreast of the chief. I walked at the chief's left, Bannack pressing me to move faster. He seemed to think we were headed for tall grass and, like the sorrel, was anxious to move out. I, too, was anxious, as hope and doubt wrestled for control of my thoughts.

The women in camp were busy. Some had built fires from stacks of dead sage and were boiling coffee before setting out to harvest seeds and berries. At the edge of camp we passed racks of meat that had curled brown in the sun. Two dogs leaped at the strips and were scolded away by a young girl in gingham dress. Squawking ravens and magpies hopped along the ground, vying for tiny scraps the women had tossed aside the previous day when they scraped fat and flesh from deer hides. The place smelled of rancid fat.

As we approached the flat where the band of horses grazed, two young herders rode toward us through the silvery expanse of bunch-grass and sage. One boy sat astride an old Indian-style saddle that consisted of two pads joined by a heavy leather girth, a hide as blanket. He'd looped a rope over his dun's lower jaw. The other herder rode bareback on a brown with flecks of red, the pony's nose humped, the underlip long and petulant.

Tendoy spoke in Shoshoni to the herders and the young men who'd followed him on foot, using his chin to indicate direction, pausing to answer questions. His sons had ridden up from camp, their high-crowned black felt hats pulled low over their foreheads. They sat on the fringe of the group and listened to Tendoy, showing no change of expression.

Tendoy said nothing to Dillard or me by way of explanation, nor did he ease our anxiety when the boys began to separate his large herd from Gabe's. He said nothing to Kitty when she rushed over from the small sagebrush corral that held Chinook and demanded to know what was happening.

During the sorting process, Gabe's crossbreeds milled about, distrustful, muscles roped with tension, first as one large group led by the bell-mare, then in smaller groups led by other mares. The lead mares bit the other horses, kicked them, and chased them off. Foals squealed as they tried to stay abreast of their frantic mothers. A stud colt chased the fillies and tried to mount them. The smell of fresh dung rode the air. Above the rest of the uproar, Chinook's loud, brassy neigh rang repeatedly across the valley and echoed from the knobby eastern hills.

The boys rode among the horses yipping, yelling, waving coiled ropes, their dark-brown skin glistening in the sun. Having made a truce, Penny and the Lemhi dogs raced around the fringes, nipping at the horses' heels.

I noticed Kitty's cow pony, Trixie, among the herd. Kitty must have brought her along as transport back to the Centennial. Lilly was there, heavy with foal. I worried mightily about her out there in all that confusion. I'd been in her condition once—heavy with child. I knew the feeling, the ultimate danger. I promised myself that Kitty would have the mare, that I'd keep special watch over her.

My heart wrenched as I saw the horses seized by a profound desire to escape harm. At the same time, it brought a sinking sensation to my stomach. If Tendoy ruled in Kitty's favor, even granted her half the horses, we'd have to drive the restless herd across the mountains. It would be up to us to keep them safe. No small task.

It took the Lemhi wranglers a half-hour to separate the herds. Then four boys drove Tendoy's herd up the valley and out of sight into a spring basin.

Tendoy had watched bland-faced through it all, as if Kitty, Dillard, and I were nowhere near. Now he let his gaze wander Gabe's herd, squinting against the sun's slanted rays. "Many of each—yearlings, mares, older horses," he said, acknowledging our presence at last. "We can divide eas—"

"You can't divide them." Tears of outrage glistened at the corners of Kitty's eyes.

Tendoy's eyes reflected annoyance. "Both man and girl speak truth. Mr. Dillard paid for half. Tendoy give him half. You, Kitty Breen, have nothing. No father. No home. Only horses to make you glad and pay your way. Tendoy knows about such things. Tendoy give you half the herd."

"But—"

I clamped my hand on Kitty's shoulder. "Hush! You'll make things worse."

"Couldn't be much worse." Dillard's words fell like stones. Yet I sensed a note of acceptance, resignation.

There was silence, a long moment of it, while Tendoy scowled at

Dillard. I stood holding my breath, Bannack's reins so tight in my hand they cut into my flesh. Every time Kitty made a move to speak, I said, "Not now."

"You do not like my decision, Mr. Dillard?"

Dillard shrugged. "Nothing wrong with it. I spent the night thinking, just as you did. I decided to let the girl have her share, but I don't have to like it." He sent me a look that said, *See, I'm not as bad as you thought.*

"You didn't speak of it—this decision of yours," Tendoy muttered.

"I wanted to see what kind of a man you were."

Tendoy's expression turned curious, even slightly amused. "Now you know?"

"Yes, now I know."

Thunderclouds had gathered in Kitty's face. I could restrain her no longer. "You can't give him something that isn't his."

"They are his," I said adamantly. "It's Gabe's doing. Accept it."

"He was sick." Kitty's eyes screamed defiance. "He didn't know—"

"Your aunt speaks the truth. You must respect it," Tendoy said evenly. Except for eyes that glittered like obsidian, his face was a mask carved from granite. The sun's fire blazed on his coppery-brown skin. "How many horses in band?"

Kitty said nothing. She probably feared an answer on her part would show acceptance of Tendoy's plan.

"Do you not know your own horses?"

She pulled in her chin and muttered. "Thirty-five."

"That mean same number for each?"

"One extra," Dillard said.

"Maybe Tendoy keep one. Pay for his trouble."

Dillard shook his head. "Not likely."

A look of speculation mixed with amusement crossed Tendoy's face. "You want more horses, Tendoy sell you some of his."

"Those broomtails? Hardly." Dillard pulled the restless sorrel around, thrust a foot in the stirrup, and threw a leg over the saddle. "Let's get to sorting."

Tendoy gazed out at the herd, taking his time to reply. It was impossible to judge whether his laconic manner resulted from natural inclination or a wish to assert his authority. "You take turns," he said after a bit. "Choose horses you want. Not stallion. We decide about him a diff—"

"He goes with me," Kitty cried. She turned rigid, fists clenched at her sides. Would there be no end to her argument? "He's Pa's favorite. The herd is no good without him." She thrust a hand toward Dillard. "This man'll use him in the mountains. Work him hard. Ruin him."

"I'll use him as your father did, to sire good trail stock." The words hissed from Dillard's tight lips.

Tendoy pushed the air to the ground in a gesture of exasperation. "Enough. I have spoken." He took a pebble from the ground, put both hands behind his back, appeared to move them around, then held the clenched fists in front of him. "Girl tell which hand holds rock. If you guess which hand, you choose first horse. We start with mares and foals."

Kitty didn't move, just stood like a spraddle-legged yearling colt daring the world. I admired her grit, but I wished she'd bend a little. Life would be easier for her if she wouldn't always meet it head-on.

"Choose," Tendoy said sternly, "or I let man have first horse."

The pink of anger in Kitty's face flushed to a deep red. Still, she didn't move.

Dillard flexed his jaw and shifted his weight in the saddle. "We're wasting time."

I, too. was losing patience. "Do it, Kitty. There's no other way."

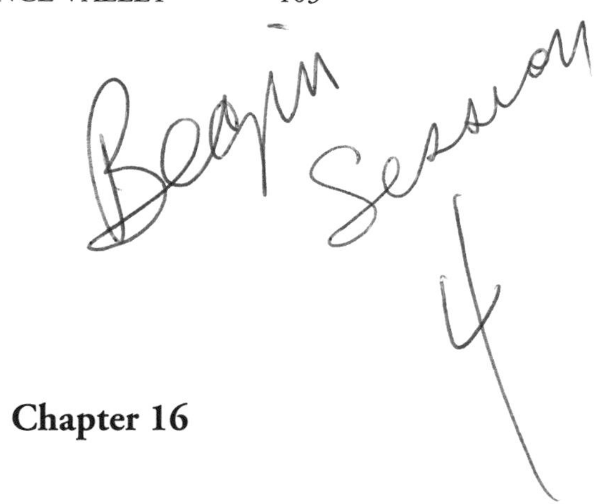

Chapter 16

This first choice of horses wasn't as crucial as who would get Chinook, but I wanted Kitty to choose first, wanted desperately for her to own Lilly. A mare about to foal deserved to be with those who cared, and I had no idea how Dillard handled such matters.

Some of the crimson had drained from Kitty's face. With a shrug that *said I'll-do-it-but-I-won't-like-it,* she stepped up to Tendoy, pointed an uncertain finger at one clenched fist, changed her mind and pointed to the other.

Slowly, teasingly, he opened the fist, revealing the pebble.

"Good!" I surprised myself with the force of the exclamation. "Choose Lilly."

Kitty shook her head. "I want the bell mare."

I could see her point. The bell mare was the dominant mare, boss of the herd when Chinook had other things on his mind. The bell she wore alerted wranglers to the herd's whereabouts. My concern for Lilly overshadowed that asset. "Lilly needs us. I have a feeling about her foal. Choose her." Kitty seemed to grapple with compromise as she scanned the herd, lip tucked beneath her teeth, but I sensed she'd do as I asked.

Allowing Kitty first choice didn't appear to add to Dillard's irritation. He looked out over the herd, gray eyes sparking keen from beneath squinted eyelids. While he and Kitty made silent choices, Tendoy spoke to the sons slouched on their drowsy horses a short distance away, indicating a steep-sided draw a quarter-mile to the south. A rock fence with a rope gate across the mouth formed a corral that would hold the horses Kitty chose. Dillard's would remain on the outside. Following Tendoy's instructions, two of his sons trotted their ponies toward the corral, the other toward Gabe's herd.

The horses knew something was afoot and didn't like it. They'd been one herd too long. I found myself rooting for them as they struck out across the sage to avoid being cut from the rest. Their panic squeezed at my heart and raked at my nerves—the squeals, whinnies, bulging eyes, taut muscles, steaming manure, and boiling dust. Riding Trixie, Kitty slid a lasso over some of the horses. So did the boys. I stayed abreast on Bannack to see that the lassos did no harm. Not until the stringy Indian ponies outstripped them did the crossbreeds turn against their will and run into the corral. Tendoy's sons pulled the gate taut behind them.

Once inside the corral, the horses ran in circles, kicked up their heels, and boxed each other, raising clouds of dust. Kitty had chosen Lilly, and I worried about her safety in the crush of bodies. Some of the spring foals, now gangly adolescents, had become separated from their mothers. They sped back and forth, squealing in front of the gate until reunited with their dams. Some of the colts and fillies in the corral were offspring of the bell mare Dillard had chosen. She trotted back and forth in front of the corral fence, bell clanging, trying to entice them to jump to freedom. Her shrieks and their answering squeals split the air. Shorty's brays of abandonment traveled from camp to join the bedlam.

In the small sagebrush corral, Chinook charged back and forth, snorted and pawed sod, stomped at the fence and bugled. His reddish-brown coat gleamed like fire in the sunlight. He seemed more a creature of the gods than born of the earth.

Tendoy stood tall amid the sage, watching it all, an enduring monument to the past. He caught the attention of one of the herd boys and made a wide arc with his arm. "My grandsons take Mr. Dillard's horses down the creek," he said as I rode up to him. "Now we look at stallion."

Dillard had dismounted to tie his denim jacket behind the saddle and was wiping the sweat of the roundup from his face with a blue bandana. We tethered our horses to a pair of junipers and followed Tendoy, as did the three sons mounted on their ponies.

Kitty had tied Trixie near Chinook's corral and stood at the gate made of rope and sage. Penny and the Lemhi dogs lay in the shadow of the rock fence, panting heavily after their run. Every now and then Chinook stopped his pacing and leaned across the gate to nuzzle Kitty's shoulder. Despite the trek through the mountains, his injury had healed into a thin, ridged line that wavered between knee and fetlock. As we neared the gate, he wheeled and thundered around in circles.

"Call him," Tendoy said as he stepped up to Kitty.

She made kissing sounds until the horse came forward, blowing huge snorts of air. Tendoy held out his hand. The stallion quivered, drew his weight back, feet steady.

"*Tsaa punku*! Fine stallion. Never see better. Gabe not show me." He made a sound that mixed a grunt with a chuckle. "Maybe he think I steal." Tendoy's deep voice seemed to calm Chinook. He pricked his ears forward and stretched his eyes wide. The chief ran a hand along his neck. "My stallions not so strong as this one. Maybe not so smart."

"Where are they?" Kitty asked. She stood as close to Chinook as the gate would allow, as if to stake her claim on the horse.

"Stallions in Idaho. Three sons stay to feed them and sheep. Take turns with these sons." He grinned toward the three men sitting on their horses. "Tendoy boss. He always come to hunt in Medicine Lodge." The sons laughed as if at a family joke.

Tendoy returned his attention to Chinook. "This horse fit to carry big chief like Joseph of the Nez Perce. He once my enemy. Now my friend in sorrow. He would like this horse."

Kitty lay her head against Chinook's neck, a defiant eye on Dillard. "He's my favorite, Pa's too. He'll sire some great foals. My herd'll soon be as big as ever."

"You're forgetting I bought him, young lady," Dillard muttered wearily.

"He's not for sale." Kitty's eyes spit fire.

"Tendoy decide what for sale, what not for sale." The chief's face hardened. "Man should have stallion, not girl. Stallions for men."

Resentment sent blood rushing to my cheeks. "Kitty's as good as any man. She rode Chinook all this way by herself. To say nothing of trailing thirty-four other horses and half-a-dozen foals. Gabe wanted her to have the stallion." Actually, Gabe had said nothing about Chinook. For Kitty's sake, I had to assume he wanted her to have the stallion. It seemed that I, too, had my heart set on keeping the magnificent animal. I'd seen many thoroughbreds in my life, but none as handsome nor as endearing as Chinook, though he could burst into a fury when protecting his harem.

Tendoy stared at me with narrowed eyes. I gave him back stare for stare. "Granddaughter say Mr. Dillard pay three thousand dollar on stallion. Half price. If he pay you other half, you give him—"

"What if I bought the horse?" The words escaped before I'd given them any thought. I had no idea how or when I'd get the money.

Dillard looked stunned, Kitty bewildered. Tendoy seemed skeptical.

"You have money, Mrs. Tate?" he asked.

"No, but I could pay over time."

"You agree, Mr. Dillard?"

"Of course not. She told me she's hardly making ends meet."

"Is true?" Tendoy asked me.

"Yes, but . . ." I could think of no further excuse.

"You have three thousand to pay, Mr. Dillard?"

Dillard reached for his wallet.

Kitty threw her arms around Chinook's neck. "He can't have him!"

Tendoy frowned at Kitty, his chin thrust forward. When he spoke next, it was as if he pondered each word carefully. "Tendoy see you have much love for horse. Maybe we decide Shoshoni way. Fair for all."

"What way is that?" Mistrust laced Dillard's words.

"A horse race. You and the girl."

"For a valuable stallion? Ridiculous."

"You have better idea?"

"I'd just as soon draw straws. Makes as much sense."

"A bird can draw straws. I say you race. You win, the horse is yours. Pay no more money. Girl win, she gets horse, pay three thousand dollar. Little by little as she can."

"It's not fair!" Rage brought Kitty's freckles into high relief. "I shouldn't have to pay anything if I win."

At first, the arrangement appeared skewed. On further thought, it seemed fair, almost favored Kitty. She was lighter. Trixie could run a faster race. "It's more than fair," I hissed.

"You're still against me, aren't you?"

"I'm rooting for you more than you'll ever know. You're too stubborn, too sorry for yourself to see—"

"Doesn't matter who you're rooting for. There's not going to be a race." Dillard took an angry stride toward the corral gate. "The stallion's mine. I'll send you a check in the mail. Certified. If you don't cash it, that's your loss." He began to unwind one of the wires that held the mesh of rope and brush in place. "I want the papers on the stallion before I—"

"I'll give you no papers," I said staunchly. "Half the horse is Kitty's."

"Fine. You want him to service your mares, you bring them to my place in the Big Hole." He released the first wire and began to give the next one an angry tug.

"You expect me to traipse seventy miles over mountain trails each time I want to breed a mare?" I waved my arms in anger. "I'll do no such thing. You bring Chinook to us in the spring and leave him until all the mares are br—"

"What about my mares? When do I breed them? Summer's too late. My boy and I won't even be in camp." Abruptly, as if an idea had struck him, he spun to face me, gray eyes keened to the glint of polished metal. "Tell you what. You want the horse, I'll race *you* for him." He jabbed a finger toward me. "How's that for fair?"

I sputtered, not knowing what to say. It'd been years since I'd raced a horse, my body not as limber as then. I wanted desperately for Kitty to have Chinook at least half the time. If I raced and lost . . .

Kitty seemed to read my mind. "Aunt Jess, you'll lose," she whined.

Likely she was right, but her lack of confidence stiffened my spine. "I used to race Gabe and won as often as not."

"Are you going to race, or do I take the horse?" Two vertical lines trenched the space between Dillard's brows. His eyes held the spark of victory.

The look set a flare to my courage. I might not win, but by God, I'd try. "Sure I'll race. You'll eat my dust the whole way."

Chapter 17

"Enough talk. We get ready." Tendoy motioned two of his sons toward the head of a side valley that flowed into the broad sweep of sage.

I peered out from under Gabe's plainsman's hat at what appeared to be a two-mile course up the valley. There was a thin scattering of sagebrush, a small wash in the middle. If the floor of the valley was similar to that on the flats, slab rock would be scarce; it'd be mainly smooth float and lots of pebbles from past glaciers. Not too bad for racing. The problem would lie in soft dirt surrounding prairie dog and badger holes. The mounds wouldn't support the weight of a horse. Bannack might step into one, injuring himself and me.

"I never thought I'd be racing for a horse worth thousands," Dillard grumbled.

I wanted to say it was his idea, but I was too upset for speech. The thought of racing quivered my insides. I only half-listened as Kitty babbled advice about racing tactics, her blue eyes intense. She was worried about losing Chinook, but did she give any thought to my safety?

I'd said, "You'll eat my dust." Brash words for someone who hadn't raced for twenty-five years. I doubted my bones were up to the pounding. I thought about calling it off as we headed toward the junipers for our horses. A glance across my shoulder at Dillard's resolute face convinced me I had no choice.

Horses in tow, we walked the short distance from the junipers to the mouth of the narrow valley. Tendoy was waiting, his eyes aglitter. Kitty stood beside him, fidgeting. I closed my eyes, willing all the strength of my spirit to join hers, willing in Bannack the same fierce desire to win.

Opening my eyes, I looked up at the sky, which earlier that morning had lifted my heart to peaks of rapture. Its dome was high, clear, without feature except for several buzzards wheeling on the upper air currents, searching, searching. The sun shone warm. The wind of open spaces blew strong.

Tendoy was explaining that two of his sons would station themselves at the turn-around point at the head of the valley. The other son would draw the starting line near where we stood.

Benito had strolled up from camp and stood to one side, looking bemused. His white teeth flashed in the sunlight. The Lemhi women had received news of the race. With children and dogs, they flocked to the valley's north rim, where they could look down on the entire course. They chose vantage points in such a deliberate way, I sensed races had been held there in the past. One woman rode a horse, a baby in a cradleboard across the withers. Two others carried cradle boards on their backs. Older women found outcrops of rock where they could sit and watch the children chase dogs through the juniper and sage. Indians loved horse races. Likely they were betting on it in small ways among themselves.

I mounted Bannack and walked him, preparing for action, trying to ease my nerves. Except for my extreme misgivings, it reminded me of when Gabe and I were children. In my mind's eye, I saw us prancing our ponies around, boasting who would win the race, ready to chance a fall or broken bone. As I looked over at Dillard warming up his sorrel, I saw not a lanky, sun-bronzed Texan riding a western saddle, but Gabe in his later youth sitting a light racing saddle, his face alive with excitement, the finely dressed ladies and gentlemen in the stands cheering him on. No Maryland aristocrats here, but Gabe would have enjoyed the spectacle to come, as well as the high stakes of the gamble.

Tendoy's son had drawn the starting line on a swath of bare ground where decades ago buffalo had rolled in the spring mud. Later, wind-storms had filled the circles with blowing sand. The other sons had stationed themselves fifty feet apart at the head of the valley. Dillard and I would race up the south side of the wash and make a turn around the man designated for each before we raced back to the finish line.

Tendoy and Kitty walked up to the starting line. The spectators on the rim one-hundred-fifty yards distant set up a clamor. It made Bannack nervous. He tossed his head and danced around. I rode him in small circles to quiet him, then cantered in a wide oval. Now and then, I kneed him into a spurting gallop to ready him for the race. I'd control him more with my knees than with the reins.

Like Bannack, the sorrel knew something momentous was about to happen. It showed in the skittish way she moved and in the way she rolled her eyes. She and Bannack skylarked around, trampling the sage, filling the air with its sharp scent. Dillard and I turned them in circles before we brought them to the line drawn in the sand and gathered them for the start.

My heart thumped against my ribs. "It's up to you," I said to Bannack. "Give it all you have."

Tendoy raised his arm and brought it down like a cleaver. Bannack hesitated a brief second. I stung his flanks with the reins and kneed him into a run. I didn't have enough voice to urge him on. My heart and lungs had lodged in my throat.

The women and children made up for my silence. They yipped and yelled on the north rim. Sensing their excitement, Bannack lengthened his stride. Ground squirrels ducked into their holes as he steamed past.

We were already a quarter-mile up the valley, running neck to neck with the sorrel. Dillard was hunched over the mare's withers, keeping his weight forward. His face was grim, determined. Now and then he slapped the mare's flanks with his reins and said, "Giddyap, there."

We slowed when we reached the soft, sandy soil of buffalo wallows and prairie dog mounds, then sped up on the hardpan. Driven by a crosswind, the dust we churned into the air drifted onto the north rim, where the children raced along, their legs stretched full stride in a futile attempt to keep up with the horses.

A family of sage hens exploded from a clump of brush. A coyote ran from its den and dashed across our path. Bannack seemed undisturbed by the coyote, but the sorrel shied. I glanced over my shoulder and saw her two lengths behind.

I forced voice into my throat. "Go, Bannack, go."

His muscles rolled beneath my thighs. His hide steamed. Flecks of saliva strung from his lips into my face. He was still in the lead when he made the turn around one of Tendoy's sons and sped back down the valley, head extended, mane flying. As before, I slowed him in sandy stretches, sped forward on hard-packed ground.

In one soft spot, he broke through the surface and lunged forward. I fell onto his neck, gulping air, clinging tight to his belly with my legs. The tough little buckskin caught himself, crouched a second or two, then plunged ahead to catch up to the easy-striding sorrel. I thought I saw concern for me on Dillard's face, but not enough that he slowed to check my welfare.

To avoid another near-fall, I steered Bannack toward the south rim, skirting soft ground. He kept abreast of the sorrel, hammering the earth about twenty-five yards to her right. I lay low along his withers, legs tight against his side. Only an arm movement when I slapped him with a hand separated me from the horse.

Three hundred yards to go. Close enough to see Tendoy and Kitty at the finish line. "Hey, Bannack! Come on, boy!" I heard Kitty scream.

I couldn't tell who the Lemhis rooted for, but they went wild, screaming themselves hoarse.

I steered Bannack toward the center of the course to be in line with the rope Tendoy and his son held at the finish. "We're almost there, boy. Give it all you have."

He forged ahead with a quick-footed gait, running ahead of the sorrel's floating stride. My heart kept pace with the quickening hoof-beats, my breath so stifled I felt light-headed.

Kitty yelled, "Come on, Bannack. You can do it!"

The caterwauling on the north rim grew.

I crouched lower along Bannack's neck and whispered in his ear. His stride lengthened. His shoulder muscles bulged and rippled, bulged and rippled. His hoofs sledged into the earth.

The sorrel resented having him near. She gave a spurt and nipped his rump. Bannack shot her a backward glance and forged ahead.

Then it happened—as accidents do—without warning.

A lone sage hen burst from the brush, bounced off Bannack's head, and hit me full force in the face.

Bannack shrieked and reared. The bird flew off, flapping its wings in a frenzy of wasted motion.

The impact of the bird had stunned me, but I held tight to Bannack, keeping my weight forward. I settled him into the last few yards.

Too late.

The sorrel had crossed the finish line and was galloping off with the rope across her shoulders.

Defeat caved my chest. I'd lost Chinook. Kitty would never forgive me. As we rushed by, I saw her shoulders slump. Her face slackened with extreme disappointment. I couldn't imagine any greater than my own. It leadened my veins along with a sense of failure and the humiliation of being hit in the face by a large bird.

Tendoy waited stolid amid the sage. I slowed Bannack to an easy run and circled back to where he stood. Kitty was tramping off toward Chinook's corral. The screeching on the rim had faded.

"It doesn't seem fair," I said. "If it hadn't been for that bird . . ."

"What is fair for one, fair for the other." Tendoy brushed blown hair back from his eyes and turned them on me. Their depths held the dark-molasses-glow of sixty odd years of accumulated wisdom. "Coyote and bird each put mark on race. The Great Spirit has spoken through his creatures. I accept his will. So must you."

* * *

The bird had cost me more than the race. It had raked its claws across my nose and cheek. Blood trickled down my face. Aside from that, I was certain to have bruises, perhaps a black and swollen eye. I touched a suspicious wetness on my forehead and found my fingertips covered with bird droppings. There were some in my hair and splattered across my shirtsleeve. I turned Bannack toward the creek to wash.

He was still heaving and spuming froth when I slid from his back and allowed him to drink. White, foamy sweat stood out all over him. I ran my hand over his wet flank and patted it. A gallant horse. Willing to reach deep for that last spurt of energy.

I hurt in a multitude of ways. Besides the dredging disappointment and the jolt to my pride, my muscles and joints ached. I shook all over. I eased onto my haunches at water's edge.

I was splashing water and didn't hear Kitty walk up behind me leading Trixie. "I knew you'd lose!" she said with spleen.

I'd expected her to be hurt, angry, but I'd hoped she'd not take it out on me. I rose stiffly and turned toward her with apology. "I tried, Kitty. If it hadn't been for the bird I would've—"

"You shouldn't have raced. I told you . . ." Her face puckered. She bit her lip and squeezed her eyes shut to hold back tears.

I put my hands on her shoulders. She flinched and shrugged my hands aside. The gesture cut like a knife. “You don’t need to be spiteful. I’m just as disappointed as you are.”

“No, you aren’t. You’re glad. Now there’s no stallion to grow the herd.” She put all the sarcastic venom of her feelings into the words, all the hatred for life stored in her veins over the past few months. She must have known she was on mutinous ground, but she didn’t care.

Resentment and self-blame heated my cheeks and stung my eyes. “I didn’t want to lose Chinook. I feel just as bad as you do.”

“You don’t know how I feel!” She rubbed a fist across her wet cheeks, put a foot in the stirrup to mount Trixie, and slung a leg over the saddle. Outrage burned scarlet in her eyes. “Nobody knows how I feel, just Pa.” I noted the reference to Gabe as if he still lived. “Just you wait. Chinook’ll come back to me. He won’t hold still for having the herd separated. If he can’t break free, I’ll go get him and take him back to Pa.” She gave me a quick lashing with her eyes and clucked Trixie across the creek.

“You’re acting like a spoiled child!” I cried as she headed for the thinly timbered ridge to the east. “Life won’t always let you have your way.”

Despite the surge of anger, I understood the tie that existed between the girl and Chinook. In a way, they were of the same nature, utterly fearless, indomitable. Now she’d lost him. Still, I’d tried to win. With all my might. As I watched her ride off, her dour mood settled on me as if born in my own mind, adding to my sense of failure. How could I have taken such a gamble? A child of ten would have had more sense.

* * *

I was feeling sorry for myself, feeling a terrible self-blame, when Sam Dillard headed my way holding the sorrel at a leisurely walk. His lean hips swiveled with the easy roll born of years in the saddle, but his shoulders held the slump of a middle-aged man whose body had endured more brutish activity than it should. Circumstance had caused us to butt heads like two billy goats, but I respected the man. I liked his drawling speech and essentially gentle manner. The anger I felt toward Kitty had pushed aside much of the resentment I’d harbored for him. I pulled the wet hair from my cheeks and pretended I didn’t look a mess.

He dismounted, tried to flex his knees, couldn’t. He tried again and barely succeeded. A laugh quivered in his chest, not quite breaking the surface. “Too many years fighting the stirrups.”

“The race didn’t help matters. I’m sorry it came to that.”

"I'm the one to apologize. I shouldn't have pushed you to it." He waved a hand toward my face. "Looks like you got the worst of the crash."

"It hurt my pride more than anything else."

He pulled a feather from my hair and handed it to me with a sympathetic grin. "A calling card."

I smiled ironically. "Think I'll keep it to remind me how foolish I was."

The lashing I'd taken from Kitty's tongue had left me vulnerable and in the need of consolation. As I fingered the feather's downy edge, I sensed Dillard's nearness and felt a compelling need to rest my head on his chest and lay all my worries there, if only for a minute.

I brushed the urge aside. 'I'm terribly sorry about the mix-up over the horses."

"I know it wasn't any of your doing . . . not directly, anyhow." He glanced toward the eastern hills, the corners of his eyes creasing with annoyance tempered by amusement. "It's that little broomtail I blame. She can work up a real froth."

Kitty was riding up a ragged draw toward a round knob speckled with juniper. I imagined her on that pinnacle, looking down on those she blamed for destroying her world, shouting to the wind, *I'll get my way, just you wait!*

"She's hurting," I said. "That makes it worse."

"Hurting once in a while never did a body any harm. Helps them grow." He flicked a smile. "'Least that's what they say." He pushed the brim of his Stetson up with a forefinger and continued to stare to the east, his expression distant, not a look that saw across the miles but one that strayed into the past.

I recalled our conversation about the wife and daughter who'd died. "I imagine you know about hurting."

He shot me a quick, forlorn glance and stared once more at the tiny figures wending their way uphill. "My Josephine was just like her. She was such a tomboy, I called her Jo. She could stare down a rattlesnake."

"Did she work with you like Kitty did with Gabe?"

"I was away on the job most of the time, not around her much. Not enough to help my wife lay down the law." He gave a silent snort. "Not that it would've done any good. When I came home the girl and I were always facing off like a couple of red-eyed bulls."

"You said she died a year ago?"

"A little more than that. Bull-headed to the last." He stared at the ground, scratching a cheek. I thought I saw him rub away a tear.

"There's no pain worse than losing a child."

"You know?"

"Yes, under circumstances that . . ." I let the rest go.

We stood beside each other a while in silence, facing the rocky knob. I wanted desperately to help Kitty, felt bound by blood and affection to do so, by my own needs, by the promise I'd made Gabe. "It's not going to be easy helping Kitty come to grips with Gabe's death and all it means for her future. It's a bit much for a young girl."

"A lot of it will be up to you. Right now her future is muddied, like a cow path after a rain. When the skies clear, the trail will be there for her to follow. You'll need to keep her from straying."

I thought a while, reluctant to bring up the subject of the horses, decided to go ahead. "I was surprised you were willing to give her half the herd."

He took his time to answer, as if unwilling to admit to a soft heart. "I'd thought all night about Jo and thought helping Kitty might make up for..." He drew a long breath, let it string out slowly. "Anyway, I figured the little buzzworm would win sooner or later, so why fight it."

The scratches burning like fire on my face turned my thoughts toward the recent folly. "Why did you race me?"

"I was tired of arguing. Never did like to argue."

"What would you have done if you'd lost?"

"Well now, I don't rightly know. Maybe offered you so much money you'd sell. I would've ended up with that chestnut one way or another. I set my mouth for him the minute I laid eyes on him. Besides, he's too much horse for a little gal." He hoisted himself onto the sorrel's back and gathered in the reins. "'Spect I'll see you again before we leave. If not, stop by my place on Ruby Creek when you go through the Big Hole."

"If you'll forgive us for the inconvenience we've caused."

"I've forgiven much of it already."

"Like I said before, I'm sorry."

"Makes me wish I'd never heard of your brother's horses. Then that little gal and I wouldn't be at odds." He glanced at me across his shoulder and flicked a smile that was more a creasing of the eyes than a parting of the lips. "Nor would we."

In that brief glimmer of warmth, I sensed something I'd noticed in him before—a need, a longing, not for something hoped for, but for something treasured and lost. Whatever lay in store for us, I wanted to remain friends. We'd be driving our herds on the same trail, the distance far.

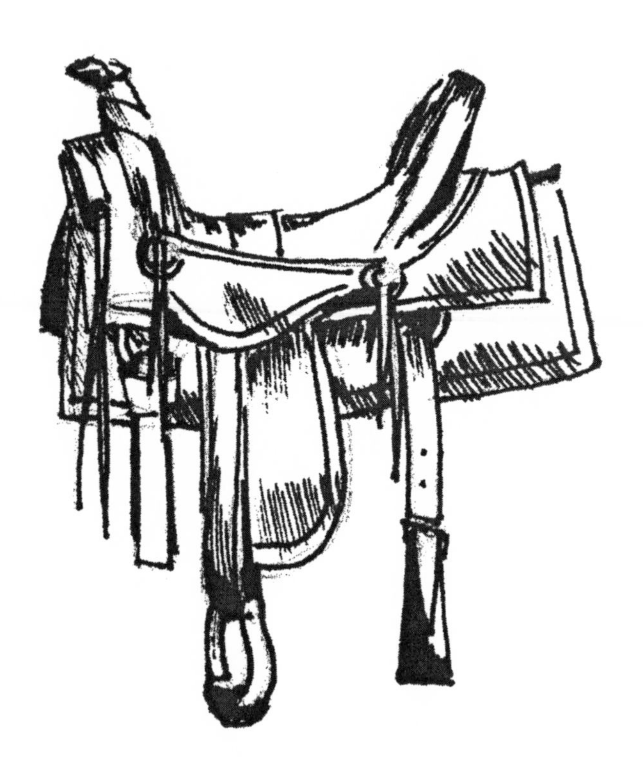

Chapter 18

Back at camp, I washed my hair thoroughly with hot water and rubbed elderberry salve on the scratches. I soaked a cloth in tea and held it on my swollen eye while I rested. I was sure Kitty would take her time on the hill.

Dillard left around noon with half of Gabe's herd. He led the string, trailing a rebellious Chinook behind the nervous sorrel. Benito brought up the rear with the two pack-horses. My heart dropped as I watched the furious Chinook fight the lead rope and scream. He kept looking back over his shoulder at the distant corral that held the rest of his mares. His muscles bulged with rage, the whites of his eyes showed—the ultimate picture of raw animal power restrained by a fragile submission to man.

I recalled Dillard's comment, "He's too much horse for a little gal," and smiled to myself. The "little gal" had brought the stallion all this way without any problem. Of course, at that time the harem had been intact.

I heard Chinook long after he'd disappeared beyond a swell in the land. I had an idea Dillard would push the herd along as fast as he could to distance the stallion from Tendoy's camp. I'd have to wait for Kitty to return before we could leave. Just as well. If we followed too close on Dillard's heels, she might decide to spirit Chinook away in the night.

If it had been possible I'd have traveled a route that took us far from Dillard, but the land wouldn't permit it. In the west, the Bitterroot Range walled the valley, forming the Continental Divide. From there, the slopes plunged thousands of feet into the Lemhi River Valley of Idaho. We'd follow the eastern base of the Divide until it left the Bitterroots and skimmed the northeast-flowing ridges of the Anaconda Mountains. Where the Divide turned to the northeast, we'd make the hazardous drop over Gibbons Pass onto the East Fork of the Bitterroot River. Before we reached Gibbons Pass, we'd cross several minor passes that connected lofty river basins, the surrounding ridges too thickly timbered and rugged for travel. There was but one route to Gibbons Pass, the same one Dillard would take to the Big Hole.

It was mid-afternoon before Kitty returned to camp, a hang-dog expression on her face. She said she'd been letting Trixie graze. Undoubtedly the truth, but I assumed it had taken a while for her to get a handle on her disappointment. She said little while we prepared to move on. I, too, had little desire to talk.

By the time we pulled out of camp, the sun had traveled two-thirds of the way across the basin of sky. Filmy clouds wisped the blue, giving the day the dreamy face of autumn. Tendoy seemed to have had enough of us and didn't bother to see us off, but I noticed him watching from the edge of camp. I hoped he'd find pleasure in the mare and six-month filly we'd left him. The roundup had stressed the mare and I feared the trip ahead would be hard on her.

The younger boys gave us a send-off of sorts. They showed off by running at a huge ball made from the inflated bladder of a large animal, butting it with their heads to see who got the biggest recoil. Other boys raced alongside our horses, yipping and yelling to spur them on.

Now that she'd made friends, Penny didn't want to part from the Lemhi dogs. The boys teased us, saying they'd keep her, but in the end they ran her off so she'd follow our string. She did so reluctantly, tail dragging. Now and then she'd stop to stare longingly at the Lemhi camp.

Kitty's horses were glad to be free of the corral. They frisked about before they settled into a string along the dim wagon track. Each foal stayed at its dam's side as if attached by an invisible cord, adding its tiny hoofprints to the mass left by Dillard's herd. Kitty led the string, ponying Shorty and the dominant mare, a dark brown named Bertie. The other horses followed the bossy mare like sheep going to pasture.

I rode drag, my nose filled with dust and the strong smell of horsehide and dung. I led an obnoxious bay stud colt that caused trouble with the rest of the horses when turned loose, a colt destined to replace Chinook. Before leaving Gabe's cow camp, the stallion had banished the colt and other two-year-olds from the herd. They'd followed as close as they could without arousing his anger. If Chinook had been here, the colt would have stayed clear of the mares and fillies. Without the stallion to discipline him, he needed restraint.

Lilly, the chestnut mare, poked along behind the rest of the herd, heavy-bellied, head drooping. Milk dribbled down the inside of her leg. I'd checked her udder before starting out. It had become tense and warm, not soft and flabby as it had been. Birth wasn't far off. I wanted desperately for the foal to be a colt, the image of Chinook. Most of all, I wanted it to be born alive and healthy.

As I rode along, thinking of the foal and its sire, I imagined them galloping free across the rolling sage and grasslands. An uncluttered landscape, this sturdy sage country, as much a part of southwestern Montana as the mountains, streams, and forests. It appealed to me as it would to a feral horse, in a way I couldn't define. It gave a sense of freedom, wild and sweet, a longing for the primeval. Beyond the sagelands loomed the peaks of the Bitterroot Range, the bare crags ribbed with avalanche gullies. They were without snow. But for how long? There was a good chance we wouldn't reach the Bitterroot Valley before the first arctic storm.

This herd of vibrant, restless horses wouldn't help matters. I watched their undulating rumps as they bent their heads to the rising track—sleek, well-muscled, shining with the good health and vitality of their breeding. Such strength. Such power. Gabe had charged me with the task of driving them two hundred miles to the northwest. Two hundred miles! A young girl in my care. An unpredictable child, single-minded in her obsession.

A sudden overwhelming sense of responsibility came to rest on my shoulders along with a vision of Gabe lying on his deathbed amid the mountains he'd come to love. My bitterness toward his deceit seemed to have faded during the problems at Tendoy's camp. I recalled his excitement in '82 when, after my father had lost the Maryland farm to bankruptcy, we'd moved west into those mountains—Gabe, Ben, and me. We'd attacked our new life with a vengeance, Gabe to buy land and cattle as he could, Ben to build a smithy in the new railroad town of Dillon, I to run a boarding-house filled to the brim with railroad men and miners. His second year in the Beaverhead Valley, Gabe had married Amy, pretty daughter of a railroad man. The union had bred a family of girls, the joy of my life, until . . .

The younger of the two living products of the Breen heritage now sped along the wagon track, stringing the herd out farther and farther. Sensing she wanted to catch up with Dillard and Chinook, I held back as much as I could. Bannack seemed tired from the race, willing to slow his pace. The stud colt had settled into the same relaxed stride. The creak of saddle leather, the rhythmic roll of Bannack's muscles beneath me, and the warmth of the sun on my shoulders, soon lulled away my concerns and brought peace.

* * *

Evening shadows flowed across the land before we spread our bedrolls along Medicine Lodge Creek. Beans heating over the sagebrush fire, fry bread sputtering in the pan, I sat crosswise on my grounded saddle to watch the herd graze in a field of nourishing, half-cured grass at the base of a reddish butte. Kitty had staked Shorty, the lead mare, and the stud colt near camp for the night and was about to turn back to the herd to check on Lilly.

"It might be good to keep Lilly near camp," I called to her.

"She won't want to foal close by. We'll watch her from a distance."

The brazen sky had turned the field a livid amber, the grass breathless, not a leaf moving. While the mares filled their perpetually hungry bellies, the colts slept on their sides or romped about like knobby-kneed children. Their slender little bodies turned and twisted and bounded into the air. They bucked and kicked, reared, pretended to box each other with their tiny forefeet. Suddenly they'd gallop wildly about in a game of chase. The mares and the older offspring looked up briefly to watch with indifference or concern, then returned to their grazing.

I remembered how the foals in Maryland would run beside their mothers, testing their stride, trying to match their mothers'. I always wondered, as did Gabe and my father, if the foal we watched was destined to become the next Derby winner, perhaps State Champion, even winner of the National.

Young things. How I loved their innocence. Their confidence. The sense the world was theirs to command.

Their hunger satisfied for the moment, the mares lay down and rolled in the dust holes of a dry wash. They writhed on their backs, kicked their heels, and twisted to scratch every inch of their hides. Lilly had more trouble than the rest. She dropped to the ground with a thud and couldn't complete the roll-over, satisfying the itch on one side only. With a big squirm and heave she thrust out her forefeet, braced against them, and lurched upward. On her feet, she gave a violent shudder to shake off the dust and caked sweat, the effort clearly more tiring for her than for the other mares. When they and their colts closed in to sniff her milky legs, she lunged at them with teeth bared, snipped a ribbon of skin from one or two, and whirled to kick them in the belly. Further proof that birth wasn't far off.

In the high country, evening closed in like a swiftly-drawn curtain, and a cold darkness flowed upward from the earth. Kitty bedded down early. I took the first shift to watch Lilly, her distended body silhouetted against the glimmering moonlight. She'd settled on her side in a patch of thick grass speckled with brush. I sat cross-legged fifty yards away, my arms folded tight across my sheepskin jacket, a blanket over my legs. Gabe's Winchester rifle rested on my lap. I'd left the revolver with Kitty.

I'd tried to get Penny to stay at camp, but she'd followed and lay curled against my legs. When the howl of wolves and coyotes quivered on an evening breeze, she growled as if in her sleep. Once, I thought I saw shadowy forms steal through the brush.

The hours dragged on, the quiet broken occasionally by the rustle of grass, the rush of bats through the air, the screech of an owl. And always those howls that sent shivers up my spine. Now and then Penny looked up, searched the darkness, and growled.

I hadn't meant to doze, but weariness overcame caution. I awoke with a start. My eyes shot open. I sensed rather than heard a sound. I'd dreamed of horses whinnying and screaming, of cougars and wolves on the prowl and the nightmare images still lay behind my eyes. Perhaps the dream had awakened me.

Then I heard the sound for a certainty. A moan, followed by a long, drawn-out grunt.

Chapter 19

I blinked toward the spot where I'd last seen Lilly. No mare. I threw off the blanket, stretched my cold-stiffened legs, and got to my feet.

Another moan. A brittle stirring of grass. Not where I thought I'd find Lilly. Farther away, toward the butte. Then, those eerie howls I'd heard before I dozed. There was something awful in that sound at that time of night and in that place.

I thought of the lantern back at camp and wished I'd brought it with me. Perhaps the fleet of tiny clouds sailing across the moon's face would pass, allowing full light.

"Lilly, where are you?"

The moan repeated itself, seeming to rise from a dark hollow west of the butte. In the moon-whitened flat below the butte, light reflected from the backs of the horse herd. I heard them munching grass. As I moved toward the hollow, they saw me and whickered softly.

Another deep, chesty moan. A hard grunt.

Holding Penny by the collar, I crept up on the moans. "Lilly, where are you?" I called softly. "Don't be afraid. It's just me, Jessie."

She was too busy bringing a new life into the world to answer. I heard another loud grunt. Steam rose from the tiny basin. At last, I saw Lilly, her back outlined against the vacant, moon-washed sky. There was a strong smell of birthing, of horse sweat and wet ripened grass. She was on her feet, licking a long, shimmering sac that encased a still body. I recalled the runt lamb and hoped there'd be no problem with the foal.

Lilly was not like the ewe. She'd given birth to other foals and her maternal instinct was strong. She continued to lick and eat the membrane until the sac moved. I heard a little bleat of a nicker. Lilly answered with a deep, gurgling whinny. I thrilled at the sounds—a thrill of relief, of utter joy at the miracle of birth. Tears leaked from my eyes.

I thought back to the times I'd sneaked into the stables to watch birthings in Maryland. I thought of all the paraphernalia we'd kept on hand to help a mare give birth—antiseptic compounds, forceps, clean towels, enema can, colic medicine, glittering-clean pails, thermometers, medicines for calming. Lilly had no safeguards for her health and her foal's. She'd completed the act alone, nature her only ally.

Lured by the babe's smell, Penny tried to pull free of my grip. I pulled her down beside me on the edge of the hollow and stroked her head while I spoke quietly to the dim shape that was Lilly. "You're a fine mother. You should be proud."

"Aunt Jessie, where are you?" Kitty's voice wavered softly on the breeze.

I murmured directions to where I sat, then we huddled together in shared anxiety and joy, watching the mare and foal in the age-old ritual of the newborn taking a hold on life. My heart swelled with the ecstasy of it all, with the feel of Kitty warm beneath my arm, her rebellion forgotten for the moment.

Lilly licked the baby, urging it to stand. It did for a few seconds, then crashed to the ground. It tried again and again, until it balanced long enough on its wobbly legs to nuzzle its mother in all the wrong places. Tired from the attempt to find a teat, it dropped to the ground, the mare beside it to rest.

Looking out over the landscape for night creatures, I saw the barren peaks of the Bitterroots washed with platinum light. The moon appeared as a huge ball rolling across the heavens, not the flat, white-paper image it sometimes had.

When I looked back at Kitty after watching the moon, I could hardly see her. "A beautiful night isn't it?" I whispered so as not to disturb the mare.

"Cold, though," she said in an equally quiet voice. She huddled closer inside my encircling arm. "It's wonderful to be here with the baby."

"And to be here with you, Kitty." I tightened my arm's clasp around her. My daughter. I wanted desperately to tell her my true identity, but I feared her reaction. Why spoil such a beautiful moment?

She looked up into my eyes. "I'm sorry I've been so hateful."

"Everyone is at times. I guess it's human nature—a way of protecting our feelings, of getting even with the world."

I turned silent, wondering if she'd always fall prey to mood swings, or if it had more to do with her age, her grief, and her disappointment. I couldn't remember how I'd acted at fourteen, though I doubted my mother or father would have tolerated disrespect.

Lilly murmured to the babe, bringing my thoughts back to nature's miracle. "It always amazes me that animal babies can live inside their mothers for close to a year, then come out ready to stand, run, jump. Human babies are helpless lumps of flesh by comparison."

"I don't ever want a baby, just lots and lots of foals, calves, kittens, puppies. Especially foals. I can't imagine not having foals to watch grow."

"You'll always have them. I promise." I made the same promise to myself. Since getting to know Chinook and the crossbreeds, I'd slipped into the comfort of my old love for horses as with a long-lost sweetheart returned.

* * *

The mare and foal rested through the cold hour before dawn while Kitty and I leaned against each other, alert for signs of predators. When the stars disappeared and a ghostly gray faded the eastern sky, the mare rose, licked the baby, and urged it to its feet. The foal prodded and probed until it found the udder, slobbered noisily, and twitched a crimped tail. It was still too dark to see true color.

Then I noticed them—three shadows the size of large dogs streaking down from the butte onto the grass at its base. The horses stirred. Whinnies cut the air. The shadows stopped their run to raise a throaty, mournful cry. Near Lilly's basin a wolf's prolonged hunting call quavered on the chill air. A pack of coyotes opened up high on the ridges to the east, a few scattered yaps, then a rising chorus of yodels that quieted slowly into silence. The blood ran cold in my veins.

Penny's hackles raised. She growled, barked.

I tightened my grip on the Winchester and pulled back the hammer. Wolves and coyotes wouldn't prey on a grown horse, but a newborn would whet their hunger. I considered shooting to warn them off, but the report of a gun would startle the mare and foal into the murky dawn and the dangers that lurked there.

Without sound or warning three furry bodies emerged from the grayness and tore along the lip of the basin. Not primed to attack, but testing the mare, arousing her anger and fear. If the wolves could get her to move from the basin, they could attack the foal. I knew about wolves from my days in the Big Hole. This was their first sortie. More would follow.

Lilly lunged up the side of the basin, neck extended, teeth bared. The wolves darted to the side and joined three others in a loose-limbed trot. Lilly returned to guard the foal.

The wolves had stopped in a group, their slanted eyes glowing in the early light. I took my arm from around Kitty and eased to my feet. "Stay here," I whispered. "Keep Penny with you. I don't want her to get hurt."

"What are you going to do?" Anxiety rasped in Kitty's voice.

"I'm going to chase them off. You try to calm Lilly."

Staying below the rim of the basin so as not to startle the mare, I crept to where the wolves had separated for the next charge. The leader of the pack took a stand to face me, her fangs bared in a savage growl. The other wolves skulked back and forth, their mottled coats like sage on the move.

I raised the Winchester, not to kill, but to frighten them off.

I was about to pull the trigger when the pounding of hoofs brought my head around. The young stud colt burst from the grayness, dragging his rope and stake. The gang of geldings and fillies were hot on his heels.

The colt plunged toward the wolves, screeching, neck stretched forward, his protective instinct firing him to action. He lashed at the wolves with his hoofs.

They darted to one side and gathered as a group, snarling, ducking their heads up and down.

The stud gave a wild scream and charged.

The wolves separated at a run and circled back to nip his heels and tail.

He whirled to spoil their aim. Put his head down and kicked. Clacked his teeth and slashed at the furry hides with his hoofs. Two wolves yiped in pain. The leader charged in anger, biting the colt's rump.

I shot a bullet into the air to end the attack and awakened the world with thunder.

Discouraged for the moment, the pack sped toward the distant Bitterroots, legs and bodies stretched full length, so many gray ghosts in dawn's mystery. The stud colt and his gang followed at their heels.

I stayed for a while to make certain no other wolves waited in hiding, then returned to Kitty and the mare. The horses returned a short time later, their breath steaming, sides heaving, the sunrise striking their coats with fire. I persuaded the stud colt to stand still so I could untie the rope at his ankle, then he whirled away to roam free and unencumbered. He was a pest, but he'd proved himself a worthy heir to Chinook's harem.

Flaming colors streaked the sky and tattered clouds flew before a high wind. Ravens hopped around the birth site, scolding. It was light enough to see the foal's chestnut coloring, a colt, not a filly. He had the same white socks on his forelegs as Chinook, the same blaze on the forehead. A switch of a tail promised the feathering of his father's. Like the sunrise, the foal touched the heart before the mind.

"Does he remind you of someone?" I asked Kitty.

"He looks like Chinook." She'd calmed the mare with sweet talk and was stroking her neck and chest. When the foal wobbled to his feet she touched his nose—always best to accustom babes to one's smell at birth.

"What will you name him?" I asked.

"I don't know. I'll have to think about it."

"You could call him Little Chinook."

"That would be too confusing. I'd say, 'Here, Chinook,' and they'd both come running."

"That's hardly possible. I mean, Dillard has Chinook."

She made no reply, just firmed her lips and turned a resolute face to the mare.

Her intentions seemed clear. Despite her change in mood, I'd have to be on the watch. There might be worse trouble ahead than wolves.

* * *

I wanted to stay a day in camp to let Lilly rest and the foal gain strength. Kitty said we'd have less problem with wolves if we moved from the birth site. She had a point, but I knew the wolves would follow if they thought it worth the effort. We agreed to move the herd slowly, to let the mare and foal rest often and allow the hungry mare to graze.

Hoping the stud colt would behave himself, I let him run and led Lilly behind Bannack—if she was loose I thought she might not follow as closely as she should. The ungainly foal staggered along at her side, covering the ground with remarkable speed. Now and then he fell, rose quickly, and gathered his awkward legs in a canter.

The trail drive continued in a leisurely manner for two days. While

Penny chased jackrabbits, I settled back in the saddle to enjoy Indian summer with its sense of waiting and suspended time. I tried not to think of the weather that lay ahead, of the chores waiting at the homestead, or of Carver Dean's arrival.

The evening of the second day, we camped north of some narrows in the Medicine Lodge Basin. They opened onto a vast grassland, to the northeast a giant, gray-headed monolith. Seeing it now meant we were a day's travel from the town of Bannack.

As they had last evening, the wolves appeared at dusk. At least we heard their mournful cries, some perhaps a quarter-mile away, others more distant. I took the first watch, letting Kitty snuggle into the warmth of her bed. When at last I traded places with her, I slipped—no plunged—into delicious sleep.

I woke to the sound of whining and expected to find Penny's tongue in my face, her breath sour from scavenging. Instead, I felt the sun in my eyes and was surprised to see it peeking over the ridge. I crawled from my bedroll and blinked at the reality of Penny tied to a sturdy willow at creekside. She tugged at the rope and whimpered, paused now and then to chew the hemp. When she saw me rise she barked an unending, relentless bark.

"All right. I'm coming." I stuffed my feet into cold boots.

She bounced up and down like an India rubber ball when I turned her loose, then ran around in circles, whining in self-pity and gratitude. I couldn't imagine why Kitty had tied her. Perhaps she'd been pestering the foal.

There was no sign of Kitty near camp. Perhaps she was searching for privacy up one of the draws.

I saw a skim of ice in the water bucket, frost on Lilly's whiskers. She and the foal appeared content. The rest of the herd grazed peacefully—no wolves or coyotes in sight, no howls in the distance. A band of mountain sheep trooped across the flats. Horned larks flitted from sage to sage.

I found a juniper for my morning toilet, spooking a Clark's nutcracker from the branches. It was when I gathered wood to rebuild the fire that I noticed Trixie was missing.

Where had Kitty gone without telling me? Certainly not to explore. Not this time of day, when we should prepare for the trail. The horses were grazing too peacefully for her to have gone off chasing wolves.

I checked her bedroll and saw the frost undisturbed on the blankets. She must have left before the cold hours preceding dawn. My thoughts flashed back to the morning in the Centennial. As she had then, Kitty had stealth in mind. She'd concealed her plan beneath a facade of sweetness. Disappointment, anger, and concern, but mainly chagrin, washed over me in alternating waves. I'd been fooled.

Chapter 20

I whistled Bannack in and saddled him. It was impossible to find Kitty's trail amid the tracks left by Dillard's herd and our own grazing animals. I had to trust the disturbing instinct that said she'd gone after Chinook.

It proved correct. I'd been gone from camp fifteen minutes when Kitty rode Trixie over a rise in the track. Sam Dillard rode beside her on his sorrel. I couldn't tell his mood from a distance, but I thought he must be furious.

"You looking for this little maverick?" he asked when they reached me.

"I certainly am. I've been worried sick. Angry, too."

They pulled up a few feet in front of me, Kitty's sullen gaze on the hands she rested on the pommel. Dillard waited for her to speak. She didn't.

I wanted to rake her up and down for leaving Lilly and the foal without waking me, for making it necessary for me to leave them, for causing Dillard more inconvenience. I held my tongue and let the harsh words wait until later. I imagined she'd already heard a few from Dillard.

He appeared tired, his face gray around the mustache and bushy brows. His squint lines deepened, as if he were smiling. He wasn't. "You'd best tell your aunt what you've been up to," he said to Kitty.

She gave me a mulish glance and without a word of explanation or apology prodded Trixie toward camp.

Dillard flattened his lips and scratched a sideburn. "Now, if that don't beat all." Exasperation put an edge on his voice. "Next time she tries something with me, I might just take her over my knee and give her a paddling."

"I hope it won't come to that. She might rebel even more."

He gave a reflective snort. "Likely you're right. My Jo wouldn't have stood for it. I never laid a hand on her. I knew it'd make her more of a renegade."

I clucked my tongue. "Two of a kind." We were still looking Kitty's way. "What was she up to?"

"I caught her taking the hobbles off Chinook."

"I knew she was going to steal him."

"You and I call it that. She doesn't. She says she didn't want him hobbled, but it was plain as a spinster's scorn to me. She knew he'd go looking for her mares." He propped a hand on his thigh and gave a wry chuckle. "Pretty foxy of her. That way the horse would do the stealing. She could catch him, claim he was an outlaw, and take possession." The first part of his statement didn't surprise me; the last did.

"That's not legal, is it?"

"I've seen it done."

"That little imp. She must have left in the middle of the night to catch up with you."

"Actually, we aren't far down the road. I had to lay up yesterday afternoon and evening. Benito's in the sack now."

"Sick?"

"We got into some bad water."

"Not the creek, I hope." If the creek had caused the problem, Kitty and I would feel it next.

"It was a hole off to the side. We camped there night before last."

I relaxed a little at the news and the fact Dillard wasn't raging. I'd expected him to be in a froth. He had every right. He seemed more tired than angry, not well enough to cause trouble. "Do you feel like eating breakfast?"

"You don't want to bother with that." He motioned toward my scared and swollen face. "Looks like you're still feeling none too well."

I'd seen my face in a pocket mirror last evening. My eyes and nose were a purplish-blue. "I look worse than I feel. I'd like your company if you can stand the sight of me. How does coffee and bacon sound? I can cook oatmeal. There's fry bread from last night."

He put a hand on his stomach. "Don't know how much I can eat." He considered for a second or two as he watched a jackrabbit skitter through the bunchgrass and sage. "I'll have some coffee. Save me putting on the pot."

Kitty had turned Trixie loose to graze and was up the creek a ways. Her beacon of orange hair marked the spot. She was sitting cross-legged at creek's edge, throwing pebbles into the water. Penny stood in the creek, dipping her head in the shallows to look for the pebbles.

Dillard and I made ourselves as comfortable as we could on the grounded saddles, drank coffee, nibbled at bacon, and peered across the breezy and shimmering Medicine Lodge Basin. High overhead, an eagle soared in lazy circles. Prairie dogs squeaked from their colony of mounds on the flats. The air was filled with the winy fragrance of fallen willow and rose leaves damp in the thickets at our backs. Despite the trouble with Kitty, I felt more serene than I had since I'd left the Bitterroot. The land and this man—when he wasn't angry—had a soothing effect.

He sat with his long legs bent, arms circling his knees, coffee cup in one hand. I sat with my short legs stretched out full length, beneath me the fleece jacket I'd folded to soften the seat.

Dillard had been watching Kitty. "A girl and her dog. A sight to soothe the beast in anyone." He pulled down the brim of his Stetson to shut out the sun and to better observe them. "The markings above the dog's eyes look like question marks. How old is she?"

"I have no idea. She was a stray. I'd guess she's at least seven."

"What about the other dog I saw at Breen's camp? You'd think he would've followed the horses."

"He belongs—belonged to Gabe. He was in mourning and wouldn't come with me."

Dillard narrowed his eyes to study me. A flicker of something I couldn't read moved in his mind. "This thing you're doing for Breen—helping Kitty—it's asking a lot."

"It's what he wanted. What I want, too. What I need above all else."

"Not many would do as much. You and him must've been close."

I bobbed my head up and down, trying not to think of my recent anger and disappointment. "We were good friends. Especially when we were kids."

The horse flies seemed to like our resting spot—marshy meadow, string of willows, lots of dung piles nearby. They'd become unbearable. I took a bottle of repellent from my shirt pocket—a mixture of castor oil, pine tar, and pennyroyal simmered to blend. I rubbed some on my hat and boots, trousers, denim jacket, and handed the bottle to Sam. He used it and handed it back.

"Do you have brothers or sisters?" I asked.

"Five. There were seven of us once. Me and my oldest brother, Bob, were like finger and thumb. We got into all sorts of scrapes. We weren't as tough as we thought. Dad always said we were too proud to cut hay and not wild enough to eat it."

"Does your brother live in Texas?"

He didn't answer for a few seconds, just stared at his coffee cup as if it held a doorway into the past and he'd walked through. "He got shot at Glorietta Pass. I did, too—in the lower back—but I lived to tell about it."

"I'm sorry," was all I could think to say. I'd always found it difficult to talk to men about their experiences in battle. I think I felt guilty for being a woman and staying home. "Weren't you a little young to be in the army?"

"I was sixteen. I lied about my age when I joined Sibley's Confederates. After Glorietta, our luck turned sour. The Yanks forced us back into Texas, and the troops kind of disbanded. I went home to help on the ranch."

Several seconds dragged by while I searched my memory for images of those difficult years. "I was just a little girl, but I remember the war was hard on us. Troops always coming through, demanding food and supplies—on their way to Antietam and Gettysburg. They raided our garden and orchards, took our stock. Ben—he was my husband, but not then, of course—he left Pa's forge to join the Yankees as a blacksmith. He was fifteen years older than I."

"He was lucky to come back . . . to you, that is."

My cheeks warmed at the remark. It seemed Dillard wasn't going to allow the dispute over the horses to color his opinion of me. I was glad of that.

He turned quiet, sipping from his cup, sucking a tooth in thought. "The war didn't amount to much in Texas," he said after a bit. "Dad did real well trailing beef over to the Confederates."

"Not many of us in the East profited from the war. My father made his money afterward. People needed good horses to replace those they'd lost in the war. Pa built up a large stable. He spent too much on breeding stock, went into racing full bore, and gambled. He was bankrupt in fifteen years. It killed him. Gabe turned out to be just as reckless with his money."

"A man has to be careful. Cattle can be just as much of a gamble."

"I'm surprised you're leaving the business. In Montana, a good cattle buyer earns a lot of respect."

He dug the toe of his boot into the sand and pursed his lips in a self-conscious way. "Anybody can buy cattle. My son has only one father. When I'm gone I want him to think I've left a huge hole in his life." A peculiar light crept into his eyes. He cleared his throat. "You feel that way about your husband?"

I thought about that, recalling the best and the worst of Ben. "For the most part. And you about your wife?"

His expression closed as he looked out across the sage. It took a while for him to say with contrition, "I should have seen it coming. I was too single-minded, too caught up in my work, always away on the job."

"In your profession, you can't help being away from home."

He ignored the comment, seeming to stare at an unendurable landscape. "I could've settled the family in the East near Rose's folks . . . near all the things that were important to her. But no, I liked the wide-open spaces. Was born into it. She . . ." He hesitated. "She was an actress, a rebel like Jo. Her parents didn't want her to go on the stage. The only way her father could keep her in Michigan was to build her a theater. Even then she went off to play New York and Philadelphia." He sighed and looked at the ground. "She gave it up to marry me."

"How did you meet—I mean, you a cattle buyer, her an . . ." On second thought I owned that Ben and I had fallen in love despite our different backgrounds—he the son of a pig farmer, I the daughter of privileged parents.

"Rose's father owned several big spreads in Texas and Colorado but he made his wealth from steel mills in Michigan. I was working on his main ranch when he brought Rose out to visit one summer."

"And you fell in love."

"She had romantic notions about the cattle business and cowboys. I thought she was pretty as a morning glory." He put his fingers together to make a steeple and studied them. He seemed to have an image of Rose behind his eyes. When he switched his attention from his hands to my face, I saw a self-righteous child looking to someone for forgiveness. "I moved her from the ranch into Denver, kept her in jewelry and fancies for the house. She gave readings and organized a theater group. Somehow it wasn't the same as playing Philadelphia and New York."

I didn't know what to say, just sipped my coffee, considering the paradox of such a marriage.

Dillard shook his head in apology. "Forgive me for rationalizing. I try not to make a habit of it. Somehow I feel the need, talking to you."

I didn't know how to take the remark, so I ran my finger self-consciously around the rim of my cup, trying to figure if he meant it as a compliment or otherwise. "When did your wife become ill?"

"Not long after Jo died. Her heart problems kept getting worse and worse. Despite her easy life, maybe because of it. Who's to say? I only know I was a cur for not being at her deathbed." He gave a sigh of release, like that of a man stretching his feet to a hearth fire after a long journey. A long moment passed before he continued. "Now, Mrs. Tate, you know about me and Rose. Tell me about yourself. You strike me as having more polish than most ranch wives."

"Call me Jessie. Mrs. Tate is too formal for these parts."

He looked out across the miles, not a house in sight, no human other than those of us on the creek. "Then I guess it's best you call me Sam."

I studied his kind, sad face and thought how fortunate I was to have his company. Life had dealt us both a blow. Perhaps in each other's company we could face the realities.

"I don't consider myself polished. I just had more advantages than most women. Despite the fact I was a tomboy, my mother insisted I act like a lady."

I continued, feeling more at ease as I went along, the words flowing rapidly. I told of my childhood in Maryland; of the finishing schools that whirled me from one elegant ball to the next; of the lessons in French and Italian, piano and voice; of the rise and fall of my father's farm. I talked about my mother's prolonged illness. My girlhood had come to an end when she took to her sickbed. I'd nursed her for four long years. No sooner had she passed on than bankruptcy sent Father to his bed. I was twenty-three, again the nurse, Gabe too busy tending the farm and legal matters to see how lonely I'd become. Ben knew. My parents hadn't let him court me because he was fifteen years older than I and "just a blacksmith." As soon as Father died, Gabe gave his permission for us to marry and the three of us moved to Dillon.

While I spoke, Sam poured tobacco from a pouch into his pipe bowl, tapped it down with a long, slender finger, and struck a match with his thumbnail. As he sucked on the stem, puffs of smoke gave off the aroma of honeyed tobacco.

"If your father went bankrupt, where'd your brother get the money to start a cattle operation?"

"Let's just say my father had some hidden assets."

"And Ben?"

"He opened a smithy in Dillon. In eighty-nine the gold bug bit him and we moved to the diggings on Trail Creek at the west end of the Big Hole."

"That's near where I bought land. I'm at the mouth of Ruby Creek."

"Then you know the creeks are fed by snows and icy springs." He nodded. "Ben developed a crippling rheumatism from working the water through the sluice. The winters were hard on him. They got down to fifty and sixty below. So we moved to the Bitterroot and took up a homestead."

"Was he able to work around the place?"

"He was too crippled. I did all the work."

"A little slip-of-a-thing like you? I wouldn't have let my wife."

I bristled a bit. "What's wrong with it?"

"It doesn't seem right to impose."

"I like working in the outdoors better than keeping my nose in the house."

He smiled, not a broad smile that would reveal his large, strong teeth, but rather a smile that merely deepened the creases in his cheeks. "There you go. I can sure agree with that." He tapped the pipe bowl on the edge of the rock to loosen the dottle, stuck the pipe back in his pocket, and rose stiffly. "I'd best get back to camp. We'll need to move on if Benito's feeling up to it. Usually I like the path as much as the destination. This time I'm racing winter." He tipped his hat. "Nice talking to you. Hope things work out the way you want."

He took a step, shot a regretful look back over his shoulder, took another hesitant step. His reluctance to leave was obvious.

I said, "Maybe we'll meet again farther on."

He nodded in Kitty's direction. "Not if I can keep away from that little fuzztail. But stop at my place before you head over the pass. Like I said, it's on Ruby Creek, where it enters the Hole. There's a rotted out prospectors soddy."

As Sam and the sorrel dropped over the rise, I was swept by a feeling that combined a sense of loss with gain and ended in turmoil. Despite the troubles we'd had over the herd, I wanted to see Sam again. It was too bad I had to keep my distance.

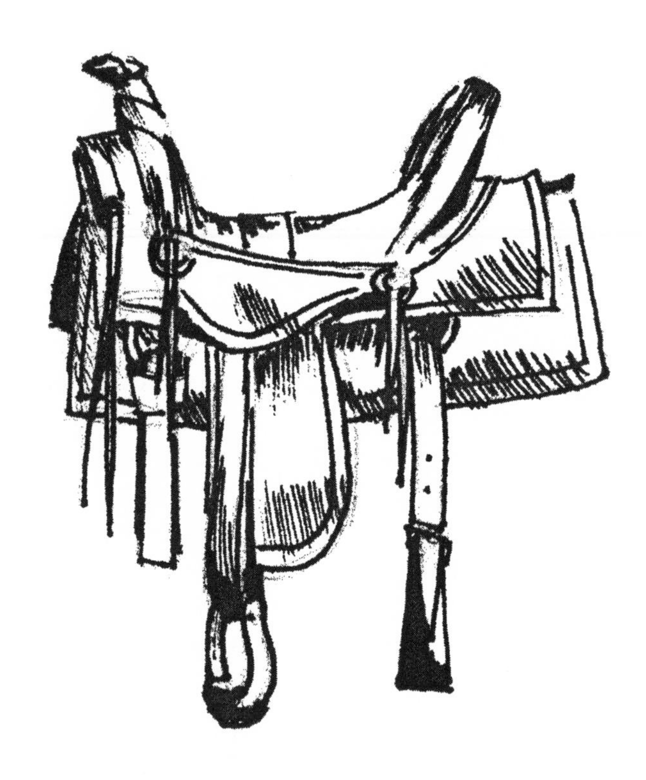

Chapter 21

I decided not to go to Kitty. I'd let her come to me. About an hour later, she did, looking like a wilted marigold. The hat could only protect the eyes, and her freckles shone dark through the burn of the sun. I imagined I looked the same. As usual, I saw myself in her—the same round freckled face, the same clear blue eyes, though the swelling around mine likely hid the resemblance today.

Without speaking, she poured herself a little Arbuckle's and added an equal amount of canned milk, then took a piece of last night's fry bread from the flour sack that held the leftovers. She started to lower herself onto a rock slab that lay beside the smoldering gray coals of the campfire, seemed uncomfortable with the move, and straightened. When she squirmed inside her loose boy's jeans, I noticed a line where the hem of her bloomers touched the inside of the dirty denim. She'd brought only one change of underwear and an extra shirt from the Centennial. When we reached the Sherwoods, we'd change and wash clothes.

I'd shaken the dust and twigs from my blankets, spread them on the canvas ground cloth, and was rolling them into a bundle. My irritation with Kitty had faded somewhat, but I looked up at her with what remained. "I'm disappointed in you for leaving camp without my knowing. For causing Sam inconvenience. It was wrong of you to try to steal—"

"I wasn't going to steal him. I was just taking off his hobbles."

I snorted in doubt. "It was just as bad that you left Lilly and the foal without waking me. With no one to watch over them. You're lucky nothing happened."

She swallowed some fry bread, wiped crumbs from her mouth with the side of a finger. "You left them."

"I had no choice. I had to find you."

She shot me a look that could scald. "I can take care of myself."

I gave the strap that fastened the bedroll a tug born of frustration and went to collect the coffee can and muslin-wrapped bacon from the fireside. I found the oat sack hidden in the camp clutter, poured a layer of oats in the fry pan I'd wiped free of grease, and whistled in Bannack and Shorty.

They came at a run and skidded to a stop, shouldering each other aside to get to the pan. When they'd finished, I staked them near camp, ready for pack and riding saddles, and poured a share of oats in the pan for Lilly and the lead mare.

"I hope you apologized to Sam," I said, turning back to Kitty. She'd tossed the rest of her fry bread to Penny and was gnawing half-heartedly on a strip of bacon.

"You call him Sam now?" she muttered sarcastically.

I let it ride. "I asked if you apologized."

She consulted her coffee for an answer. "Sort of." The freckles gave her an air of innocence, but her nervous glance spoke of guilt. The apology, if it existed at all, hadn't amounted to much.

"If we don't meet him earlier, we'll stop at his place in the Big Hole so you can give him a proper apology."

"Why are you taking his side? I thought you wanted to help me."

"I am helping you. To do the right thing." I'd expected to find her a bit humbled after being caught stealing. Instead, we were having the same old argument. I began to assemble my satchel of clothes and other odds and ends on the canvas.

"What's right about Dillard owning Chinook? He's my horse. I wanted to take him back to Pa before I . . . " She shut her mouth on the rest and stared into the dwindling fire. Her chin crinkled and started to tremble.

"Before you what?"

"Before I . . . before I . . . oh, nothing. Forget it." She pressed her lips together and squeezed her eyes shut. Despite the effort against it, a tear trickled down her cheek.

I thought she was feeling sorry for herself because she'd failed to steal Chinook. Yet I noted something else in her manner. I stopped my work.

"What's wrong?"

She looked across my shoulder toward the northern horizon. "Nothing."

"There is. Tell me."

"I—I just kinda ache," she said on a sigh.

I thought of the bad water. Possibly she'd drunk from the same hole as Sam and Benito, though I couldn't remember when she'd had an opportunity. "Is it your stomach?"

"Not my stomach. My belly, low down."

"Did you drink anywhere besides the creek?"

"It's not bad water." She gulped a mouthful of air. Again her chin trembled. "I'm bleeding . . . I'm going to die."

My stunned gaze flashed over her but saw no signs of injury. I walked over, put a hand on her shoulder, and searched her face. "Did you hurt yourself?"

The look she gave me was damp, a blend of anxiety and shame. She sniffled a few times and wiped her nose with the back of her hand. "I didn't hurt myself. The bloods coming . . ." She stared at the ground. "It's coming from inside, like Aunt Stella, Ma's sister. She bled inside. Oh, Aunt Jessie . . ." With a great sob, she sank into my arms.

A hard ball formed in my stomach as I encircled her quaking shoulders. Stella died before Amy. Kitty couldn't have been more than six, possibly seven. "Stella told you that?" I said in disbelief.

"I was listening behind the door when she told Ma."

"Stella had cancer of the uterus. You're too young for—" Reason struck like a hornet. How stupid of me not to have understood. Of course Kitty wouldn't have known. She'd had no woman around to counsel her at the right time. I thought back to the moment my mother had told me about menstruation—as sketchily as she could. "It's all about mothers and daughters," she'd said. "Our cross to bear. The womb belongs to the woman whether she likes it or not."

Kitty had lived among men. She'd dealt with cows and mares but hadn't bothered to relate nature's rhythms to herself. She probably thought such things happened only to married women. I'd had that idea when I was a girl, and I'd grown up around animals. Ignorance breeds strange notions. No wonder she'd been so emotionally wrought. On top of her grief for Gabe and resentment over the crossbreeds, a profound change had seized her body.

I urged her toward my saddle and its jacket pillow. "Come, sit down. We have a lot to talk about." I sat opposite her on my bedroll.

By the time I'd told her as delicately as I could about the facts of life and sexuality, about ways to care for herself and lessen her discomfort, she'd lost the fear of dying. The embarrassment that took its place flared into outrage.

"Why don't men have to go through all this? It's not fair."

I recalled expressing the same anger to my mother. She'd replied stoically, "Be satisfied with your lot. There's nothing a woman can do about it, so why chafe about it and make yourself unhappy?"

"I thought the same when I was your age," I told Kitty. "There are times when I still do—that is, about having to put up with the inconvenience, sometimes the pain. But you can't separate the process from that of giving birth. Bringing a child into the world is a joy a man can never know." And, I thought, losing a child, or thinking one had lost a child within minutes of birth, brought a sadness beyond enduring. Ben hadn't understood that. If he had, he wouldn't have . . . I willed the memory aside.

Kitty sat in quiet, thinking. "Did you love Uncle Ben?" she asked after a bit.

The question jolted with its uncanny tie to my own thoughts. Evidently, Kitty had made a frog-leap typical of her. I answered as honestly as I could under the circumstances. "Of course I loved him."

"I don't see how you can love a man. They just get you with child."

Ben get me with child? If only he had. God knows he'd tried. "You can't blame men. They're just part of nature's scheme. You'll fall in love one day."

"Not me. I hate men!" It struck me that as genuine as Kitty's anger might be, she was adding fuel to her temper to keep it strong.

I laughed. "You'll change your mind. I'm sure I thought that when I was fourteen." I paused, searching for something to feed my argument. "You didn't hate Gabe. How can you say you hate men?"

"He's family. Men that aren't family want just one thing from a girl."

I made a sound that was half-laugh, half-gasp. "Who told you that?"

"Nobody. I just know, that's all." She hauled herself from the saddle. "Men think women were put on this earth for them to use. I won't be used!"

I wondered what was behind Kitty's outrage. She'd lived among wranglers, some of them crude, to say the least. On the other hand, perhaps she'd met a boy she liked and was professing hate to hide the fact. Common for a girl in her early teens.

I watched her disappear behind a clump of juniper for a moment of privacy, then went about dousing the campfire. When she returned, I was throwing a sweat-stained horsehair blanket over Shorty's back. We each took a side of the pack-saddle and hauled it up.

My mind was still on our conversation. "There are good men in the world, Kitty, men who'd never think of taking advantage of a woman—well, not in the way you mean." I pulled on the saddle to shift it into the middle of Shorty's back. "You'll find one some day."

"Not likely." She bent down to fasten the front cinch, gave it a fierce tug to tighten the buckle. Shorty crow-hopped and snorted.

I leaned over to fasten the rear cinch, grunting with the effort. "Make a good life for yourself, then. All you need is grit, and there's no doubt you have plenty of that."

"That's what I'm gonna do. That's why I need Chinook."

"Sam needs him, too. He thinks he's the greatest horse ever."

"And I don't?" she said with a sarcastic puff of air.

"Of course you do. But how can you ask him to give up Chinook when he's been so patient with you? With both of us." I rested my arms over the saddle and worked for air.

"Sam doesn't love him as much as I do. Not as much as Pa." Arms rigid at her side, she headed for the pile of halters and lead ropes.

I strode up beside her and turned her by the arm. "Love has many faces, Kitty. Maybe you love Chinook too much. Selfish love becomes obsession."

She eyed me as if I were a customer for the loony farm. "What do you mean—obsession?"

"It's a deep passion for something regardless of the cost to yourself and others. Like your father's obsession with thoroughbreds and crossbreeds. He centered his life around them, yours too. Without concern for your needs."

She propped her hands on her hips and glared. "He wanted me to work with him because he loved me. More'n any mother would."

The hair on my neck bristled. I worked to keep my voice even, and to keep the words measured. "No love is stronger than a mother's. Even when the child is grown and goes her separate way, the tie remains. After nine months in the womb it can never be broken."

She looked down her nose and gave a *huh* of a laugh. "How would you know? Some old biddy tell you?"

"How would I know?" I said fiercely. "I'll tell you how. I'm a mother.

And I'm looking at the ungrateful snip who's my daughter." I'd envisioned telling Kitty the truth during some quiet moment. Instead, I'd spat it out with defiance, turning it loose to do its damage, the consequences to fall where they may. Kitty might even think I was ashamed to be her mother. As much as I might wish to reel the words in and begin again in a gentler vein, I couldn't.

They'd struck Kitty dumb. She just stood with mouth agape. I wondered what thoughts wheeled around in her startled mind.

Slowly, the color rose in her cheeks to meet her doubt-squinted eyes. "You're just saying that so I'll do what you want."

"It's true," I said staunchly. "Gabe told me when I was about to leave the cow camp."

"He wouldn't. You're lying."

"I'd never lie about such a thing. Neither would Gabe. You should have seen his pain when he told me. If only you knew how I . . ." I left the rest unsaid. She was in no mood for understanding.

"It's a bunch of hogwash. He must have said it so you'd come after me."

I sucked in a breath to keep from giving her a good shaking. "I believe Gabe. He said I was so sick when I gave birth that he and Ben thought I was going to die." It took great effort to control the spite that wanted to creep into my voice. "While I was giving birth to you, Amy was on her bed giving birth to a dead child. We were delirious and didn't know what was happening. Ben didn't want another man's . . . he didn't want a baby. Gabe did. So they switched you for the dead child." I paused to slow my agitated breathing and to bring sense to the story. "Gabe did it for Amy. She wanted a baby desperately. She was a good mother. She never knew you weren't her child. I didn't know until Gabe told me at camp."

Doubt continued to smolder like living coals in Kitty's eyes. "She was my mother. Not you. You can't make me believe . . ." She choked. Her lips quivered. "No matter what you say, I won't be your daughter. And you can't keep me from taking Chinook. One way or another he's gonna be mine!" That said, she spun on her heel, snatched a halter and lead rope from the pile, and with long, fierce strides headed for Trixie.

* * *

Kitty's resentful disbelief made me feel unwanted, definitely unloved, stupid for wanting to help. My chin dragged the ground. Yet I worried about the possibility she might try to steal Chinook and wind up in trouble with the law. Sam Dillard had said he was losing patience, and I believed him. I needed his drawling words of advice and found him flickering in and out my mind. I wondered if he thought of me and scolded myself for the wondering. I was a woman, with a woman's yearnings, but this was no time for silly notions. Appeasing Kitty and keeping her out of harm's way would be an almost impossible task. For now, riding with the herd between us, there was no chance to spread balm on the wound, nor did I have the desire. Not yet.

Sam and Benito had forged ahead with their herd. We saw no trace of them except for a blackened campfire and the mass of hoofprints. The wagon track had become more distinct, and ruts turned from it toward old campsites. Here and there, the prints of wild horses crossed the track. The hoofs were unshod, untrimmed, bits of hoof missing. I glimpsed two wild herds watching us from the sage-covered foothills and noticed stud piles on the crests. The stallions ranged wide, prancing, crests raised, to inspect us from a distance. I'd read recently that almost one million wild horses roamed the West. Many were descendants of those the Spanish conquistadors had brought into the new world. Others had run away from settlers and army units. Because of the herds keeping watch on us now, I decided it was time to let Lilly follow on her own and put the stud colt on lead before he took off after the strange mares.

The old track had left the creek to join a well-traveled, east-west wagon road. We followed it west for a few miles, through dust three inches deep, and turned north at a fork in the road. A sign pointed toward Bannack, the town for which Gabe's buckskin had been named. I leaned forward and stroked his neck. "We're coming to the place where you were born. I wonder if you'll recognize it."

Ben's fascination with gold mining had taken us to Bannack several times. The town's luck had waxed and waned since it burst into life in 1862, a wild and ruthless camp of gold-crazed miners and outlaws. The single street running up the gulch had teemed with hard-working, hard-swearing, hard-drinking men and those who did them service or did them dirt. When gold petered out, the town almost gasped its last breath. Help had come in the form of dredges that pumped new life into the town. The latest dredge was electric powered and efficient, the first successful gold dredge in the world.

Our path to the Big Hole wouldn't take us into Bannack, but a long day's travel had brought us to within four miles of a spur road that led to the town. A strong wind had whipped our shirts all day and raised a haze of dust. Above the haze, wind-stretched clouds striped a cobalt sky. The immediate countryside had turned dull and unappealing. Prospect holes pocked the low, desert-like hills and gulches. Abandoned miners' soddies warted the base of the slopes. Range cattle roamed thick.

I heard trouble before I saw it. The bugle of horses—stallions from the deep, blaring sound of it—punctuated by lighter, excited whinnies.

I hurried to catch up with a sullen Kitty. "Slow down. Sounds like trouble ahead."

The cause for the uproar became evident when we topped a rise in the road. Sam and Benito had driven their herd about three hundred yards east of the road into a cattle-free basin thick with bunchgrass, likely to make camp. On the edge of the herd, two stallions slashed at each other in a fury of powerful horse flesh. One was Chinook, a lead rope dangling from his glistening red-brown neck. The other horse was a dapple gray mustang with tangled white mane and tail, a dorsal stripe down his rump. Their fierce trumpeting said they were trying to kill each other.

The rest of the herd milled around in panic. Mares shrieked. Foals squealed in their baby voices. Farther off, three yearlings ran around in circles, kicking, bucking, manes and tails flying. Though frightened, they were too curious to go far. A half-mile away, on the crest of a hill, the mustang's herd paced back and forth, nickering. The wind put an extra edge on the animals' nerves.

Benito whirled about on his dun gelding and slung the end of a lariat at the mustang. Sam had dismounted and held a coiled snake whip in his hand.

"I have to break up the fight!" Kitty yelled.

I envisioned her trampled by angry hoofs. "No! It's too dangerous." I thrust the stud colt's lead rope into her hand. "Keep the herd together."

"Chinook's mine! I'll take care of him."

I spun Bannack around to face her and snapped an order like a seasoned trail boss. "Do as I say!"

Chapter 22

I prodded Bannack into a gallop down the sagebrush slope toward the battling stallions. Two hundred yards behind me, Kitty yelled at the herd to keep them from following. She'd have her hands full keeping them bunched. I heard her whip snap the air.

Bannack had his own case of the jitters. He quivered beneath me, snorted and whinnied. He wasn't alone in his anxiety. My heart throbbed as if it would leap from my chest. Deep within me lurked a hatred for violence of any sort, especially between animals. I feared for the beautiful chestnut. He could be killed, at the least, torn and maimed. Like a grizzly sow defending her cub, I was blind to danger. My senses riveted on one purpose—saving Chinook from harm.

The dapple gray was a handsome specimen, larger than most wild horses, at least sixteen hands. His shoulders and neck were as massive as they were muscular, as opposed to Chinook's long, graceful neck and body. He could charge like a battering ram. Chinook made up for lack of girth with agility and the remarkable strength of his long legs. He used them to rear and lash out with vicious hoofs, to spin and kick with his hind legs.

Sam moved toward the stallions, cursing, cracking the rawhide whip in the air. His long drooping mustache and grizzled hair blew in the wind.

"Don't whip them!" I yelled as I rode near. "It'll rile them worse."

Sam let the eighteen feet or so of braided whip loop at his feet. "Stay away. You can get—" He clamped his mouth shut as Chinook screamed and whirled to lash at the mustang with his hind feet. The mustang sprang aside to avoid the slamming hoofs.

With a sharp flick of wrist and arm, Sam sent the rawhide humming through the air. The popper snapped within inches of the mustang's rump, the crack as loud as a shot from a small rifle. The mustang spun to see what was trying to bite him. When he saw Sam, he laid back his ears and snorted.

Bannack fought the reins in his desire to cut and run. I spoke to him quietly and patted his neck to bring him under control. "It's all right. S'awright."

I tried to appear relaxed as we circled the stallions. Inwardly, I churned. They paid me little notice. They were too busy facing off.

Sam lashed out with the whip. His aim was off, and rather than hit the mustang, the popper snapped near Chinook's chest. The stallion pulled in his chin and seemed to swell. His eyes sparked.

"I yelled, "Don't use the whip. You'll hurt him."

I saw Dillard's lanky frame tense, could almost feel the heat in his face. "Stay away! You'll get stomped."

"I know how to calm them." I kneed Bannack toward the stallions. They were tired and screamed less often. The stench of their sweaty hides drifted on the air. Blood trickled from their wounds.

"It's all right. S'awright," I murmured as I circled them.

They jerked their heads around and snorted, their flared nostrils wet from exertion. I headed for the mustang, an arm outstretched in a staying gesture. He circled in place, muscles tense. His eyes bulged white as marbles.

I reined the buckskin back and forth between the seething stallions. They pawed the ground and tossed their heads, unsure how to react.

"S'awright, s'awright," I said over and over.

The gray continued to circle in place and storm. Yet little by little, jockeying Bannack around to keep Chinook from darting past, I forced the mustang back. When he stood about thirty feet away, I brought Bannack to a stop.

"All right, boy. Fight's over. Go cool off." I held out an arm, fingers pointed downward, and flapped my hand to wave the wild stallion back.

Sam had come up behind Chinook and was speaking to him, trying to calm him. The chestnut stood with head hung, panting heavily. The mustang retreated farther, blowing deep lungsfuls of air, his eyes still fired with rage. I advanced slowly, pushing him back. He was exhausted from the battle, clearly hurting. Flaps of crimson hide lay open on his shoulder. Scars knifed across his neck, flanks, and legs. He limped on his hind leg as I herded him toward the wild harem tromping about in the distance. When he showed a willingness to leave on his own, I stopped to watch, alert for a change of mind. Before long, it was impossible to distinguish his dapple gray from that of the rolling sage. Unlike Chinook, he'd have no one to tend his wounds. Part of me blamed him for attacking Chinook. Another part hated to see any animal hurt, especially such a prime specimen.

When I returned to the scene of battle, Sam was examining Chinook's wounds, stroking his flanks. Chinook stood with sides heaving, his glazed brown eyes intent on the departing mustang. He wasn't as battered as the gray, but blood streaked his neck and rump. My lungs filled with the air of regret.

Kitty hadn't been able to keep her horses on the hill, nor Benito to keep Sam's herd bunched. The hollow ring of the lead mare's bell rose above their mingled confusion.

Their alarm hadn't escaped Chinook. Suddenly, as if he'd considered his next move all along, he whirled, tearing the lead rope from Sam's hand, charged into the combined herds, and bit the bell mare in the rump. As she put her head down to kick, he darted to the side, came around and seized the top of her neck, then forced her to run along with him.

When she was under way, he gathered the rest of his harem, snaking around them, his nose a few inches above the ground, his neck stretched full length, weaving.

Kitty's herd tore after the bell mare for fear of being left behind. Sam's sorrel and the pack animals flew along with the rest. Stirrups and packs jounced up and down, lead ropes and reins strung along the ground. Chinook rounded up the four as he did the rest, lunging, biting, weaving his neck in and out like a whiplash. Penny's yipping added to the bedlam as she ran after the horses and nipped at their heels.

Leaving Sam on foot, I joined Penny in the chase, as did Benito and Kitty, yelling and swinging lariats. Despite their considerable skill, they continued to miss the mark. I was glad. My sympathy was with the stampeding horses. For their sakes, we had to capture them sooner or later, but I didn't want them burned by ropes. I was relieved when Lilly and the foal stopped to rest. Sam was afoot. He could catch Lilly and ride her. At the least, he could keep the foal from being killed in the rush of bodies.

Chinook was quick to turn and twist, gathering the mares whenever they darted to the side. I doubted the herd would let us capture them soon. Their thunder ripped through the broken landscape. Their hoofs sent miniature dust devils spinning into the gusty, dust-filled air.

Up and down the sagebrush hills we rode, catching sight of the herd on a crest, losing them as they lunged into the next draw. The clanging bell on the lead mare gave the only clue to their whereabouts. As far as I could tell, in their cross-country charge they were headed straight for the town of Bannack.

Chapter 23

When Kitty, Benito, and I topped a ridge, the diggings along Grasshopper Creek lay stretched before us in a trough that cut through the hills. We pulled up to look the situation over and saw Chinook streak easterly down the gulch searching for an escape route. He found no easy way across the piles of tailings and switched directions, colliding with the herd as he whirled around.

I urged Bannack down the slope. Kitty and Benito rode abreast.

Chinook saw us closing in and tore upstream in the direction of town a quarter-mile away, its single cramped street lined with stores and cabins. The frantic herd raced after him, manes and tails flying like flags in a wind. The lead mare's bell clanged.

The first person to hear them pounding along the gulch was a woman working a pump handle on the edge of town.

"Look out! Horses!" she screamed as she clung to the side of her cabin.

"Christ a'mighty!" said one of two men straddling a bench in front of a saloon. He took his drunken partner by the arm and dove through the saloon's batwings.

Three horses tied at the hitch rail swung their rumps around to avoid being rammed. One of them jerked his reins free and joined the stampede, stirrups swinging. Close to 150 hoofs churned the dusty street. Some clattered along the boardwalk. One of the larger mares crashed through a rotten timber and went to her knees. I feared she'd broken her leg, but she righted herself, yanked her foot from the shattered wood, and trotted off.

Kitty, Benito, and I kept our distance. It wouldn't do to drive the horses too hard. They'd already panicked, a danger to themselves and everyone in the narrow street. They humped along like waves on the spine of a flooding stream, the powerful chestnut leading the surge.

Two freight wagons, startled mules in harness, waited in front of a mercantile. "Holy Ned!" cried a lad on the driver's seat. He dove head-first onto the great, pillowed body of a woman fixed to the walk in fright.

"Get off me, young—" The woman's cries were lost in the splintering of wood.

Several horses had collided with the wagons, bashing the sideboard of one, ripping the grub box from the other. One of the mares ran off, streaming a canvas scarf from her neck. Blood streaked her flanks. Another fell to the ground, spurting blood from its chest.

"Oh, Lord! We've got to help them," I yelled to Kitty.

"Not until the rest are safe. We can come back then."

"*Sí*, the girl knows what is best," Benito said from my left side.

I rode on, hoping there'd be no more casualties to horses or property. If Sam had been there he would've had a fit.

We churned past cabins with square-hewn logs and lime-chinked walls, a frame church with a Gothic ribbed window, a cafe that wafted the aroma of coffee and spicy stew. There were false-fronted stores, gaps between them where buildings had once stood. Wild-eyed men and women poked their heads through doorways to watch the herd thunder past. Horses in a corral kicked up their heels and raced around squealing. The mare's bell clanged on.

The saddle on Sam Dillard's pack-horse slid beneath his belly and hung there with its pack, threatening to throw him off balance. He dug in his heels and looked helplessly after the herd. One of the townspeople would have to help him. We'd return for him later.

The saddle on the sorrel was still square on her back. As she ran past a jail with thick log walls and sod roof, a prisoner stuck an arm through a barred window. "Hey you, Red, come back. Gimme a ride outta here."

I hoped we wouldn't end up sharing the man's cell. Running a herd of horses through town was no trivial matter. The townspeople were furious, cursing at us as we rode past.

One man shook his fist. "You damned-well better come back and pay for this mess."

"I'll do what I can," I yelled over my shoulder, knowing full well I hadn't the money.

West of town the gulch widened, and we encountered mounds of tailings, flumes, and ditches, the road running up the middle. A dredge hummed away on the creek's south bank. Nearer the road, gleaners looked up in surprise from digging in old prospect holes. One man, too close to the road for comfort, clawed his way from a hole and dived into another filled with sluice water. He came up dripping mud, angry as a wet hornet.

"What d'you crazies think you're doing? Take your goddamned rodeo somewheres else."

A little farther on, the herd swarmed around the base of a hill into the path of a schoolmarm sending her pupils home. "Come here!" she screamed at those standing in the road.

The young ones raced to her side and gathered around her on the schoolhouse steps. A few of the older boys ran alongside the herd, laughing, daring each other to grab a ride. None of them did, though they could have if they'd tried. The horses had slowed to a weary trot.

The road steepened as it wound up the gulch, allowing a clear view of Chinook as he lunged ahead of the herd. He was about to ram into three horsemen, sauntering along in no hurry. When the sound of the stampede reached their ears, they reined their horses up onto the side of the road.

One was an older man, one a boy Kitty's age, the other a boy in his late teens. The boys were mounted on striking black and white pintos.

"It's the Sherwoods," Kitty said with relief in her voice. She drifted back to speak to them.

Soon the older man pulled alongside me on a huge black gelding, his suit of dark gray cheviot dusty from the road. He let slip an instant of surprise at my swollen face and touched the brim of his Stetson. "My name's Hal Sherwood. Kitty tells me you're Gabe Breen's sister." His voice had a hollow, head-in-the-barrel quality. At the sound of it, Bannack spun his head around, pricked his ears, and nickered as if he knew the man.

"You must be the friend Gabe and Kitty talked about. I'm Jessie Tate."

Sherwood's large eyes slanted downward at the outside corners, accentuating a wide, prominent nose. They stared at me in curiosity. "Kitty says she's bringing the herd to my ranch. I'd like to know why."

"She's bringing half of them. The other half belongs to Sam Dillard. He owns that sorrel." I pointed toward the saddled mare trotting ahead of us.

"He's back on the main road a ways. On foot. The herd got away from us."

Sherwood brought a snort up from his barrel chest. "I'd say that's a lean call."

"As for why we're doing it, that's too long a story for now."

"Guess I can wait." He jerked a thumb to the west. "My place is 'bout a mile up the road, near the forks. There's a big corral I use for roundup. We can drive 'em in there. Me and my boys will take point and swing. You and the other two bring up the drags."

Putting spurs to his black, he soon closed on the front ranks and dogged the bell mare. Chinook darted off the side of the road, jumping sage and leaping boulders to keep from being trapped within the herd. Amazingly, his halter rope was still in place, though broken to a shorter length.

A quiver of fear ran through the herd when they realized more wranglers were taking part in the drive. Some of them splashed muddy waves from the shallows of Grasshopper Creek. One group of mares and foals bolted up the north slope.

Chinook fell back to bite rumps and snake his neck. Benito closed in, circling his lasso in the air. He threw, missed. Chinook pulled away from Benito and clacked his teeth at the bell mare's side. Sherwood dogged her heels.

A quarter-mile away a monster corral loomed like a gigantic trap at the intersection of roads, its pole gate hanging open. Ranch buildings cluttered the flat behind it. In her panic, the bell mare burst into a run that would take the herd straight toward the corral.

Chinook charged ahead to turn the mare, whipping between her and the gate, nipping her to force her back.

Single-minded in her fright, the mare slipped past him into the corral, her bell clanging wildly. The rest of the herd jammed in behind her, all except Chinook, the stud colt and two of the geldings. Benito took after the geldings. The stud colt streaked off to the north toward some low-lying hills.

The younger Sherwood boy yelled, "Hey, Kitty, bet I can lasso that colt before you can."

"Like fun you can." Forgetting Chinook for the challenge of the moment, Kitty raced after the colt, lariat circling in the air.

Sherwood and the older son had dismounted and slammed the gate shut on the herd. The horses reared and pawed against the railings, jostled and bit each other. Chinook charged back and forth outside the corral, screaming. The bell mare shouldered through the pack and whinnied over the fence at the stallion. He gave a furious trumpet that brought shrieks from every horse in the corral.

Several ranch dogs came at a run, hackles raised, and nipped the stallion's heels. Sherwood rapped out a single word to call them in and went for the lariat tied in a loop on his saddle.

The rope missed its mark and fell across Chinook's back. He reared, his eyes filled with fear of ropes that sizzle through the air to hold him fast. A second later, he was powering across the flat toward the sagebrush hills in the south.

"Sonofabitch!" Sherwood coiled his rope and put a foot in the stirrup.

I waved an arm to stop him. "I'll go."

"You'll need help with that rebel."

"No! He's tired and hurt. We shouldn't press him. He'll accept me. He has before."

Chapter 24

The ranch seemed to have kindled a spark in Bannack's memory. He didn't want to leave. Every now and then he'd stop to whinny toward a pasture that held several excited horses. We were a half-mile from the ranch before he'd continue in the direction I wanted without balking.

As we cut through the bunch grass and sage, squirrels poked their heads from their dens and sat upright, flicking their tails. Antelope had replaced the Medicine Lodge's mountain sheep. They'd scurry across the flat to look us over, stop at a safe distance, and raise their noses to get our wind

Three-quarters-of-a-mile to the east Sam Dillard walked the main road, his denim-clad figure etched dark and lean against the light-gray hills. He was leading Lilly while the foal gamboled along at her side.

Sympathy for the three traveling the dusty road swept my feelings, especially for Sam. All he'd wanted was a good string of horses for his son, a little peace of mind, and escape from his feelings of guilt. Now he was on foot, undoubtedly bone-weary, disgruntled, frustrated, buffeted by the wind. All that without knowing Chinook was on the loose.

I found the chestnut a few miles from the ranch, lying in a bunch-grass swale. He startled at the sight of me, raised his head and shoulders and thrust out his forelegs in an attempt to rise. Failing in that, he blew a great sigh and settled onto the grass, eyes and ears alert. His rusty sides heaved in and out. Blood oozed from battle wounds on his neck and flank and beaded along his mane to the ridge of his back. Flies had gathered on the wounds.

I tied Bannack to a sage bush on the lip of the basin and walked into the swale, rustling the dry grass. Grasshoppers that had survived the cold nights lit on my pants. I didn't take a lariat with me. I didn't want Chinook to think I was out to capture him. I'd need to get close enough to reach the halter rope.

Chinook tried once more to push off from the ground and fell back with a grunt. I spoke to him softly for several minutes before I crept to his side. As I kneeled to stroke his flanks, he drew his head back and snorted, but relaxed at the feel of my hand. His wide-spaced brown eyes lost their fright. A whicker rumbled lightly in his chest.

The smell of blood and sweat was strong as I stroked the underside of his neck. "You poor dear. I wish I had a magic potion that could make you well."

He seemed to remember I'd tended his injury at Gabe's camp. He mouthed my denim jacket and the brim of my hat, knocking it to the ground. When he ran his soft lips over my hair and cheek, an even greater love swelled my heart.

While I checked his wounds, I sang an Irish lullaby to soothe him. "Too-ra-loo-ra-loo-ra . . ." He dropped his chin and closed his eyes.

Three of the long gashes on his neck and flank lay open, in need of stitches. The injury from the Centennial, healed into a thin ridge, seemed slight compared to the wounds of battle. I imagined Sherwood kept disinfectants, ointments, oiled thread, and curved needles on hand to close wounds. Most ranchers did. We'd need to watch for infection. Sam might have to lay up two or three days to let Chinook rest. That wouldn't help the man's mood.

The sun hung low in the western sky and cold had begun to seep from the ground. I thought of the fleece jacket tied back of my saddle, but I was reluctant to leave Chinook. He might gather strength and run.

I took a firm hold on his lead rope and scooped my hat from the ground. I was stuffing it on my head when Bannack whinnied and pricked his ears to the north. He flared his nostrils in and out to sniff the gusting wind.

"What is it, Bannack? What's out there?"

He gave a loud, rib-rippling neigh and trotted around the sage bush, jerking on his rope.

The scents that had aroused Bannack's interest hadn't escaped Chinook. He rumbled a deep nicker, both question and warning. With a huge grunt, he thrust out his forelegs and lurched to his feet.

Emboldened by Chinook's interest, Bannack tugged even harder at his rope, snapping the branch in two. For a moment he paced along the lip of the basin, whinnying, trailing the branch and raising dust. Then, without so much as a glance in my direction, he spun off toward the north, galloping toward a narrow gap between hills.

"Get back here!" I screeched. I doubted he would. The familiar smells of his early years had captured his imagination. He'd chosen to forget I lived. Now I'd have to lead Chinook to the ranch on foot or try to ride him. I decided on the latter.

Keeping a short lead, I pulled Chinook to the foot of an embankment and hauled myself part-way up the steep incline. When his swerving back came close, I leaped on board. My leg must have struck one of his wounds. He took off as if a bee had stung his rump.

"Whoa, there. Whoa!" I yelled. Unable to square myself, I clamped one leg over his back, an arm over his neck, and rode his side, clutching the lead rope with my left hand. I was certain I'd fall.

The stallion's canter became a gallop as we sped through a maze of low-lying hills. Not until we'd burst onto the broad valley that stretched across the mottled half-dusk was I able to pull myself to a balanced seat.

In the distance, Bannack ran hell-bent-for-leather toward the ranch. I pulled on the halter rope to turn Chinook in that direction. He fought the move. The smell had spooked him into running like a demon despite his injuries, despite exhaustion from the long chase across the countryside.

Just north of Bannack I spied three large specks coming toward us. Judging from the way they traveled evenly abreast, I thought they must be horsemen. I leaned over Chinook's neck. "Do as I ask, boy, or they'll come after you with lariats."

Chinook collected all the information he needed from the air and gathered his muscles into a gallop. The gallop turned into a run, then an incredible floating gait that seemed more of the air than of the ground. I had no way to control him, simply leaned over his neck and clung to his flaring mane. His hoofs slashed at the ground, reached out, slashed, reached out, each foothold sure, unerring. He slowed a brief second to check on the horses hammering in from the north, then surge ahead as before, hoofs reaching—slashing—reaching—slashing. My blood quickened. My muscles rippled in rhythm with his.

We'd reached a series of dry creek beds, called washes, which sent crooked fingers across the flat. Most of them we cleared in one leap, others we crossed with a lunge down the near side and a lunge up the far bank. Chinook had little trouble maintaining his speed until he came upon a wash too wide to sail over, too narrow to plunge in and out, the banks on each side undercut and crumbling.

His muscles flinched beneath me. He was going too fast to stop before he reached the wash. The bank crumbled beneath him as he gathered his muscles in a great leap to the far side. An inner force seemed to propel him forward, upward.

My heart roared. *Make it, Chinook. Make it.*

For a long breathless moment we hung suspended between earth and sky, between safety and disaster. During that thundering silence I closed my eyes to strengthen my will, to strengthen Chinook's.

It seemed an eternity before hoofs struck the earth. My eyelids flew open. Chinook's front legs had taken a purchase on the far bank. He clawed at the loose rock and sand.

There was a sound of crumbling earth and rock, the thud of a thousand pounds of horse flesh hitting the floor of the wash. A burst of air from Chinook's lungs. I felt the crushing pain of his weight on my leg, a stabbing pain where my head struck a rock.

Then numb blackness.

Chapter 25

I emerged from the darkness bewildered, hurt, and shivering. As the haze left my eyes, I saw the legs of a horse planted in the rocks and pebbles that were my bed. He was hovering over me, his breath warm on my cheeks, his liquid brown eyes focused on my face. When I stirred, he mouthed my hair and clothes, leaving them wet with saliva. A chestnut stallion. He looked as if he'd run into a barbed wire fence.

I shoved his muzzle aside and rose onto an elbow. The change in position made me retch. My head swam and felt as if it would burst. When I explored a lump at the back of my head, blood smeared my fingers. My leg ached, but I saw no blood on my pants leg. Nothing seemed broken. Bent over, retching, I hauled myself to my feet. The world spun around. About to faint, I dropped to the ground.

"Oh, Ben! Why aren't you here to help me?"

I don't know how long I lay there before the memory of Ben's death glimmered through the throbbing in my head. Then, as events of the immediate past sparked into life, I recognized the horse as Chinook and remembered his fall. He stopped sniffing me and stood rigid, ears pricked forward, listening to hoofbeats gallop in from the northeast. I sat up, but before I could grab his lead rope, he dashed away to circle on the floor of the wash. When he'd gathered momentum, he leaped the crumbled bank of the wash and clattered off into the growing dusk of the southwest.

The other horses pounded toward the wash. Men yelled. My heartbeat quickened.

A hundred yards from where I sat, two horsemen crossed the wash in a blur of dark cloth and denim, black and tan horse-hide. A third set of hoofbeats slowed to a walk as they neared my place of accident. I froze, then breathed a sigh of relief as Sam Dillard rode over the embankment, sitting tall on his sorrel.

"I can think of a better place to take a siesta." His thin face was drawn but smiling.

I was embarrassed, humbled, holding my stomach. I gave a sour laugh. "A pillow would help."

"Sorry, didn't think to bring one along." He threw a leg over the mare's rump.

"How did you get here so fast? I saw you on foot way over there." I motioned with my arm. "Maybe I was out longer than I thought."

"Sherwood spied me and brought my mare. After we took Lilly and the colt to the ranch, we lit out after you. Benito, too." He broke off, coughing the dry hack that resulted from swallowing too much dust, then went on in a scratchy voice. "We thought you might be having trouble with that rascally stallion of mine."

"How did you know I'd fallen?"

"We saw him drop into the wash. Risky to ride a stallion bareback." He untied his fleece jacket from its place behind the saddle and pulled it around my shoulders. The wind continued to howl across the barren ground, and I shook, despite the jacket. No promise the wind would cease.

"Have you seen Bannack?" I asked.

"We passed him a ways back, on a tear. The kids can take care of him. They're on their way in with the stud colt." Sam squatted down beside me, his clear gray eyes filled with concern and something akin to tenderness. "Are you hurt?"

I shrugged. "Not much. I bumped my head." I put my hand on the lump. It had grown larger, bloodier. My brains felt as if they were trying to pound their way through my skull. "It's made me sick to my stomach."

"Nothing else hurts?"

"Not really." I saw no point in mentioning my leg. Likely it was just bruised.

"You're lucky. Riding a racer bareback is like keeping your seat on a fence rail during a bad quake."

"I would have fallen, saddle or not. He tried to jump too far."

"If you say so." Doubt crinkled his eyes. He took my hand. "Can you stand?"

I pushed feebly on the ground with the other hand. The wrist seemed strained.

"Here, let me give you a boost." He hooked an arm under my elbow and gently hauled me to my feet.

I stood, a bit wobbly. My head reeled. The nerves in my leg shrieked. Yet Sam's arm brought comfort, a sense all would be well.

"No broken bones. That's good," he said in his soft drawl. "We'll get you to the ranch and do something about that burl on your noggin."

I'd been so concerned about myself, it struck me for the first time that Sam had chosen to help *me*, rather than ride after his stallion. I felt a rush of gratitude and something else I dared not give a name. "Shouldn't you try to find Chinook? He's bleeding."

Sam glanced in the direction Chinook had taken. "Sherwood and Benito know what they're doing. Likely they'll bring him in. If not, Chinook'll find a hidy-hole until it gets plumb dark, then sneak back to the ranch to check on his harem. We'll catch him in the morning."

* * *

As we rode up to the ranch, a post wagon rumbled in from the flats and stopped at the barn, the sod roof prickly with cactus and burr-weed. The building was a log affair, low and rambling, unremarkable in the muted light of late afternoon. Deer antlers and the pronged skulls of antelope had been thrown onto the roof in a heap, along with a few Bighorn curls and the rack from a moose.

Oblivious to our approach, three weary-looking wranglers slid from the wagon and entered the barn. Two shepherd pups had jumped from the wagon ahead of them and were greeted raucously by Penny and the older Sherwood dogs. The corralled horses set up a chorus of welcome for Tawn, Dillard's sorrel, and for the team pulling the wagon. Shorty brayed like a lost soul in an alien land, letting out so much air with each bray that his ribs looked as if they'd cave in.

Dillard headed for the house, a two-story log building with tall spectral windows. No garden softened its stark lines, except for a few scraggly lilacs along the foundation, their leaves turning a rich mauve. Half the shakes on the roof were skewed to one side or the other. A gust of wind scooped dirt from the turn-around in front of the house and scattered it across the roof, slamming the loose shakes. Another gust shredded smoke rising from a stovepipe that thrust its sooted arm from a large cabin at the rear of the house. From a huge dinner bell hanging from the porch roof, I judged the cabin to be the cookhouse.

Sam reined Tawn in at the main house and knocked at the door. No answer. He pushed the door open and yelled. Still no answer. He returned to the mare and helped me down. "You go in the house. I'll water and brush Tawn and check on the horses in the corral, then see what we can do to make you feel better. Hal says he's a widower, but the boys must be around here somewhere. They'll know where the medicine's kept."

I thanked him gratefully, told him where he could find the medicines in my pack, and watched him ride off. I was about to hobble inside when angry shouts erupted west of the house. All I wanted was to lie down with my head on a pillow, but the fact one of the voices was Kitty's prodded me numbly around the corner of the house.

I found Kitty leaning against the six-foot fence of a breaking corral, a pout on her face. The Sherwood boys were inside the corral staring-down a long-tailed roan tied to a snubbing post. It was swinging its rump around, stomping its hobbled feet, and jerking back on the rope, its bulging eyes fixed on the boys. Its unkempt mane and tail said it was a mustang. From the piles of dung circling another post, it appeared the horse had been tied in the corral for several days with a little hay and water, common practice in the West for breaking wild horses. The boys had managed to hobble the horse and put a hackamore on him, as well as a saddle blanket and a saddle that wasn't much more than a pad with stirrups. The older boy had fastened spurs to his riding boots.

I hobbled up to the fence and stood next to Kitty. She studied my scratched face in question. "What happened to you?"

I explained briefly. Very briefly. It hurt my head to think.

"What about Chinook?"

"Benito and Mr. Sherwood have gone after him." I tried to sound casual and confident of the outcome. A loud grumbling turned my head toward the boys. "What's going on here?"

"Lance is showing off."

The older boy grimaced around a hand-rolled cigarette that dangled from the corner of his mouth. "Not showing off. I gotta break this mustang."

The younger Sherwood stood at the snubbing post, a grudging expression on his face. "Lance won't let me try," he said with obvious spleen.

Lance gave an arrogant toss of his head. "Pa gave *me* the job not Mike. I'm going to earn my living taming broncs."

I opened my mouth to reply, but Mike cut in, "I know as much about it as he does. I'm gentler with 'em too."

"Lance doesn't believe I can break a mustang." Kitty intended the words for me, but directed her scornful glance toward the older boy.

"She does an amazing job." I'd watched her break the mustang in the Centennial.

"Couldn't break this'n," Lance said as he crept up to the horse. "He's pure poison. He'd kill her."

"Too bad. With care he'd be a nice-looking animal."

Lance wrinkled his nose. "Nothing but an overgrown rat."

"These overgrown rats are far tougher than the stock most ranchers breed."

Lance countered with a snort. "Tell that to my pa." He closed the gap between him and the nervous mustang. "Steady, you flea-bitten nag. We're gonna have us some fun."

The roan seemed to know what lay ahead. He pulled back on the snubbing rope, rolled his eyes, and squealed. Replies from horses in the big corral ripped the air. Lighter neighs rose from the barn.

Lance edged toward the horse. "Steady now. Steady."

The roan screamed and jerked back on the rope, throwing himself to the ground in a blanket of dust. Writhing, squealing, snorting, he struggled to free himself from the hobbles and rope that held him prisoner. He got to his feet several times and threw himself just as many. One last muscle-wrenching effort brought him to a wobbly stand that allowed him to drag himself around, squealing. Dust choked the air.

"I don't torture the horses I break," Kitty yelled.

"What've you been breaking? Namby-pambies?"

Moving deftly to avoid being stomped on, Mike removed the hobbles while Lance twisted the roan's ear with one hand and held tight to the rope with the other. As Lance swung onto the seat, the horse froze, his muscles bunched, nostrils flared, eyes rolled. He didn't seem to realize he was without hobbles.

"Get the rope, Mike!"

Mike sullenly flipped the rope from the snubbing post. Lance dug his knees into the horse.

The roan took short, chopping steps until he discovered he was no longer bound, then shot skyward in a long, curving deer-leap.

"Bet you can't stay with him," Mike taunted.

Lance was too busy trying to keep his seat to answer.

The roan leaped around and around, bowing his body in the air, his hind feet drawn under as if he were bent in half, front legs stiff as crowbars, driving hoofprints into the dust. In a sudden change of tactics, he reared, trying to shake Lance from his back.

"You wall-eyed son of a stud!" Lance dug in with the spurs.

Maddened, terrified, the horse gave a bawl that rasped at my nerves and tore at my feelings. The air filled with a mass of whirling mane and tail. Hoofs sliced out in all directions. Shrieks split the air. Lance hurtled to the ground like a meteor, plowing dirt ahead of him, crumpling his hat beneath him. The cigarette flew from his lips.

He hauled himself to his feet, wiping the dirt from his mouth. "Sonofabitch. Time you'n me settled this argument." He grabbed a snake whip lying on the ground.

I groaned as the heavy whip hummed through the air and snapped into the mustang's hide. He tried to escape but could only race along the fence while the blacksnake writhed back and forth in the air.

The terrible rage that swept me shoved aside pain and fatigue. "Don't whip him!" I crawled through one of the gaps between rails. Kitty was ahead of me, running toward Lance. She lunged for the whip.

Lance pushed her aside, yelling, "Beat it, you stupid brat."

"You'll have to whip me too." Kitty ran around the corral, protecting the roan's bleeding flank with her own slight frame. Lance followed in circles, twitching the whip on the ground, looking for an opening.

I stole up behind him, and when he pulled the whip into a backswing, I seized the stock. "You'll ruin him. Let Kitty quiet him."

Lance spun, drilling holes in me with his eyes. "I'll bust him any way I want."

"Afraid Kitty'll show you up?" Mike taunted.

"Damn it, stay out of this."

For a long strident moment, Lance stood immobile, glaring at Mike, Kitty, and me. Seeming to arrive at a decision, he jerked the whip from my hand, coiled it, and sauntered over to the fence. There he leaned against a rail, the whip looped over an arm, and rolled a cigarette. Rebellion sulled in his face.

Kitty took Lance's retreat as a cue to demonstrate the proper way to tame a mustang. Following the same procedure she'd used with the mustang at the Centennial, she crept toward the terrified horse whistling a soft tune. She continued to whistle until he let her stroke his flank. When he'd stand in place she slipped the saddle and blanket from his back and rubbed him all over gently many times, first with her hands, then with her hat. Mike sat on his heels near the snubbing post and beamed at her success. Lance leaned against the fence in brooding silence. I found an empty oat pail, turned it upside down and sat on it, cradling my head, too tired to move into the house.

Forty minutes had dragged by before the roan stopped his quivering and his frantic breathing. Kitty stroked him a while longer. "I'll let him stand," she said to Mike as she tied the horse to the snubbing post. "I'll ride him tomorrow."

"I'll ride him now!" Lance pushed off from the fence and swaggered toward the saddle lying on the ground, a fresh cigarette stuck in the corner of his mouth. His heavy eyebrows twitched with a nervous bravado.

Kitty thrust out a hand to stop him. "I just calmed him down."

"Awww, what's it gonna hurt?" Lance's eyes held the almost hysterical glitter I'd seen in people obsessed with their own ideas. He stooped for the saddle.

Kitty grabbed his arm. "He'll come undone."

The glitter in Lance's eyes flared with something I read as a surge of daring. Leaving the saddle, he strode toward the horse.

"It won't hurt to wait," I shouted. He ignored me.

The roan saw him coming and flattened his ears, crouched, and snorted. The veins in his cheeks stood out like ropes.

Lance slipped the snubbing rope from the post, gave a powerful thrust with his legs, and landed belly crosswise on the mustang's lurching back.

Furious, Kitty grabbed the hem of his jacket and dragged him to the ground. Leaving him to choke on the dust, she shadowed the frightened horse, saying over and over, "Easy, fella. Easy, there. Don't be afraid."

Lance rose to his knees, coughing and swearing, and watched Kitty with hate-filled eyes. With a leap, he shoved her to the ground.

She twisted to face him, screaming and clawing, fighting the fists that battered her head and shoulders.

The dogs had heard the brawl and came on a run. They tore around the youngsters, barking. Horses whinnied and raced back and forth in their enclosures.

I tugged at Kitty's arms, Mike at Lance's, yelling at them to stop fighting. Dust boiled into the air and made us cough. I stopped to retch.

Kitty and Lance went on scrapping in the dung, dust, and hay.

From behind us came the sound of galloping hoofs. A glance over my shoulder told me Hal Sherwood had arrived and was throwing a leg over the saddle before his horse came to a stop.

He scrambled over the fence, shouting, "What in the blazes is going on?" Without waiting for an answer, he grabbed Lance by the belt, dragged him over to the fence, and stood with an arm on each side of the boy so he couldn't escape. "What are you doing, fighting a girl? I taught you better'n that!"

"Kitty was trying to help him with the mustang," Mike taunted. "He was jealous."

"I was not. The nosy brat spoiled—"

"You're the one that spoiled it." Kitty sat on the ground, wiping dirt from eyes and mouth. A scratch oozed blood across her forehead. Mats of filth clung to her clothes.

"I could've ridden him out."

"Sure you could. When cows climb trees."

The jibe set a match to Lance's hatred. He ducked beneath his father's arm and made a quick move toward Kitty as I helped her from the ground.

Hal lunged at the boy and took a vise-like hold on his shoulder. "You hell-cat. Simmer down." He turned toward me, working to relax his face muscles. His ride had left the smell of saddle leather on his clothes. Tobacco juice trickled from the corner of his mouth. "Suppose you tell me how this started."

I told the story in as judicious a way as I could. It wasn't easy. My head ached. Besides that, I felt a terrible anger toward a young man who'd whip a horse out of spite, embarrassment for a girl who'd brawl in the dirt like an unlicked cub. Hal managed to keep them quiet until I told of Lance's attempt to mount the horse bareback.

At that, Kitty stabbed a finger in the air. "I told him to stay off, and he wouldn't."

"Dumb dodo. I just wanted to see if that cloud-hunter was ready to ride."

"Yeah. Now I'll have to gentle him all over again."

"Like blazes you will." Lance made a move to shove Kitty, but Hal pulled him around by the collar.

"Enough of this! I don't want to have to ear you down."

"Aww, let me ride him, Pa. I'll show him who's boss."

From Mike came the first two lines of a bronc busters' tune, sung in a taunting, wavering tenor. "Many was a bronc never got rode. Never was a rider never got throwed."

With a roar, Lance pulled free of his father's grip and threw a punch at Mike that sent him to the ground with a bloody nose.

"Whoa there, boy." Hal swung out a ham-sized palm to grab Lance's arm.

Lance dodged, took several running steps toward the fence, and climbed to the top rail. There he turned and yelled at Kitty, "You ain't gonna get the best of me. See if you do. You, too, Mike." Without so much as a "may I" he mounted his father's horse and sunk in his spurs. At the feel of sharp metal, the clean-limbed black dropped into a short, easy lope, stringing a trail of dust across the flats.

Chapter 26

I dug deep for words that would express my regret for the trouble Kitty and I had caused, telling Hal I thought we should leave. He wouldn't allow it. He knew all about his son's mean streak and offered his own apology. He also knew about head injuries and said I should stay at the ranch a few days to rest.

Proving the sincerity of the invitation, he stomped the dirt from his feet and urged me into the roomy parlor. The floor had been swept after a fashion, but dust filmed a dining table and chairs. Newspapers and dime novels were strewn here and there. A frayed rug braided from scraps of wool was dusty and worn.

Sherwood lit a kerosene table lamp and motioned me to a sofa, the original avocado green soiled and faded to the color of a near-ripe olive. "You'll be warmer in here than in the bedroom."

"Do you have any laudanum?"

"'Fraid not. My wife used to keep it on hand. I just use whiskey when I hurt. Want some?"

I refused politely and lay my head on a firm green velveteen pillow, pulled a crocheted afghan tight around me, and let my gaze wander the room. It settled first on a small organ that stood in a dim corner, a beaded lamp on its lid. Several portraits stared vacantly from the kalsomined wall beside the organ, their expressions somber. A picture of the family showed the parents, Mike, Lance, an older sister, and two older boys, all with hair of varying shades of brown. Mike seemed to have inherited his mother's appealing face. His hair was coffee-brown, as were his eyes, and his eyebrows as graceful as a dove's wing. His legs were too long for the trunk of his body, an adolescent build, no more fat on him than a lizard. On the other hand, Lance had his father's build, heavy in the trunk, with short legs. His brown eyes turned down at the outside corners like his father's, his nose prominent.

Hal built a fire in the Franklin stove and lit a lamp hanging in the adjoining kitchen. I heard him work a pump outside the house and bring several pails of water into the kitchen, heard him drag what sounded like metal tubs from a kitchen cellar. Wood thudded on metal as he shoved fuel into the range's firebox.

"I've put a kettle on," he said when he came from the kitchen. "It'll whistle when the water's hot. There's tea in the cupboard, maybe a cinnamon stick. I've set you up with water and tubs for a bath and washing clothes when you're up to it. There's a basin for washing that poor face of yours." He shrugged off my murmured thanks and pushed his way outside against the wind.

It wasn't long before Sam came into the house with my pack of personal belongings. I told him where to find the packet of laudanum and he brought it with a glass of water and a smile. After washing the cut on my head and applying carbolated ointment, he left to eat supper at the cookhouse. I had no appetite.

Because Chinook had eluded Hal and Benito, a search was planned for tomorrow. Though exhausted, Sam and Benito would ride into town after supper to collect the horses that had been left behind and pay for damaged property. That accomplished, they could take part in the search. Sam wanted to pay for all the damages, but I insisted I'd pay for half when I reached the Bitterroot. The check for three thousand dollars he thrust upon me as payment for Chinook—despite the farcical race in the Medicine Lodge—would cover the cost of damages and leave ample funds for Kitty's future. It would even cover the amount Ben owed Carver Dean.

I'd learned much about Sam while observing him that day. I'd warmed to his humorous play on words and to the simple gestures that turned potential problems into gentle vapors. It was his firm way of handling a crisis that I most respected in him. I could imagine why his father-in-law had trusted him with his cattle business. In that respect, Ben had been like Sam, a man respected by others. Yet both men were capable of terrible anger if victimized, the rage not always voiced, but seething beneath a calm exterior.

I'd noted something else in Sam's manner, something I'd glimpsed several times. Shadows from the past seemed to haunt the ready smile and quick joke—more than grief and self-blame, a much deeper guilt. I hoped the coils of misdeeds hadn't shackled his heart and conscience as they had Ben's and mine.

The fight in the corral had temporarily distracted me from the ache in my leg. Now it claimed my attention. The calf had begun to swell and turn the color of a newt, the skin tight around my knee. I should take Hal's advice and rest for several days, but I didn't want to wear out our welcome. It would be uncomfortable to face Lance. More uncomfortable to face an early blizzard on the trail. The bad-weather season was nearing, with more than a hundred miles between Sherwood's ranch and my homestead. I longed to be there, longed for things familiar and the comfort of my daily routine. That, despite the fact Carver Dean might be waiting on my doorstep, ready to plunder my life.

* * *

My eyes cracked open dryly to the light of a new day driving the gray from an east-facing window. My head seemed stuffed with cotton. My ears buzzed. Where was I? A look around the room brought a glimmer of remembrance—Ellen Sherwood's room, the daughter in the portrait, now the wife of a preacher in Billings. Hal had settled me in the room when he returned from supper. The door had been closed all night and the warmth from the parlor's Franklin stove had gone elsewhere.

The other rooms in the Sherwood home had the look of a widower's den, the furnishings made for utility, no attempt at neatness. On a ranch like this, cowpokes and neighboring ranchers would tromp in and out, mud and manure on their feet, dust on their clothes. Hal Sherwood seemed the type who'd want them to feel at home, not afraid they'd soil the dainties.

Mrs. Sherwood had flavored this bedroom the way her husband had flavored the rest of the house. Though in need of a dusting, it smacked of feminine fancy—satins and laces, ruffles at the window and bed. Doilies threaded with pink ribbons topped a cherrywood chiffonier and dressing table. Roses and violets in raised relief coiled around a china pitcher and wash basin. Ben would have called the frills "fummadiddle," objects and decorations that served no useful purpose.

It dawned in my foggy head that someone had turned on the lamp.

Kitty? A look over the side of the bed showed the trundle bed had been pulled from under the massive four-poster, the bedding rumpled from someone sleeping there. The stupor from the laudanum had been so complete, my exhaustion so great, I'd slept like a winter bear and hadn't wakened when she'd entered the bedroom and pulled out the trundle.

There was the sound of Mike's and Kitty's voices coming from the kitchen into the parlor. A brief conversation, then Kitty opened and closed the bedroom door and settled at the dressing table, hugging herself against the chill.

I sat up, dizzy-headed, fingering the gauze that covered the bump on the back of my head. I felt like a rug that had been hung on the line and beaten with a hoop. "Good morning."

Evidently Kitty had thought I was asleep. She gave my reflection in the mirror a startled glance and answered me with a grunt.

"You need to stay warm." I tossed her a shawl Hal had loaned me the previous evening.

Grudgingly, she wrapped the lavender wool around her shoulders. "Your face looks better," she said to my image in the mirror. Her tone was as brittle as the air in the room.

"That's good news." I studied her reflection in the glass. She'd given her face a thorough scrubbing, and it shone with the vibrance of youth and outdoor living. "You look rested."

She made no reply, simply untied the shoelace that bound the end of her braid and worked a brush through the rippling waves. The rays of the rising sun pierced the window and set fire to the carrot red in her hair. "Brushing makes your hair shine." I hoped to encourage something she indulged in rarely.

Another grunt. "Think I'll wash it before I ride after Chinook."

A face scrubbing? Hair wash? Cleanliness was a new concern. "Will you have time?"

"Mike and Lance have chores to do before we go. Sam needs to take care of the horses that ran into the wagon. They're pretty bunged up."

I'd observed Mike Sherwood and Kitty after the fight in the corral and knew he was the reason for her concern about appearance. It was clear they liked each other but didn't know whether to hide the fact or show it. What Kitty couldn't conceal was excitement that glittered amid the sorrow and rage that had burned in her eyes for days.

I couldn't blame her for taking a shine to Mike. He seemed a nice boy, quiet, kind to animals. And he liked to sing. Last evening I'd opened the tall, single-paned window a crack, and the sound of a guitar along with a sour-sweet blend of male voices and a woman's brassy contralto had drifted in from the cookshack. Kitty's lovely, clear soprano had floated above the rest, reminding of my young voice and the portly Italian my mother had engaged for a singing teacher. I was glad Kitty had stayed for the evening round of music and song. Let her sing while she could. Life sobered one soon enough, saddling a person with duties beyond imagination. Let a girl enjoy her youth and be merry. Still, when I thought of her affection for Mike, it was all I could do to keep from throwing an arm around her and declaring to the powers that force a child to bloom into adulthood, "Not yet. You can't have her. She's mine."

Kitty set down the brush to study her image in the mirror, turning her head this way and that in a critical way. "I hate pimples," she said as she fingered a small eruption on her chin. "They make me look ugly."

"That's not true. You're pretty. You'll be even prettier when you're sixteen or eighteen. It takes time for nature to make the most of a girl's features." I recalled I'd begun to worry about my features when Kitty's age. I'd slicked my hair and pinched my cheeks before going out to the stables where Ben had his blacksmith shop. When Father wasn't around I'd watch Ben shamelessly while he worked.

"Have you had breakfast?" I asked, sickening a bit at the thought of food.

"Not yet. Mike says seven o'clock prompt. Clare doesn't like the food to get cold."

"Who's Clare?"

"The cook." She snickered. "She's something else."

"Guess I'd better dress." The thought brought me no joy.

"Sam says you need to stay in bed."

"I want to look for Chinook." I envisioned the stallion out in the wilds, wounded, frightened, undoubtedly bewildered by events. I worried that the search would be in vain, that Chinook's intelligence would keep him at a distance. It seemed unjust to deprive such a remarkable animal of his freedom. Yet the wilds held danger even for him.

"You'll get sick if you go." Kitty's frown said she was more interested in excluding me from the search than in my welfare.

To prove her wrong I sat up and slid my legs over the edge of the mattress. Pain shot up my right leg from ankle to thigh. My head spun around. I fell back.

"See what I mean?"

I grumbled a sigh. "Who'll be going?"

"Mike, Lance, Sam, and me. I'd just as soon Lance didn't, but his dad said he has to go 'cause he knows the country best. He goes out there looking for mustangs."

I wondered at the wisdom of having Lance along. He might take revenge on Kitty, or she might start trouble. "Hal won't be going?"

"He's getting ready for roundup. Benito offered to help. Hal's short on hired help."

Kitty pushed the trundle into place, took her jeans from the floor where she'd tossed them, and held them up for inspection. Usually she paid no heed, simply yanked them on regardless of their condition.

"They're dirty. So's the other pair I brought along."

"I'll wash them when I get to feeling better." I wondered where I'd find the energy. "Maybe Mike has a pair you can wear until yours are clean."

"Aunt Jess! That'd be too embarrassing."

I shrugged. "Just a suggestion." I couldn't escape the fact she'd called me Aunt Jess. When would it be Mother? Or would it never?

She backtracked slightly. "If I decide to wash them, I'll do it myself. I don't need your help."

The snide words hit me like a smelly fish in the face. I was too groggy to work up a froth, so I ignored the remark. No use starting an argument. I was too dull-witted for battle. Besides, Kitty was already at war with feelings that tore at her teenage heart.

Dressed in dirty jeans, boots, and denim jacket, she stopped to inspect herself in the mirror and fiddle with her hair.

"Aren't you going to braid it?" I asked.

"Nope. At least not till I wash it." She went to open the door and turned back, her hand on the knob. She stood there for a minute, staring at me with eyes that cut like a scythe. I thought I was about to feel the lash of her tongue. Instead, she asked tersely, "Do you like Mike?"

Considering her attitude toward me, the confidentiality of the question took me by surprise. "Uh, he seems nice enough. He's polite. Why?"

"Oh, nothing. Just wondered."

"Do *you* like him?"

"Yeah—sure. He doesn't tease me like some boys, isn't mean or braggy. I don't know . . ." The pain and uncertainty of adolescence seemed to have shoved aside some of her more disagreeable impulses.

It pained me to think a boy could give Kitty the companionship she wouldn't allow me, but I was thankful for Mike in a way. I watched with bittersweet amusement as the girl who fancied him flitted out the door on wings. It seemed she was turning into a young lady despite herself, an idea almost as frightening as the possibility she'd remain a reckless tomboy.

The possibility she might never accept me as her mother saddened me, bringing with it thoughts of Gabe. I hated him, loved him, cursed him, wept for him. He'd sent me on a mission for his sake and Kitty's, more and more for my sake as the days passed. I'd fulfill my vow. Strange thing about vows—they coiled around one's heart and conscience, driving one to achieve the impossible. Before I'd delivered Kitty and the herd safely to the Bitterroot, I'd likely learn more about the impossible.

Chapter 27

It wasn't until early afternoon I felt like facing the day. I bathed, put on a denim skirt and blouse Ellen had left behind, then hobbled to the window to check on the weather. The few cloud puffs I'd watched scud across the blue a few hours ago had bred legions that amassed into a sodden gray sky. Not a day for washing and drying clothes. That would have to wait until tomorrow. Just as well. Kitty had relented and borrowed a shirt and jeans from Mike. Her own filthy clothes would need to soak overnight to rid them of the smell of dung from scrapping in the corral.

I needed coffee. I was sure to find some in the cookhouse. Ranch cooks always kept a pot heating on the stove.

I found Clare, the cook, washing the dishes from the mid-day meal, her round midriff pressed against a pan of hot, sudsy water on a worktable. A pan of rinse water steamed beside it. Clare was a huge, dark-haired woman with a couple of long black hairs growing on her chin and brown eyes sunken in the pillows of her cheeks. The tight bun on the back of her head pulled at the skin of her temples. Her size made it difficult to tell her age—anywhere from thirty to forty-five or fifty. The spots on her apron were more telling. They declared the ingredients in the dinner menu. Those, along with the thick smell of coffee, fried steak, baked beans, and biscuits that filled the room, left little room for conjecture.

I took a cup from the rinse pan and shook off the excess water. "We've made extra work for you."

"I'm used to having extras." A cheroot bobbed up and down in Clare's lips as she spoke. "Seems strange when I don't. Folks come on foot, horseback, some with nothing in their pockets but a hole. We don't ask a man's business or history. Just take him at face value."

"True Montana hospitality."

"'Spose you and your hubby do your share."

"*I* do. Ben passed away four years ago."

Clare swung her head around with a puzzled look. "I thought Sam was yours."

"Sam?" The idea brought a pleasant warmth to my face. "He's just traveling our way."

Clare gave a snort. "I thought them looks on his face when he talked about you being hurt meant more'n if he was your ball and chain."

The flush on my cheeks grew warmer. "What looks?"

"Reckon I been around cowpokes long enough to know when they have a hankering for a woman—not me o' course." She trumpeted a laugh. "Never had to worry about men laying hands on me."

Avoiding comment, I wiped a towel over knives and forks. My right leg ached and I shifted my weight onto the left, trying to find a point of ease. Noting my discomfort, Clare pulled a stool from beneath a work counter and set it in front of the pan of rinse water.

"You look peaked. Best sit down before I have to scoop you off the floor."

The heels of a large pair of men's shoes poked from beneath Clare's gingham skirts as she took a dipper of water from a bucket in a corner of the kitchen. She poured the water into a teakettle and pulled the kettle onto a hot stove lid. The stove's radiated heat made me feel I, too, had been set on the lid to boil.

"A cup of tea will give you a boost," she said with a toothy, tobacco-stained smile.

"I'd rather have coffee."

"Coffee it is, then."

The kitchen was separated from the dining area. It held two utility cupboards and a large dish closet with dishes of various faded designs staring through the open door. Under a window stood a sink cluttered with bowls and pots waiting to be washed. A butter churn and cream separator sat beneath the sink. Immense coffee-pots sat at the back of the stove, likely half-filled with old grounds to be boiled up again when a fresh brew was needed. Clare filled a cup from a pot with brown stains trickling down the sides.

"Kinda funny 'bout you and that man," she said as she set the coffee cup in front of me. "Thought you was traveling together."

"We're just headed the same direction. Actually, it's more complicated than that, but that's the gist of it."

She clamped the cheroot in the corner of her mouth and dipped her puffy red hands into the dishwater. "I'd do it if I was you—travel together, I mean. Makes sense. Might keep that stallion from running off again. You could catch you a good man while you're at it. Get you some ball and chain jewelry."

"I don't need a man," I said in a half-hearted exclamation.

"Life ain't much without one." I detected regret in her voice and in the way she flicked ashes from the cheroot onto the floor.

"Sometimes life isn't much with one," I said, then added hurriedly, "Not speaking from my own experience, of course."

She shot me a knowing look. "'Course not." She paused to concentrate on scrubbing the bean pot. "Hope Lance don't find that stallion before the others do. You might not get him back alive."

The comment set off alarm bells. I'd worried about Lance hurting Kitty. Maybe he'd do it through Chinook. "Why do you say that?"

"That stud stole a couple of our pasture mares in the night. Hal's mad enough to paw sod. As far as he's concerned, a man's loose stallion is no better'n a mustang. Welcome as a rattlesnake in a cowboy's boot."

"What about Mike?"

She smiled with affection. "That pussy cat? Never. He loves animals too much. His father's been in ranching too long for that. He says there'll always be trouble on the range as long as there's mustangs. He'd like to kill the lot."

I cringed at the sentiment, though I'd heard it many times. Most ranchers hated the wild horses for feeding on the range grasses, the stallions for stealing mares. But they didn't hesitate to capture them for their own mounts, or use the worst of the lot for hog feed, chicken feed, and dog food. They used the hair for mattresses, riatas, and hackamores. The hides made chair bottoms, floor coverings, water buckets, and clothing. Ranchers with the skill to capture them and the means to keep them corralled had used the wild herds to their advantage ever since the start of the migration west. It seemed to me things had balanced out more on the side of the ranchers than the mustangs.

* * *

I stayed in the cookhouse a while longer, listening to Clare spout a running commentary on the Sherwood family past and present, smoke from her cheroot twining upward to envelope flies clustered on the ceiling. Much of what she said was told in fun, all of it with kindness, except for remarks she made about Lance. It seemed he was the black sheep, "wild as a trapped coon."

When I returned to the cabin I spent the time worrying about Lance and fretting over the fact that Sam and the youngsters hadn't returned. My leg throbbed beyond enduring, so I took some laudanum. Then I dozed.

When I woke, rain pelted the shake roof with the thud of stones. Wind shrieked around the doorframe. I'd no sooner opened my eyes than the back door slammed open and boot heels punched across the kitchen floor. Hal strode into the parlor, his face a storm about to break.

"Those damned boys! Not home yet. I told Mike that if he was going to go skylarking around he'd have to come back in time to do the chores."

I sat up abruptly and jerked to my feet, wincing. A gust of wind squealed inside as I pulled open the door and watched the sky leak. Water dripped from the eaves in fits and starts. Beyond the yard, rain made a felty beat on the bare earth of the turn-around. Instinct gnawed at my stomach. Not a good time for Sam and Kitty to be out.

I turned back to pace, limping, in front of the Franklin stove. "Something's wrong. I'm sure of it."

"I know two boys who'll go without supper if they don't get back soon." Hal had dropped onto a chair of cowhide laced to a frame of steer horns, his legs stretched out before him, his head against the backrest, Stetson on his lap. A bald spot like a tonsure crowned his gray-brown hair. His jowly face and down-turned eyes resembled those of the stuffed moose behind him on the wall.

Hal was still grumbling. "I might even make those hooligans go without—" He broke off as the front door groaned open and slammed back on its hinges.

Mike Sherwood stepped into the room, dripping water from hat and coat, and forced the door shut against the wind.

"Where in the hell have you been?" Each of Hal's words hung in the air, given a punch rather than shouted, the impact more ominous than if he'd yelled.

Mike hung his wraps on hooks beside the door and stood with a hip slung out, a thumb in the pocket of his jeans. His gaze darted from the floor to his father and back to the floor. His brown eyes were lidded, unrevealing. "We've been looking for Kitty."

"Did you find her?"

"Nope."

The news struck me with the force of a sledgehammer. "She's lost?"

"'Fraid so. We went—"

Hal's thunder cut off the rest. "What sort of fool thing is that? Losing the girl?"

"You know how the country is around the Rocky Hills. All cut up." Mike edged over to the stove and stood beside me, his back to the warmth.

"Why in the devil did you go that far? You knew you were supposed to be back in time to do your chores. Now we've got a girl lost in the storm."

I added to the alarm. "We can't let her wander all night."

"Nothing else we can do ma'am," Mike said sheepishly. "We looked for her until it was plumb dark."

Anger and worry had gotten to Hal. He pushed off from the chair, yelling, "How in the blazes did you lose her in the first place?"

Mike shrugged. "I don't know. We kept seeing that stud off a ways. Each time we got close, he disappeared faster than a quarter at a poker game. Kitty, she wanted to keep chasing him. Lance said we should separate and try to trap him."

Lance said! He could have suggested that hoping she'd get lost.

"Where did you see her last?" I tried to keep suspicion from my voice.

"Near a hill that stuck up above all the rest. We were supposed to meet there if we couldn't find Chinook. Anybody could've found that hill ag—"

"Stupid idea," Hal said with a hiss. "That country can fool a person. Canyons go every which way." He paused as if struck by a sudden thought. "Where's your brother?"

"Feeding the horses."

"Let you face the music alone, did he? Sounds like Lance. I'll give him a piece of my mind." He started for the door.

Before he reached it the door swung open and another sodden rider stepped inside. This time it was Sam. The expression on his face matched Hal's.

"Where in tarnation did you kids go?" he asked Mike. "We were supposed to meet, remember? I waited for you till it was pitch black."

Mike repeated his explanation, flushing and stammering.

"Damned kids showed no judgment," Hal said. "Losing track of a girl in country she doesn't know. It fools even us, and we've been there a lot." He stepped toward the door. "We'll all ride out in the morning, take the hired hands. The bunch of us ought to find the girl." He turned to look at Mike accusingly. "Hope you realize you'll cost me a day. I'm already behind getting ready for roundup."

"No need for you to take time," Sam said. "I can find her. Maybe the boys can show me where they last saw her."

"I'm going too," I injected with force.

"What about your head?"

"It's fine," I lied. The leg was of more concern.

"I need Mike," Hal said hurriedly, "but I'll send Lance. He's not much help to me when he's in one of his sour moods. I'll send the roundup's bean master and his helper. They'll be riding in this evening. Nothing for them to do until roundup." He took hold of the door-knob. "We'd best get out to the cook-shack. Clare's already madder'n a hornet to be holding supper."

"Uh, Pa . . ." Mike said before his father could open the door. "Thought you ought to know. Chinook's got three mares with him. The extra one looks like that new mare of Farley Mead's. Guess he stole her, too."

"Damn! What next?"

Chapter 28

The rain pounded against the windows and drummed on the shake roof. Unable to sleep, I lay listening to the sky release its load of moisture. I hoped Kitty had found shelter. Not that she wasn't accustomed to suffering the rain—she worked outside in all kinds of weather—but rain added a miserable dimension as well as a chance for exposure that could lead to pneumonia. I stretched my imagination to its fullest, groping for possible reasons for her disappearance, but found none to ease my anxiety. I was so close to taking her into my home and offering her love that I couldn't bear the thought of losing her.

A hundred other worries nibbled like gnats at my peace of mind. I thought about Chinook, that elegant thoroughbred, confronting dangers that lurked in the wilds, running from men who might consider him an outlaw, his injuries open to infection. I worried about winter, soon to put its lock on the world, and about the countless repairs waiting at my place in the Bitterroot. I thought of the runt lamb, hoping she'd put on enough fat to survive the hounding winds. I thought about Kitty's crossbreeds, wondering if I could find pasture for them. And I had Carver Dean to consider. It shriveled my insides to think that leech would suck my livelihood once again, that he might tell others the dark secret from Ben's and my past.

Longing for sleep, I tried to let the monotonous pelting of the rain lull my senses. At home, when I wasn't worried about calves and lambs being born or hay to be gathered, rain seemed like music on the roof above my bed. Not on this night. Giving up on rest, I slipped Gabe's denim jacket over my flannel nightgown and went into the kitchen to boil a pot of coffee. Everyone else was abed. A blend of whistles, sputters, and grinding snores came from Hal's bedroom, not a sound from the boys' room upstairs.

I stoked the firebox with wood Hal had set on the scarred linoleum beside the stove, and while the fire took hold, I washed the teakettle and coffee-pot with a sliver of soap I found on the sinkstand. The fire would satisfy two needs, to heat coffee and to drive the damp chill from the room.

As I prepared the brew, I found myself thinking of Sam and needing his company. I couldn't imagine how the deep regard I held for him could have wormed its way through all the other feelings that had torn me apart of late, but I sensed it had a strong hold on me.

As if my thoughts had flown to the bunkhouse where Sam had made his bed, a few minutes later he stepped through the back door, wet as an otter. I caught the quick scent of pipe tobacco.

He stomped the mud from his boots, drawing sharp, quick breaths. "It's a beast out there," he said around the pipe stem.

"What you need is some coffee."

"Sounds good."

He hung his jacket on a hook beside the door and set his hat on the table. Beneath the white hat line, his face was burned a rich bronze from the high-altitude sun. He'd been a nice-looking man. Still was.

He ran long, tapered fingers through his grizzled hair. "I saw the light on. Figured somebody else couldn't sleep."

"I was worried about Kitty."

"Then we'll worry together." He pulled a chair from the table and sat with his long legs crossed at the ankles. The boots were not the ones he'd worn at the start of the trip. The leather in these was wrinkled, mellowed with age to the shade of rich old cedar. The dust in the creases had turned to mud.

I poured coffee into brown mugs that had started to craze and took a chair opposite Sam. He sucked on his pipe, drawing fragrant smoke from the bowl. I warmed my hands on my steaming cup. The old cast-iron stove radiated a bone-drying warmth for legs and feet.

Sam and I sat a while, thinking more things than we said. When we finally settled into conversation, we spoke first of the weather, of Hal Sherwood's generous hospitality, then of Kitty lost in the hills.

"I know the search will cost you more time." I cooled my coffee to blow away some of my regret. Sam didn't look up, but his shoulders lifted as if he were holding his breath to keep from saying something he'd rather not. "I just wanted you to know I'm sorry."

"Don't you worry about this old Texas lizard. It's just as much my fault. And Chinook's." He shot a sour look at the cup sitting on the table's chipped blue paint. "That stallion's getting to be more problem than he's worth."

I gave a wry smile. "I'd be glad to take him off your hands."

"Oh, no, you don't. I wanted him. I'll step in his manure if I have to."

That settled, we sat a while in the gray silence of the room. Sam stared at me from beneath hedgy brows and scratched the stubble that blackened his chin. I fiddled with the tail of my night braid, acutely aware of those melancholy gray eyes fixed on me. Though they were aimed my way, they saw, I thought, a different scene.

"Why are you staring at me?"

"Just thinking. Rose had a lot of red in her hair, too. Hers was darker though, kind of chestnut." He gave me another second's scrutiny. "Your face is sunnier, friendly to the world. Rose didn't let many people get to know her, just her theater friends." There was more sorrow in his voice than blame.

"*You* got to know her."

"That's the sad part. I don't know as I ever did. It was as if she was acting a part. She was good at that." He clasped his hands over his stomach, rubbing the thumbs together in thought.

"Weren't you happy together?"

"At first—you know how newlyweds are. She pretended to want what I wanted out of life. I was selfish. Didn't see the pretense. When the little ones came along, she kind of—oh, I don't know what you'd say—got tied up inside herself, acted like she'd been deprived of everything she'd dreamed of."

"Maybe she was."

He seemed to chew on that thought for a while. Light flickering from a cracked seam in the stove deepened the care lines that ridged his brow. "I tried to make amends, moved her to Denver and all. It didn't seem to make any difference. I think she liked playing the martyr. I got so I felt more resentful than sorry for her."

"Sometimes it's hard to tell who's the real martyr," I said, reflecting on my own bitter-sweet past. "Each person has to bend a little, has to meet the other half-way."

"Well . . . I suppose neither of us was good at that. But I'm learning." He looked up with an expression of quiet amusement, one common for him. Sometimes it was cynical. This time I thought it rose from humility.

Once more he fell silent, sucking on his pipe. The rain drummed on the roof. Tiny splatters came through a crack in the ceiling and landed on the stove with a sizzle.

"Did you and Ben get along?"

The question surprised me. It took me a while to reply, then with a shrug. "As well as most couples—better than some. There were moments when . . ." I thought of the stubborn devotion that had caused me to keep Ben's terrible secret over the years. I'd often wondered at the sanity of such a love, wondered if it was worth the cost to true contentment and peace of mind. Gabe's confession had added fuel to my doubts. "I suppose we loved each other more than we should, perhaps more than either of us deserved. We shared desperate times and made a good life for ourselves despite them, maybe because of them."

Why was I confessing all this? Because Sam had opened himself to scrutiny? Because I thought he was as entitled to explore my character as I was to invade his? Perhaps my feelings for him were nibbling at my defenses. Whatever the reason, the confessional had begun. Difficult to say where it would end.

"There weren't hard times for Rose and me," he said in a pensive way. "Not the kind you mean. Our problem was too much time apart."

"Sometimes distance helps."

"Not in our case." He took the pipe from his mouth and blew a ring of smoke toward the ceiling in a manner of regret. "Was Ben good to you?"

"In the way you mean. He was affectionate, generous. Never lifted a hand to strike me. But as I said, there were times . . ." I doubted I was ready to reveal my deepest pain in this bloodless guilt-letting. I changed direction. "It was hard for Ben to take adversity in stride. He hated to lose control. Hated it when things went wrong, hated it when something caused needless work."

"All of us men have some of that in us."

I nodded, recalling that particular quality in Sam during his confrontations with Gabe and Tendoy, recalled it in my father and brother. "Ben went beyond frustration. When he'd worked things out for himself, he'd follow his decisions whatever the cost to himself." And ultimately to me, I reminded myself with a pang of anger and regret.

"I imagine it was hard on you when he died."

I pulled my thoughts from those of blame and let them wind toward Ben's death. "I should have done more to ease his pain, though I don't know what. It seemed I was always making poultices, brewing special teas, massaging. I'd become so used to tending his needs, I felt at a complete loss when he died."

"I have that feeling, even though Rose and I were at the end of our tether."

I knew each of our hearts was lonely and afraid, and I wanted to say something about shared grief. I couldn't. Instead, we sat in the dusky room, me thinking my thoughts, Sam thinking his. On the edge of my musings, the range's firebox snapped in rhythm to the tick of the wall clock. A mouse skittered across the floor and darted beneath the door to the root cellar. The wind splattered rain pellets against the window.

I watched Sam's down-turned face grow more somber with each passing moment. His jaw firmed, his lips tightened under the mustache. His chest swelled in and out with the intensity of his breathing.

"I don't like to control other people's lives. Never wanted to control Rose, nor Jo." This new direction he'd taken resulted in a lower, near-furious cast to his voice. "I guess that's one reason Jo got to be so independent. The one time I put my foot down, it cost her . . ." As his face creased with remembered anguish, he put a hand over his lips to hide the fact he was close to tears.

When he went on, his voice shook with a mix of remorse and anger. "She wanted to marry the bastard! I said I wouldn't allow it. Told her I'd found him rolling in the hay with a neighbor gal. She wouldn't believe me. Said I'd lied because I didn't like the man. Said she was going to marry him whether I'd let her or not. She went tearing across the Platte on her horse to find him, the waters rumbling over the banks, sweeping half the county ahead of them. She couldn't . . ." His voice caught in his throat.

The outpouring had cost Sam a great deal emotionally. Despite his efforts, tears spilled over his eyelids and rolled down his cheeks into his mustache. He took out a handkerchief and blew his nose.

I wanted to comfort him, wanted to tell him despair would pass with time. A half-truth. My heartache of yesteryear still enveloped me like a cloak.

I reached across the table and rested my hand on his. It felt cold, despite the warmth of the stove. "Don't be so hard on yourself. You have a son. You're giving of yourself for his sake. That should count for something."

He looked up, flicking a damp, rueful smile. "It was Rob's idea. He could tell I was hurting, that I needed a way out."

"Tell me about Rob. What was he like as a boy?"

I'd hoped the question would turn Sam's mind from his self-blame, but it took time for his thoughts to switch direction. The result was a marked change in the pitch and volume of his voice. Not shattered nor furious now, but quiet, drawling.

"He was just a regular kid, special to me because he was my boy. Smart like his mother."

"Don't belittle yourself."

"'Spose I'm smart enough. Not as much education as I'd like. Sixth grade."

I let that pass. "How did Rob become a surveyor?"

"He never did take to ranching. Loves to ride, mind you." He raised a hand for emphasis. "We've had us some great trips into the Rockies." He smiled, obviously reflecting on those times. "Anyway, he studied engineering at the college in Fort Collins. Then his grandpa loaned him the money to start his own surveying business. He's done real well. The government contract will last several years."

"I imagine you're looking forward to spending time with him." He nodded, smiled. "When will he arrive in Montana?"

"April." He gave a *huh* of a laugh. "'Spect I'll have to put my nose to the grindstone, but it'll be good to be in the mountains. Here, a man feels free."

I thought about that, recalling an Indian-summer day in the Medicine Lodge. "There've been moments on this trip I've felt free and giddy as a jay, like I didn't have a problem in the world."

"I guess that's the bright side of all this. Got you onto a horse and into the mountains."

I hadn't thought of it that way, but it was true. If it hadn't been for Kitty and the horses, I'd never have seen the Medicine Lodge and wouldn't be sitting here with Sam. In that moment of discovery, that opening of a life

I'd refused and now accepted, I realized I'd caught the thread of something I'd forgotten and had begun to weave it into my heart's cloth and into my vision of what might be.

In my mind's eye, I saw Kitty and myself in the Bitterroot, content in each other's company, the herd of crossbreeds frisking through the fields, lively and sleek. The picture remained in my mind until a different scene jolted me back to reality. I saw Kitty, lying prostrate on a mountain-top, shivering, sodden from the storm, perhaps injured from a fall, or lifeless, and felt a sudden dropping of my heart.

Sam studied me over the rim of his cup. "Why are you crying?"

"Kitty."

"We'll find her. Don't you worry." He drank the last of his coffee and set the cup down with a loud clack. "Seems to me you've taken on too much to help your brother. Accepting the herd and the responsibility for Kitty."

"I want Kitty. I've wanted her for years."

"Guess I can understand that. No children of your own."

No children of my own? If only he knew. Wretchedness poured from my heart as it had many times in the last week.

Sam scraped his chair across the floor to sit beside me and patted my arm. "There, there. She's all right. That little niece of yours has spunk."

I turned toward him, quaking, my face contorted with misery. "She's not my niece, Sam. She's mine. My own child."

Chapter 29

Sam's cheeks slackened. For a moment he was speechless. "Kitty yours? She calls you Aunt Jess."

"I told her just two days ago. She doesn't believe me. I didn't know until I was about to leave the Centennial. Gabe confessed on his deathbed."

More bewilderment on Sam's part along with a trace of suspicion.

"It was none of my doing." Moisture spurted from my eyes.

"Now, Jessie." Sam patted my hand and clucked his tongue. "Want to tell me about it? You listened to my dark secrets. It helps." Then with a brittle grin, "Kinda like a dose of castor oil."

I considered that with unwanted amusement while I tried to control the spasms that balled my stomach. I'd kept the circumstances of Kitty's birth hidden in the pockets of my soul for so long, the telling would not be easy. Like prying away the bars of a prison.

I began slowly, hesitantly, forcing the words from my lips. "Kitty's father had a room at my boarding-house in Dillon . . . Hubert, a mining engineer. A strange man. More intelligent than most. Ruthless in some respects. I could tell he liked me more than he should. I gave him no encouragement and avoided him as much as possible—not easy in a boarding house. I think he was lonely. The town was new, there weren't many women." I paused, filled with a loathing I'd banned from memory.

Sam sat on the edge of his chair, holding my hand, the feel of his palm warm now, comforting. "Did he force the issue?" I nodded. "You gave in?"

"Of course I didn't! I-I was terrified. How could you think me that—that loose?"

"It's not always a matter of being loose. Circumstances sometimes . . ." He gave an apologetic shrug. "I'm sorry. Go on."

After a shudder of reluctance I continued slowly, deliberately. "Ben had left the smithy in charge of his helper for a month and gone prospecting with a mining partner, Carver Dean." I swallowed to rid my mouth of the name's putrid taste. "One night, just before they returned, I'd gone to bed and forgotten to lock the door to my room. Hubert came in . . . I couldn't stop him from . . ." How could I go on telling the story to a man? I'd never even told a woman.

Sam, too, seemed embarrassed. He averted his eyes and shook his head. "Jessie, I don't need to hear this."

"You said it would help."

"Yeah, but it's sort of like twisting a knife."

"Let it twist. The canker's been growing inside me for too long. If you don't mind listening. If you won't think me evil."

"I'd never think you evil." The squint lines quickened into an expression of tenderness.

I hesitated, digging deep for the courage to go on. "I tried to stop Hubert, tried to scream, but he stuffed a cloth in my mouth. He even . . . he even had a knife." The memory of the sharp steel at my throat affected me like a cold wind from the north. I bit my lips to stifle the image.

"Bastard!" Sam firmed his grip on my hand. "Did you go to the sheriff?" The question seemed a way to eliminate further details. I was glad.

"He would have accused me of being a whore, of bringing it on myself. A woman has no credence in such matters. Not with the law. Not even with her husband." I paused to calm the breath that pulled at my lungs.

"Ben must have wanted to kill the man."

The reality of the statement clamped onto my throat. All the years of keeping mute sealed my lips. Yet I wanted desperately to purge myself of the secret that had haunted my days. I told myself I had nothing to fear. Ben was no longer with me, no longer subject to the law.

I began warily, certain Sam would think the worst of me. "I didn't tell Ben the day he returned from his trip. He might have thought me unclean, unfit to be his wife. You know how men are."

The planes of Sam's face drew tight. He scratched a cheek. "I'd like to think I would have been different. But who's to say? We male animals don't like our territory violated." A pause. "When did you tell Ben?"

"I didn't. That night he found Hubert's handkerchief under our bed and went into a rage. He climbed the stairs to tell Hubert he had to move out. Next morning . . . when I went to clean Hubert's room, I . . ." I put my hand at my forehead to fight a sudden dizziness. I felt as if I'd dissolve into the wooden chair.

"It's all right," Sam murmured. "You don't need to go on."

"I do. I've waited too long." I drew a deep breath to clear my head and continued in a trembly voice. "I found Hubert hanging by the neck. There was a suicide note on the dresser. It told of an unrequited love, no name of the loved one. I was devastated. I blamed myself until . . ."

"It was justice where Hubert was concerned, I'd say."

I shook my head in grim dissent. "The sheriff called it suicide. I wish it had been that simple." I stared absently at the creaking stove, seeing the frightful scene on the heat-whitened metal. The scent of burnt pine that lingered on the edge of my awareness became the smell of coal smoldering on Hubert's grate. Rather than the stove-pipe that shoved an elbow through the ceiling, I saw Hubert, hanging limp from his belt, his head jerked to one side, his face ashen.

I squeezed my eyes shut on the image for a brief second, then hurried on with the tale, letting the words tumble out to be rid of them. "I found a button from one of Ben's shirts on the floor—a wooden button he'd made himself—he liked wooden buttons. There must have been a struggle. Later, I found the button missing from his shirt and sewed another in its place."

"What did Ben say when you confronted him?"

"I didn't. Our marriage was strained as it was. I never told him I knew."

Sam sucked in a lungful of air and held it while he rubbed his fingers along his wide, drooping mustache. "Maybe they fought when Ben told Hubert to leave. Ben might have threatened to turn him over to the law. Hubert hung himself after that."

"I wish it were so. Hubert was a cad, but no coward. He came into the kitchen in the wee hours of the morning, needing matches. I couldn't sleep and had gone to fix myself some tea. He left without saying a thing. Ben must have followed him upstairs."

"Seems circumstantial. What about the suicide note?"

"Printed. Carefully. Too carefully. Hubert had written checks for his rent and written me notes. He never printed."

For a while we sat without speaking. Sam still held my hand, rubbing his thumb over my skin. My story had erased all expression from his face. His eyes held no clue to his feelings.

"It must have been hard on you to keep the secret all these years."

"I loved Ben, though his act of murder and his—" I caught myself before I revealed an even darker secret, "though it lessened my love. He'd killed a man to avenge my honor. I was as much to blame for Hubert's death as he. I might as well have helped to slip the belt around his neck."

"Don't blame yourself. You've gone through enough." Sam stared at me, frowning. "I take it no one ever found out."

"Ben's mining partner, Carver Dean, knew. He had a room next to Hubert's and heard me scream. He was there before anyone else. I was stooping to pick up the button."

A nod of understanding. "He'd seen it on Ben's shirt."

"I made excuses for it being in the room, but Carver didn't believe me. Despicable man. He'd long suspected Hubert's interest in me."

"Despicable? I'd say he was a loyal friend. He could have turned Ben over to the sheriff."

"Loyal, no. Greedy, yes. Ben never said anything to me, but I'm sure Carver used the secret as a sword over Ben's head. Ben bought all of the equipment to work their claims and stood the cost of the trips. He brought less and less of his earnings home from the smithy. Then Carver talked Ben into selling the shop so they could work the claims on Ruby Creek full time."

I continued in bitter remembrance of those winters on the creek. "As soon as the first snows fell, Carver would go south and leave Ben in charge of the diggings. I tried to take care of him, kept him from the sluice boxes as much as I could, but Ben didn't like to be babied. When his hands got so crippled from the ice water he couldn't work, Carver sold him the land in the Bitterroot. At an exorbitant price. I found the bill of sale in Ben's wallet after he died." I'd revealed all I'd cared to about Carver Dean. The telling of the murder had been enough. It'd wrung the life from me. I leaned an elbow on the table to hold my head aloft and felt my temples throb.

Sam shifted on the chair. His shoulders raised on a groan of dismay. "I hope Ben deserved your loyalty."

"In most ways he did."

"Kitty is Hubert's child, then."

I nodded.

"How can you be sure?"

"Ben had been gone for a month. When he found out about Hubert, he stayed away from my bed."

A rueful smile tightened Sam's lips. "He must have known when he saw you . . . I can imagine how he felt about you carrying Hubert's child."

"He wanted me to—to deal with it. I wouldn't, though at first I hated the seed growing inside me as much as Ben did. As the months passed, and my body bloomed with new life, I came to love it as if it were Ben's child. He didn't. He hated it more as time passed. He drew inside himself and would seldom speak. We were like two strangers living together. I could hardly stand it." I dropped my gaze, recalling those dark days. The little strength that remained drained away.

"How did Kitty end up with Gabe?"

Even more than the circumstances of Hubert's death, the events surrounding Kitty's birth tore my feelings to shreds. How could I speak of it?

Sam waited for my answer. I gave none. "Ben wouldn't let you keep her?"

"I—I didn't know at the time. It wasn't until Gabe was on his deathbed that I learned the truth."

"How could you not have known?"

I stared at the wall, aflicker with lamplight, and saw emblazoned on it that night of the birth. Not as I recalled it—I'd been too near death for that—but as Gabe had described it to me.

"I almost died giving birth. There were complications. I was delirious for several days. During that time, Gabe's wife gave birth to a stillborn child. She'd been in labor two days. Ben thought it a way to rid himself of a child he despised. He and Gabe conspired . . ." For a moment I thought I couldn't possibly continue. My lips trembled. Sam waited patiently. "Amy lost consciousness when the child was born. She didn't know it was dead. Ben conspired with Gabe to make a switch. They buried Amy's child as mine and put Kitty at Amy's breast. I was too ill to . . ." I couldn't go on.

"Did Amy know who the child was?"

"No. Amy was a dear, a wonderful mother. I don't blame her."

Sam shook his head sadly, said nothing.

"I despised Gabe when he told me. I wanted to—God help me—I

wanted to strangle him. I ranted and railed until some of the hate left me. Gabe wept like a baby."

Sympathy creased Sam's face. His eyes glassed with moisture. "Why didn't you tell Kitty sooner?"

"When Gabe told me, she'd already run off with the horses. You know how grieving and rebellious she was when we found her. It didn't seem the time. I decided to wait until we were on the trail. Then something came up that forced the truth from me. Kitty was furious, unbelieving. I think she hates me all the more for it." I flipped my hand toward the dark unknown. "Now I might never win her over. She's out there. Heaven knows where."

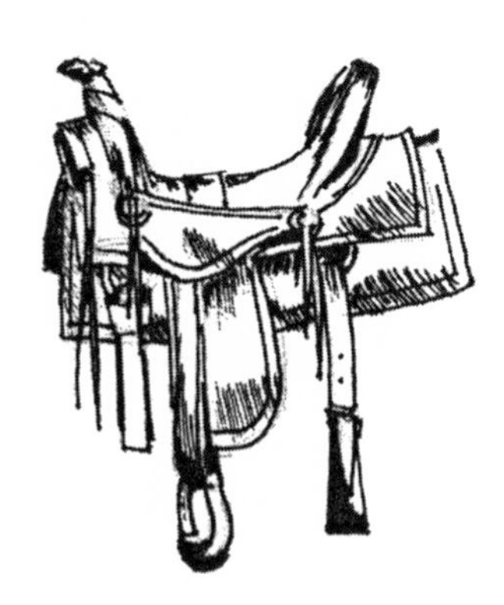

Chapter 30

When the five of us rode out from Sherwood's ranch, an omen of the coming winter shivered on the air. Nearly three weeks had passed since I'd left the Bitterroot, October just around the bend. The wind had driven the heavy, udder-shaped clouds of last night from the valley and left dusky brown clouds in the shape of bird's wings hovering over the peaks of the Pioneer Range. The sky was cold and withdrawn, a pale gray. An angry glow remained in the east where the rising sun had disappeared behind a thin cloud layer. The rest of the sky was sullen under the leaden grayness. It acted as a hand held above the eyes, increasing the visibility at ground level. The wintry sky forecast snow.

Mist rose from tiny creeks, where the frosty air breathed across them. Ice fringed their banks. The loss of warmth from the earth was like the slowing of one's heartbeat. It dampened the inner processes that warmed body and soul.

The horses sensed the change in the weather. They'd balked at being saddled and bit each other. Now they danced about and wanted to run. It was difficult to hold them in. My sore leg gave me fits from rubbing against Bannack's hide. Sam would send me back to Sherwood's if he knew. At breakfast he'd watched me as secretly as he could, his eyes filled with a subtle mix of anxiety and caring that resulted from our night of confession. Now, when he wasn't watching, I draped the leg across the horse's withers and rode with one foot in the stirrup. The swollen knee wouldn't tolerate the bend for long, and I let the leg hang loose for a while.

One thing about the cold, it demanded one's attention. No room to reflect on yesterday's happenings. It took all one's efforts to stay warm. I was thankful for the gloves I'd found in the pockets of Gabe's fleece jacket, and thought about Kitty in her denims. Last night I'd fretted about her getting wet; now I worried about her freezing. Enough to gray one's hair in a twinkling—find Kitty before she turned to ice, find Chinook before some trigger-happy ranch hand put a bullet through his heart. The fact Lance and the roundup cook had tucked rifles in their saddle scabbards heightened the worry. We all carried revolvers to signal when we sighted Kitty or Chinook—one shot into the air. Rifles seemed unnecessary, unless the owners had other intentions.

Since Lance knew the country best, he'd planned the strategy for the search. In between sarcastic comments about outlaw horses and girls who got themselves lost, he told us the outfit would fan out, an eighth of a mile between each rider, and head southeast over the flats and jumbled hills to intercept Kitty or Chinook if they'd headed back from that direction.

It was eleven o'clock when we reached the knob where the searchers were supposed to have met yesterday afternoon. Lance pointed out the spot where he'd last seen Kitty and Chinook and indicated the direction of a roundup catch-corral into which we hoped to drive Chinook and the mares. We separated to make a wide circle through the broken ridges and valleys, planning to return eventually to the bristly knob if we found nothing.

The splintered landscape allowed little chance to keep others in sight, a fact that had undoubtedly led to Kitty's disappearance. Evidently Sam was afraid I too would lose my way. He insisted on riding a path that paralleled mine by a hundred yards or less. For that I was grateful. If I happened to find Kitty injured, I'd need help. We headed southeast, Lance a quarter-mile or more to our right. The rest spread out due east.

Thus far we'd encountered large herds of longhorns, the soil ground to powder by their hoofs and pelted into slick puddles by last night's rain. It was impossible to tell horse tracks from the prints of cattle. As we approached a barrier ridge that walled the badlands from the flats we'd just crossed, we saw fewer cattle, more wildlife among the scattered juniper and pine. Deer trails criss-crossed the hillsides. Pellets lay on the ground, some so fresh they steamed. Two bucks, their necks swollen for the rutting season, challenged each other, pawing up the sod, trapping their antlers together. Other bucks rubbed the velvet from their antlers on the rough limbs of juniper. Flocks of bluebirds and robins on their way south had stopped to feed on the berries.

Toward the top of the ridge we crossed the muddied tracks of a large horse herd. As far as we could tell, they were unshod mustangs. Several sets of hoofprints in the shelter of trees were not as affected by the rain. They told a different story. Two were unshod, three shod—a large print, three middle-sized ones, and a small shod print that could have been Trixie's. It seemed possible Kitty had come upon the small group, at least seen the tracks, and followed them.

The hoofprints led us up the rocky ridge and over a bare saddle. Coyotes, a couple of wolves, and a canine of in-between size, possibly Penny, had followed the horses' trail. The wandering tracks of a huge sow bear and two cubs appeared here and there. They zigzagged across the crest of the ridge, seemingly without direction, from rocky outcrop to bristle of timber, to trough of boulders, and back again. The bears had left scat that carried traces of rodent hair and the hulls of juniper berries. I saw where the sow had overturned rocks and punky yellow logs in her search for grubs and other creatures that liked dark places. A fresh scattering of dirt showed where she'd dug into a ground squirrel's tunnel.

The saddle opened onto an easy slope covered with sage and tall, browning grass, its broad sweep broken by juniper and thickets of stunted aspen. Just below the saddle, the horse prints divided. Those of the wild herd forked to the right, keeping to the crest of the ridge. The smaller group headed straight downward, following terraces that dipped gently toward a dark furrow in the landscape.

Sam and I sat motionless for a while to consider the situation and to let our mounts blow. A cold, fickle wind filled the air with the smell of autumn grass, of juniper and sage. There was a strong odor of deer. Now and then the wind flushed the scent of cedars from beyond the terraces where the natural staircase dropped into a canyon.

We descended the gentle steps until they ended in a bench that stretched from one deep gulch entering from the right to another entering from the left. The gulches met at the foot of the bench to form the canyon. Prospect holes pocked the rocky fringes of the bench. In the middle of the flat, tipi rings looked like giant bracelets in the grass.

Sam swung an arm to indicate direction. "Think I'll cut over to the right so I can look down into that gulch. You can do the same with that one coming in from the left. We can circle around and meet at the foot of the bench. See that outcrop in the middle, with the pine on top?" I nodded. "That's a good spot. I'll see you there in a little while."

"Same signal if we find anything?"

"Yeah, one shot if it's Kitty. Not if it's Chinook. You might spook him. Just come to the meeting place and we'll plan a strategy to catch him or drive him to the corral." He reined the sorrel around. "Remember there's a bear around. If you see her, give her a wide berth. And stay in sight as much as possible."

I would have followed Sam's advice, but a series of rocky spines cut between me and the rim of the gulch, blocking my path. I'd need to travel three or four hundred yards to skirt above them. A shorter route led through a boggy spring, at its base a copse of stunted aspen. The aspen would take me from Sam's view, but that route would save considerable time.

Bannack gave a little jump when he felt the bog's spongy soil give way beneath his feet. He heaved and humped through the mire, lurched over tussocks of grass and moss.

The main arm of the bog oozed down from a source near the rim and entered the aspen thicket. Another, shallower, arm made a turn around the upper side of the grove and continued a ways down the bench. We were crossing the shallow arm a few yards down from the turn when we saw her. I had an instant, mind-shattering impression that froze my blood—a huge cinnamon-colored sow bear with two half-grown cubs. The cubs were chasing each other through clumps of short willow on the edge of the aspen thicket. The sow's round rump was toward us, her feet sunk into the mud, her massive head bent over a mossy tussock, munching something. When she turned her muzzle, I saw her lips wrinkle from the taste of her meal.

Her putrid smell crazed Bannack. He tossed his head, snorted, and leaped sideways, sinking into the bog.

His snorting brought the sow's head around. She gave a sharp woof, sending the cubs into the thicket, and turned to face us. At first she stood four-square, sniffing the air, focusing her poor eyesight on us. Then she rose on her hind legs, waved her snout, and sniffed.

As she reared, I noted a carcass lying on the ground at her feet, slightly larger than a coyote, a hole in the skull, the back strap gnawed free of flesh. Not much left but bare bones and strips of black and white fur.

Oh, Lord! Penny?

At first doubt, then certainty. We'd tracked Trixie to the area. Penny would have been with her.

My chest caved with a mix of outrage and grief. A terrible rage boiled up within me. I drew the revolver. I wanted to kill this horrid thing that had desecrated the dog. Wanted to stop her from destroying again.

The only safe place to shoot a bear was in the head, and there was no certainty she'd die immediately from that. I'd heard of bears shot several times who'd charged and maimed the man holding the gun. A wounded bear was twice the danger.

My heart stopped a second in fear, then sprang forward with rage that flowed along my arm to the finger poised on the trigger.

Bannack's heaving and humping made it impossible to aim the gun. I slid around in the saddle, trying to keep my balance while he lurched through the mud, frantic to reach the far side of the bog. He was about to get a purchase on dry ground when the sow charged.

She hurtled toward us with the speed of a locomotive, splattering mud in the air. The bellowing mouth held me transfixed. The tongue showed red, the teeth sharper than a ripsaw. Fright drenched my scalp with sweat. The savage part of me shoved aside fear, wanting to kill the beast. The gentler half thought of the cubs—they needed their mother.

I was still clinging desperately to Bannack's humping back when the bear swerved abruptly and circled back to where she'd started. A test run, calculated to scare us off—or to taunt us while she decided whether it was worth the effort to attack.

Bannack didn't wait to find out. On dry ground now, he stretched his legs full length, putting distance between us and the bear. I glanced over my shoulder and saw the bear follow a short ways, then stop to watch us. Next time I checked, she'd turned back and was lumbering into the thicket.

When I reached the rim of the gulch, I reined Bannack to a stop. There, I could slow my breathing and the angry, frightened racing of my heart.

Though I tried, I couldn't shake the image of Penny's ravaged carcass. What worse death than to have a bear clamp its razor-teeth onto one's skull, to have its hot, smelly breath accompany one into oblivion? I could only hope she'd died instantly.

I preferred to remember Penny as I'd last seen her, offering an easy grin and wag of the tail. Intensely loyal. Protective. Cattle and horses could give her the slip, but she'd been a joy.

I sat longer than I should, suffering spasms of grief. If I was to make a successful search for Kitty and Chinook, I'd need a clear mind. I tried to shove Penny and the bear from mind, tried to force calm into my veins.

Comparative calm brought a sudden jolt of panic and a blinding bolt of despair. If the bear had killed Penny, perhaps she'd . . . I shriveled at the thought. I had to find Kitty, had to make sure she hadn't met the same fate.

Sam had reached the far side of the bench and was heading up the rim away from me, studying the ground as if he'd seen tracks. I gathered my feelings as best I could, stroked Bannack to reassure him, and headed down the rim of the left-hand gulch, scanning the rocky draw below us, pausing now and then to look over my shoulder toward the aspen grove.

When I reached the foot of the bench, I reined Bannack toward the outcrop of rock, following the lip for a view of the timbered canyon. I was surprised to find the bench didn't drop abruptly. Instead, another series of open terraces descended to an aspen meadow before they plunged into the canyon.

Directly below us, a wire-grass spring spilled rivulets down the hillside to collect in the meadow as a tiny creek. Scattered cottonwoods and aspens grew along the creek, protecting its banks. A hundred yards east of the creek, a group of four horses stopped their grazing to lift their heads. One was larger, sleeker than the rest, all of them dark in the gray light of the impending storm. Chinook and the mares.

When they wheeled and stood facing the west, I thought the horses had seen me, but my binoculars showed them standing stiff-legged, ears pricked forward, eyes turned toward the trees growing along the creek.

I turned the binoculars toward the creek and saw Lance's black and white pinto tied within a clump of aspen. What I saw next sent a hot wave of anger up my spine. Lance stood in the fringe of trees, rifle at his shoulder, the barrel propped in the crotch of a limb. He was aiming at the horses. He must have known he'd find them there and had circled around ahead of us.

Chapter 31

Outrage over Penny still simmered in my veins. The sight of Lance intent on killing Chinook fueled it into a boil. My mind locked on two purposes—one, stop Lance from firing; two, spook Chinook from harms way.

I fired my revolver in the air and cried in a half-yell, half-yodel, "Ai-ai-ai-ai-ai!" The savage yodeling filled the basin with its fiendish sound, echoed from gulch to gulch, and shrieked on down the canyon. It startled Chinook and the mares into a milling run.

Alarmed by the explosion at his ear, Bannack tossed his head and pulled on the reins. I turned him in a tight circle and nudged him with my heels. As we charged down the slope toward the trees, I fired my revolver and continued my fierce yodeling.

A few longhorns tore from the trees and scattered into the canyon. A bull snorted onto the bench. Chinook was about to disappear into the left-hand gulch.

The report of a rifle slammed into my ears and clawed at my nerves. Dirt spit from the rim of the gulch, a few feet from Chinook. Another missed shot roared across the badlands.

A look toward the grove told me Sherwood's black sheep was about to escape. In running for his pinto, he'd tripped on an exposed root and was groping for his rifle in the underbrush.

I reined Bannack to a stop behind him and aimed the revolver at his back. "Stay where you are!"

"Who's gonna make me?" Rifle in hand, he leaped to his feet and ran into the open to skirt the trees.

I sent a bullet thudding into the ground beside him.

"You ain't gonna shoot me," he said on the run. "You're too chicken."

He was right, I had no stomach for killing. But I didn't mind using a whip. I knew how from the many times I'd driven the bull to pasture. I holstered my revolver and pulled on the thong that kept the snake whip coiled on my saddle. Taking a firm grip on the stock, I raised the whip over my shoulder.

There was a loud crack as I lashed out with the braided rawhide. It coiled around Lance, binding his arms to his sides. He grabbed the popper with one of his fists and gave it a jerk. I held tight to the stock as I slid from Bannack.

In the second it took my feet to touch the ground, Lance spun away from me, letting the whip drop from his waist. I gathered in the rawhide and sent it humming through the air. Again it coiled around the running boy.

"You got no damned right to do this."

"Just giving you what a killer deserves."

"That stud's a pest. Deserves to die."

"Like Kitty."

"What d'you mean?"

"You didn't try to find her." Accusation growled in my throat. "You wanted her to spend the night in the wilds. I found her dog. Killed by a bear. It might've killed—" Several shots and excited whinnies from the head of the gulch Sam was following brought my attention around. Had he shot? If so, at what? One shot would have meant he'd found Kitty. There were too many for that.

Lance seized the moment to spin out of the whip, then sped along the edge of the grove toward the shadowy form of the horse tied within the trees. I sliced the air with the rawhide. The popper snapped against Lance's shoulders. He cried out, stumbled.

I caught up to him before he could rise. "Tell me what you know about Kitty or I'll give you the whipping of your life."

He staggered to his feet, swearing. "The dumb busybody deserved it. Ought to keep her nose out of other people's business."

"Deserved what?"

He made a move to leave. I cracked the popper at his feet.

He ran a hand under his leaking nose. Wind-reddened eyes shot me a surly look that ended with a murky smile. "I sliced into the cinch a ways."

I knew what he'd intended. The cinch would have broken after a few hours' ride. When it did, the saddle would have slid from the horse. Kitty might have hit her head, even broken her neck. Rage flared in my eyes and clogged my throat.

Lance started for his horse on a run. I followed, a madwoman, lashing out again and again with the whip, the sound like picket fire. I'd allow time for Lance to regain his feet and start off, then I'd raise the whipstock over my head and lash out again, letting the rawhide deliver my outrage. My shoulder muscles and the ligaments around my ribs threatened to tear loose from the force of my thrusts. Sweat dampened my armpits.

Twice the popper struck Lance's thigh, snapping blood onto his jeans. Each time it struck, he stumbled, swore. "Stop it! Damn you!"

When he darted into the trees to untie the pinto, I gathered in the whip and let him haul himself into the saddle. "You're a disgrace to your father," I said with rasping breath. Then, as the boy cleared the trees and galloped into the open, "Don't ever show your face to me again."

By the time I'd whistled in Bannack and mounted, Lance had turned up the terraced slope that led to the bench. I followed to make certain he left the area. When we reached the pine-studded outcrop, I reined Bannack in, hoping I'd seen the last of the rascal. The bear bolstered that wish. As Lance swung across the bench and headed toward her thicket, she exploded from the trees, bellowing, and chased him along the rim of the gulch into the rows of spiny ridges. Last I saw of him, he was bent over his horse's neck, holding on for dear life, the irate bear on his tail.

I stayed there for a moment, trying to slow my heaving chest. As the heat of anger drained away, my conscience came alive to the fact I'd horsewhipped a man. Maddened to think someone would do evil to a girl. My girl. I'd lost my head.

The brief insanity had left me limp, dazed, aware once more of the pain grinding in my leg. The weather was closing in. The wind that had swirled aimlessly all afternoon had settled into a west wind and was rising. It froze the sweat that dampened my forehead. The leaden sky that swallowed-up life had taken on the form of thousands of woolly-backed sheep. Snow clouds. A flake fell on my glove and melted. I looked up and saw more flakes falling, large, like fluffs of goose down. I had to find Kitty before snow covered all traces.

How could I leave without knowing why Sam had shot or how he fared? With a welling up of tenderness, I knew I cared terribly what happened to him. I knew I loved him and that nothing would be the same again. But I loved Kitty as well, with the deep, abiding love of a mother deprived. If she died, part of me would die with her. I felt torn in a hundred directions. I wished Gabe had never become ill, that I'd never left the Bitterroot. I wished to heaven this nightmare was just that, a dream.

* * *

The sky was falling around my shoulders. A time for decision. I reasoned that if Kitty was following Chinook before she disappeared, she wouldn't have dropped into the timbered canyon. Horses preferred the open, where they could see danger approach. I set my course to the northeast. I'd cross the gulch into which Chinook had fled, then continue across the maze of hogbacks and ragged draws that scored the land.

Typical of arctic storms that roared down from Canada and joined ugly weather that blew in from the Pacific, the west wind that had ruffled Bannack's mane and stung my nose a few minutes earlier had slid into a fierce northwester that howled in at an angle and cut through my trousers to the skin. Bannack turned feisty and hard to manage. His nervous hoofs clacked on the freezing ground. When the wind tried to snatch my hat, I took the bandana from around my neck, rolled it diagonally, lay it across the crown of my hat, and tied it under my chin.

The snow had changed to tiny pellets, blown horizontally. They bit my face and burned. One violent gust nearly blew me from the saddle. Bannack threw back his head and jerked on the reins.

I stroked his neck. "Easy, boy. Easy. No time to panic."

The next blast sent Bannack sideways onto his knees. At the same time, a muffled squeal split the thick air. Four horses loomed in the mist, blurry humps in the blowing white, a lighter gray than the snow-whipped cedars—Chinook and his mares, their coats speckled with snow. My heart raced at the sight of them, so close, yet like ghosts in that obscure world. Their tails whipped between their legs as they trotted off. They were going downhill to the northeast. I wondered why they weren't running with the wind, as horses were prone to do. Perhaps they were taking a familiar path, one they'd followed yesterday. It might lead me to Kitty.

Bannack had regained his feet and was stumbling through the slippery snow. I angled him into the wind, urging him in the direction Chinook and the mares had taken. They were lost from sight, their tracks blown over with fresh snow.

Bannack hesitated. I dug my knees into his ribs. "Come on, boy. Keep going." The wind tore the words from my lips and sent them flying into the snow, clouds, and mist that shrouded the landscape.

We plodded on, snow plastering our windward sides. Nothing. No sign. No tracks. Nothing but smothering white.

I had a frantic sense it was useless to go farther. If I did, I was certain to lose my way. I'd search for Kitty and Chinook as soon as it cleared, before the wolves and coyotes left their dens. In the meantime, I'd find shelter from the storm. But where? The wind was searching out every nook and cranny. I could see only a few feet ahead of me. We'd crossed several gulches since we'd left the bench. Now we descended into another. In the bottom, the gusts swirled in every direction, making it impossible to determine the angle of the wind.

I was chilled through to the bone. My teeth chattered and ached. My body shook. Ice coated my cheeks. They felt as if they were freezing. I bent low, shielding my face and eyes against the blizzard.

It was impossible to see where we were going, nothing but swirling snow. I reasoned if Bannack caught a familiar scent on the wind, he'd find the way. I eased up on the reins and touched my heels to his side. He plunged through the drifted snow in leaps as if he were hobbled, up one slope, down into another draw. Discouraged, unsure which way to go, he stood with his sides heaving, blowing plumes of foggy breath. The whining wind drove into us from all directions.

I leaned forward and patted his neck. "That's all right, boy. Rest a while." My breathy words made puffs in the air that were immediately tattered by the screaming wind.

Though barely heard, my voice must have comforted the horse. He dragged himself up another slope and into the open, into the merciless snow-wind battering in from the northwest. I knew I should stop. It would be better to stay in one spot and let Sam come looking for us. But how would he know where to look? Besides, he might have problems of his own. I considered holing-up in the next draw, huddling against Bannack for his warmth, but then I realized we might be drifted over with snow, smothered, frozen to death.

Feeling swallowed and lost, I kept bending my mind toward Kitty, needing my help. I'd promised to care for her. Wanted it desperately. Now I might never have the chance.

Chapter 32

Ben had always said survival began in the mind. I closed my frosted eyelids and tried to relax, told myself I'd be all right, that I'd find my way. *Just keep moving.* I'd studied the map that morning and knew if I kept the wind at the right angle, I'd eventually reach Grasshopper Creek and the town of Bannack. If the wind changed direction it could throw me off course.

The cold had clawed deeper. It had even cooled the fire in my leg. My brain was numb. I had no idea how far we'd strayed, or how long we'd been gone. It seemed an eternity. There was less light, the day drawing toward evening.

In places, the gale had scoured the ground to bare earth. In others it had piled the snow into drifts as high as a man's waist. Bannack plowed through one drift, stumbled into what appeared to be a wash, and fell. I pitched forward over his head and had to flail around in the snow to right myself. The cold had stiffened my injured leg, the swelling tight against my jeans. I doubted I could climb into the saddle. If I walked, I might stay warmer, though my riding boots would give little protection against the cold.

Get moving, Jessie. You can't stand here until dark.

I brushed balled snow from my jacket, pulled my hat into place, and with Bannack's steamy breath on my neck, wallowed out of the swirling snow and mist to the top of the wash. The wind shrieked and howled violence, driving the snow in one horizontal direction. As I angled into it, I had to turn my face aside. I could hardly breathe. I hadn't the faintest idea where I was going, but I had to move or freeze to death. I'd known ranchers who'd frozen to death trying to reach their barn after feeding cattle, heard of travelers turned to icicles in their wagons. I'd heard of people sleeping themselves to death. Not from exhaustion, but from the hypnotic spell of the drifting snow.

Keep moving, Jessie!

I did for a while, shoulders hunched, teeth clenched. My good leg had turned wooden. I dropped into what must have been a swamp or a creek and slugged through icy water that rose to my knees.

The blizzard eased a bit as I climbed from the wet, allowing a glimpse of furry shapes in the white. They resembled a picture I'd seen of a misty group of polar bears. The dampened sound of their movements and their snorting trembled in the air, then blew away on a fresh gale.

Bannack nickered in answer to faint whinnies, pulled free of my weak grip on the reins, and disappeared into the storm.

"Bannack, come back here!" The words seemed to go no farther than my lips. "Bannack, come here!" Useless to call. The horses had moved beyond my ability to see or hear.

Again I felt swallowed, lost to everything that breathed, that pulsed with life. Despair fixed my mind on Kitty. She was out there somewhere, needing me. Of what use to survive this ordeal if I lost her?

I started off again, shaking all over, teetering on my feet. I could no longer feel the cold. The stinging white pellets seemed to have penetrated my skull. They swirled in my head like the winter scene in a glass paperweight. I dropped onto the drifted snow, lulled by a great need to sleep.

I don't know how long I'd lain there when a chesty whicker dragged me from my snowy sleep. Soft lips mouthed the upturned collar of my jacket and the soggy brim of my hat. They brushed saliva against my cheek. I opened my watery eyes onto the frosted muzzle of a horse, the nostrils blowing steam. Our foggy breaths joined and swirled around us. Bannack? The voice was too deep. No bridle on this horse; instead it wore a halter with a rope three feet long, frayed on the end as if it had broken. If not Bannack, then who? My head swam, too fogged to consider the possibilities.

Another whicker, two firm nudges on my shoulder. The horse seemed to sense I shouldn't stay huddled in the snow. My spirits lifted to know something living stood at my side, offering help, telling me not to lie there, not to let myself freeze to death. Using the rope, I pulled myself to my feet and let the horse drag me blindly along on my wooden legs. Nearby whinnies sliced through the storm. The horse answered.

It was nearly dark now. Little light reflected off the snow. I went forward several yards, stopped, turned my face from the storm, and gasped for breath. Even with the horse to lead me, I couldn't take another step. I fell in a heap at the base of a drift, the wind howling over the top. I could see the horse's legs nearby. It dipped its muzzle to my face and blew a plume of breath.

The rope I'd wrapped around my glove jerked me to my senses before it pulled free of my hand. The horse whickered.

Keep your eyes open, Jessie. Mustn't sleep! That would be the end.

The snow appeared to be thinning. The wind had died a bit. The horse seemed determined to stay with me. A blessing.

Try again, Jessie. Try again.

I moved but had no physical sense of it. Only intense will prodded me forward through darkening space. I sensed the horse beside me rather than saw it, felt the warmth of its body, its cloudy breath, felt its muzzle at my shoulder when I lagged behind.

The tiniest speck of yellow flickered through the blowing white. I blinked my eyes. The speck remained.

A light? Oh, please, let it be!

"Hello there! Helloooooooo."

I moved a few steps, cried again, "Hello there. Hellooooooo."

The effort had sapped all sound from my throat, sapped all my will. A terrible need to sleep washed over me. It swept me into a whirling haze, swept me onto the deep, soft blanket of white. Strange, but I thought of what people would say when they found me dead. When they found Kitty dead. Dearest Kitty. Hot tears stung my eyes.

An image of Sam burned through the shroud of self-blame and self-pity. What would he say if he found me frozen stiff in the vast white? Would he think me stupid for losing my way in the blizzard? Or would his heart swell with regret? If only he'd come and lift me in his arms, as he had the day I had fallen. If only he'd carry me into the shelter of some old soddy and build a fire to warm my soul.

A whicker. The muzzle soft at my cheeks. In my frozen, disjointed mind, the horse's face translated to Sam's thin, dark-haired features, to his caring eyes. I heard his sweet voice drawl softly, "Don't worry, Jessie. I'm here. I'll see you through."

No sooner had Sam's features blurred into that of the horse than the vision returned, this time with my father's stern, gray features. "Don't give in, Jessie. Show the kind of stuff you're made of."

My father's anxious countenance wavered into Ben's craggy face, his words offering comfort. "Come, Jessie. I'll take care of you. Give me your hand." My hand? I couldn't feel it, had no strength to raise it.

Ben's face dissolved into a dizzying mist that cleared slowly to an image of Gabe's hollow-eyed gaze, his parched lips saying, "I'll be with you, Jessie . . . sailing on the clouds . . . riding the ridge tops."

Oh, Lord!

"I've failed you, Gabe. Forgive me. Heaven knows I've tried . . ." Suddenly I felt too weary for self-blame, sorrow, or regret, too weary to glimpse phantoms in the snow. I wanted desperately to sleep, to forget failed vows.

Chapter 33

I awakened to an unpleasant smell, such as that left after burning a disgusting weed. As my mind groped toward consciousness, I became aware of someone rubbing my hand and the sound of someone breathing quickly through their mouth. I felt as if I were clawing my way from a bottomless pit for a view of the world.

My eyelids wavered open, the feeling like the scratch of sand on my eyeballs. My sight cleared, then dimmed, cleared and dimmed until it focused on a round face the color of Yeng Sang's, on long black hair pulled back tightly from the scalp into a braid. Black, shallow-set eyes peered anxiously into mine.

"Good, you live." The man's lips stretched into a grin, revealing large square teeth.

He sat on his haunches beside me, bent forward with concern. Loose-fitting gray pants covered his legs, above them a padded shan-type jacket over a long shirt. He seemed young, but it was difficult to tell a Chinaman's age.

"Where am I?" The words slothed from my mouth, thick as molasses.

"Sing Lee's cabin."

I made a hazy survey of the log hut. A dingy coop with sod roof. No windows. Snow sifted through the cracks between logs. The light I'd seen must have come through those cracks.

My eyelids closed beneath the spell of a lamp's flickering light. Half-conscious from my snow sleep, I found it hard to think, but I knew I must.

There were questions I wanted to ask.

I opened my eyes a crack and continued my foggy survey. A woven mat lay along the opposite wall, shabby blankets rolled at one end. A few simple garments hung on pegs above the bed. A pine slab set in front of the pallet for a table held an oil lamp shaped like a gravy boat, a bowl with chopsticks, small opium bottles, and a long-stemmed pipe. A tiny wisp of smoke curled from the pipe.

"How did I get here?"

"I carry you. I hear you call. Hear horse go 'nnnnnnnn.'" He imitated a whinny.

"Where is he?"

"One outside." He pointed to the door. "A buckskin."

"Were there others?"

"Many stand where I find you. They go off. This one follow Sing Lee." He laughed quietly. "I think he smell hay we keep in shed for mules."

Just like Bannack to think of his stomach. "What color were the others?"

"Hard to tell in snow. I think they same ones I saw on bluff yesterday."

Likely Chinook and his gang. He seemed to have traveled in circles, stealing mares at night, escaping to the safety of the badlands during the day. Bless his heart, he must have been the phantom horse who'd kept me moving.

"Where is this cabin?"

The Chinaman seemed puzzled. "Here, missee. Where you lie." Like other Chinese I'd known, he had difficulty pronouncing r's, substituting various vowel sounds.

"I mean where in the mountains?"

"Grasshopper Creek." This time, the r's had the sound of l's.

"Are we near the town of Bannack?"

"'Bout six miles that way." He swung an arm toward one of the walls, I had no idea which of the four directions.

I closed my eyes, struggling to think, opened them again. The Chinaman seemed to grapple with a concern of his own. His anxious gaze picked at every detail of my features, as if searching for clues to my condition. "Hands warm now?"

"Not quite."

He started to rub my hand. I drew it away as gratitude battled with a revived sense of propriety. "I can rub them together myself."

"You feel toes?"

I'd gathered enough of my wits to know sensation had returned to my limbs. Agony crept into them as my blood began to move again. The fire had started to smolder in my injured leg. "They hurt."

"Good, you wiggle toes. Move arms and legs. I fix tea. Make you warm inside."

A cupboard made from wooden crates stood in the corner opposite my clothes. It held a clutter of personal belongings and utensils for cooking. Beside it stood a bucket of coal and a brazier filled with red-hot embers, a steaming kettle on the grate. A dishpan and pail of water lay nearby along with an earthenware jug.

Sing Lee pulled little cloth sacks from the cupboard, took pinches of this herb and that, and dropped them into a wire-mesh tea strainer, then set the strainer in a crockery teapot with hot water to steep.

While he worked, I wiggled my fingers and toes. The fight to bring my blood back to life seemed endless. The more I woke and moved, the more pain flowed through my veins. I felt the fire's warmth on my cheeks and felt it grow against my good leg.

Sing Lee set the teapot on the slab table and put a few lumps of coal on the brazier. While the water soaked up the herbs' full flavor, he sat cross-legged on his pallet, arms folded across his chest. I closed my eyes to rest.

When I opened them, it seemed his gaze had never left me. He poured the tea into a drinking bowl and set it on the table near my bed.

I took a sip. "What's in it?"

"Juniper berries, sage, ginger root."

"It's soothing. Refreshes at the same time." I studied the man's bland face, becoming more curious. "Why are you here on Grasshopper Creek?"

"We work old diggings. Ten of us."

"Are you finding any gold?"

He shrugged. "'Nuff for food and clothes. Send some home to family in China. White man give up too easy. Chinaman dig very deep, work very hard for gold."

I knew about Chinese endurance. They'd left behind famine and hardship in China to grub for fortune in America. For years, they'd spaded and washed the gravel bars, ferreting through old claims and diggings for specks of gold the original owners held in disdain. If they discovered promising color as yet unfound, the white men would drive them off. Many

Chinese had abandoned the gold mines to turn their diligence to cooking or washing white men's clothes. Their backs had built the railroads and performed other services white man wouldn't consider. Now sentiment had turned against them. People said the Chinese took jobs from American citizens. It was likely only the earlier immigrants would remain in America. Most of those clung to tradition—in the clothes they wore, their language, food, and medicines.

I seemed to be lying on one of those traditions, the same sort of woven mat as that across the room. I raised my head to see what covered me and realized suddenly that I lay naked beneath the shabby blankets. The thought of Sing Lee removing my clothes made me stammer, "W-Where are my clothes?"

He pointed to a shadowy corner behind me. I twisted to see my jeans, shirt, and jacket hanging from pegs on the logs.

He seemed to sense my embarrassment. "Clothes wet. Keep you from getting warm. You excuse please."

I quickly changed the subject. "Whose bed is this?

"Uncle's. Shun Lee."

"Where is he?"

"In town. Buy food. He mebbe back in morning. If no more snow."

He studied me intently. "What you do out in storm?"

"I was looking for my nie—my daughter." How difficult to change the terms after all these years. "She lost her way yesterday." The short chronicle nudged me back to other dim corners of reality. "I have to go . . . have to find her."

I rose, pulling the blanket around me. Pain shot up my swollen leg, forcing me to lie back on the pallet. A moan of agony escaped my lips.

Sing Lee squatted beside me, his hand on my shoulder. "You lie still. I think I know where girl is." He fingered my hair. "Hair like yours? More color?"

Relief flooded my heart, on its tail a foreboding. "Where is she? Is she all right?"

"In cabin down creek. With boss man and his woman."

"Thank God!" Tears welled in my eyes and ran down my cheeks. "I want to see her." Again I tried to rise, fell back.

"You stay on bed. Leg bad. Mebbe freeze."

"It's not frozen." I explained that a horse had fallen on it.

"Shun Lee make good salve. I get." Sing Lee brought a flat, round tin from the cluttered crate and handed it to me.

I eyed the tin doubtfully, opened it a crack, and sniffed. The smell was acrid with sage, cedar, and scents unfamiliar to me. It reminded of a salve Yeng Sing made from herbs he collected from the countryside. Each Christmas he'd send me home with a tin, along with a bottle of his cough syrup—cinnamon bark, ginseng root, spikenard, comfrey root, blood-root and gin.

I took another whiff of the salve. "It smells medicinal."

"It work good. You rub on leg. I bring girl here."

The blizzard had calmed somewhat, yet snow drifted inside when Sing Lee opened the door. The draft nearly snuffed the flame in the oil lamp. I could hear him speak to Bannack, heard the buckskin nicker and stomp his hoofs.

Sing Lee peered around the door frame. "Horse want to come in," he said with a chuckle, and closed the door.

A nice man, I thought. Gentle. He'd kept me from dying. He and the phantom horse that had breathed life into my cheeks.

Chapter 34

Kitty lived. Thank God! Thank all the hosts who look over us mortals. Thank the blessed horse who led me to her. Thank the phantoms in the snow.

Would she have forgotten her hatred and be happy to see me? Or would she blame me for failing her? Would my yearning continue? I'd thought it intolerable when I'd postponed the truth, the anguish mine alone. I wondered now if continued silence would have been the better course, the true test of my mother's love.

These thoughts wheeled in my weary mind while I finished my tea and rubbed the salve on my leg. It was so swollen I couldn't bend it. No walking for a while. The color was about the same, like raw meat. It itched as well as burned. The salve set it on fire and warmed me all over.

I heard voices outside the door and a nicker. I pulled the blanket tight around me.

The door squealed open and Kitty blew inside, a bundle of animation, dressed in borrowed shan, pants and padded jacket. Rough patches of red splotched her cheeks and nose. I imagined mine looked the same. She tossed a forked tree branch—a makeshift crutch—onto the floor and dropped down beside me, the smell of the cold outdoors on her clothes. Her blue eyes, glassy from the wind, were stretched wide and smiling.

She was smiling!

A greeting tumbled out as she threw her arms around me, blending tears and laughter. "Oh, Mom, I'm so glad to see you."

A gasp. A lurch of the heart. "What did you say?"

"I said, I'm glad to see you." She kissed the words onto my cheek.

"I—I mean, what did you call me? I thought you said Mom." The name sent a thrill clamoring through my veins.

She pulled back to look me in the face, her eyes suddenly timid and wary. "I . . . I've been practicing for when I saw you. It just slipped out. I've been so scared. I thought I might never see you again."

For a moment we stared, assessing the other's feelings. Of one thing I was certain: The blizzard that had joined us in strong affection had been worth all the fright, all the agony.

I pulled her head onto my shoulder and held her in a mother's embrace. "I'm so glad you feel that way. I was afraid . . ." I swallowed at a thickness in my throat, wishing I could find the words to express the fullness in my heart.

Sing Lee had been standing to one side, his expression a blend of puzzlement, joy, sympathy. He held a bundle of clothes. "Pardon, missee. Boss's woman send you clothes. I go now so you can dress. Spend night in boss's cabin. Girl sleep here with you. Plenty coal for night. I come in morning. Cook rice."

I thanked him fervently for all he'd done. He bowed his way outside, grinning, shrugging his jacket up around his shoulders.

Kitty hobbled over to the cupboard for a cup and poured herself some tea while I slipped a shan over my nakedness. The pants could wait until later. It would be a strain to pull them on over my leg, and there were blankets to cover me. After enduring such fear that I'd find Kitty dead, that I might not live, I craved conversation.

"Come, sit beside me." I patted the edge of the pallet. She limped across the cramped room and set her cup on the table, then settled on the blankets, one leg crossed, the other stretched out before her. I pulled up her pants leg and saw her ankle was bound with short splints and rags. It had the same smell as Shun Lee's salve. "What happened?"

She gave one of her careless shrugs. "The saddle slipped off Trixie and I fell on my ankle. Some buzzard-head cut the cinch."

"I know who. I gave him a whipping he'll not forget."

"Lance?"

I nodded.

"That loco-brain. I could've been killed."

"But you weren't, and now I have you." I circled my arms around her and gave her a squeeze. She didn't resist. "Did you have to walk, or did you fix the saddle?"

"Trixie took off when the cinch broke. I saw her later with Chinook."

"The great protector. He must have followed you as much as you followed him." I adjusted my leg for comfort and kissed Kitty on the forehead. "How far did you go before you found this camp?"

"Maybe three miles. I spent the night in a leaky prospector's dugout. I left the saddle there."

"I worried about you." I pulled her closer, letting my love melt around her. "I met a sow bear with cubs . . . saw what was left of Penny. I was scared to death the bear had eaten you."

She looked up, mouth ajar. "Penny? She's in the boss man's cabin, gnawing on a bone."

"Oh Lord, I was certain it was she, the same color fur."

"Likely some sheepherder's dog."

"So all of us are safe. I hope Sam is too. Sometimes things do turn out for the best."

"Except for my ankle and your leg. Sing Lee told me about it. Does it hurt a lot?"

"I'm afraid I'll have to stay off it for a while."

She looked into my eyes and smiled. "I'll take care of you."

"How nice." I felt her heart beat against mine as she snuggled inside my arms. Utter bliss.

"I'm sorry I've caused you so much worry. Sorry you had to make this trip."

"It's for myself as much as for you, dear girl. I'm just thankful I'm taking you home."

"First we have to catch Chinook." The thought seemed to unsettle her. She slipped an arm free and reached for her cup. "Have you seen him?"

"Today, during the storm. I'm sure he was the horse that kept me from freezing. He must have known you were here." I went on to tell her as much of the experience as I remembered.

"He's pure gold. We just have to catch him. Pa will be real upset if we don't." Still that reference to Gabe as if her were living. A long pause. "Aunt Jess—I mean, Mom—I don't understand why Uncle Ben gave me to Pa. Did he hate me that much? What should I call him, Uncle Ben or Father?"

"There's no reason to change. He's dead." And he wasn't the real father.

She fixed her inquiring eyes on mine. "Did he? Hate me, I mean?"

"I'm afraid he despised you even before you were born."

"Why?"

"It's not a happy tale."

"I don't care. I want to know."

She curled tight against me as I told about the past, leaving out details that would startle, keeping mute about the hanging. She didn't interrupt, but her ragged breathing told of her feelings.

"I'm so sorry," she said when I'd finished. "I've been mean to you. For no reason."

"You were hurting, dear child. I knew that." I leaned my head on hers with a sigh of release. "Everything is all right now. My father used to say that mistakes don't matter as much as what we do about them."

"I guess that's where Pa heard it. He says the same thing." Suddenly, her cheeks drew taut. She bit her trembling lip.

For a moment we huddled silent in our comforting embrace, no sound but Bannack stomping outside the door and the wail of the dying wind. The smell of burning coal had swallowed that of opium.

"Do you ever feel lonesome," Kitty asked at length, "even when you're with someone else . . . even with a lot of people?"

"I've felt that way much of the time since Ben died." I paused, wishing thoughts of the dead hadn't come to haunt our reunion. "You miss Gabe a lot, don't you?"

She nodded against my shoulder, taking a while to go on. "I thought maybe . . . since you'll be laid up with your leg . . . I might . . ." She seemed unsure of her ground and let the rest trail away.

I said nothing, though I felt the stirrings of curiosity. The silence lengthened. Possibly more stock-taking on her part. Patience on mine. I might as well wait; I was going nowhere.

When finally she spoke, she did so warily. "I'd like to ride back to the Centennial, see how Pa's. . . if he's . . ."

The words squeezed my heart. "It'd serve no purpose. Your father's in his grave. I told you that."

"How can you be sure he's dead?" She pulled away, doubt strong in her face and manner. "He wasn't when you left."

"No, but—"

"Then there's a chance he isn't." Conviction glittered in her eyes. "I don't think he is."

"Kitty, he is, believe me."

"How can you possibly know?"

For God's sake, Jessie Tate, tell her the truth. You must. Otherwise she'll never accept her father's death as fact, will never be at peace.

I took her hand and felt it tense, cold. Her expression was one of misgiving. I closed my eyes for a second, summoning the courage to speak. "Gabe planned to take his life. I heard the shot when I rode out. I didn't go back because he was frantic that I find you."

Her lips parted in shock. Her eyes stared in disbelief. "He wouldn't! Not Pa."

An odd tremor passed through me as I recalled that morning. It seemed unreal. A bad dream. Someone else's nightmare. "It was one of the most difficult things I've ever done—letting him keep the gun. He couldn't stand the pain any longer . . . so much of it . . . for so long. I couldn't deny him."

For a long, excruciating moment Kitty stared at me with accusing eyes. Then, as the truth took root, they softened with understanding. She lifted them toward the ceiling. Sobs shook her frame. Slowly, she leaned toward me and crumpled into my arms.

I stroked her head, gathering my shattered thoughts. "It was for the best, dear. It would have been a matter of days. This way, the decision was Gabe's."

Her nod was so slight, I could barely detect it. But somewhere the tiny germ of acceptance had sprouted in the darkness of grief. It seemed she knew the past was behind, that life was changing for her, as it was for me. Everything changed in this world. Past joys and grievances eventually faded away. I was changing, accepting Gabe's dreams for Kitty and the herd as my own. I hadn't expected it. In some ways I hadn't wanted it. But it was happening.

Kitty's thoughts had been wandering along some shadowy path. "Did you love your mother more than your father?" she asked without preamble.

I thought back, searching my garret of memories. "Not the love one feels because of a smile or touch. Mother wasn't a loving person. Most of the time she was too busy planning parties and having important guests to dinner to bother with us children. Then the war intervened . . . she lost my brothers and sisters to cholera. For a while she was wrapped in grief. Our nanny, bless her Irish heart, taught us what it meant to love."

"What about your father?"

I pondered that. "The attention he gave us centered around the horses—the teaching—the demand for perfection. Not much outward show of love there."

"I wish Ma—I mean Amy—was still alive. We could all three be together."

"I do, too. How I wish it for all our sakes." I'd given myself over heart and soul to Kitty's care, but she and Amy had been dear to each other. If Amy had lived, Kitty might have developed into a different girl, more well-rounded, a happier person, not so single-minded and rebellious as under Gabe's sole care. Fate had deprived her.

"At least you're not alone, dear. I'm here. So are Amy and Gabe in a way. They're watching over you." I recalled Gabe's last words. "Gabe said he'd be looking down from the clouds, riding the ridge tops. He'll never abandon you. Nor will I."

She didn't reply, letting silence speak for her sorrow. I retreated into my own thoughts of dear ones who lived in a pocket of my heart.

For a while, Kitty and I sat in communal mourning. Then we spoke of the problems ahead, of solutions, compromises, until weariness closed on us like a clenched fist. Kitty rolled out the blankets on the pallet across the way and lay on her side facing me, her hands folded in the curl of her legs. She looked serene lying there in slumber, her face childlike, angelic, the skin smooth as a babe's. Her orange hair lay in a frizzy veil around her shoulders.

I watched her for a long while, love and empathy swelling within me. Unable to resist, I reached across and pulled a strand of hair away from her eyes. She made a little sound, moved her head slightly, but didn't wake. Until that moment, I'd never fully realized the depth of the hole her loss had left inside me.

I thought of the vow I'd made to take the herd to the Bitterroot, at the time more for Gabe's benefit, now more for mine and Kitty's. The concentration of will had driven me beyond myself until I was stronger than I knew or aimed to be. Thus far, the journey had tested me to the utmost—my loyalties, my feelings, my courage. No telling what stones lay ahead in the trail to test me further.

Chapter 35

I woke at first light but Kitty slept on, lost in the deaf marmot-sleep of a weary teen. Sing Lee returned shortly after dawn to boil rice. He offered me the use of a covered pail and scolded worriedly at my decision to go outside for my toilet, but my inhibitions reared at the thought of his tending me like a bed patient.

The wind had died as the blizzard wound down and snow had settled where, before, the gale had scraped the earth bare. The hills slept beneath a white meringue. The brush and evergreens wore frothy white coats. Mist shrouded the creek and crawled over heaps of mine tailings toward the bench that held Sing Lee's cabin.

Down the creek from the soddy, a hill shot skyward from the bench, ending in a knob with a cockscomb of pine. A skirt of bitterbrush at its base would serve my needs. I held the brush in my sights as I stumped along on my tender leg, pain the price of modesty.

A panther screamed in a timbered canyon to the north, the cry enough to make the hair on my scalp leap to attention. Out in the Rocky Hills, wolves and coyotes howled a chilling echo. When Bannack nickered from his tether near the soddy, four horses shrilled an answer. They emerged from the misty creekbottom and bunched nervously on the rim of the bench, Trixie among them, her reins dragging on the ground.

A loud trumpeting split the air as Chinook trotted from the mists in all his wild, regal glory and came to a stomping halt a few yards away. His eyes glittered. His muscles bulged, ready for flight. His breath plumed in the frosty air.

"Good morning," I said with great feeling. "You seem in fine fettle." I held out my hand. He nickered softly and circled me, snorting.

Some of the wounds from his battle with the mustang had formed long ridges of jellied crimson, and others had scabbed over. The flaps of hide on neck and flank had stiffened, but I saw little swelling. I'd need a closer look to detect infection.

I limped toward him, extending my hand, hoping to seize the broken lead rope. His eyes drilled holes in me. His muscles quivered, nostrils flared. "I want to take you home," I said as I reached for the rope. "I'll give you a ton of oats."

He backed away, stiff-legged, blowing, bobbing his head. The mares edged toward the foggy creek bottom, whinnying. Chinook wheeled and ran toward them, snaking his neck. With grunts and whinnies, he bunched them, sniffed each mare, and touched each muzzle. When they gave sign they'd not run, he whirled to face me.

I eased toward him, holding out my hand, hoping fervently he'd stay. "I want to thank you for saving my life. I'll be forever grateful." He seemed ready to bolt.

The mares were first to run. They snorted and tossed their heads, leaving dropped dung to steam in the chill air. They didn't go far. I'd aroused their curiosity.

Chinook shot them a backward glance and blared an order, then turned my way. He seemed torn, desirous of my affection, yet loathe to relinquish his freedom and his mares. His nostrils flared in and out. His eyes sparked.

"It's all right, beauty. I won't hurt you." From my jacket, I fished out a bag of raisins I'd forgotten during yesterday's misadventures, dumped a few into my hand, and held them out.

Chinook edged toward me, fluttering his lips, his gaze fixed on my hand. A chorus of whinnies rose from the sopranos along with the sound of their stomping. Chinook glanced over his shoulder and trumpeted.

"Come on," I said, "the raisins are for you, not the girls."

He stood his ground, made no move to come closer.

I decided to try indifference. "Suit yourself, I'll leave you alone." I tossed the raisins into the snow and turned away. If he chose to bolt, I might never catch him. I could only hope he'd follow the raisin trail.

I'd gone a few steps when I heard him snuffling in the snow. A few seconds later, a loud whinny rumbled at my shoulder, startling my breath away.

I turned with a joyous grin. "Decided to follow, did you?" Bobbing his head, he mouthed the pocket where I'd stowed the bag of raisins.

He made no attempt to leave as I fed him the rest. When I stroked his neck and rubbed the muscles in his shoulders, he relaxed visibly. His eyes softened to the deep, liquid brown of molasses. Whickers vibrated in his chest. He mouthed my hat, my braid, and brought his lips away with a strand of strawberry blond hair. I threw my arms around him and lay my head along the soft curve of his neck. Marvelous animal. He'd bartered his freedom for my eternal devotion.

* * *

Shun Lee returned in mid-morning, riding one mule, leading another loaded with packs. He and his nephew delivered the supplies to their countrymen down the creek, then returned with a cowhide they used for skidding ore across the snow. Soon after, I sat upon the hide like a mound of quartz swaddled in blankets. Each leg of the hide was tied to a rope, the end of the rope looped around the horn on Bannack's saddle, the rope long enough he wouldn't kick me in the dragging.

Sing Lee rode Bannack, though he had some frantic moments when Bannack tried to rid himself of the devil-hide stalking his rear end. Despite her injured ankle, Kitty rode Trixie bareback, leading the subdued Chinook. The sun sparked fire onto her hair and his chestnut coat. Shun Lee marshaled the parade, riding one mule, ponying the other for Sing Lee's return to camp. The mares followed in line, feeling the promise of the day. They kicked up their heels and humped their shiny backs. Their many colors reminded me of an Indian tale that credited the Four Winds for the gift of horse color—gold from the east wind, red from the south, black from the west, gray from the north wind. White signified the spirit of the wind. Surely, Chinook was born of all Four Winds, the Sun God and Thunder God to boot.

Snow hid the rough track that wound along the bluff above Grasshopper Creek. Ruts were visible only here and there, where the contours of the hills had served as barriers to the storm. In some places the drifts were two feet deep, and the animals plowed through on the trail Shun Lee's mules had made earlier that morning. The sun held little heat and touched my cheeks without warming them. The cold air searched out the openings in the blankets and chilled my toes.

We arrived at the Sherwood ranch in mid-afternoon amid a bedlam of whinnies, snorts, and brays, my rump sore from the ride over submerged rocks and ground-hugging brush. The rest of the search crew had dragged in just before us after spending the night holed-up in the Rocky Hills. I felt sympathy for the roundup cook and his helper, felt avenged in the case of Lance.

We were still at the corral when Sam straggled in from the southeast, his sorrel pulling Kitty's saddle behind her in the snow. My heart leaped at the sight of him, safe, alive.

He made noises about how he'd worried about us, how thankful he was we'd found safety in the storm, how grateful he was to have Chinook returned. His gratitude overflowed into a generous gift of money to the Lees for their trouble, which they accepted with great humility.

Later, after I'd taken a sponge bath in the kitchen and made myself half-way presentable, after Sam had treated Chinook's wounds, he brought my supper over from the cookhouse and served me on the parlor sofa. The dishes returned to Clare, we now relaxed, I with my legs horizontal, Sam across the room on the leather settee, the cowhide worn a dark-brown, nearly black from years of use. The fragrance of burley tobacco drifted over the newspaper he held in front of him. Dust motes swirled in the drift of smoke and lamp light, creating a dance of perpetual motion. Strange—from the moment I'd met Sam I'd expected him to carry a pipe rather than the smelly cigars of merchants or the hand-rolled cigarettes of cowboys. Ben had smoked a pipe.

Clearly happy for the fire in the Franklin stove, Penny and one of the older shepherd dogs lay on a braided rug near the hearth. They snored and fluttered their lips. After my fright over the bear, it warmed my heart to have Penny near, though it hurt to think of some sheepherder grieving the loss of his companion.

A hard cord had started to form along the outside of my leg. Despite Sing Lee's ointment, perhaps because of it, the leg itched to distraction. Heat from the fire made me want to claw the skin away. To keep myself from it, I'd asked Kitty to find a darning ball and yarn. I vented my annoyance by stabbing gray yarn across a hole in one of my socks.

Kitty hadn't returned from the cookhouse, where the men were finalizing plans for tomorrow's roundup. There'd been something in her expression when she left for supper, a near-wildness mixed with a look of guilt that led me to believe she wanted to be with Mike while she could. There was no chance trouble would flare between her and Lance. Hal had booted the boy from the ranch when he heard about the cinch and told him to find work where he could.

I let Sam enjoy his rest, speaking only in reply to comments he made about items in the newspaper. When the mantel clock chimed the half hour, he folded the paper and lay it on the cowhide. Rubbing his face, he slid down on the seat and leaned his head against the headrail in one of the loose, graceful poses that seemed natural for him. He blew a long sigh.

"Tired?" I asked.

"Worn to a nubbin."

"It's all my fault."

"Wasn't your fault." He twitched a smile that was wry-mouthed and squinty. "I have to admit, though, you sure know how to give a man a case of the bejabbers. I thought I'd lost you."

"It was stupid of me not to wait, but I was frantic about Kitty." I went on to explain in detail about the sow bear and the dog's remains, about Lance's admission of guilt. "By the way, was that you I heard shooting at the head of the draw?"

"'Fraid it was. The cowman in me went berserk." His face turned sheepish. "I'd been following a panther's tracks. It'd dragged something. I thought it might be—well, you know, that it might be Kitty." He grimaced. "Turned out to be a little heifer. Found the cat gnawing on it. I saw red. Shot and missed. The cat took off up the gulch. I rode after it, shooting. Finally lost track of it way up on top when it sneaked into a jumble of boulders." He sighed and scratched his head. "Guess I went loco for a while. Forgot what I was about."

"Didn't you hear me shoot, or Lance?"

"The wind was blowing mighty strong from me to you. Must've blown the sound down into the canyon."

"The fact we were below the bench didn't help."

"I just wish you'd waited for me. We could've faced the storm together."

It was my turn to look sheepish. "It was a day for foolish impulses." Then defensively, "But I found Kitty and Chinook."

He slanted a look at me from under his shaggy brows. "I didn't mean any blame. It's just that I'd hate to have lost you." Our eyes met, held, wavered, held again. "It just wouldn't seem right without you and Kitty on my tail."

"Always bedeviling, causing concern."

"Helping me out of scrapes."

"Mainly you helping us. Like bringing that saddle of Kitty's."

"That was luck. Just stumbled onto the soddy where she stayed. Leaky old box. Least it kept the worst of the wind off." He straightened on the seat and stretched a yawn. "Think I'll sleep tonight. How about you, with that leg?"

"I'll take some laudanum."

"It's that bad?"

I could have said it felt like a furnace. "I'll be able to start home in a couple of days." Home? Well over one-hundred miles to the northwest, much of it through the steep-sided mountains Lewis and Clark had found so daunting.

"Whoa, now." Sam raised a staying hand. "You aren't going to fork a horse until that leg is ready, with a couple of extra days' rest for good measure. I don't want you getting blood poisoning half-way down the Divide."

"My neighbors will think I've run off and left them high and dry."

"They didn't expect you back until after your brother died, did they?"

"No, but . . ."

"There you go. They'll think he's still alive. No reason to hurry."

I gave a snort of doubt. "Tell that to Hal. I'm afraid we've outstayed our welcome."

"I'd be happy for you to stay at my place. I can pick up a wagon in Bannack. You can ride to the Hole."

"Don't go to that expense."

"I need to buy one anyway."

"I don't know, I—"

"I'll clean up the old soddy. There's a cook-stove for heat. Needs some new parts, but it'll do. I'll put the door back on the shack to keep it warm." His lips spread into a smile that showed, I thought, a sudden inner contentment.

"I wouldn't think of having you go to all that trouble."

"Need to do it anyway." He dropped his gaze to the scuffed toes of his boots and sucked a tooth. When he looked up, his eyes had filled with uncertainty. "Maybe you don't want that."

"I'd hate to impose." Actually, the thought of staying with Sam brought a pleasant warmth. Not just to be in his care, but to speak of common interests, to learn more of his past and of his plans for the future. Just to talk about the weather would be nice.

"No trouble at all. I'd hate to have you slip through my fingers before I have a chance to . . ." Again, he dropped his gaze. This time, he pulled self-consciously on the lobe of his ear.

"I'd like to spend time with you, too. I didn't know how much I . . ." I averted my eyes, letting the rest of the thought remain unspoken. It seemed neither of us had the courage to say what was in our hearts. "I can't lie around too long, worrying about my place, wondering if we'll make it down before the next snowstorm. But I'll stay a few days, if you don't mind." I tried to keep my voice from betraying just how much I longed to be with him, how much I'd miss him when I left. I saw our friendship slipping into a thing of the past, relegated to cards sent at Christmas. I wanted to keep that from happening.

I began to polish the words that would frame a new subject and in the process left some of my apprehension behind. "You ought to consider wintering the horses in the Bitterroot. The temperature can drop to fifty or sixty below in the Hole. Snowstorms are beastly."

I went on to tell of Ben's and my experience living on Ruby Creek and Trail Creek, telling of the time it had taken just to keep warm—chopping wood, stoking fires that gave off barely enough heat to fight the icy drafts. I told of having to bundle myself in woolens to stay warm inside the soddy, how on the worst nights, I'd put my pillow over my head with just a crack for breathing.

Sam listened with lips pursed, seeming to weigh each word. Weariness aged his face, the lamplight turned his ruddy skin sallow. "The Bitterroot isn't cold?"

"It can get to twenty below. But the cold doesn't last. Some winters there's hardly any snow in the valley, just in the mountains."

"And in the Hole?"

"It can pile up several feet. Your horses will lose a lot of fat and energy. It's hard for them to fight disease. You really . . ." I left the rest unsaid as it dawned on me I was begging, close to insulting Sam's intelligence, the last thing I wanted to happen. "I'm sorry. I have no business—"

"'Course you do. Don't think I haven't considered it."

He turned quiet once more, rubbing his chin and scratching his sideburns. I worried that I'd argued my cause too hard and thought it best to let silence help him sort out his feelings. Still deep in thought, he rose to the north-facing window beside the settee. Holding the muslin curtain aside, he stared onto a twilight scene that included the clothes-line and a corner of the cookhouse, as well as cottonwoods growing along Grasshopper Creek as it wound through the brushy hills toward the timbered heights.

I knotted the yarn, clipped it, and pulled the sock from the ball. "Something I said bothering you?"

"Oh," he muttered, sighing, "not really." He continued to stare outside. "I could rent pasture. We could keep the herd together. It'd be easier on Chinook. You could use him for stud."

My heart pounded at the thought. I tried not to let my excitement show, to be even-handed in my reply. "I doubt you'll be sorry. If it doesn't work out, you can always change your plans. As for renting pasture, I'd guess you'll have quite a choice. Last winter was hard on the ranchers. They're in need of cash."

Letting the curtain close, he turned toward me, eyes uncertain, distracted. "'Course my boy and I will have our geldings and three-year-old fillies with us a good seven months out of the year, working out of the Hole. You can keep Chinook at your place while I'm gone. Kitty can break my two-and three-year-olds and train them to saddle. I can buy the horses she's already broke if she's willing."

"I can't see her refusing a ready market. Gabe expected her to sell a few as army remounts."

"I could rent enough land for you to run a small herd of cattle if you'd like. No sense my running any. I'll be away too much of the time." His voice lacked surety, as if he were trying to convince himself as well as me.

"I have little sympathy for raising beef cattle. I hate the branding, the dehorning, the separation of cows from their calves." I'd pulled another sock onto the ball and flashed the needle across the hole, rattling on with my comments to keep pace with my excited pulse. "I'll stick with dairy cows, raise an orphaned Hereford or two for beef. One nice thing about raising sheep for their wool, I don't have to kill them."

I wasn't sure Sam heard my rambling. He seemed intent on his own thoughts. He began to pace the room, the sound of his boot heels loud on the bare floor, muffled on the braided rug. Smoke from his pipe wreathed his head and banked along the ceiling.

I chattered on. "All this will please Kitty. As it does me. Breeding and training horses creates life, fulfillment."

Sam continued to pace, looking sideways at me from time to time in a squinty, inquiring way. I tried to keep my smile within bounds. My internal workings were a different matter. Pleasure over the future translated from an inner trembling to a shaking of my fingers that made it difficult to drive the thread into the heavy sock.

"If it works out," he said from deep in his musings, "next winter I could buy a place near yours and put up a nice cabin. Then maybe . . ." He stopped wearing out the carpet to stare out the window. Just for a moment.

Spinning to face me, he raised his arms in a gesture of frustration. "Aw, I'm just star-gazing. It's not right to bend my boy's plans all to hell without talking to him. A plan is worth eight eggs if both parties don't have a hand in it."

My insides quivered. My stomach felt as if it would sink into oblivion. Surely all the talk hadn't come to naught. Words were slow to leave my lips. "I agree, you should speak to your son. But as for the bending, there's not a dream ever dreamed that hasn't been battered and hammered into shape as life went along. Witness the fact you're here in Montana, that I've taken on the responsibility for Kitty's herd."

The lines at the corners of his eyes deepened as though he were smiling, but I thought it reflected intense concentration instead. He seemed to argue with himself, his resolve to take shape and harden. He pulled the stool from the pump organ, set it in front of the sofa, and sat. I caught the scent of tobacco and saddle leather that hovered around him.

He took the darning and set it in the basket, then held my hands a long moment without speaking. A peculiar light had come to his eyes. "Could you ever grow to love me, Jessie?"

I stopped breathing as alternating waves of apprehension and joy swept through me. Love wasn't something one could put into words. It was a need, a longing of the spirit. I managed only a soundless whisper. "I've already begun to love you, Sam."

"Then maybe, someday, you and I . . ." He searched my face, his expression urgent, not far from desperation. It seemed I could see through his large gray eyes into his soul. They seemed to stare into mine. "Someday, maybe next spring . . ." Again he faltered. I wished he'd get on with it, before my heart flew from my body. "There's something I have to do first. I . . ."

"Yes?" My voice trembled.

"I want to visit Rose's grave, Jo's too." His look splintered on mine. "Maybe then I'll be free to ask."

Anticipation drained away, leaving a mix of disappointment and relief. I'd thought he'd . . . but I, too, needed time to think, to accept the complexities of a deeper relationship, time to bend my ways. Still, I'd hoped.

It took several seconds to gather my wits. Sam stared at my hands and stroked my fingers. A feathery sensation rippled across my numbed feelings. "When will you go?" I said heavily.

"As soon as I get the herd settled in the Bitterroot." I heard the same regret in his voice as he must have heard in mine. "We ought to have corrals and sheds finished on Ruby Creek by the time you're well enough to ride into the Bitterroot. If not, Benito can stay behind and do what's left. I'll probably leave for Colorado the end of October. Rob will be in Denver, expecting a report on my progress."

He looked up then, his eyes warm with tenderness and promise. He reached out with his long fingers and ran them over my cheek under my chin, their touch as soft as cattail down. "Don't you worry. I'll be back in the spring. Wild horses couldn't stop me. Just don't forget to think about me while I'm gone."

Forget him? After all we'd been through? We'd sat at the same watch-fires, facing doubt and fear. We'd confessed our pasts. Those times were etched in my heart, to remain forever.

Chapter 36

While at Ruby Creek, I didn't see as much of Sam as I would have liked—he and Benito slaved from dawn to sunset, building corrals. When he did come to the soddy to make sure I was following orders, he hovered over me making fussing noises, obviously worried about the continued swelling in my leg. He insisted I drink my fill of willow bark and sage tea. He also pointed out the need to keep my leg elevated, no matter how I tired of the position, and the need to cover the leg with my fleece jacket, fleece toward the skin. He always made a joke or two to cheer me, his laughter never loud or unseemly, just a twinkle in his eyes and a twitch of a smile.

And there was Kitty. My joy. My child. She sat beside me talking about subjects we'd never dared speak of before, of girl things, woman things, of our hopes for the coming months and years.

It was mid-October when the icy breath and fog-gray clouds of an advancing front told us we must head for lower elevations. My leg had healed enough to ride Bannack, but to save it stress, we'd take four days for the hazardous trip into the Bitterroot, normally a two-or three-day ride from Gibbons Pass.

Home! My lambs. The young orchard bearing its first apples—apple trees were one of my passions. Autumn leaves spicing the creeks that frothed down from the mountains. The swelling rush of the Bitterroot River. The saw-toothed peaks of the Bitterroot Range veiled with gossamer clouds etched black with sunsets. To the north the broadening valley, beginning to settle with farms where not long ago there was wilderness, the fringes thick with forests. And my bed. Feather soft. I yearned for my own bed and kitchen. Even the specter of Carver Dean looming on the horizon did little to dampen my spirits.

* * *

As we rode up the long drive onto the wooded bench that held the homestead's cluster of buildings, I felt as if a zephyr had lifted me from the saddle and filled my soul with new-found life. My big yellow dog, Duff, came at a run to warn off the invasion of horses with a frenzy of barking. When he saw me in the lead, he leaped up and down and spun around and around with joy. I slid from Bannack, handed Sam the reins, and told him where to pasture the horses. Assured the intruders meant no harm, Duff put his paws on my shoulders—usually not allowed—and ran his tongue over my face. I kissed his forehead.

At the same time, the two mother cats and their new kittens ran from the barn, mewing. While the mothers rubbed on my trousers, I scooped up the kittens and buried my nose in their soft fur. The hogs squealed in their pens near the barn. The Rhode Island Reds scooted toward me and clucked for grain.

The reunion wouldn't have been complete without a tour of the field behind the barn. I hugged each cow around the neck, smelling their sweet hides, scratched the curious sheep behind their ears and told them how delighted I was to see them. I picked up the runt lamb, struggling to lift her new weight, and held her close to my heart. My twenty-year-old buckskin, Zeb, came at a gallop and craned his neck to look behind me, expecting to see a pan of oats. Giving up on that, he gave my hair and woolen hat a slobbery bath. I set the wriggly lamb on the ground and gave Zeb his share of hugs, soaking up his warmth.

All the animals appeared well-cared for, the garden cleared and spaded for the winter. What a blessing to have good neighbors.

Ben had bought the site from Carver more for the setting than to raise large bands of livestock. It lay south of a creek that tumbled down from the mountains into the Bitterroot River. The jagged spine of the Bitterroot Range hovered in the west, the Sapphires to the east, each within what seemed a stone's throw. Twilight had dropped a purple hush over the land. The sound of riffling waters reached my ears unfettered by the daytime whine of the nearby sawmill.

Timber covered most of the parcel, leaving little grazing land. For now,

I'd turn the crossbreeds into the ten-acre hayfield back of the sheep pasture. There was enough stubble to last a few days, time enough to buy hay from one of the large ranches in the upper valley, not much time for Sam to look for land. But I'd worry about that tomorrow.

The cabin beckoned like a near-forgotten friend. Too crippled with rheumatism to do the work himself, Ben had hired men to build it of logs. They'd stacked them wide enough and high enough for a roomy sitting room, bedroom, kitchen, and loft, and hewed them on the inside with a broad ax.

We were all tired enough to crawl into bed without supper, but once I'd reacquainted myself with the house, I fixed us a bite to eat. Soon after, we settled ourselves for the night, Sam and Benito on bunks in the loft. Kitty breathed heavily with sleep on a pallet spread on the floor of my bedroom. Beyond the window, the moon flooded the fields and forest with a platinum light. A night breeze fluttered the lace curtains.

I lay quiet, soaking up the comfort of my feather mattress, and loosened the braid I was too weary to tend before I dropped onto my bed. I hadn't yet dampened the oil lamp on the nightstand, and it shone on a wedding picture of Ben and me. We hadn't had the funds for an expensive wedding and dressed simply in the traveling suits we'd bought for the trip west. After four years without him, Ben still seemed extraordinarily near. Despite demons of the past, I woke sometimes in the early hours and stretched out for him, forgetting I lived with his ghost. Other ghosts lived within me—my father, incredibly strong-willed, ruled by obsession, and Gabe, the mirror of our father, but more amiable, dearer to my heart, until his confession. They lived in me, neither censuring nor sympathetic. Perhaps now I could come to terms with their flaws, with the passion for horses that had disrupted the lives of those they touched. All three shadows—Ben's, Father's, Gabe's—fell long over my days and nights.

Now another man had crept into my life. He, too, was strong-willed but from what I'd observed, not given to obsession. A man immensely appreciative and sensitive to my needs. What kind of shadow would this man cast on my life? At the moment I could imagine nothing less than a blithe shadow that beckoned me into a future filled with promise.

* * *

Afraid the herd might graze the stubble field down to nothing, Sam left right after breakfast to lease pasture. Benito had volunteered to trim the saddle horses' hoofs and reset shoes on those in need of them. Kitty had gone out with curry comb, brush, and her own skinny fingers to remove burrs caught on the horses' manes and tails when they traveled the weedy foothills of the Sapphire Mountains. Their tails were a tangle of spiny burrs and hair. The manes were almost as bad. The forelocks were mats that rose like Indian head-dresses from their foreheads.

Dressed in the loose comfort of my yellow calico, I concentrated on the house. Shut tight, though not tight enough to prevent dust from filtering in through cracks in the logs, the air inside was stale. I threw open the windows, trying not to disturb fly traps spiders had glued to the frames. Flies were a problem this time of the year. They crawled inside, looking for crannies in which to sleep away the cold months.

I swept the floors and dusted the collection of odds and ends that served as furniture. Desperate for clean underwear, I built a fire in the cookstove—a large cast-iron one with overhead warming ovens—filled a washtub with water from the pump out back, and set it on the stove to boil with chips of lye soap. While I waited for the water to heat, I mopped the floor. It was made from puncheons, split thick and hewn on the upper side, ice hard and golden yellow when scrubbed.

The mother cats had claimed two of the kitchen chairs. They sat purring in sunlight that lanced through the window. Their kittens scampered around on the floor, clawed and spit at each other. Duff had taken a shine to Kitty and had followed her into the field with Penny.

When the water had boiled, I set the tub of sudsy water on the worktable in the center of the kitchen—a collection of cupboards, work tops, and sinkstand similar to Clare's kitchen. The walls were lined with pans, saws, rifles, a rack for hats and coats. The room was afloat with familiar sounds and smells—the snap of coals, the perpetual tick of the wall clock Ben had given me on our second anniversary, the tap of a woodpecker drilling the logs for insects, the smell of burning pitch, and the antiseptic smell of lye.

I was running a pair of bloomers over a rippled board when I heard a light knock on the door. Carver flashed to mind.

I twisted my head around. "Who is it?" I said with a hiss of panic.

"Yeng Sang."

Relief turned me limp. "Come in. Come in."

The door opened slightly. "Ah, Missee Tate. Good, you home."

"You're a sight for sore eyes. Please, come in." I wiped my hands on a towel and went to show my guest inside.

Rufus, Gabe's dog, had shoved past Yeng Sang and was wagging himself almost in two, nudging my hand. The cats bristled on their chairs. The kittens scrambled behind the wood box. I held Rufus' blue-gray head and kissed it, told him I was glad to see him.

I pulled a chair over for Yeng Sang to sit. He did, bobbing his head politely according to Chinese custom. "Let me fix you some tea."

I put the teakettle on the hottest stove lid and found a box of tea crackers as yet unopened. Rufus followed as if glued to my side. I gave him a cracker.

"How did you get Rufus to come? He wouldn't follow me when I left."

"At first, I think he not come. When I bury Mister Gabe, dog sit all time by grave—three, four days. It take me that long to clean cabin, pack things I know you want of Mister Gabe's, things from my cabin." He paused, looking at Rufus with sadness. "I guess dog smell Mister Gabe on things in pack. When I leave, he follow."

The story tugged at my heart, filling my mind with images of the morning I left the Centennial—of a dying man's last hymn and of the revolver that foretold the end. I felt compelled to ask the question I'd been anxious, yet loathe, to have answered. "When did Gabe die?"

"Right after you leave. He . . ." Yeng Sang left unsaid the part I needed to hear.

"I'm sorry I let you attend to the burial. It's tormented me, leaving Gabe in that condition."

"Missee Kitty need you. Not Mister Gabe. He at peace with ancestors in heaven. You take good care of Kitty, then Mister Gabe look down on you with joy."

I couldn't bring myself to ask the specifics of Gabe's death, nor did Yeng Sang seem willing to speak of them. The circumstances must have torn him apart, yet I couldn't help wondering why it had taken him so long to reach us; we'd been delayed a good two weeks. "Did you have trouble along the way?"

He dropped his gaze and broke into an embarrassed grin. "I stop at friend's in Lakeview . . . drink too much rice whiskey . . . play poker at saloon . . . many days . . . I lonesome for Mister Gabe." He took a leather pouch from the pocket of his loose-fitting pants and set it on the table beside the tub. "I win, much win. I give it to you for take care of Kitty."

I shook my head briskly. "No, you need it. You have no job." I handed him the pouch and set a mug of tea in its place.

"You do Yeng Sang dishonor."

"But I—"

He held up a hand to stop my protest. "At Lakeview, I play poker for you, for Mister Gabe, for Kitty." He reached within his shan and brought out a money belt. His lips spread into a broad grin. "This Yeng Sang's—full of gold dust, some silver money. Most I win from Chinese miners in Big Hole. I stay long time. We all get sick from too much opium and whiskey."

"I'd still rather you keep the pouch."

"You think Yeng Sang evil?"

"Of course not. You're a dear friend, loyal as they come."

"Then you take money."

I thought of the money Ben owed Carver—I'd returned Sam's check, since we intended to share Chinook. I thought of the need to provide a home for my daughter. "I'll accept it for Kitty's sake."

I put the pouch out of sight in the cupboard, set a plate of crackers on the crowded table, and sat where I wouldn't have to peer around the tub at Yeng Sang. It steamed the smell of soap and cotton.

"You'll stay here, of course."

"Two, mebbe three days." He sipped tea from the mug, seeming to savor it with reverence. "I stop at log camp few miles back. Big boss want me to cook for men." He darted me a sly grin. "Men want chance to win back their money."

"What money?"

"Money they lose to Yeng Sang in poker game."

What an enigma, this gentle man. Willing to work his heart out for an employer, just as willing to give in to his personal demons during leisure hours. I'd hoped to have him with me, to benefit from his words of wisdom and to enjoy his wry humor. "I'm glad for you, sad for me."

"I come see you often."

"Please do. There's much I want to ask you about Gabe, things he might have kept from Kitty."

He dropped his black-eyed gaze to his cup and closed his eyes while he inhaled deeply of the tea's steaming fragrance. He looked up then, his face serene. "How can I speak of Mister Gabe? Some things I know with my mind. Some things I know with my heart. His joy and sadness, his anger, his fears. How do I know the cause? He may dream he is a bird and soar to heaven, or dream he is a fish and dive to the bottom of the ocean. Who is to say whether he was awake or in a dream? It is better to forget these things, the changes in life. Mister Gabe has walked into the pure, the divine, the One. Let him rest."

* * *

Unlike Yeng Sang, I had no sound faith in a hereafter. But his arrival had brought an unexpected serenity. A feeling of resolution. I could bid Gabe's phantom a final good night.

I spent the late afternoon cooking for Sam's return. I breaded steaks and put them on to fry, potatoes and onions in another pan, stirred a pot of beans I'd set at the back of the stove early that morning. Carrot salad waited in the cooler in the spring-house. As if presenting me with a welcome-home gift, the hens had outdone themselves. I'd made a rich golden mayonnaise and slid a custard into the oven. Yeng Sang baked pies from McIntosh apples picked from my young trees. The kitchen floated in the fragrance of apples and cinnamon. The lid on the coffee-pot popped up and down, releasing a dark aroma into the mix.

As soon as the pies were baked, Yeng Sang rode down the valley on his paint horse to see what Darby and Hamilton had to offer. Darby, three miles north of the homestead, was a small village of houses, post office and store, school, saloons, livery. Hamilton was larger, with a bank and hotel, an opera house, several saloons, buildings that were headquarters for Marcus Daly's stock farm and lumber operations. An acquaintance of Yeng Sang's owned a cafe in town—I'd heard he kept a poker table going in the back room. Still, I wondered if the town would welcome Yeng Sang. There was growing sentiment in the valley against imigrating Chinese, a fear they'd take jobs from white men.

As gambling was available, I doubted Yeng Sang would return in time for supper. Sam had promised he would. Benito was in the barn, waiting for me to ring the dinner bell. Kitty was out by the creek, reading, taking a much-needed rest after a frustrating day with the burrs.

I didn't want to start the gravy until Sam returned. Wondering if he had, I looked through a window that opened onto lilac bushes, a patch of grass, and the vegetable garden. The barn and pastures lay beyond. A roan was tied to the hitch rail. Someone was at the pump, working the handle, sloshing water over his face and hands, his back toward me. Not as tall as Sam, yet the build familiar. A spark of recognition sent the sting of nettles shooting up my spine.

Instant reactions—dry the hands, make sure the revolver on the wall was loaded. Leave the strap open on the holster. I started to smooth my hair as I did when company arrived unexpectedly, but I caught myself. I didn't care how I looked for this man.

By the time Carver Dean knocked on the door, I was ready. I handed him a towel as he walked inside, a rough slab of a man with a dark, weedy beard and shrubby eyebrows that covered much of the face. A bulbous nose, yellow-brown eyes. I'd never seen him dressed in such a fine suit—a brown herring bone with a yellow scarf and opal stick-pin, a bowler to match the suit. I wondered if he'd dressed to impress the citizens of the valley or to impress me. I thought I knew the answer and writhed inwardly.

He rubbed the towel over his face and threw it across the back of a chair. "Smells good in here. Looks like I'm in time for dinner."

My mouth stiffened. "Darby has an inn. You can eat there."

"Now, is that any way to treat an old friend?"

I wanted to say I'd just as soon open my home to the plague, but let it go at "You're no friend, nor are you welcome."

"I have business with Ben."

"Ben's dead."

Carver seemed shocked. I doubted grief had caused the reaction. Likely, he realized an end to his blackmail. "When?"

"Soon after you left for Alaska." I glared daggers. "If you've come to collect a debt, you'll have to show proof."

After the unexpected news, it took Carver a moment to gather his cunning. "Uh . . . sure. Have it right here. An IOU." He slipped a piece of paper from among the folds of his wallet.

I read it with suspicion, saw the signature was Ben's. "Why did he need the money?"

The question seemed to catch Carver off balance. He thought for a second before he stammered, "I—I—uh, don't know. I think it was to buy a plow."

"Couldn't have been. The neighbors went in with us to buy a plow. I paid for our half by tutoring their children." I waved the IOU under his nose. "This is worthless and you know it. You threatened Ben to make him sign it. You wanted to grind him under your heel once more before you left for Alaska."

Carver had brought his fluster under control. His face took on its usual callous expression. "Not true."

"Don't lie. You didn't figure on Ben dying."

He sucked in his cheeks and rubbed a sideburn. "Then you'll have to pay. A wife's responsible for her husband's debts."

"You'll not get a dime out of me."

His eyes narrowed to amber slits. "Better reconsider. The sheriff would like to know you were an accomplice to a killing."

"I wasn't."

"You knew what Ben did."

"So did you!"

For a long, thorny moment we exchanged glare for glare. His eyes leaked murder. I felt like a firebrand, as if my touch could set the room aflame.

I saw something sinister move in Carver's mind. He slid onto the edge of a chair, pulled a cheroot from his vest pocket, and sniffed it without taking his sullen gaze from me. "Got a match?" I took a tin of matches from the windowsill and tossed it onto the table between the settings of brown stoneware and cutlery. He lit the cheroot and blew smoke. "Nice dress. You always did look pretty in yellow." He waited for a word of appreciation. I gave none. "Sit down." He used the cheroot to indicate a chair.

"I'd rather stand."

"You sure don't make it easy for a man." He motioned toward the stove. "How about a cup of that Arbuckle's? The smell's driving me wild. I always said you make the best pot of coffee in Montana." It was obvious he'd changed tactics, trying to flatter me to get his way.

I poured his coffee, resisting the temptation to pour some in his lap, then backed to the end of the table near the parlor door.

He blew on the coffee. A sip of it made his lip curl. "Too hot." He set the cup down. "Sure you won't sit?" I shook my head. "You're headstrong. I like that in you, in any woman. Need it to survive in this world." He sucked on the cigar, blew a curl of smoke toward the angled ceiling. "I've admired you over the years, Jessie. Was jealous of Ben. You didn't know that, did you?"

He waited for a reply. I gave none. Just stood clutching the back of a chair with an angry grip. I wished he'd leave me in peace.

"You need a man around this place," he said with a glance out the window. "You shouldn't have to do chores. I could hire help." He took his gaze from the window and turned it on me. "You could act the lady you are. We could even move into town if you'd like. Maybe the big city—Seattle, San Francisco. The city's a good place to live. Nobody knows you. A man can make up any kind of a past he wants."

"What have you got to hide beside blackmail and meanness?"

The remark jarred a harsh laugh from him. "I'll ignore that. Comes from not knowing me very well."

"Well enough I don't want to know more."

His lips parted on teeth stained brown from tobacco. What appeared to be a smile was in fact a sneer. "You're no spring chicken. You can't be particular. I've got more to offer than Ben did."

"Don't flatter yourself."

He didn't give up easily. "I've plenty of cash. I could make you a comfortable life, show you the pleasures of the big city."

"I wouldn't marry you if you owned Seattle. Not after what you did to Ben. I've been praying you lay dead on some mountaintop, no one to care if you lived or died."

Outrage flared so suddenly in his face, I was afraid he'd leap up and slap my face. Instead, he slapped the table, jolting the tableware into a clatter. "Ben was a murderer. He could've spent the rest of his life in jail."

At that moment, the back door groaned open slightly and Kitty poked her head inside, the door blocking her view of Carver. She seemed distracted by something happening outside. "I'm going up to the barn and help Benito," she said. "He's having trouble shoeing Trixie. Be long before supper?"

I tried to keep the residue of anger from my voice. "No. Don't get started on anything big."

"Who was that?" Carver asked as the door closed.

"Kitty."

"Just visiting?"

"Gabe passed away."

"Mmm." He rubbed his fingers across the chin hidden beneath his beard, eyes speculative, glinting fire. "It'd be a shame to tell her she's a bastard, that Gabe and Ben lied to her."

"She already knows. You can't hold that sword over my head." The heat of resentment sucked sweat into my armpits and a damp film onto my neck and face. I turned to the stove, looking for something to give my attention so I wouldn't have to face the man. I opened the firebox, took a short poker from the side of the stove, and bent to stoke the coals into flame.

Before I could straighten, I heard the floor creak behind me. Thick fingers ran along the back of my neck and ears. My nerves shrieked at their touch. "Take your hands off me."

He didn't. Instead he took a firm grip on my shoulders and began to knead. "Don't pretend you don't like it," he said with a coarse laugh. "Every woman has cravings. Despite what you say about me, I bet you'd love to take me into your bed." His voice was crooning, laced with mockery.

The thought of going to bed with Carver brought beads of sweat to my upper lip. My heart pumped hate and fury. I whirled, shoving his hands away. "I'd sooner take a rattlesnake to bed."

His expression turned savage. One eye twitched at the corner. "Maybe you'd like me to spread it around Darby that little gal of yours is a bastard, that her stepdad was a murderer." His voice was low, the anger barely suppressed, the effect louder than screaming.

"You wouldn't!"

"Try me."

Rage boiled up within me. I wanted to hurt this man, wanted him out of my life forever. Before I was aware of it, I'd swung the poker at him, striking his face. He swore. There was a faint odor of burning flesh and hair.

He grabbed my hand and with an iron-fisted squeeze forced the poker to the floor. "A real wildcat, ain't you." He laughed at me in such a mean, scornful way, I wanted to spit in his face. Better yet . . .

I spun toward the wall at my back, pulled the revolver from the holster, and aimed it at Carver, my thumb on the hammer. "If you say a word to anyone about my affairs, I'll have you put in jail."

He sneered a laugh. "I'd like to see you try."

Outrage found its way to my trigger finger. Only the front door slamming back against the wall kept me from shooting the man.

Kitty's hurried tread punched lightly across the parlor floor. "Mom, we can't find—" She'd started the sentence before entering the kitchen, stopped abruptly when she cleared the doorway. "What happened? Who's this fella?"

"I'll tell you later," I said without turning. "Mr. Dean was just leaving."

"My coffee, remember?" He made a move to sit.

I jerked the gun barrel toward the door. “If you aren’t out of here by the time I count to three, I’ll—”

“You’ll what?” With a contemptuous laugh, he sat, then bent as if to scratch his leg.

I recalled he usually carried a knife or a small pistol in his boot. “Put your hands on the table!”

He straightened, reaching for his cup. “I’d rather put them around your lovely neck.” Then, with a lewd grin, “Better yet, I’ll put them around your—”

An explosion from my gun roared from the ceiling and walls, engulfing us in maddening sound. The burst deafened me for a few seconds and made my heart leap about. The smell of gun-powder filled my nose. I shook from the jolt of the blast, from the insolence that had snapped at my nerves and blinded me with fury.

At the same time I’d shot into the floor at Carver’s feet, Kitty had given the tablecloth a jerk, spilling coffee onto his vest. He got to his feet, swearing, brushing his vest. “Watch what you’re doing, damn it!”

“That’s nothing compared to what you’ll get if you don’t leave.”

Kitty took the poker from the floor and held it up in threat. “You heard her, mister.”

The bully in Carver yielded slowly, then with oaths, snarls, and glares. When he finally stomped outside, grimacing at us over his shoulder, Kitty and I followed, weapons ready.

“I gave you a chance,” he said from the back of his roan. “Now you can take the consequences. If I were you, I wouldn’t show your face in Darby for a while.”

“You can’t hurt us with your gossip.” My voice held more conviction than I felt.

“Yeah, we can take care of ourselves,” Kitty put in. “We’re a good team, aren’t we, Mom?”

“Yes, we are.” I smiled across at her, affection building on anger as I recalled the distance we’d come on our journey of the heart, one calamity after another keeping us apart. “Couldn’t be better, dear girl,” I said, choking on the words. “Couldn’t be better.”

Chapter 37

Sam and I had decided to say goodbye here, at my place, rather than at Darby, where he and Benito would meet the stage. Benito would then pony Sam's horse back to the West Fork of the Bitterroot where Sam had leased pasture. Too distraught about Sam's leaving to work in the house, I'd decided to dig daffodils from around the foundation of the house and separate the clumps. I kneeled on an old rug to keep the skirts of my bottle-green wool from the dirt. From here, I could watch the drive for Sam's arrival.

The sun was two hours past its zenith, mellowed from noon's crocus-yellow into the soft amber of late October. It shone on the river bottom, where cottonwood leaves flickered glints of copper amid the pines. West of the homestead, past the thick woods that clothed the foothills, the jagged skyline of the Bitterroots demanded my gaze. A few clouds in the shape of sailboats lazed across the peaks on an east-flowing breeze, a tight armada, touching fore and aft.

At the edge of the woods, the leaves of my young apple orchard held the rose and yellow hues of autumn. Downed by blackbirds, a few red apples lay rotting on the grass. Bees and wasps swarmed around the fermenting fruit, their buzzing loud enough to reach my ears. I felt saddened at the dying off of nature. The season was made for melancholy, as was the farewell that lay ahead. The parting with Sam would be difficult, almost as wrenching as my farewell to Gabe, though in a different way. I hoped I'd not live in the aftermath of moments missed, of things I should have said but hadn't or had said poorly. I'd wait for his return as patiently as I could, knowing, for his sake, he must fulfill his obligations to the past.

Kitty had turned Chinook into the corral at the side of the barn, where he'd spend much of the winter. She was there, running a brush over his gleaming red-brown hide. The teenage son and daughter of my good neighbors had come to visit. They played with the dogs and took turns with the brush. I'd first invited them to the house two days ago and was pleased with Kitty's delighted approval of the pair, pleased with their friendship toward her. It was as though she was starved for the company of those her own age. It seemed the ordeals of the journey across the wilds had cleansed her of rebellion, at least for the moment.

I was glad Chinook would spend the winter at my homestead. The memory of his unselfish devotion would stir my heart forever. I wanted Lilly and the foal near me as well, and Kitty had three yearling colts she wanted to keep under close watch. All but Chinook grazed in a small field that bordered the drive. When they set up a chorus of whinnies and ran down the field, I thought Sam had arrived at the base of the hill.

Chinook's bugle rang out across the canyon and echoed from the rocky cliffs east of the river. The dogs ran from the corral and barked a welcome, tussling with each other as they sped down the drive.

I rose, dropped my garden gloves to the rug, and shook out my skirts. From the porch, I took a gift Kitty and I had bought in Darby and wrapped in white tissue paper. By the time I'd reached the garden fence and walked through the gate, a sorrel had trotted onto the bench with a paint on lead, their shoes ringing on rocks in the drive. Not Sam's horse, but one I knew from the man astride her back—Sheriff White. On the paint sat Yeng Sang, a hang-dog expression on his face.

I'd worried about Yeng Sang since the night he'd failed to return from Hamilton. I'd even felt slighted, thinking he might have gone to his new job without stopping by, though his pack of belongings remained in the barn.

I set Sam's gift across the corner of the fence and watched the sheriff ride within a few feet. He tipped his bowler—a blond man of medium height and stature, dressed in black worsted, a silver star pinned to the coat. His features were ordinary, except for the small blue eyes that stared from the tanned face, so light a blue they were almost white. We exchanged greetings.

He jerked a thumb to the rear. "This here Chinaman says you'll vouch for him."

"Vouch for him? What's he done?"

"Got in a fight over a poker hand. I had him in jail a couple of days. Do you know him?"

"He worked for my brother for years. He's an unselfish, caring man, and a dear friend."

"Is he staying with you?"

"I wish he were. He has a job at the log camp up the East Fork."

"Guess he was telling the truth." The sheriff coiled the lead rope and handed it to Yeng Sang. "You're free to go. Just don't show your face in Hamilton.

Yeng Sang bobbed his head in thanks to the sheriff and me. "I bake you pies one day soon, Missee Tate. Now I go. Boss wonder why I not come to work." Nudging the paint in the ribs, he headed for the barn to collect his belongings, his black queue swinging.

The sheriff seemed in no hurry to leave. He sat with a hand on his hip, studying me with his ice-blue eyes as if I were suspect. I squirmed beneath his gaze. I knew him only slightly from the two times he'd stopped at the school on his rounds of the upper valley.

"That fella the Chinamen had the fight with—Carver Dean—he was telling me some interesting things about you, Mrs. Tate. He said I oughta look into them."

A freezing sensation crept from my toes up my spine to my scalp. My throat tightened. "What would that be?"

"Something about a murder over an illegitimate child." He removed his bowler and scratched his thatch of blond hair. "Since your husband's dead, I consider that past. But if there's something I need to know . . . well, you'll tell me, won't you?"

The ice left my veins, replaced by a sensation of heat, as if I were burning at the stake. "Th-there's nothing to tell."

"Glad to hear that." He stuffed the hat on his head and turned his horse-part way around. "The fella said he'd spread some gossip. Seemed to be mad at the world. I wouldn't worry about folks around here. There isn't a one doesn't have a skeleton in his closet or a black sheep in the family."

"Thank you for understanding."

"You might get that Chinaman to bake me a pie. I have a weakness for apple." With a grin and nod, he prodded his horse toward the drive.

Spurred by a different anxiety, I hurried to stop him. He reined in the horse. "Is Carver still in the valley?"

He gave a little *huh* of a laugh. "Funny thing about that fella. If he hadn't gotten into a fight, I might never have known he was in town. Seems he's wanted in Canada for mining fraud and assault with a deadly weapon. The Mounties are sending a man to pick him up. I guess you won't have to worry about him for a while." He jabbed a heel into the sorrel's ribs. She grunted and gave a lurch. "You take care, Mrs. Tate. I'll stop by one of these days to see how you're doing."

* * *

A few minutes later, Sam and Benito rode onto the bench amid the same chorus of snorts and whinnies that had greeted the sheriff. Benito pulled up his dun at the fence and spoke to the rowdy horses on the other side. He tipped his hat to me from there. It was obvious he wanted to let Sam say goodbye in private. Actually, we'd said all that needed saying in the way of plans for the winter and the possibilities that offered themselves on his return. His stop today was for a final smile and one last touch. Once more, I tore myself from my bulbs.

Sam tied the sorrel to the fence near Benito's dun, took two slender packages from his saddlebag, and walked over to meet me. He was dressed in a blue serge traveling suit, embossed boots, and black bowler. The red silk neckerchief that circled his neck was held in place by a beaded Indian ring. He tipped his hat and complimented me on my dress—I'd worn green to please him.

Kitty sauntered out from the corral and joined us, smiling.

"How's Chinook?" Sam asked her.

"Just fine. He's eating up the attention." She turned to me, secrets sparkling in her eyes. "Give him the present, Mom." I was pleased that "Mom" had replaced "Aunt Jessie" for good.

I handed him the tissue-wrapped package, which contained a royal blue neckerchief with red flecks. "It's not much. Just so you'll think of us from time to time. We both chose it." He started to pick at the ribbon. I told him he needn't open it now, unless he'd rather.

"Well, now, I will wait until later, when I can enjoy it in leisure. I do thank you. Though I doubt I'll need a present to remember you by." His smile was tender. "Here's something for you, Jessie." He took one of the thin brown-paper packages from under his arm and handed it to me. "And you, Kitty." He handed her the other. "You can open them when I've left."

"I never could wait to open a present." Kitty tore at the wrapping and brought out an oak-framed charcoal drawing of Chinook. She held it up for me to see. "Isn't it a beaut." Then to Sam, "Who drew it?"

"'Fraid I did."

"You're kidding me."

"I'm an old pencil licker from way back."

Kitty studied the drawing a long moment, her face turning bleak. Abruptly, she threw her arms around Sam and buried her head on his chest. "Thank you so much. I . . ." Her voice choked. She started to quake. "I'm sorry I caused so much trouble."

He patted her on the back, clucking like a mother hen. "Now, now, no need to cry. All that's past. Time to look ahead."

"I hate myself. I'm nothing but a—"

"No need for blame. There's been too much of that already, too much ahead waiting to test our mettle."

"I know, but—"

"No buts, either. We have a bit of the Irish in us, you and I. That makes us fighters. Nothing can ever knock that out of us." He gave her a squeeze, then took one arm from around her and pulled me into a communal embrace. "It just goes to show," he went on, "it's never too late for a person to change direction, never too late to learn."

"Wish it'd been easier," Kitty murmured.

"Life's like that. You have to go through things, experience them. You have to suffer in all kinds of ways before you get the answers. But no road is ever impassable if you put your mind to it. And you don't have to hog it to yourself. There's room for everybody."

I knew his decision to move the herd to the Bitterroot was born more from concern for Kitty and me than for the horses, more from concern he'd err in judgment as he had with his daughter. Knowing this, my heart swelled with affection.

I beamed into his face. "I'd say we've all learned a lesson."

His features creased into the warmest smile imaginable, then slowly turned wistful, as if he yearned for something beyond asking. Slowly, tentatively, he bent to kiss my lips.

Sensing it was time to leave, Kitty gave Sam one last hug and turned toward the corral. She took a few steps and turned back briefly with a reluctant wave. "Have a good trip. I'll miss you."

"I'll miss you." Sam watched Kitty scurry off, then turned his sweet-sad eyes on me. "You haven't opened your package."

Fumbling open the wrapper, I found an exquisite likeness of Lilly and her foal. For a moment I couldn't speak. When I did, my voice was thick with feeling. "It's lovely, Sam. I'll cherish it always."

I'd expected some sort of humor to lighten the moment. Instead, Sam laid the picture and his gift across the corner of the yard fence, then took my hands and held them against his chest. I felt how strong and warm they were, felt their affection, the kindness they'd shown others over the years, the years of labor they'd endured.

"I love you, Jessie. Don't forget that."

"I love you." I took one of his hands and held it over my heart for a long while, then put it quickly and tenderly on my cheek before I lay it at his side. The tears that welled into my eyes made him swim out of focus in his fine suit.

"Now, now. No need to cry." He took off his bowler, rumpled his hair in a manner of intense reluctance, then set the bowler in place at an angle. "I'd best be going or I'll miss the stage." He leaned close and kissed each of my damp cheeks. "Spring isn't that far off, Jessie. Likely I won't be able to wait for the snows to melt. I'll come wading through, yelling, 'Hey Jessie, want me or not, the old hoss is back.'"

We walked together in silence to where Benito and the sorrel waited. The colts frisked about inside the fence, pestering Sam's mare and the dun. Chinook's colts. Beloved stallion. Gentle with kittens, yet spirited, his courage beyond belief, a healer of wounded lives. His splendor lived in the colts. Gabe's spirit lived in them and in Kitty. Proud youngsters. Fearless. They breathed hope for the years to come.

Sam mounted his mare, turned toward me for an instant and flicked a sad smile, then prodded the sorrel down the drive. The last I saw of him was his hand extended in farewell, sinking below the drive's horizon.

Surely, I told my plunging heart, just as destiny had guided us safely to the end of one trail, it would lead us along the promising path into tomorrow. As inevitably as I'd watch icy fingers put a lock on the land, I'd smell daffodils and hyacinths on the warm, sweet breath of another spring and feel the joy of Sam's return.